MacArthur
Must Die

Also by Ian Slater:

MacArthur Must Die

A NOVEL BY

IAN SLATER

DONALD I. FINE, INC.
New York

Library of Congress Catalogue Card Number: 93-72583
ISBN: 1-55611-383-8

Manufactured in the United States of America

10 9 8 7 6 5 4 3 2 1

Designed by Irving Perkins Associates

In memory of my father, Lt. D. J. Slater, 25th Battalion, Darling Downs Regiment, and all those who fought against the Imperial Empire of Japan.

ACKNOWLEDGMENTS

I would like to thank my brother Robert and Professor Charles Slonecker who is a colleague and friend of mine at the University of British Columbia. Most of all I am indebted to my wife, Marian, whose patience, typing and editorial skills continue to give me invaluable support in my work.

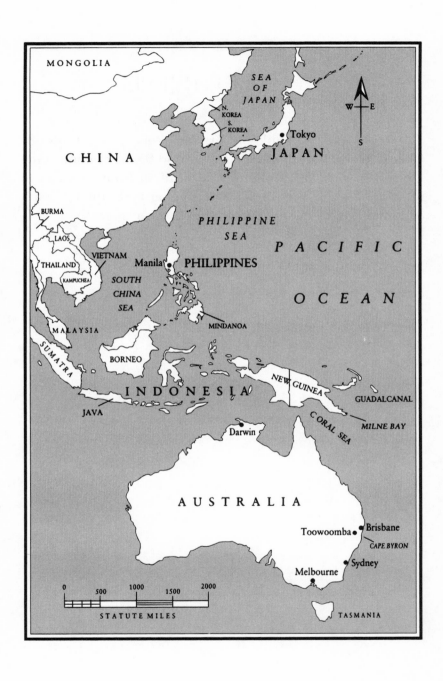

PROLOGUE

Tokyo—Early Fall, 1942

In his office at General Staff Headquarters in Ichigaya district, war minister Gen. Hideki Tojo, having given orders for no interruptions, sat chain-smoking as he pored over his map of Southern Command. To the left of the map there was the red folder marked CARP, the naval intelligence proposal from Col. Onê Heiji, now standing respectfully at attention before him. Another intelligence report to Tojo's right informed him that the Americans were at work on some kind of superbomb —top U.S. physicists were disappearing from their usual residences and being shipped to a place somewhere in the American southwest called "The Poplars"—"Los Alamos" in Spanish.

Tojo's eyes, partly hidden by the thin-rimmed spectacles, moved down from the Japanese main islands to the great southern arc that swept twelve thousand miles from Burma in the west to New Guinea in the south to the Aleutian Islands in the far northern reaches of the Pacific. Japan controlled it all, so that the Allies did not have a single base from which they could strike the sacred homeland, but time was of the essence. If Gen. Douglas MacArthur, who had promised, "I shall return," was allowed to continue working his way from Australia, breaking through Nippon's perimeter and in the process tying up more than a million of the Imperial Army's troops in the Southwest Pacific theatre, then quite clearly it would be easier for Adm. Chester Nimitz, who was operating from the Central Pacific, to sweep in and take the Marianas, Tinian, Saipan and then Iwo Jima and Okinawa in the Ryukyus. From there American bombers, the B–17 Flying Fortresses and the

1

new giant B–29s, would have fighter escort and could reach the Japanese homeland with the new bomb.

If Tojo was to prevent this, he would have to get agreement for Heiji's project from the general staff. He must have a good argument, and Heiji was the resident MacArthur expert.

Deep in thought, Tojo ceased pacing, mesmerized by the map. Already MacArthur had destroyed Horri's south sea army. The war minister's voice was more highly pitched than usual. "Your suggestions?" he asked Heiji. He wanted reassurance that an I-boat, of which the navy was desperately short, should be used on the CARP mission—by which he meant: Was there no other way to stop MacArthur?

Normally Heiji knew that the answer would have been to advise sending in more troops, more ships, more planes, but this had not worked as Milne Bay and Buna had so painfully demonstrated. MacArthur was different. That was the whole point of Operation CARP. Tojo must be made to understand what he, Colonel Heiji, the resident MacArthur expert, already knew: that there was simply no other commander in the Pacific like MacArthur.

Heiji flipped open the file. He skipped the photographs of MacArthur with his now famous corncob pipe, his sunglasses, which he seemed to wear in all kinds of weather, the determined jaw, and pointed out how MacArthur had graduated from West Point with the highest marks of the century, how he had accompanied his father as a special aide to Tokyo in 1905, observing the Russian-Japanese War, had seen action in Mexico in 1914 at Vera Cruz, had commanded the Rainbow Division in World War One, had been decorated thirteen times, and in 1919 was the youngest commandant of West Point, then the youngest major general to serve in the U.S. Army. Heiji also pointed out to Tojo that MacArthur had served in the Philippines as garrison commander from 1928 to 1930, that he had become chief of staff of the U.S. Army in 1930, and had advised the Philippine government in military

affairs since 1935 as field marshal until 1941 when Roosevelt
had recalled him to active duty as U.S. Commander, Far East.

"I know all this," snapped Tojo. "So do the chiefs of staff.
You are not here to give history lessons. Have you no better
intelligence for me?"

Colonel Heiji bowed quickly. "Some of our Filipino spies
were among the Fili-American troops on Corregidor, general
—in the Malinta Tunnel."

"So?"

"Before he was ordered out to Australia by Roosevelt, Mac-
Arthur sent an aide to search the island for ammunition—two
seven-millimeter bullets, an odd size, with which to load his
father's derringer."

Tojo looked blank.

"A small American pistol, general."

Tojo waited. "Yes?"

"He loaded the pistol and—" Heiji opened the file for the
exact page of the report. "And he said, 'They will not take me
alive.' "

Tojo, hands clasped behind his back, walked slowly to the
window overlooking the busy street below. He nodded
thoughtfully. MacArthur's action was precisely what a Japanese officer would be expected to do. *"Bushido. Hara-kiri?"*

"Yes, sir. No other American general, no other Allied general, would say such a thing. Percival at Singapore, King in
Bataan, Wainwright . . . all surrendered rather than die."

Tojo's glasses caught the glint of late evening sun, momentarily making him appear eyeless.

Heiji then quietly, respectfully, placed a singed book before
the war minister. "The fall of Manila was so rapid MacArthur
only had time to take a handful of personal effects. This is an
old textbook, printed in 1920. Military strategy. Our intelligence unit found it in MacArthur's hotel suite in Manila. He
loves hotels," said Heiji. "He had a very large library there."
Heiji turned the book so that Tojo could better read it. "This

is a passage on the growth of our military. It is in his own hand."

"Read it."

"Yes, sir." Heiji turned the book back toward himself. "It says, 'Japanese are superb in attack—poor in defense. Reason: have not been taught defense because it smacks of surrender and surrender for a Japanese is unthinkable. If something is unthinkable you cannot plan to prevent it.' " Heiji paused and cleared his throat. He was surprised to see that his white glove, holding the folder, was unsteady. He continued reading. " 'This is the key in any engagement with Japan. Attack is always the best form of defense in dealing with the Jap. He has not planned for it because he cannot imagine it.' " Heiji closed the book and put it smartly back under his arm.

Tojo stopped pacing and gazed intently across at the flag-staff and the gardens beyond.

Heiji continued: "When he was chief of staff MacArthur was often known to wear our traditional *yukata*. In summer he used a *sensu*."

Tojo was surprised, and this information, this new vision of the American general in a Japanese robe and using the Oriental fan, small enough details in themselves, showed an affinity of mind that Tojo found alarming in its implications for out-thinking the Japanese.

"He hates Europe and loves the Orient," Heiji went on. "Like his father he has spent many years studying the East. No other American commander begins to understand us as he does. This is why he defeats us."

Tojo nodded slowly. Heiji was right. There was no other way. MacArthur was simply too dangerous. To attack his army would not be enough. American reverses in New Guinea had already proved that.

Tojo lifted the CARP folder. "One thing I do not understand, Heiji. In preparation for our southern conquest our maps of Asia and Australia are the best in the world. Our agents have been collecting such intelligence for years in preparation for our victories. Why would you not use your agents in Australia?"

"They were not trained for it, general. Besides, they are gone. Interned. The Australians have imprisoned anyone of Japanese origin. The same as in America and Canada. Worse, in fact. This is why I prepared my plan."

Tojo was eyeless again behind the mirrored discs. He was looking out of the window far beyond the ancient city. "It is full of risk, this CARP."

"Yes, general," Heiji admitted freely, "but as you have so often told us, all great ventures are so."

Tojo sat down. "I will support you—press for an agreement from the general's staff immediately."

"Thank you, sir." Inwardly Heiji sighed with relief.

"It will require someone of exceptional abilities," said Tojo. "He must be fluent in English, resourceful, and if at all possible someone who has lived in Australia—familiar with the area."

"Exactly so!" agreed Heiji, not revealing the fact that having already sifted through hundreds of possibilities he had found the right man.

CHAPTER ONE

Fishing village on Honshu, Japan, October, 1942

"Tomokazu—Tomokazu—"

It was his mother calling, her voice tense with fear.

"*Hai?*—Yes?"

"A message has come. You've been ordered to Tokyo. To Imperial Headquarters." She was convinced that Tomokazu's time spent in Australia as an exchange student had finally put him under suspicion—that he would be handed over to the *Kempetai*—the thought police.

Tomokazu Somura stood rigidly at attention in the light blue kepi and overalls of the civilian defense force. At five feet five he was several inches taller than Colonel Heiji. It made him uncomfortable.

Heiji did not waste time. His office overlooking the dockyard's giant gantries was coldly functional, as businesslike, with its metal desk and steel cabinet, as his manner was abrupt.

"Are you claustrophobic, Somura?"

"No, sir," answered Tomokazu.

Heiji nodded. "Your file says in 1941 you spent eleven months as a student in Australia at the technical college in Toowoomba—not far from Brisbane. Correct?"

"Yes, sir."

"Good. You will attend a five-month crash course at Hiroshima Naval Academy—Eta Jima. I-boats—submarines. Beginning this afternoon. You will earn the rank of first lieutenant. Understood?"

"Yes, sir."

7

Eta Jima was Japan's West Point. It would be hell, Tomo-kazu thought, first light to midnight—every day. And the high, starched choke collar of the cadet's uniform—every day.

Heiji gave him the file of the operation war minister Tojo had called Operation CARP after the fish believed to bring good luck. "You are bound in absolute secrecy to the imperial general staff and to His Majesty the Emperor. The slightest infringement will mean the immediate death of yourself and your family. Understood?"

"Yes, sir."

"Over here."

It took a few moments for Somura to recognize the mockup of Brisbane halfway down Australia's boomerang-shaped eastern seaboard. The meandering shape of the Brisbane River with its wide S-shaped curve and the city nudged his memory, but as yet there were no name flags. It was only when he saw the long, sharp, triangular shape of North Stradbroke Island and South Stradbroke beyond the city plan that he knew it was Brisbane, only eighty miles from Toowoomba, where he had been an exchange student in aeronautical design until he had been summoned home for what had been called family reasons. Heiji had paid attention to every detail. There was even a replica of the big sign for Seppelts Wines by the river.

"MacArthur's headquarters are here at Lennon's Hotel." Heiji's finger moved forward from the red facade representing the brick front of the four-storied hotel, three blocks to the northeast, to the ten-storied AMP Insurance Building.

"He works seven days a week. You must commit the route to memory. It is in the file. He is heavily defended and so you will only get one opportunity along the route. Understand?"

"Yes, sir," but Tomokazu Somura was only beginning to understand. He was stunned, but knew he must hold his emotion in check. It hit him, finally, with the force of a karate blow —he had been chosen to assassinate the most legendary of all the American generals, the man for whom Eisenhower and

Patton had merely been aides. He, Tomokazu Somura, was being ordered to kill an American god.

Heiji intoned matter-of-factly, "We must stop him before he gets stronger and wins more stepping stones in the islands. Air bases from which he can bomb the homeland . . ."

"Yes, sir."

"The plan itself is simple. It is also dangerous. But . . ." Heiji hesitated, recalling what war minister Tojo had so often said ". . . all great plans are so."

Somura had difficulty swallowing, his throat dry as parchment.

"We will land you by submarine on a part of the coast you are familiar with from your student days in Australia. You will make your way into Brisbane, and you will carry out your mission. Once in the city decide which of the three intersections on his daily route you wish to use. We cannot tell you that from here. The submarine will rendezvous off the same place you land and take you off." Heiji waved his hand. "That is the broad plan. In the next few months we will fill you in on the details. There are many. We have much to do."

Somura heard Heiji's voice at a distance, as if he were talking to someone else.

"To begin with you should become familiar with the necessary small arms. The Nambu, number 94, eight millimeter. It is the best I think." He waited.

"Yes, sir."

The colonel looked hard at Somura. "You do not seem pleased?"

"Yes, sir, I am. It has happened so . . . all so quickly, if the colonel permits . . ."

The thin line of the mouth broke slightly. It was the nearest Heiji could get to a smile as his short body leaned awkwardly over the metal table and he slapped Somura's shoulder. "I chose you from all applicants—not only because of your background in Australia but also because of your family. They have always served the emperor well."

Somura knew better than to be insolent, to point out that he had not exactly been an applicant but had been urgently recalled to Japan, supposedly by a dying grandfather, only to find his grandfather was well and that he, Somura, had been conscripted into the imperial defense forces.

"Above all, you know the area," Heiji continued. "But as importantly you are also familiar with their customs, the climate, the food, the drink, their idiom of speech. Such matters can mean the difference between success and failure." Heiji turned, a frown crossing his face. He was not sure Somura understood the magnitude of the honor. The colonel's head rose imperiously, his fingers taut, pressing down against the steel table's edge. "It is the most important mission I have ever conceived. General Tojo has personally commanded it. The emperor himself . . ."

Somura bowed. "I am honored, colonel."

Heiji nodded, apparently appeased. He pulled the CARP file back toward him, and for the first time Somura saw the colonel seemed uneasy.

"As I have already indicated, Somura, I will not insult you and tell you it is not a dangerous mission. But if you train well, if you practice the timing, the escape route, you will stand a fifty-fifty chance. Those are far better odds than many of our warriors have faced in the south sea detachments."

"Yes, sir." Tomokazu, eyes straight ahead, hesitated momentarily. "Colonel, if I may be permitted a question."

"Yes."

"As the American navy now controls the Coral Sea will it be possible to penetrate their defenses—to get me there?"

"After the Battle of the Solomon Sea three of our midget submarines made it as far south as Sydney Harbor. We are still sinking Allied ships off the Australian coast. Our I-boats

are the largest submarines the world has ever seen. If anyone
can make it, they can."

Tomokazu said no more on the question, acknowledging
that Heiji had not answered, or rather could not answer, it
with any real certainty. He left Colonel Heiji's office, heart
pounding from the shock—and excitement—of his assignment. Of course he knew he would not be able to . . . see
Elizabeth . . . he could not even hope to see her, much as he
longed to.

It had been toward the end of 1941 in the Australian spring
when the two of them had stood silently on the high verandah
overlooking the parade ground that bordered the Toowoomba High School yard and lay in the dip a few miles west
of the range's rim. They could see the column of cadets
marching, the slouch hats moving in unison, the obsolete
rifles above them, bayonets piercing the twilight like the protective spikes of some long animal moving into night.

He took her hand hesitantly at first. They had been in love
for only three months, but at this moment they felt as if they
had been together forever, yet not long enough. Now he held
her hand firmly and she responded, squeezing gently. "Tom
. . . I'm scared. First all this Hitler business and Mussolini
and now . . . ."

"Shush," he said, "don't worry so."

"They'll call you up."

"My birthday isn't till next month," he said, to give her
hope she did not feel.

"If they call you up you'll go, won't you?"

He was silent.

"*Won't* you?" she repeated. Her hand tugged insistently on
his. She looked up at his seemingly calm, brown eyes.

"I haven't joined the cadets here, have I?"

"But would you go?" she pressed. "Back to Japan if you were called up?"

"I would have to."

Her hand withdrew from his, not quickly or angrily but slowly, reluctantly. "I think men like war," she said abruptly.

He stroked the long, soft blond hair and lifted her chin. She was crying. "Everything will be all right, Elizabeth. I will write to you every week. I promise—"

"Are you sure it's not just your family's plan to get you back? Away from me?"

"Yes. No. My grandfather is ill. They don't expect him to live much longer. I must go. We are very close. Please don't worry. In a month or so I will be back here at school—"

"I'll die if you aren't."

"Elizabeth." He was pleased. How could he not be? As his fingers trailed through her hair she touched his forehead, then mussed the neat part until it disappeared. When they kissed he could feel the spreading softness of her breasts, and she, his hardness against her.

The sergeant major's voice could be heard in the background through the gathering darkness. "Atten-hun! . . . S-lope arms!" There was a metallic sound as the hundred rifles rose in the three platoons, up to the cadet's right sides, over to their left, heads never moving, as if the guns had a will all their own.

"I mean it," she said. "I don't know what I'd do—"

"I will come back. Japan is not at war with anyone. And as soon as my grandfather's funeral—"

"Pre-sent arms!" In the near darkness the cadets slapped the rifle stocks in concert, lifted the Enfields forward, the magazines crashing in place like distant artillery, trigger guards to the front, the hundred right heels banging hard on the asphalt.

"S-lope arms! . . . Or-der arms!" Now the rifle butts thundered to the ground, and Elizabeth held him tightly. No matter what he said, everything pointed to war in the Pacific; it wasn't only in the papers, it was in the air. Everyone seemed to be waiting for something to happen, though no one knew precisely what or when. She saw the regular army sergeant major dismissing the Tech cadets—Tech a derivation of the high school's original status as a technical school. In the gathering darkness Elizabeth could tell from the way he walked that unlike the cadets the sergeant major was an older man, in his fifties, many of the young men already away fighting the Germans and Italians in the Middle East. Below she could see, silhouetted against the last of the evening light, the slouch hats streaming off the parade ground toward them, the hats' left sides pinned up so as to be out of the way of the rifle barrels when marching. It also meant, or so she'd heard from one of the girls, that the army always kissed you from the left side. A roll of raucous laughter spilled out from the darkness as obscenities flew back and forth, some of the cadets disappearing toward the bike shed among the long, black, spidery stilts that supported the library and helped cool it in the hot summer. Some of the cadets started up the cement stairway that led to the verandah, their heavy boots clumping loudly.

He had taken her hand and stepped back quickly through one of the tall pull-up windows into the blackness of an empty classroom. They stood in silence as the cadets in their khaki drill filed past toward the lockers on the far end.

"You don't have to be afraid," she said.

"I am never afraid," he told her.

She could not see his eyes in the darkness but knew he was looking straight at her. "Then why do you hide? Some of them are your friends."

"*Some* of them."

War . . . it was as if something was moving toward them, like a bush fire out of control. As they walked up Margaret Street past Queen's Park, Elizabeth made herself aware of everything around her, determined to remember this night. Ev-

erything seemed peaceful enough. Here in Toowoomba, a
town of forty thousand halfway down Australia's east coast
and eighty miles inland, October's spring moon was swaying
high above the camphor laurel trees, the thick, polished green
leaves pushed to and fro by a gentle easterly. The breeze gave
Toowoomba, at three thousand feet, cool relief. But in the
valley immediately to the east, where the dense eucalyptus
range dropped suddenly and dramatically and flattened out
toward Brisbane and the sea, it remained hot and humid.

Up past the Church of England Boy's Grammar, one of
the many private schools serving the vast farming and cattle-
station areas to the west, the breeze became even cooler and
for a moment Elizabeth was sure she could smell the sea
mixed up with the usual eucalyptus air of the bush, whose
sizzling sound came from the cicadas' nonstop chorus. The
unexpected chilliness was a good excuse to snuggle up, not
that she needed one. "Remember—" she began, "the weekend at the coast? At Byron Bay?"

"With your mother," he said. "While your father was
away." The tinge of bitterness, he could tell, had hurt her. "I
will never forget," he added quickly, slipping his arm about
her. "The most easterly point in Australia," he added in a
mocking, instructional voice. "Most people think Point Danger thirty miles to the north is the farthest east but surveyors
have discovered . . ."

She giggled softly at his imitation of the "believe it or not"
tone of the geography teacher in whose class they had first
met. In Byron Bay, a hundred and fifty miles away to the
southeast, they had walked along the long, sweeping crescent
beach up to the pass between the big scraggy rock and the
shore and on out beneath the high, grassy cliffs to the black
cape. Far below the dazzling white lighthouse, "the largest in
the Southern Hemisphere," he teased, they would sit behind
a natural honeycombed surf barrier of rock, their hair blowing in the free ocean wind that pushed enormous breakers

toward them, exploding towering walls of water in crescendos of foam and spray that leapt and swept down over them in a salty rain.

It was there only three months before, on her seventeenth birthday, that he first told her how much he loved her and where she had allowed herself to hope they would get married. She still dreamt of it but she knew that it would be impossible. She had thought of making love to him, even of becoming pregnant, but she'd been brought up to believe that men didn't want you "used." Besides, Tomokazu, the almost too perfect gentleman, never pushed her—which made the arguments with her mother even worse. And she knew that her father would never let them get married even if her mother relented—which she wouldn't. Her mother would not go against her father. The only reason they'd been allowed to see one another at all was that her father was away on his yearly trip up north in the sugar country cutting cane on contract and doing other odd jobs. Elizabeth asked her mother to promise that she wouldn't tell her father until he came home and she had a chance to explain herself. Not even her girlfriends understood, their parents telling their own kids that Elizabeth Lawson "wasn't playing with a full deck."

From her bedroom window, Elizabeth's mother, Sarah Lawson, saw them kissing in a tight embrace just inside the door on the bungalow's verandah. She felt bad that she had broken her promise to Elizabeth. She had written to Bluey telling him, well not really telling him, only saying that Elizabeth was no longer going out with Bruce Keely and had been going fairly steadily with a new boyfriend. Sarah wouldn't have told Bluey anything but she knew he'd find out sooner or later and better it come out gradually rather than all at once. Not that it would make much difference how he found out; she knew he'd hit the roof anyway. To Sarah, Bluey was a good man, a good husband and a good father to Elizabeth and young Frank, but he had his rules—and Elizabeth had broken the toughest one of all by falling in love with a Jap. Sarah watched them kissing again and felt a sweet longing and her arms crossed, unconsciously caressing the memory. She felt for her daughter. She watched them part, and left the window.

The night Tomokazu left for Japan Sarah heard Elizabeth crying in her bedroom.

CHAPTER TWO

The early morning light pierced the purple bush, casting golden shafts through the blue gums, making even the scrubby, faded lantana bushes look bright and new. It was an illusion, for later in the day as the sun climbed higher and the steam train snaked its way along the valley floor the bush took on a harsher aspect, only the smell of the eucalyptus remaining unchanged. By late afternoon, here and there in the deep shaded gullies that cleft the abruptly rising range a lone wallaby could be seen bent by a water hole, standing stockstill, his ears twitching nervously as the train laboriously chugged its way higher and higher toward Toowoomba's lip.

In the last carriage Bluey Lawson—"Bluey" because of his red hair—rested his heavy boots on the seat opposite, the sweat visible on the chest of his navy blue singlet as he stared eastward down over the smoky haze of the Lockyer Valley, its far-off sprinklers twinkling beneath a cloudless blue sky. Eighty miles due east, over the darker smudges of the Minden and Marburg ranges, lay Brisbane, the state of Queensland's capital, and just beyond that the Pacific Ocean, but Bluey's thoughts were a hundred miles south of Brisbane, along the great sandy beach running to the jagged fist of Cape Byron.

Like so many men born and raised inland, Bluey Lawson badly wanted to live by the sea, and if all went well he meant to sell the house in Toowoomba and retire there. He planned to buy one of the secluded fibro-cement cottages by the bay and spend the rest of his days fishing for the quick-silvered taylor. But from the headlines in the *Courier-Mail* he reckoned things were looking pretty bad. Hitler's armies had the Allies on the run and if the Japs started acting up, Australia stood on its Molly Malone, its seven million against seventy million

17

Japanese. 'Course the big naval base at Singapore should stop them dead in their tracks. The Japs weren't supposed to be much chop anyway; they copied everything. The fact was, however, that it was pointless thinking about the future until things settled down. Right now you had to look life square in the face; no good pulling the wool over your eyes. As a cane cutter, sugar being vital to the Australian economy and to help feed the troops overseas, he'd been given exemption from the first call-up for the Middle East. But if trouble started in the Near East then he'd most likely be conscripted, or volunteer, as his father had for Gallipoli, and be sent out of the country. If that happened he'd never save up enough to pay off the mortgage, let alone put enough away to move to the coast.

Anyway, he told himself, Toowoomba wasn't bad. Some said it was the prettiest city, town really, in all Australia; lots of gardens, more bearable than most places in summer, and to the west there were the vast alluvial plains of the Darling Downs, one of the richest crop-growing areas on earth, which also meant there was lots of hunting in and around the big sheep and cattle stations. It was these big spreads that sent all their kids to the Toowoomba boarding schools. Sometimes Bluey thought there were as many schools as pubs, and there were plenty of those, which he was eagerly looking forward to.

Walking down the street from the station toward Daley's pub, Bluey saw old Mrs. Ling. Godstruth! She was still trotting out, shopping for vegetables early in the day as she had since—he couldn't remember a time when Toowoomba didn't have the Lings running the Chinese café on Margaret Street. They were descendants of the Chinese who had flocked to work the Australian gold fields in the eighteen hundreds. "Morning, Mrs. Ling."

"Hi hi. You been gone?"

"Yeah, cutting cane."

"Make lots money, eh?"

"Yeah," he said. "Gonna buy you out, Mrs. Ling."

She laughed. "Any day. Yes, sure."

She was piling a box of cauliflower heads and papaya in the old pushcart. He hoisted it up for her. "There you are, Mrs. Ling."

"Ta."

"How's the family?"

She redistributed the load. "Here good. Bad time home. Hong Kong."

"How's that?"

"Japanese make much trouble China you see."

"Ah," said Bluey, picking up a fallen cauliflower. "Don't worry about them, Mrs. Ling. Any trouble in Hong Kong, the Brits'll send a coupla ships up from Singapore. Big naval base. That'll clean 'em up."

"Hope so."

"Know so. You say hi to Mr. Ling for me."

"Yes. Sure."

Inside Daley's Hotel the public bar was jam-packed, the laborers having knocked off for the day, the stale smell of spilled beer on sawdust permeating the solid line of men leaning up against the bar, legs on the brass runner, elbows cocked, air thick with blue white smoke, the steady roar of voices punctuated now and then by raucous laughter. Two big blade fans turned lethargically above the smoke, shifting it to and fro like heavy mist. Through the obscenities and more bursts of laughter an announcer could be heard giving the latest race results from Eagle Farm in Brisbane.

As the evening wore on, Bluey was pacing himself carefully, sticking to the seven ounces rather than the little fives that went down much faster and could make you blotto before you were ready. In the midst of the loud commotion, telling his stories about the wild north, he clean forgot about his promise to his wife Sarah in his last letter that this time he'd be home for dinner early after having been away so long. In spirit he was still cutting cane and ending the day as all cutters did.

It was around 9:30 when Mick Riley, one of Bluey's mates, noticed that Marge, the barmaid, now had a helper, an older woman, late forties, not bad looking and painted with peach rouge and dark lipstick. Mick was staring at her when he saw Rolston, a bookie's penciller with beet red face and barrel gut, pushing through the throng toward them. Mick tried to head him off by shepherding Bluey away. "Let's go out to the beer garden. Like sardines in here." But it was too late.

"Hey, Lawson," Rolston yelled. There was a malicious grin of anticipation on his face. "How's your son-in-law, mate?"

"C'mon, Bluey," said Mick, turning toward the garden.

"What's he on about? Son-in-law?"

"Ah—take no notice of 'im. He's pissed."

"Yeah," said Ted, another friend of Bluey's. "He's pissed."

"Hey, Lawson. How's your son-in-law?"

"I haven't got one."

"Just kidding. I hear Elizabeth's got a new beau?"

"A what?"

"Come on," insisted Mick. "He's full as a boot."

"A new boyfriend," Rolston pressed, taking another swig from the schooner. "Heard she's given young Keely the brush-off." Rolston cupped his hand and bent down to Bluey's ear. Before he'd finished there was a crash, then the beer glass clattering, miraculously unbroken, rolling empty along the floor. The bar's roar subsided temporarily but before anyone could say anything Bluey was gone, punching open the swing doors, leaving Rolston stretched out cold in the sawdust.

"Pissed again," someone shouted.

As Bluey strode up Ruthven Street into the twilight, two old Toowoomba friends said hello but Bluey didn't hear them. Past the Commonwealth Bank on the corner of Little Russell

Street he hopped into a black-and-white taxi, something he hadn't done in ten years. Taxis were too expensive for anything but emergencies.

"Elizabeth!"

"Oh, Bluey"—His wife, Sarah, ran in front of him as he stood silhouetted against the frosted louvers, whipping off the broad bush hat, flinging it aside onto the frayed lounge chair.

"Leave her alone, Blue—she's upset."

"*She*'s bloody upset! *She*'s upset!" He turned on Sarah. A fly buzzed annoyingly about him and suddenly his hand shot out. For a second Sarah thought he was going to hit her. He never had before but she'd never before seen him so angry. His hand snapped shut into a fist and the fly stopped buzzing. He threw it at the worn linoleum floor and switched on the verandah light, the sudden illumination causing Sarah to turn away.

"And you, you let it go on. Behind my back!"

"For God's sake, you were away! If you were home more often—"

"If I was home more often it'd take me a year on odd jobs to make what I make up north in three months. So don't come that act with me."

"I tried to talk to her."

"Never mind bloody well talking to her. Tell her *no*. That's it! No, final, finished!" He swung sharply toward Elizabeth's room.

Sarah stepped in front of him. "Blue—Bluey, it's over. He's gone. He had to leave—his grandfather got sick. I don't think they'll be seeing one another—"

"Hey, what's going on?" It was Frank, their sixteen-year-old, staggering out sleepily in his pajamas. "Hi, dad."

"G'day," said Bluey. "For Christ's sake, cover yourself up."

Frank groggily pulled the fly slit tighter. "What's the big row about?"

"Your sister. And I would've thought you'd had more brains for a start."

"What? I can't tell her anything. She won't listen to mum. 'Sides, none of my business."

"Tom!" Bluey turned to his wife. "That's what *you* called him in your letters. Tom! That was bloody sneaky for a start."

She pushed back the straggly piece of hair with her left hand, pulling her dressing gown tightly around her. "Well, that's what Elizabeth calls—called him."

"You know what I mean. Why didn't you tell me his full handle, eh? I didn't hear it from my family. Oh no. That ratbag Rolston tells me. In front of everybody at the pub. Comes up and whispers in my bloody ear. 'Hear you're going to be growing rice,' he says. Didn't know what the hell he was on about. Then he says"—Bluey's eyes were glistening with rage—"then he says, 'Tomo'—"

"Tomokazu," said Sarah.

" 'A Nip!' he says. 'You're kid's running around with a Nip!' I couldn't believe it. I dropped the bastard."

"Oh, Bluey." Sarah sat down heavily. "You didn't hit him?"

"Then I saw the bloody light. Tom . . . bloody Tom's a *Jap*."

"Hello, dad."

Elizabeth, at five foot three, was the smallest in the family. Bluey looked down at her. She had her hair done in long, blond braids resting on her light skin that contrasted with her pale blue eyes and blue nightdress.

"Put your dressing gown on, love," said Sarah. "It's getting cold. You too, Frank."

"Ah, mum, it's hotter'n—"

"Don't argue," snapped Bluey. "Do as you're told. Now."

Frank slouched away, yawning. "I'm going to bed. 'Night."

"I'll make some tea," said Sarah, starting off to the kitchen.

Bluey stood there looking down at his daughter. She *was* the most beautiful girl, almost a woman, he'd ever seen. Just a year ago she'd been all awkward angles and bumps and her thighs, he'd thought, were getting too big from too much grass hockey and sports in general—almost boyish in appearance—but now the transformation had passed. She was in full bloom, her breasts developed, the legs thinned out, tummy firm, and her face free of the acne crisis of two years ago. "What've you done?"

"Don't be angry, dad, please."

He wanted to be angry, he wanted to be furious, but felt his rage beginning to desert him. Elizabeth sank into the lounge chair. "She said she wouldn't tell you—"

"Don't call your mother 'she,' " he said, his voice falling by the second.

"Sorry, but she promised—"

"She didn't tell me. I heard down at the pub." He was becoming louder again. "About my own daughter, I had to hear it—"

"You want a sandwich, Blue?"

"I don't care."

"What do you want on it?"

"For Christ's sake, Sarah—I dunno—peanut butter'll do." He opened up his tobacco tin and, pulling savagely at the dark navy cut leaf, began rolling his own, the palm of his right hand rhythmically kneading, punishing his left. "Well, your mother says it's over."

Elizabeth sat up quickly. "He's gone home for a while, his grandfather's—"

"Well, I'm glad. It'll be easier—"

There were tears in her eyes. Damn it, he hated tears from his daughter, or Sarah, for that matter. "Now look, girl, I don't—Sarah, where's that tea?"

"Coming."

"Look, it's for your own good."

"No, it isn't," she said. "It's because he's Japanese. Because he's not white. You hate anyone—"

Bluey's hands stopped rubbing the tobacco and his right finger jabbed at her. "Now that's not true. That's *not* true. I don't care whether a man's black, yellow or bloody brindle. But you can't mix 'em. It won't work."

"How do you know it—"

"No *ifs* about it, Elizabeth. Look, up north I've been workin' all day next to an abo mate of mine, Joey—Joey's a prince. Better than half the white men I know but he has to live with a white woman of his in a shanty near Childers. They just don't—"

"Tomokazu's not aboriginal. And even if he was I don't see—"

"That's not the point—"

Sarah came in with a small tray. She put down an enamel mug of tea and the sandwich for Bluey, then returned to the safety of the kitchen.

"Sweetheart," Bluey said, "it's not just you. If it was just you and this bloke Toma . . ."

"Tomokazu," she said clearly. "Tomokazu Somura."

"Yeah, well, Somura. If it was just the two of you, you might make a go of it. But when you had kids—"

"What if I never have kids?"

"Elizabeth!" It was Sarah.

Bluey forced a conspiratorial smile for his daughter. "Now don't have her on."

"I'm not." She looked straight at him. "What if I don't *want* children?"

He studied her face, half convinced she was baiting him but not certain. It was a conversation he couldn't have imagined a year before. They really did grow fast. Too fast.

"All right." He sat back. "If you didn't have kids you'd still have to live in this country. I say again, I don't care what color a man's skin is." His hand motioned somewhere beyond the house—westward toward town. "I saw old Mrs. Ling this morning. Can't get better people than the Chinks. But, Elizabeth, like it or not, this is a white man's country and everywhere you'd go you'd have to put up with people talking behind your back. Hell, it's bad enough between us and the Protestants. I don't care one way or the other meself. Half my mates are Protestant but, well, you know what it was like at the convent. Every time the kids from South School would go past yours you'd be pelting one another with bunya nuts." He laughed. He didn't mean to but bunya nuts always made him laugh. Anyway, he thought, it might loosen things up, help her see reason.

"I didn't pelt anybody, daddy."

"That's not the point. It's what other people—"

"I don't care what people say."

"Yeah? Well, you say that now, kiddo, but believe me that's all right when you're here safe and sound. Me putting the bread and butter on the table and your mum making ends meet." He pulled out a cigarette paper. "When you get out there it's a different story. For starters he'd be flat out getting a job."

"They let him in the country to study," she said. "To study at the Tech—at the high school. When he comes back he'll go for his senior certificate and go to uni in Brisbane."

"They let him in to study, yeah, but letting him stay's a different story."

"How about the Lings, then?" she persisted. "And the East Indian man, the one who comes around selling vegetables in the cart. How about them?"

"Government didn't know where they came from or how they got here. Snuck in during the gold rush. Besides, that was years ago. Point is, no more'll be coming in. We've got a White Australia Policy, same as the Yanks. Only difference is, they don't call it that. He couldn't get a job here, Liz, and even if he could . . ." He began tapping in the end of his cigarette with the tip of a wooden matchstick . . . "I'm not saying I agree with it, Liz, I'm just telling you that's how it is."

"We could move to Japan."

"Elizabeth!" A cup went down with a bang on the kitchen table.

"Now cut that out," said Bluey. He turned toward the kitchen. "This tea's a bit strong, Sarah. Could fill your fountain pen with it. How about some hot water?"

"Hold your horses."

Bluey leaned forward. "Liz, I'm only telling you what a Japanese father would tell his son. You must know that. You're bright enough." He paused. "You must know how it is, kiddo."

Silence.

"It wouldn't be any different over there, sweetheart. Probably be worse. They hate the whites. Look at this Tojo." He sat back, drawing deeply on his cigarette. "There's race hatred for you. He'd like to kill every white in Asia. You'd be ostra . . ."

"Ostracized," she said softly.

"Yeah. Worse than here. Believe me. For starters there's a hell of a lot *more* of them than us." He picked up the enamel mug, took a sip, and put it down on the table, reaching for her hand at the same time. She drew away.

He sat back, remembering all the times he'd held her as a child; she'd always been his favorite. "It's not only Aussie, it's everywhere. In thirty, forty years maybe people'll laugh at it all. Think we were all a bunch of yahoos. I dunno, but right now it's not going to change. That's life, Liz. Even if you don't have kids. I'm not saying he's a bad bloke. Your mum says he's a decent sort and she's a pretty good judge." He grinned toward the kitchen, raising his voice. "Even if she can't make a good cuppa!"

Sarah came in from the kitchen and put her arm around his

shoulder. The tension remained. Elizabeth still looked un-forgiving. There was another long silence.

Finally the tautness gave way in her face. "He's really very kind, daddy," she said softly. "When you meet him I know you'll . . ."

Bluey coughed and put the mug down, spilling some of the tea. He took her hand. "Doesn't really matter a fig what I think or anyone else. He's a Jap and there's going to be a war. Tojo's talking fight every day. Same as Hitler. He and Hitler have signed a pact. That's why I'm home early. An army guy came 'round and told all the cane contractors to wrap it up as soon as they could. If the Japs start throwing their weight 'round the army'll need everyone, probably ship us to Singapore to stop them."

"Bluey—" Sarah began.

Bluey held up his hand.

"That's how bad it is, Liz. You can't marry a Jap."

She broke down then, convinced she would never see him again.

Some weeks later on a hot December night after having had only one letter from Tomokazu and no mention of when he might return, Elizabeth knelt to say her prayers. She began with several "Hail Mary's," then stopped. For a moment, in panic, she couldn't recall Tomokazu's face. It had happened before. It was perverse. Was it already an unconscious attempt to forget him, to push away the pain? Was her father right? She tried to fix the gentle almond eyes in her mind's eye, the shy smile he gave when first he'd had difficulty pronouncing the last part of Eliz-a-beth. She would tease him and he would have her try to pronounce "Asahigawa"—a place in Honshu —and they would laugh a lot. It was a love ritual they had made and kept.

"Dear God," she had prayed, "please bring him back."

She tried again to remember his face in every detail but again it blurred away into generalities and instead she saw a face she didn't want to see, a face from innumerable newspaper photographs: the bald round head, the thick bushy moustache and the rimless glasses, the chest of medals and the samurai sword. Tojo—the minister of war, the one they called the "Razor."

It had been on the night of December 8.

As she had prayed, the *Kido-Butai,* the six-carrier strike force four thousand miles away, was racing through the darkness at twenty-six knots toward its launch points at twenty-six degrees north latitude, longitude 158 degrees west. Here, across the dateline, it was early morning, Sunday, December 7, 1941.

Shortly before 6:00 A.M. the red pennant with the white circle rose halfway up the mast of flagship *Akagi* (Red Castle) signaling "Prepare for Takeoff." High above the deafening roar of aircraft straining at the chocks, the pennant, fluttering strongly in the battle gray dawn, reached height then dipped. The forty-three Mitsubishi Zeroes were the first to take off, then the forty-nine Kate-Nakajima bombers quickly coming into the V-formation behind the protective screen of the fighters, then the fifty-one Vals, Aichi 99 dive bombers and finally the forty Nakajima 97 torpedo bombers. At 7:49, approaching Pearl Harbor 275 miles to the southwest, Air Commander Fuchida broke radio silence to broadcast the message "Tora . . . Tora . . . Tora!" ("Tiger . . . Tiger . . . Tiger!"), signaling Admiral Nagumo, commander of the Kido-Butai, that the Japanese had taken the Americans by complete surprise.

A few minutes before 8:00 A.M., as the first signal to raise morning colors on the U.S. warships sounded, the attack began. By 8:30 the battleships *West Virginia, Arizona, Tennessee, Maryland, Nevada, Oklahoma* and *California* either had sunk or were afire. The battle fleet was crippled. Now the Japanese Imperial Staff's secret plan of southern conquest could proceed unimpeded by the U.S. Pacific fleet. It had cost the Japanese less than 300 men—the U.S. more than 3,000 killed and wounded.

CHAPTER THREE

Worried about her father, who after the most meager basic training at Wacol Military Camp near Brisbane had been rushed to Singapore in late January, Elizabeth, along with the rest of the world, was stunned by the speed of the Japanese advance. In distances covered, the German blitzkrieg paled by comparison. Looking at the maps of the Pacific and East Indian oceans displayed daily in the Brisbane *Courier-Mail* and Toowoomba *Chronicle* she, like everyone else, found it difficult to believe at first that so much had fallen so fast across an area twice the size of the United States. On the Wednesday only two days after Pearl Harbor, defying all known tenets of naval strategy, the Japanese, who already ruled Manchuria, much of Indo-China and Formosa, humiliated Britain and gave Churchill his greatest single shock of the war when Japanese warplanes dove out of the sky over the South China Sea killing 800 British sailors and sinking the battle cruiser *Repulse* and battleship *Prince of Wales* en route to relieve Singapore. It was the first time in history that a capital ship under steam had been destroyed by enemy aircraft. Simultaneously the Americans were being attacked in the Philippines. Then Hong Kong fell, then Malaya, then, almost unbelievably, on February 23, Fortress Singapore surrendered, its massive guns still pointing seaward unable to turn to contest the unthinkable that had become the reality—a Japanese assault from the *landward* side. When General Percival's surrender party walked forward with the white flag, 138,000 Allied prisoners of war fell into Japanese hands.

Sarah Lawson tried to find out about Bluey. Elizabeth wrote a letter to the local Labour minister of parliament. He was sympathetic but replied that it was "utter chaos in Ma-

laya" and with Singapore gone nothing in the way of records
had yet been retrieved. He apologized as he did to hundreds
of others, but amid the confusion of the massive Allied collapse he could do nothing at present, he said, "to ease the
pain." They could only "wait, hope and pray."

CHAPTER FOUR
Western Malaya

"You are disgrace."

Colonel Kiho, immaculate in neatly pressed khaki shirt and light tropical issue helmet, was looking down on them from the cool verandah, waving the long bamboo cane. The two prisoners, an American and an Australian, stood at attention, their eyes squinting in the harsh glare of the sunbleached parade ground, which only a month before had been part of one of Malaya's largest rubber plantations. The two men knew better than to answer unless a question was asked, and that if they did speak they must first bow respectfully to the Japanese commandant. A Canadian POW had been beaten unconscious ten days earlier for speaking before told to do so.

The Japanese guard with his long rifle, his face in the shadow of the field cap's neck guard, was standing stiffly on the second of the six steps leading up to the shady open verandah of the old plantation house. Bluey Lawson knew there were six steps because he'd counted them at least a hundred times during the four hours they had been standing in the small white pebble courtyard. Whenever a finger of shade reached out toward them the guard, waiting till the very last second, would prod them a pace back into the blazing sunlight and 105 degrees. Had they been in Singapore, at the massive Changi Prison down at sea level, the humidity would have sweated them into exhaustion and by now, Bluey knew, they'd be mercifully flat on the deck. The only reason that he and the American, a pilot out of Manila, and the other fifty-odd ragtag POWs behind them in the two platoons were still upright was because the plantation was in the hills near Selangor where the air was drier. Spreading out from the house the rubber trees blurred into a cool green ocean, which Bluey felt he could almost touch. Only twenty yards either side and they could be in the reviving shade. But only if they obeyed and survived. Now the Japanese had moved a three-ton truck up, and through the canvas flaps that hung down its back he could hear a low, monotonous buzzing.

"You in Changi," Kiho went on, "you not work. Here, plenty work. Honor. But you disgrace. No honor."

The American, a mere skeleton hanging in torn khaki, was near collapse.

Lawson's hand reached out to steady him. "You all right, mate?"

The Japanese guard stepped forward, transferring his rifle to the left hand, slapped Lawson's face, then stepped back. The American crumpled to the ground, his emaciated arm sticking out from his side at a grotesque angle like a broken wing. Colonel Kiho stepped down onto the third step, a mosquito bothering him as he addressed the parade, telling them they were bad soldiers, bad men who shamed their comrades.

Kiho genuinely could not understand the Americans or the Australians. He could not understand any of these white men. They surrendered in droves from Hong Kong to Manila—so many that even dispersal into these makeshift camps throughout the occupied territories wasn't enough—and yet as prisoners they acted arrogant and unashamed. Kiho had decided that such behavior was a pathetic attempt to regain esteem for their race, acting in defiance of the victors—the yellow men who had swept them aside in the great southern offensive. They were trying to regain honor through defiance. He had heard about the same thing from Changi, from where these and other prisoners had been sent to help harvest and transport the rubber. At the big camp at Changi such disciplinary measures as Kiho employed also had to be taken.

Still, in the matter of prisoners of war, Kiho had to admit Nippon's forces were more fortunate than Hitler's. In the

Reich, escaping POWs could sometimes reach Switzerland, Spain or Portugal. Here, where could they go? The jungle was the prison. Even so, some tried to escape into the steaming rain forests. Kiho did not understand it. It was a soldier's duty to fight to the death, but if captured he forfeited all honor and had to submit to the victor, to imprisonment and forced labor. Kiho did not believe himself a cruel man; he did not support, like some other officers, the policy of the Chinese Experiment in Manchuria where thousands were summarily executed and experimented on. If punishment was meted out indiscriminately its point was lost; there was no reason for good behavior, no difference in the prisoners' minds between behaving and not behaving. No reward.

Kiho saw the American was moving at his feet and shouted to the guard. *"Hai!"* The guard stepped forward and helped the American to his feet. Kiho ordered the guard to put his water bottle to the American's parched lips. Kiho saw the Australian, L/Cpl. "Bluey" Lawson, looking at the bottle. He motioned to have the bottle passed to Lawson, who began by sipping but then took a long gulp. Foolish in this heat, Kiho knew, and ordered the bottle taken away. It was the same old problem—the white man did not have the restraint of the Oriental in such climates. The soldiers of Nippon were no more natural jungle fighters than an American from New York or an Australian from Brisbane. But the Japanese had been trained, and were disciplined. Kiho looked beyond the two prisoners at the other POWs, the ones who were left standing.

"Last day," Kiho said, shaking the bamboo cane, "prisoner run away." He gave an order and the truck's tailgate fell open, revealing the bullet-torn corpse of the man, the loud buzzing Lawson had heard caused by swarms of flies in a black mass about the dead man's mouth, nose and eyes.

"Silly!" said Kiho, indicating the corpse. "One man in jungle not last long. Japanese soldiers always find. You know rule." The cane shot out toward the dead soldier. "He know rule!"

All Lawson could hear was the buzzing of the flies.

Kiho, his Adam's apple plainly visible above the immaculate, open-necked khaki shirt, gave another order and the guards around the perimeter of the parade ground brought the rifles to port, the bayonets glinting, a square of steel around the tattered khaki assembly.

When they had come to pick out the two of them, Bluey had tried to figure which it would be this time, tall or short. Sometimes you had a chance to crouch a little or stretch, depending on what you thought their preference was. But you couldn't really predict—the American beside him was barely five feet three, Bluey close on six feet.

Now Kiho threw away his stick, which clattered noisily on the tiny stones. The guards held the American's arms out behind him, forcing him to the gravel, and pushed Bluey Lawson into the same position. Kiho drew his samurai sword and lifted it high, its blue steel momentarily disappearing into the sun, then fell. Then it rose and fell again—and the two heads, eyes open, frozen in shock, were rolling in the dust. Someone was retching in the ranks behind. The headless torsos, spouting blood now, pitched forward, jerking, kicking in spasm, sending pebbles and fine white dust into the still air.

That evening Colonel Kiho wrote to his wife Miyoko how the Americans and Australians were so difficult to comprehend, like children who persisted in going against their betters. Sometimes, he confessed, he doubted whether it was possible to really understand such inferiors.

Kiho forwarded to Kuala Lumpur, and from there to Tokyo, whatever intelligence he had managed to gather either by direct interrogation of Allied prisoners or by other means —in some cases Allied positions had been overrun so quickly that maps and papers that should have been destroyed along with tanks, planes and artillery had been captured intact.

But today Kiho had nothing of special interest for either
Rabaul, the southernmost headquarters in New Britain just
east of New Guinea, or for Tokyo's intelligence headquarters.
All he was sending them was the usual shoulder patch insignia
of the prisoners under his command, the one from the executed prisoner Lawson, a rectangle, navy blue and light blue
separated by a diagonal line, bottom left to top right, signifying a Darling Downs regiment from the northern Australian
state of Queensland.

CHAPTER FIVE

Thailand fell, then Burma; Borneo was taken, the Dutch East Indies were gone with another 60,000 Dutch, British and American prisoners, and then the New Hebrides were taken. Next on the target list was New Guinea, the great iguana-shaped island that would be the springboard, if the Japanese Imperial Navy had its way, for the invasion of Australia just ninety miles south across Torres Strait. Tojo had told the Japanese people that "Japan will dispose of Burma, China, India, Netherlands Indies, Australia and New Zealand in that order." On February 19, only ten weeks after Pearl Harbor and 4,000 miles away, Darwin, Australia's largest northern port, was bombed by Fuchida, again from the carrier *Akagi*, using 188 planes, only one less than were used in the first wave on Pearl Harbor. The port of Darwin was demolished, the U.S.S. *Peary* sunk together with sixteen other U.S. and Australian ships either sunk or damaged. Civilian casualties were higher than at Pearl Harbor. A week later, February 27, seventeen warships of the Imperial Japanese Navy under Rear Admiral Takagi in the biggest naval battle since Jutland engaged sixteen warships of the combined British, American, Dutch and Australian fleet in the battle of the Java Sea. It was an Allied disaster. In less than eight hours, without the loss of a single ship, the Japanese sank half the Allied fleet. Java fell. Four days later, on March 3, Broome and Wyndham in Western Australia were bombed.

In Australia anxiety turned to fear, to a sense of crisis, fueled by the knowledge of the lightning savagery of Japanese troops who had gone berserk in Singapore, bayoneting prisoners in hospital beds and raping, then mutilating, nurses,

37

and castrating Allied prisoners before putting them to death. In just seven months from December, 1941, to July, 1942, the Japanese had conquered nearly everything before them. Now, only Australia, vast in size, as big as the continental United States but with a small population, stood between the Japanese and total victory in the Pacific.

So for the Allies, Australia had to hold not only for its own sake but because as England was to Europe, Australia was to Asia, the springboard for an Allied comeback if one could be mounted in time before the speed of the Japanese assault severed the vital supply line between the U.S. and Australasia. As Australian prime minister John Curtin warned President Franklin D. Roosevelt, only Australia stood between Japan and the United States's west coast. The danger had become apparent when on the night of February 23–24, 1942, the Japanese sub I–17 shelled the oil installations off Santa Barbara and Allied shipping continued to be sunk off Australia's east coast.

For Elizabeth Lawson the thought of going to school in these times was nightmarish. The Tuesday after the Pearl Harbor attack she had walked across to Herries Street and down past the grammar school, taking the back way along the creek. It was already hot and, for Toowoomba, unusually humid, thunderclouds merging in a dazzling white barrier far to the west, spreading all the way south over the New South Wales–Queensland border. By the time she reached Tech she was already flushed and perspiring, her white uniform blouse sticking to her like a second skin. Using the side entrance she walked slowly, then hurriedly as she saw a group of students approaching from Queen's Park. Only in the relative privacy of the washroom did she feel safe, not realizing until several minutes had passed that she had now trapped herself if someone wanted to corner her with taunts about the Japanese. She had stayed there, relishing the cool of the thick cement walls, composing herself for the ordeal. When the bell sounded her heart was pounding so hard she was sure her blouse showed it. She emerged, into the fierce light.

"Elizabeth?"

It had been Elaine Foster, an old friend from her subsenior year, and two others from her math class.

"Yes?" She would challenge them as she had defended Tomokazu to her father.

Elaine had smiled and moved forward. The other two had touched her, briefly, awkwardly, and the three girls embraced her.

She was grateful for that, as she heard, "bloody slant-eyes" from one of the boys, late for first bell, as he rode through the gate.

On parade one of the masters led the school in morning prayers ". . . that we may prevail over the forces of barbarism . . ." but she prayed for Tomokazu, convinced he could never be part of barbarism; besides, he could only have arrived in Japan a few weeks before the sneak attack on Pearl Harbor. There was no way he could have been connected with it. She silently finished with a prayer that peace would come soon.

But only war came.

The Japanese were on a winning run and now as Elizabeth and her class helped to build one of the air-raid shelters in Queen's Park across from the school she was already hearing talk of the "Brisbane Line," 2,000 miles long stretching east to west right across Australia, from Brisbane halfway down the east coast to Perth all the way to the far southwest of the continent. The top part, two-thirds of the country, was to be surrendered after a policy of scorched earth, and whatever meager resources there were would be concentrated to fight the Japanese south of the line.

* * *

On the western side of Luzon, in the rugged, parrot-beaked peninsula called Bataan, Gen. Douglas MacArthur's stubborn Fili-American army had held on, the remainder of his troops dug in and crowded on Corregidor, the rocky, tadpole-shaped fortress two miles to the south of Bataan, where massive American guns guarded the entrance to Manila Bay, just as Singapore's massive British guns had guarded Malaya. Now, as General Homma's Fourteenth Army closed the pincers, one arm pushing down from the north onto Bataan, the other attacking Corregidor in the south, MacArthur, already a hero and awarded decorations in World War One including six Silver Stars for gallantry, had become the lone symbol of Allied defiance. Determined to fight to the last, buying precious time for the Allies, MacArthur had already accepted that, with no relief in sight, he, his wife and four-year-old son, along with the army, would die.

Roosevelt, however, decided he was needed elsewhere and ordered him to get out and head south to Australia, where a new army might be marshaled and trained for what FDR and Winston Churchill had now decided must be the Allied counteroffensive. On the night of March 11, 1942, MacArthur, his wife Jean, their son Arthur and his Filipino amah, Ah Cheu, along with several of MacArthur's aides, had boarded PT 41, one of four PT boats MacArthur selected to make the dangerous dash to Mindanao 500 miles to the south on the first leg of his daring 4,000-mile escape.

In the darkness, as the PT boat pulled out from Corregidor past Cabra Island on its port bow into the South China Sea and down through Mindoro Strait, it struck heavy seas in the pitch black night. As dawn broke on the racing diamond formation of the four boats, one of the PT skippers, as Lt. John F. Kennedy would do a year later, thought he saw a Japanese destroyer bearing down. Unlike Kennedy, he was mistaken but didn't realize it before he had ordered General Quarters and almost torpedoed PT 41 emerging ghostlike from the early morning mist.

It was only the first of a number of close shaves for MacArthur as the Japanese tried to stop him before he reached Australia. Japanese lookouts on nearby islands had lit bonfires, the traditional signal that someone was trying to get through the straits. None of the PT boats made the halfway rendezvous at the Cuyo Islands on time and had to run in daylight, risking discovery and attack from Japanese aircraft. Shortly after leaving the island of Tagauayan, one of PT 41's lookouts spotted a Japanese warship on a collision course. The PT skipper, his boat at full speed, managed to quickly change his heading and evade detection. Then, just after sunset, Japanese coastal batteries on Negros Island heard the roar of the 4,000-horsepower Packard engines, and soon stalks of searchlights were piercing the darkness. Shortly before dawn on March 13, PT 41 reached the north coast of Mindanao. MacArthur's party had only just sat down to eat by the airfield, waiting for the B-17s to arrive from Australia, when an old Filipino woman arrived, shattering security by asking to see Mrs. MacArthur: Japanese patrols were reported heading for the airfield at that moment.

At dawn on March 17, as the B-17s approached the end of their 1,600-mile flight to Australia, Japanese fighters were scrambled to shoot them down but lost the B-17s in the predawn darkness. Flying across the Timor Sea approaching Darwin, their destination on the Australian central north coast, MacArthur's pilot was informed that Japanese bombers were pounding Darwin and that MacArthur's B-17 would have to land some fifty miles south, at Batchelor Field. Fatigued but happy after the long flight, the general, it was later reported, turned to an aide and said, "It was close, but that's the way it is in war. You win or lose, live or die, and the difference is just an eyelash."

MacArthur boarded another plane, this time a C–47 transport, to take him to Alice Springs in the heart of Australia and then on to Melbourne, another 2,000 miles. The takeoff was sudden and violent, throwing the general and his party hard up against the fuselage. The reason: a flight of Mitsubishis was closing in on Batchelor Field. Again the Japanese had been only seconds late.

After resting at Alice Springs in Australia's red center, Mac-Arthur went due south to Adelaide on a train journey that took another two-and-a-half days through the arid, fly-infested deserts of central Australia, but by now the secret of his arrival was out. Already America's most celebrated soldier, MacArthur was greeted in Australia as a savior—the man who had slowed the Japanese advance, buying precious time in the dogged defense of Bataan and Corregidor while the bulk of Australia's troops were away fighting in North Africa and the Middle East. The news of his arrival in mid-March sent the country into a kind of hysteria. In America The New York *Times* of March 18 proclaimed:

MACARTHUR IN AUSTRALIA AS ALLIED COMMANDER
MOVE HAILED AS FORESHADOWING TURN OF THE TIDE

Approaching Adelaide, MacArthur, tired and battle weary but knowing that reporters would be insistent for a statement, scribbled his famous message of hope on the back of an envelope:

The President of the United States ordered me to break through the Japanese lines and proceed from Corregidor to Australia for the purpose, as I understand it, of organizing the American offensive against Japan, a primary object of which is the relief of the Philippines. I came through and I shall return.

On April 9, came the devastating news from the Philippines that General King, his Fili-American troops starving, desperately low on supplies, had surrendered Bataan. More than 75,000 men laid down their arms to the Imperial Japanese Army. Tojo now claimed that "Japan is determined to destroy the United States and Great Britain." On the death march to Camp O'Donnell more than 7,000 American and Filipino prisoners died from disease and brutality. Men who stumbled and fell from fatigue were bayoneted to death while others were forced to dig graves and bury their comrades alive. As the emaciated prisoners stumbled through the jungle heat along the dusty roads, Filipinos openly wept, many risking their lives to try to snatch the odd prisoner and hide him from the straggling columns.

One of the rescued Filipinos, before he managed to escape south to Australia on one of the hospital ships, was Carlos Pacis. His real name was Romulo Pacis, and some said "Carlos" was a name given him by the staff of the Sacred Heart Hospital in Manila, where he had been an outpatient on and off for "acute anxiety" between 1929 and 1931. Whatever the reason, he became known as Carlos and was one of the volunteer Filipino guerrillas who, after throwing away their uniforms, had managed to get out before the Japanese fleet had completely cut the southern escape route from Bataan and Corregidor.

Seven of his countrymen had been chosen to be in the welcoming guard at Spencer Street Station where MacArthur arrived in Melbourne on the last leg of his escape from Corregidor, but Carlos, too ill at the time, was not one of them. Recovering from tuberculosis contracted in the jungles of Luzon during the worst part of the fighting, he had been given noncombatant duties in the officers' mess at St. Kilda Barracks. Still, he had been one of the spectators at the station and he would remember it all his life. Amid all the red cap bands and scarlet collar tabs of the big brass, MacArthur stood out in plain soldier's khaki, neatly pressed, the thin brown army-issue belt girding his tall, fit frame, his chest, unlike that of most of the other general staff officers, without any of the medals that had been awarded him. Only the crushed and worn gold oak leaves on the famous cap, and the four tiny silver stars on the collar of the safari jacket signified his military rank, the highest then attainable by most professional soldiers.

Carlos had watched the general on that Saturday morning of March 21, when just after 10:00 A.M. he stepped forward through the cheering thousands that were pressing against the bobby-helmeted Victorian police, through the small army of correspondents toward the big microphone of the Australian Broadcasting Corporation.

The crowd became silent. At that moment the general spoke not only to Australia and America but to the world. Carlos, his short frame straining on tiptoe, could not see, but a policeman, spotting the Filipino now proudly back in uniform, motioned him to the front, where he could see MacArthur clearly. Behind the general stood his wife, his son Arthur and the Filipino amah. Taking a piece of paper from his pocket the general, in characteristic mellifluous stentorian tones, began to speak.

> I am glad indeed to be in immediate cooperation with the Australian soldier. I know him well from World War days and admire him greatly. I have every confidence in the ultimate success of our joint cause; but success in modern war requires something more than courage and a willingness to die: it requires careful preparation. . . . No general can make something out of nothing. My success or failure will depend primarily upon the resources which the respective governments place at my disposal. My faith in them is complete. In any event I shall do my best. "I shall keep the soldier's faith."

Carlos would say he was struck by the phrase "careful preparation." The general was right. That was the key.

There had been thunderous applause and cheers from the

spectators spilling out onto Flinders and Collins Streets and down behind them as far as the Yarra. It was, the Australians said, a great speech, a ray of hope in the war-torn darkness. In England, thousands were queuing for hours to see the Movietone reels of MacArthur's arrival, British newspapers dubbing him another Horatio Nelson and an American Sir Francis Drake—"our greatest hope in our greatest need." Thousands of children were being baptized "MacArthur," and in Arkansas, at Little Rock, MacArthur's birthplace was to be blessed as a national shrine. An American reporter in London declared that in Britain such rapturous attention had not been lavished on any man "since the days of Valentino." And in Washington, a boulevard would now bear the general's name.

Elizabeth had listened, too, and nine days later heard the broadcast when MacArthur was awarded the Medal of Honor, presented to him at a dinner given by Australia's prime minister in Canberra. The static from the national capital 900 miles to the south surged into the Lawson living room, but they still could hear the words of the general giving them new hope that just possibly the Japanese might be stopped:

> . . . I have come as a soldier in the great crusade of personal liberty as opposed to perpetual slavery. My faith in our ultimate victory is invincible, and I bring you tonight the unbreakable spirit of the free man's military code in support of our joint cause. . . . We shall win or we shall die and to this end I pledge the full resources of all the mighty power of my country and all the blood of my countrymen.

Elizabeth saw that her mother had tears in her eyes.

"God bless him," she said quietly. All of Australia was sharing that sentiment.

No one had mentioned Tomokazu since the war began. It

was understood that he was never to be mentioned. Elizabeth even hid the Japanese doll he had given her and she knew that like the doll, her love must hide, go underground and wait out the war's hatred. Even so, she was torn in the tug-of-war between loyalty to her country and her love of Tomokazu. The only thing that made it bearable was her conviction that Tomokazu could not have taken part in any of the fighting. Even if he had been conscripted there would not have been enough time for him to be sent off in the southern army. His skill in aeronautical design would, she hoped, keep him at home and out of it. She just could not share her country's blanket hatred of the Japanese, and besides, hadn't even some of the Aussie soldiers who had gotten out of Malaya said that *some* Japanese officers had tried to intervene to stop the brutality and rape . . . And then she would become confused, guilty about her feelings for him, longing for him and yet terrified of the impending Japanese intervention.

Guilt and fear and loneliness swirled around her. Where was he? Where was her father? Her brother Frank? What would happen? They said MacArthur would reverse things, but now there was more bad news from the Philippines. After bombarding Corregidor with up to 15,000 shells a day Admiral Yamashita had forced a surrender on General Wainright. The U.S. Stars and Stripes was hauled down and the white flag run up once more and another 11,000 troops taken prisoner. On June 1, 1942, Elizabeth woke up to find her mother in shock. Three Japanese midget submarines, the type used in the Pearl Harbor attack, had penetrated the defenses of Sydney Harbor over two thousand miles south of New Guinea and had torpedoed the S.S. *Kuttabul.*

Some two months later, on July 20, 1942, MacArthur moved his headquarters from Melbourne, south of Sydney in the southeastern corner of the country, up to Brisbane, halfway up the 3,000-mile eastern Australian coast—much closer to the Japanese-held islands.

CHAPTER SIX
Toowoomba

It was mid-July, just before MacArthur's move, when the two well-dressed very polite men appeared at Mrs. Dalgetty's front door. Though their shoes were dusted by Toowoomba's red volcanic soil she could tell immediately they weren't from Queensland. Being July it was midwinter but it was an unusually warm day and only colder southerners would be wearing suits. Their accent was softer, more English, from Melbourne probably. They told her they were from ASIO. Mrs. Dalgetty, trying to cover her hair curlers with her scarf, said she didn't know what they were talking about. They showed her a card.

"Australian Security and Intelligence Organization," the taller man said.

"Quite a mouthful," she told him.

Only the tall one smiled. The other one looked south from the Mount Lofty area down onto the town and back again along the range top.

"We're checking on aliens, Mrs. Dalgetty. Their associates. Understand you had a Japanese boarder?"

"Yes. Nice boy."

"Could we come in?"

"All right. Can't talk for long. Have to pluck a chicken for the weekend."

"We won't take long."

They took half an hour. Without asking directions, they walked past the cramped kitchen smelling of cabbage and through the dingy lounge cluttered with cheap china ornaments, its garish orange linoleum clashing with the yellow wallpaper. They turned right through a dark hallway with an

47

overburdened coatrack into the second bedroom in the far left corner of the house. By contrast the nine-by-nine room, its windows running south and west, was airy and neat. A lowboy with mirror attached stood to the left of the door, the clothes chest on the opposite wall facing the lowboy, and the bed, its base a sturdy iron stand and its coarse blue woolen blankets tucked tightly beneath the hard mattress, stood along the southern wall. A single pillow was covered in brown calico, and a pair of shoes, size seven and a half, were waiting on a gray kangaroo-skin rug, so worn in the middle that it shone.

Mrs. Dalgetty nodded at the shoes. "He was coming back, you know, that is, till the war started. Went home to see family. Illness."

The smaller of the two nodded. "Things certainly seem arranged as if he'd meant to come back."

"Yes," she said. "Left a deposit on the room."

The taller man went through the old cedar lowboy: a checkered sports coat, two pairs of the latest cuffed slacks, new white linen shirts, beige shorts and long white socks. An old beat-up Slazenger tennis racket was propped in the corner of the lowboy, two of the gut strings broken and curled, and there was a photograph of him in a pair of overalls standing by a Tiger Moth at Toowoomba's aerodrome. The underwear was "Chesty Bond."

"All Aussie brands," the smaller one said.

"Well, they would be, wouldn't they?" said the other.

"All the latest fashion, I mean," said the smaller, who now appeared to Mrs. Dalgetty to be the boss.

"Yeah," replied his colleague, sitting on the edge of the bed, sifting through the immaculately arranged drawers. "Quite the boy 'round town."

"Oh, no," said Mrs. Dalgetty. "He wasn't flashy at all. He was neat and clean, I'll give him that. Nip or not."

"Write home much, did he?"

"Don't know."

"Get much mail?"

"No. Now and then, y'know."

In one of the drawers they found an old Royal Automobile Club of Queensland touring map of southeastern Queensland running onto the lush Northern Rivers district, which lay just south of the Queensland border hugging the New South Wales coast, and souvenir stickers of Byron Bay, Southport and Brisbane.

"Go to the coast much, did he?" asked the boss, showing the stickers.

"Yes. Well, once or twice. Brisbane a few times and northern New South—Byron Bay, I think. With his girlfriend and her mum."

"Elizabeth Lawson."

"You do get around," she said. "Yeah, he went with Elizabeth. As I say, only once or twice."

"What was his name?"

They had known exactly where his room was, had gone straight to it without any help from her, yet now they were asking his name? It could only mean that one of the snoopy neighbors had been shooting off their mouth—and all they knew apart from where his room was was that he was a Jap going out with a white girl.

"Tomokazu," she said. "Tomokazu Somura."

"Can you spell that?"

They wrote it down. When they left she saw they took the map and a small bunch of notes face down and held together by an elastic band. The small one turned at the door. "We'll send these back to you. Don't say anything about our visit."

Outside the rickety front gate the smaller one took out a pipe and began stuffing it with Navy plug. "What do you think, Len?"

"Looks clean as a whistle."

"How about the girl?"

"No point is there?"

"No. For now." He pushed the moist tobacco deep into the bowl, fussing with the edges. "Better cover ourselves, though. Keep an eye on her. Routine surveillance, known associate of alien. Local man can handle it. Post office can check surveillance of incoming mail."

"No bloody mail from Japan," said Len. "I'll bet you a fiver he was just what Immigration said, a Nip on a student visa at the Tech studying aeronautical design."

"Yes, guess you're right. Probably stuck at home designing battleships."

"Yeah, with *our* scrap iron." The small one read one of the notes dated November 14 of the previous year. He shook his head. "Ah, nothing here. 'My darling Tommie,' et cetera. Just a bunch of lovey dovey crap. Written before the Jap got called home."

"Sounds like he had a bloody good time over here. More pussy than he could handle."

"Yeah," said the smaller one. "Dirty little bitch."

Mrs. Dalgetty took a protesting chicken from the coop by its legs, put it on the block and chopped off its head. Mrs. Cohen, watching from next door, was watering her papaya tree. Toowoomba was too cold for papaya, the temperature often falling below freezing in winter, but Mrs. Cohen insisted on having a go. "Had visitors?" she called out.

"Yes," answered Mrs. Dalgetty, hanging the chicken upside down on the washing line to bleed. "Coupla coppers. Security dicks."

"From Brisbane?"

"Pull my other leg. In all that garb? Melbourne, I'd say. Sniffing around Tomokazu's room. Thought he might have been a Jap spy."

"Well, you can't blame 'em."

"Suppose not. That bloody Tojo. All his fault." What she meant was that now she'd definitely have to find someone else to rent the room.

CHAPTER SEVEN

MacArthur was shocked to discover that Australia couldn't even be called a garrison, let alone a springboard. With most of the country's troops overseas in the Middle East or rotting in Japanese camps, he had only one Australian division scattered through northern Australia and New Guinea and only one American division in the whole country, while some of the Royal Australian Air Force planes were Tiger Moths from post-World War One. On top of this the Japanese had captured over eighty percent of the world's rubber and the huge oil fields of the East Indies—the very material without which the Allies could not hope to win a modern war.

Worse, the Japanese had now reached the northern coast of New Guinea. Conventional logic said to dig in, to train what few troops he had, and ready the air force and what naval contingents there were to defend Australia in a last-ditch stand. Instead, MacArthur told Australia's prime minister Curtin that he would have no part of the Brisbane Line strategy. It was defeatist. It had to go or he would resign. Curtin gave in.

Now in his Brisbane headquarters, after listening to the horror story that was his aide's firsthand account of the New Guinea jungle: a green hell, larger than Texas, made up of man-high, razor kunai grass, impenetrable swamps, the precipitous jungle-covered 13,000-foot Owen Stanley mountain range, the swamps of rampant typhus, malaria and dysentery that made it the worst fighting country in the world, MacArthur, incredibly, called a press conference. He entered the press room and promptly informed the assembled correspondents that rather than digging in and waiting for the Japanese, he would attack!

Like his own staff, it was the last thing the Japanese expected. Following intelligence reports, MacArthur sent the now-returned veteran Seventh Australian Division to Milne Bay in Papua on the eastern tip of New Guinea, where he anticipated the Japanese would attack in order to secure vital forward air fields for their Australian offensive. The Japanese landed on the night of August 25–26, and the battle was joined in the fetid, steaming jungle surrounding the bay. For eleven days and nights in a ceaseless downpour the fighting raged with artillery, naval bombardment, tanks, flamethrowers and bayonets. Finally the Japanese were pushed back into the sea and with them, for the first time, the aura of Nippon's invincibility. Leaving half their troops dead on the beaches and in the surrounding jungles along the twenty-mile-long bay, the remnants of the Japanese marines withdrew on the night of September 5–6. Word that the Japanese could be beaten after all spread quickly as far as the beleaguered British army in Burma . . .

When Elizabeth Lawson first read the news she thought that perhaps her nightmares of invasion would go away, and they did. But not her thoughts of Tomokazu. Now she allowed herself to dream of them together again, aching for him, wanting him in her arms.

Pressing overland from the north coast of New Guinea, a large Japanese force under Gen. Tomitaro Horii was moving over the divide of the Owen Stanleys, marching toward the strategic Port Moresby on the southern, Australian side of New Guinea in another attempt to take the island.

MacArthur's forces were outnumbered by five to one. Being September, it was the spring of 1942 in the Southern Hemisphere, approaching the time of the monsoons, the period of continual and torrential rains called "The Wet"—in terrain where a half-mile progress a day was the most you could expect, where muddied pathways allowed only one man at a time on the 13,000-foot-high Kokoda Trail.

Along with the rain came blackwater fever, dengue fever, bush typhus, yaws, hookworm and the ever-present, all-pervasive malaria, so that companies were fighting with most of their complement running high fevers. And there were Jap snipers, lashed high in the trees in order to sleep and living on C rations of rice and water, virtually impossible to see and capable of stopping an entire division dead in its tracks by pinning down the advance patrols. Still, encouraged by the Japanese reverse at Milne Bay, MacArthur's Allied force counterattacked, and Horii lost 10,000 out of a force of 14,000, including his own life. To secure the victory MacArthur needed his troops, the Australian Seventh Division and the American Thirty-second, to effect a pincer on Horii's retreating army around Gona and Buna on New Guinea's northeastern coast. But the Japanese dug in, and the Allies bogged down.

MacArthur now ordered General Eichelberger to take Buna or not come back alive. Tojo's orders were just as explicit. *MacArthur must be stopped.* Tojo was far from alone in his determination to end the growing Allied advance. Imperial Headquarters, angered by MacArthur's daring escape from Corregidor and now alarmed by his reemergence in the field, demanded that Buna be held at all costs. Apart from national honor, without New Guinea vital bases would be lost from which Nippon could bomb MacArthur's staging areas in Australia.

Young Frank Lawson was part of the Australian–U.S. counterattack on the Gona–Buna front in late December of 1942. By now the Allies knew that *kofuku*—"surrender"—was the most despised word in the Japanese vocabulary. The Japanese soldier's field manual was very clear: to surrender was beyond contempt, the worst thing a Japanese could ever do, not only a betrayal of self but, much worse, a betrayal of family and, above all, a betrayal of country. It could never be justified, and the last bullet should always be saved for oneself. The Allies knew that to take Buna would mean rooting out the last Japanese in the last bunker . . .

It was the night of January 1. On both sides of the line the bunkers, varying from waist to shoulder height and big enough to hold two to six men, were dug out of the rotting jungle earth, the evacuated soil being used to form a ridge a foot or so high on three sides of the bunker. Coconut tree trunks and other logs were placed across the bunker, resting on the three raised ridges of dirt, then more logs across these until high enough for protection from shelling. The log-tiered, layered roof was covered in dirt and bush camouflage leaving a foot-high slit facing the enemy. Through this a constant watch was maintained throughout any given line of bunkers, especially at night, and in as many as possible a machine gun was mounted. A soldier never left the shelter at night, and used his helmet to defecate and urinate in and took turns to stand guard. As the bunkers were usually impervious to mortar or artillery fire, even at close range, the only sure way to clean them out was to lob a grenade through the slit or to use a flame thrower—the man packing the flame thrower became a walking bomb.

It was a long way, over 1,500 miles, from a peaceful summer evening in Toowoomba, sitting at Picnic Point watching Tabletop Mountain turn purple with the setting sun. But right now Frank tried to forget about home, about what his mother and Elizabeth were doing, about where his dad was, and concentrated on trying to learn the trick of staying alive. In building his bunker before dusk he'd been especially careful. Despite the sweat, the rain, the awkwardness of moving his stocky frame in the confined space and the swarms of mosquitoes, he'd made a Z-shaped entrance to the bunker he was

sharing this night with Corporal Pierce as they waited for supplies and reinforcements before closing in on Adachi's last
troops in New Guinea. Frank knew that if a Nip managed to
spot the bunker from the direct flash of the Bren gun and
lobbed a grenade into the entrance at the rear, the explosion
would deafen him for a while and start his ears ringing but
the grenade couldn't roll around in the acute angle of the Z if
he'd made a good job of it, and the crawl space should take
the impact of the shrapnel.

His spade struck metal and for a terrifying moment he
thought it was a mine. Nothing happened. He looked closer.
It was a rusted tin of Moringa's Drops and broken glass from
a bottle of Suntory whiskey, its English-language label promis-
ing "Old Vat 7 Years."

"Hey!" he called out to Pierce. "We're smack on top of a Jap
rubbish dump!"

"Great."

The tropical sun fell abruptly behind the blackish green
peaks of the Owen Stanleys, and the jungle began its nightly
danse macabre of misbegotten shapes, all of which seemed to be
moving, and the mosquitoes came in hordes. The sticky repel-
lent kept some of them away, and the Atabrine tablets that
turned a man's skin yellow kept out the malaria, but eyelids,
nostrils and ears were still vulnerable to attack, and occasionally, despite orders for silence, Frank could hear a sharp
smack from somewhere along the line where the buzzing onslaught had driven someone beyond the limit. They had taken
a sapper out the night before, a young bloke from Oakey,
crying with the itching—a massive allergic reaction to the
hundreds of bites that peppered his face. "Lucky bastard." A
uniform was no protection even for those who had changed
over from the wide, flappy Bombay Bloomer shorts into full-
length trousers. The stingers could penetrate damn near anything.

Pierce tried to get some sleep, seeking refuge beneath a

coarse blue army-issue blanket, but soon it was soaked with his perspiration and he could hardly breathe. "Jesus Christ." He gasped for air and sat up. Some of the men in the Darling Downs company had tried to wear the head netting that hung down from the slouch hat, their heavy helmets, like their gas-masks, long ago discarded as too heavy and cumbersome. The trouble with the netting, which made everyone look like a beekeeper, was that in the Turkish bath of New Guinea's coastal humidity the intense heat was as bad as the bites. The choice was steaming suffocation or the never-ending itch.

To the east through a grove of blasted coconut trees that looked like so many umbrellas stripped ragged and unfurled in the moonlight they could see the occasional white line of surf spilling over a coral reef a hundred yards or so offshore, and beyond, a burned-out enemy landing craft washing idly to and fro against the reef, its turret swaying with each swell of the sea.

Then the Japs started up; the English-speaking voices coming through the jungle in the tinny tones of crude amplifiers. When he had first arrived in the islands Frank thought the veterans from Milne Bay and the U.S. troops from the Solomons were having him on when they told him about the Japs' verbal attacks. Now he knew differently. "Hi, Aussies! Think about your girlfriends, Aussies, and your American allies back home. They sleep while you die. Americans have more money, Aussies—much more money. Buy more things for girls. You die tonight, Aussies. Remember Gallipoli."

That was one mistake, the mention of Gallipoli. It stopped Frank from being just angry and made him brave. His grand-father had been an Anzac in the Australia–New Zealand Army Corps, landing in the Dardanelles, and for Australians there was no greater call to courage than the mention of the stubborn defeat in the face of the Turks on the cliffs of Gallipoli Peninsula in 1915.

"Remember Gallipoli, Aussies . . ."

"Remember the fucking Alamo!" someone shouted back.

"Stupid bastard," whispered Pierce. "The Alamo, what's that got to do with the price of figs? That was a Yank fight."

Frank shook his head. Fifteen hundred miles from home, and his outfit and the Japs trading crazy insults over a swamp.

They waited. Soon the Japs would start insulting the politicians, which was sort of funny. On Guadalcanal they were telling the Americans that Roosevelt ate shit. Tonight it would probably be Prime Minister Curtin's turn. Someone, again in defiance of orders, sang out, "The Emperor eats shit!"

But tonight there were no insults of Curtin or FDR or Churchill. This first night of the New Year they started the stuff that really was scary. Somehow, no one was ever really sure how, they periodically got hold of the battalion lists, usually after having overrun Allied posts farther up in the islands, then they'd match the shoulder patch insignia from the POWs with the troops they were fighting in the field. The result would be the same once they'd ID'd the regiment opposing them: they would start in with the Christian names. They had done it in Bataan and it had unnerved the Americans too. You knew they weren't sure whether you were there at the front or not. You could have just as easily been back in the field hospital at Moresby with "break bone" fever or typhus or dysentery or yaws or wounded. But knowing this didn't help. When you heard your name called out in that dark place, fear crawled into the bunker. And when they got the nicknames correct, it could damn near paralyze you. Nerves at the brink, often short on rations, always short on sleep, you'd sometimes fire a round or a burst to steady yourself, to get it off your chest. It did that. It also told the Japs exactly where you were.

"Johnny Pierce! Corporal Pierce from Gatton!" They pronounced it "Gat-ton" instead of running the two t's together, but it did the dirty trick.

"Jesus Christ . . ." began Pierce. The moon was pearl white, passing through a cloud like a galleon in full sail.

"Say your prayers, Johnny. Bayonet for you, Johnny. No more love to make for you, Johnny. Bayonet for you, Johnny." The high-pitched voices were getting closer.

"Don't worry about it, Johnno," Frank whispered. "It's all bullshit."

"We're coming, Johnny!"

"Yeah," said Pierce. " 'Course it is."

"You got the magazines ready?" asked Frank. He could feel them on the left side of the Bren gun.

"Yeah," said Pierce. "Right beside you."

"Thanks. Don't let'm—"

"No more love to make, Johnny."

Frank saw the bush move. He pulled the trigger. The Bren gun stuttered forward into the blackness.

"Hold your fire!" It was the sergeant major.

Without warning the moon was swallowed by high cumulus, and Frank could no longer see the breakers at the edge of the sea. For some reason they had given him a sense of security—a horizon in the pitch black night.

"Give me a helmet," he whispered quickly. He opened his fly and urinated in it. If the Japs were in battalion strength, 400 or more, the Bren's barrel, unlike the water-cooled Vickers, would get red hot and the urine might have to be used to cool it. It could mean he might get to use an extra magazine and that could mean his life.

The "banzai" came in a concerted roar and suddenly the jungle was alive, shaking. A flame erupted from the darkness, streaking toward a bunker to Lawson's right.

In three bursts Frank brought down four of them, and Pierce, banging away with his .303, took care of another two. Behind them they could hear the hollow thumps from the four-inch mortars, and farther back, the deep crunching of their twenty-five pounders, the shells now screaming overhead toward the Japanese staging areas, but it was more bluff

than anything else, the exact enemy positions being unknown.

"Grenade!" Frank shouted.

It toppled high on the roof, exploded, dirt pouring down.
Instinctively Frank had wanted to duck below the slit level but
his training told him no. That's when they rushed. He fired a
long burst through an arc of forty-five degrees, the Bren's
heat washing back over his face like a hot fan. Something fell
ahead in the darkness and there was a bluish tongue of flame.
The Ariska's bullet whistled through the slit, passing between
them, thudding into the earthen wall. The Bren stopped.
Frank's right hand swept forward, taking off the banana-
shaped magazine and replacing it with a full one, all in one
forward-and-backward motion. He snapped it in, pulled back
on the cocking pin and disregarded the drum sights. At this
range you did it by feel.

Now the artillery had stopped—the Japs were too close.
The moon reappeared and in its glow he saw the glint of steel.
The wave was overwhelming them when Frank heard, "Fix
bayonets" from behind the bunker. There was a thump beside
the bunker to the left of him. He saw a crumpled and groan-
ing soldier. "Take the Bren," he said, pushing it toward
Pierce. Out through the Z entrance, his elbows moving fast,
Frank pushed himself through the soft fallen dirt, crawled
round the rear of his bunker, momentarily exposing himself
to his own troops, and dragged the wounded man back, half
pulling, half pushing him into the bunker. And then everything went black and he pitched forward over the other's
body . . .

Blazing sun. When he came to, his head heavy as stone,
throbbing, nauseated, he found himself looking dumbly at a
Japanese bayonet, its owner yelling at him and pointing
toward an X-shaped cross of coconut logs. Around him he
could see other filthy, exhausted Australian and American
prisoners. Johnny Pierce was next to him. "Ran out of

ammo . . ." began Pierce. "Had to give it up. They thought you were—"

The Japanese guard smashed Pierce's face with his rifle butt. Pierce reeled sideways. As they were hauled toward the coconut crosses in the clearing and lashed to them, the jungle seemed to Frank to have been transformed; it was extraordinarily bright, green and beautiful, purified by the rain. Then his heart began banging his chest. He'd heard about what they had done at Milne Bay but he thought of his father watching him, of his granddad who had won the Military Cross . . .

The Japanese platoon, what was left of them, about twenty in all, formed two lines, like a rugby lineout. Lawson noticed one of the Jap's black canvas boots was split at the ankle. The officer, a lieutenant, was wearing a bowl-shaped cork top; the troops wore the light khaki cotton field caps.

The lieutenant gave a short speech in Japanese, then a translator told them surrender was the act of women. When he gave the word, two of the Japanese, one from the head of each line, ran forward, rifles fully extended, yelling the usual *"banzai."*

Johnny Pierce cried out almost immediately, but for some reason young Frank Lawson did not make a sound when the bayonet first hit him, and it was only after the Japanese paused and pushed for the secondary thrust, when they said that the bayonet must have splintered his spine, that his scream seemed to fill the whole jungle. Then the rest of the Japanese had their go, careful not to hit the heart, as this way it took much longer.

Buna fell to MacArthur's forces the next morning, January 2, 1943. Of the 20,000 Japanese who had invaded New Guinea, more than 12,000 now lay dead. Soon the rest of New Guinea would fall to MacArthur. After the fighting, during which Allied losses were higher than those of the much more publicized battle of Guadalcanal—it was safer reporting from a ship at Guadalcanal whereas in Buna you had to go ashore to see the action—the tide seemed finally to be turning against Japan.

To stop their reverses, they decided they must stop MacArthur.

Brisbane HQ told Sara Lawson that her son, Franklin Thomas, like John Pierce, had been killed in action near Buna. Beyond this, no details were given. Three days later, after elements of the American 126th Regiment relieved Gona and got some Aussies from the Darling Downs regiment out, the details filtered back and Toowoomba was simply too small to protect Sarah and Elizabeth from the truth. When they were told, Elizabeth remembered only sitting and staring at the louvered windows. She lost track of time, it must have been hours, her mind refusing to accept it. The doctor gave her and her mother some pills. Elizabeth dimly remembered taking them, obediently, like a child; her mother had no recollection of the doctor ever being there.

After that, when she forced herself to comprehend what had happened to her brother, Elizabeth knew her father was right—and she would tell him so when he came home—she would never marry a Japanese. Not now. Not ever. She told herself this as forcefully and as often as she told herself that she hoped she would never see him again. Then why didn't she dream of her father, who was missing and whom she missed so terribly? Why did she, in her dreams, continue to go to Tomokazu?

CHAPTER EIGHT
Honshu, Japan

Before going to his father's house, Tomokazu, in keeping with
ancient custom, first made his way through the grove of whis-
pery bamboo and approached the *inkyo*, the small attached
bungalow behind that of his parents. It was made of the same
sand-colored slatted wood hewn from the giant pine forest
that had clothed the great mountain since the beginning of
time. Far below, through the translucent mist, the lakes glistened like mother of pearl as, dressed in black mourning
robe, he placed his Western-style shoes on the tatami mat and
greeted his grandparents. With deep reverence he told them
he would go shortly to the family shrine and say prayers to the
kami, the gods, for his ancestors. And as a sign of his venera-
tion for his grandparents, and their parents before them, he
bowed before them, left bean cake at the *inkyo*, bowed low
before the emperor's picture, keeping his arms still by his
side, and quietly left. He would not mourn his ancestors too
long, however; to do so would be unworthy and even worse,
an abnegation of his faith in the *kami*. Death was an interlude.
This was not only his belief but the belief of all his family, of
the whole nation. It was Shinto. When one died one passed
through the great *torii*, the gateway to another time, to join
the gods, one's ancestors, and so it was as futile as it was child-
ish to shed tears. One was forever on a journey and in this
earthly part of it one needed only think of service to the emperor, the son of heaven. If one did one's duty to Him it was
enough. The *kami* would know. One's pain in body or mind
was of no consequence. Which was why from an early age one
learned and talked about cutting the belly, *hara-kiri*, if honor
and the gods required it. And if one wasn't of the samurai,

63

honor could always be found by plunging into the crater of Mihara, thereby beginning a new life with the *kami*.

Elizabeth had talked about it too—"afterlife," the Christians called it. Tomokazu knew that to try to understand the mystery of it all was foolishness, as foolish as trying to explain how one was still the same person this year as last but also different. Shinto understood this, which was why Tomokazu hung the tiny mirrors in the holy black camphor tree together with the yellow prayer ribbons. In the mirror one saw one's ancestors, one's gods, and knew at that moment how one could also become a god and live forever in one's children and in their children as they looked in the mirror and saw you, and so in death one merely entered the great mirror, the serene sea that followed the typhoon, one's end on earth merely hastening one's journey through to the higher reality of the *kami* as one passed from a mirror image where left seemed right and right seemed left, into the place behind the mirror into the truer reality of another room. The military acknowledged this profound truth too: on ending one's earthly interlude one was promoted to the next highest rank.

But for all his tranquility of the moment Tomokazu felt a sadness too. A lack, really. Without his love there would be no one of their spirit to look into the sacred mirrors—no one to pass through the bright vermilion *torii* that seemed on fire against the emerald green of Nippon's forest and the blue of her seas.

In his parents' house he sat silently as his mother prepared tea, she in turn quietly observing the boiling water in the small iron stove inside the square moat of protective ash. When the water began boiling she transferred the water into the stone bowl of powdered tea and began whipping the mixture with the bamboo whisk. They ate sushi, and to signify their joy at his being home, his mother presented a treat, a *saba,* a special Osaka sushi topped with pickled herring and dark green seaweed.

Tomokazu watched his younger sisters playing nearby with gaily painted *kokeshi* dolls that he had brought them from northern Honshu. He had given one to Elizabeth. Over a year ago he had mailed her a letter during the long hot stopover in Port Moresby in New Guinea. He had not put on any return address because he could not be sure where he would be for the next few months and he did not want his parents to know how he felt about her—until the time was right. They would not understand. For them all whites were still barbarians and worse, exploiting Asia and capable of the most terrible atrocities against its peoples. Tojo had made this clear with newspaper stories resurrecting the cruelty of the Americans in the Spanish–American War. Tomokazu could only hope that Elizabeth had received the letter. Now he knew that she had been right after all; that flying back to Japan he was flying into war and away from her—perhaps forever. His mother had feared war too but she knew that like all Yamato, all Japan, he was always at the emperor's call.

Tomokazu poured tea into his bowl and, swirling it gently, washed down the last grain of rice so as not to show offence.

"Next weekend," he told his mother, he would visit again.

She nodded, pleased. His father said "good," which for him was a mouthful. By contrast his two small sisters kept badgering him, giggling, clinging to his robe, asking what it was he did that was so "secret" in Yokosuka. Like all Japanese children they were still in *ameru*, the period of indulgence, but by now, Tomokazu thought, they should begin to understand responsibility. He told them that he drew things and that he could not say any more.

Did he ever fly? they asked.

"Sometimes," he said, and that was enough, no more questions. When they persisted he told them that like all the workers at the Yokosuka works he bowed each morning to the emperor's picture and sang "Kimigayo"—the national anthem. When they still kept at him their father finally spoke up. Did they want the *Kempetai,* the thought police, to come? The laughter died.

The light was fading, the colored lanterns were not yet lit, and in the twilight chill Tomokazu's heart felt empty as a bowl. He walked down from his parents' home toward the Inland Sea, passing a sacred camphor tree covered in the white paper blossoms of Shinto horoscopes and the multicolored *sembazuru,* the colored paper strips, hanging like leis of frangipani. The dusk silhouetted a tiny rocky island crested by wind-dwarfed pines, and for a moment it reminded him of the pass at Byron Bay. But that was 4,000 miles away—another time, another country. A long line of seaweed strips set out to dry fluttered like wet ribbons in the rising sea breeze. In the near-darkness he saw a young woman hurrying by with a lamp, then heard laughter. Some of the villagers were gathering to go fishing. He watched the cormorant birds, up to half a dozen per boat, set upon the water, each attached by a cord about its throat to the fishermen controlling them from the boat. From each bow a long pole arched over the sea, a burning golden fire at its end luring the fish upward where the cormorants dived and caught them and were hauled back to the boat, the cords choking and so preventing them from swallowing the fish before the fishermen could retrieve them.

He had told Elizabeth about it once, how different it was from the fisherman's life in Byron Bay. She had thought it was cruel, using the birds this way. It had been their first real disagreement and he decided it should be their last—there were many things that neither of them would understand in the other's culture, like the Christian god and *kami,* which for all their similarity were finally not at all the same. In death the Christians hid everything that reminded them of death. In Yamato one went to meet it, one saw it each day in the mirrors of water—one's death staring back at one from the other side of the earthly existence.

More fishermen pushed off from the beach and soon lights were bobbing everywhere: fires on water like the ghosts of rising suns. And thoughts of his mission replaced the image of Elizabeth.

CHAPTER NINE
Brisbane—Victoria Barracks

Perspiring heavily in the hot muggy air, Carlos Pacis, trying to suppress his cough, was shaving carefully, learning the mystery of the new Gillette safety razor he found, to his delight, was indeed safe and did not threaten to butcher you if you suffered from a slight tic, which he did whenever he was especially anxious. He had a photo of MacArthur up by the mirror. The tall general always looked magnificently aloof, next only to God, cane in hand, the long, aquiline nose, the suntanned closely shaved face, the deliberative, fearless eyes. Carlos remembered on Corregidor how the general had disdained the air-raid shelters, refusing even to use the protection of the tunnel, confident, it seemed, that he would go only when his Maker decreed it. And yet the general was not disdainful of other men's fears. He seemed to understand their weaknesses without making them feel weak or ashamed. He was compassionate. He was the bravest man Carlos knew and Filipinos loved him. Carlos could still recall the great speech at Spencer Street Station in Melbourne.

But Carlos had also heard the speeches of the Japanese: the white man—the British, the Dutch and the Americans—had dominated the Pacific far too long. If the Asian peoples were to govern their own destiny, now was the time to act. Carlos certainly did not love the Japanese but they had given the yellow man new pride and had destroyed the myth of the white man's superiority. When Singapore, "the city of the lion," had collapsed within a week, the truth of the Japanese prophecy was clear. Only a fool could not see the future.

Carlos stared into the mirror. He was a soldier, and like his grandfather and his father, he wanted his country to be *his*

country, governed by his own people. Philippines for the Filipinos—not for foreigners. The British would not stand for it
in their own country, would they? And certainly not the
Americans. The Americans had fought for their own freedom.
Now it was time to win the Philippines for the Filipinos—not
for foreigners. Better for the moment the Japs who at least
promised independence; better them than the whites. The
Greater Asia Co-Prosperity Plan had promised to put an end
to white imperialism. Besides, the Japs were winning. One
had to be practical, to adjust to the new reality. Hadn't the
Americans done the same? The ones who had been English
until the English were beaten became Americans if they had
any sense.

He ran his hand carefully over his chin. He was satisfied. It
was important to shave well. He would stand a better chance if
he looked clean and well-kempt and not like some beggar
from the Manila slums. MacArthur would always welcome a
Filipino; he loved them as much as they loved him. Carlos
explained to his image, the other Carlos, that it was nothing
personal against the general—it was for Filipino independence. MacArthur above everyone understood the fight for
freedom . . . he himself had sympathized with the rebels in
the outer islands, hadn't he?

Well, Carlos would no longer run like a dog delivering the
cocktails in the evening "blue hour" on the patio of the Manila Hotel. No more bowing like a servant in response to the
snapping of impatient white fingers. No more being used like
a vassal in your own country. He knew MacArthur was not
one of them. The general, he'd heard, had even stopped
drinking when the war began, to focus all his energy on de-
feating the Japanese. But he was, nevertheless, the greatest
symbol, the upholder of white rule in the East, and now the
message of Buna was being heard, that if the Japanese could
be defeated, the symbol might return and never leave. And if
MacArthur returned, so would the whites. It would be the old

way back again, and the chance for his people's independence would be lost forever.

Carlos's duty was clear. MacArthur must die.

In time, he believed, he would be a hero like his grandfather, who had fought the Americans in the Philippines in the Spanish–American War. A statue even, and instead of Manila's Dewey Boulevard there would be the Avenida de Pacis. He rolled it on his tongue. It sounded very good, noble. It even had a heroic ring. Like MacArthur.

He would have preferred a grenade but he knew that if he requested such a thing, or any other weapon, from the Australians they would wonder why. One did not need a weapon to tend the officers' bar. A knife, yes, but then the difficulty would be getting close enough. At least two guards with Tommy guns accompanied the general almost everywhere, in and out of Lennon's Hotel and to and from the headquarters in the Insurance Building. The only way was to appear normal, relaxed, eager to shake the hand of the great man. Any show of nerves would alert the men with the guns. It would have been infinitely easier on Manila's Dewey Boulevard, from which Carlos used to see the great man striding, pacing back and forth on the patio of his six-room penthouse, the blue and gold of the West Point robe occasionally catching the late evening sun. But then there had been no good reason— then the Americans were fully ensconced and besides, the idea had never occurred to him. But now the Japanese had changed it all. At first almost everyone in Manila wanted to help the Americans fight them, but now that the Americans had been defeated in the Philippines, new opportunities presented themselves.

He must be brave, like MacArthur. He would wear his decorations from the Filipino militia. He would join the usual crush of autograph seekers that gathered whenever MacArthur's Cadillac or Packard arrived and departed in front of his hotel and headquarters. He must rehearse. He stood back from the mirror. He must advance quickly yet not too quickly, eager but not too eager. First he would hail the general, like so, and MacArthur would smile, recognizing him at once as a Filipino and brother-in-arms. Still, if they saw you produce a knife you would be dead. To be brave was not enough. One must also be cunning—"preparation," just as the general had said.

Carlos had finished shaving and now he sat on the edge of the big enamel tub, thinking hard as the tap dripped, dripped, with the ritual sound of a funeral drum.

Chapter Ten

It was the evening of February 10, 1943. Being early fall in Australia, it was still light at 8:00 P.M. as Carlos Pacis waited by Lennon's Hotel, watching the main entrance beneath the striped canvas awning that had been erected especially for MacArthur. By now the general should be on his way back from his headquarters at the AMP Insurance Building. Carlos looked at the jeweler's clock on the corner. 8:01. He took the small black tube, six inches in length, from inside his shirt. Pulling off the top section, as one would a fountain pen, he clipped it to the other end; the blade, which he had painted black so as not to glint in the light, was three inches long. It was all he required. The Roman legions, he had heard from Father Maviros, had had the shortest swords for a thousand years and yet they had conquered all of the known world, including Britain, by concentrating above all else on one tactical movement—a quick two inches of steel into the heart. One thrust and that was all that was needed to kill your enemy. At 8:02 the shiny black Packard, two outriders ahead to stop traffic, made its privileged U-turn in George Street and drew up at the entrance to the hotel. Carlos stepped out from the shadows, his medals clinking, a pad of white linen paper in his left hand, the "pen" in his right. A group of young autograph hunters streamed out of the lobby.

"General! General!"

MacArthur, still in summer uniform of light khaki shirt and tie, khaki pants and the proudly battered Bataan cap, turned and saw the Filipino. In the spill of light from the hotel's lobby he transferred his cane from his right hand to the left, preparing for a handshake.

Carlos's right hand went up . . . One of the two guards looked at the pen, saw the blade, stepped in between the general and Carlos, and fired. The Thompson roared, bucked, spitting a long blue-white flame. There were screams and Carlos Pacis was dead on the pavement, his medals shiny with his own blood, the rapier-sharp knife still clutched in his hand.

Within seconds, except for the tall cool figure of MacArthur, it was pandemonium. The reporter on the MacArthur beat scooped the story. "While everyone else seemed panic-stricken," the reporter wrote,

> . . . screaming and running, the guards trying to push the general into the safety of Lennon's lobby, MacArthur, brushing off all entreaties, walked slowly over and looked down at the dead Filipino in the dark pool of blood. As he gazed upon the Filipino's medals the commander in chief seemed more saddened than angered at the action of a man for whose country the general is fighting so valiantly.

The MP who shot Carlos said later that strangely enough it hadn't really been the knife that had alerted him—it was the man's eyes. "Almond shape," the MP explained. "He looked like a Jap."

When Colonel Heiji heard the news at Imperial Headquarters in Tokyo he called Carlos Pacis a mad son of a slut, and sent for Tomokazu Somura. Now MacArthur would be even more heavily protected, a veritable phalanx of armed guards about him. After Pacis a frontal attack by Somura or any other would-be assassin would be almost certain suicide, a tailed attack that would be ended in another hail of machine-gun bullets. Heiji had nothing against suicide, providing it succeeded in eliminating the target, but following the Filipino's insane attempt, security around the general would be doubled. And, he told Somura, "The Australians are already suspicious of anyone with a different skin. Now any nonwhite who gets within a hundred yards of MacArthur will be shot on sight."

"Except his Chinese servant," said Tomokazu, who had read the CARP file carefully and knew that MacArthur himself had no color prejudice.

Heiji grunted. After the Filipino's stupid failure he knew that his original plan of sending in Somura to shoot MacArthur close range, face-to-face, could not be justified. The old Japanese proverb applied: "Once bitten, twice shy." Damn the Filipino!

Heiji briskly dismissed Somura, as though it was somehow Somura's fault, and sat brooding in his office into the late evening, vowing not to leave until he had thought of an alternate plan that would satisfy Tojo and the chiefs, one that had a reasonable chance of success. Beside him and below the emperor's picture was a signed photograph of his hero, Yamamoto, author of Nippon's first great victory against the Americans at Pearl Harbor.

He sat silently, gazing at the steel desk, studying its form, its symmetry, which reflected the higher reality and symmetry of nature, letting the stillness help him to reach the higher plane where pure thought was possible. He imagined himself before the admiral: Yamamoto was demanding a more daring yet calculated plan, reminding Heiji that only cowards turned tail at the first sight of difficulty. Finally Heiji thought he perceived a way, and now was thankful for Carlo Pacis; as the beauty of the iris, the flower of the warrior, was nurtured by dung, one's success was born in the death of another's failure. He went over the CARP file once again, asking himself one simple question above all others: When is any supreme commander least public and most private, as private, that is, as a supreme commander can be in war?

It was then that he conceived what would later be called "Heiji's surprise."

CHAPTER ELEVEN
March, 1943

Standing on the vast Kure docks beneath a gunmetal sky, Heiji extended his hands toward the long, sleek shape as if he had personally conceived and nurtured it to its maturity. "The Allies have nothing like them," he said. "The nearest is the Narwhal, almost ten years older and with nothing of the endurance."

Somura had to admit that 14,000 miles was an unheard-of operational range. Even the Germans couldn't match Nippon's achievement. Compared to the huge Japanese I-class creation the German U-boats were midgets and not nearly as fast.

"A hundred and twenty yards long," continued Heiji, "and over thirty feet wide. The first even to try the concept were the British with the 'Mutton-boat,' the M2. But they gave up years ago after she sank off Dorset." Heiji began walking down the wharf. Below them Somura could hear the slapping of the tide against the maze of turpentine logs. "We took note of the British sinking, of course," said the colonel. "One explanation was that the hydroplanes were defective. Another that a hatch had been opened prematurely before she had fully surfaced. Personally I think it was the hatch." He stopped halfway down. "The French tried a few years later with the Surcouf." Heiji was holding his head high, reminding Somura of a bird that frequently puffed itself up, so much so it seemed in danger of exploding. "It was very beautiful, the Surcouf," Heiji said, "very big and fast. Not as fast as ours, of course. Anyhow an American freighter accidentally rammed and sank her for us a year ago."

Heiji stood with hands akimbo, breathing in the sea air. It

was intoxicating. If his new plan, his *odorokino okurimono*—his unpleasant surprise, as he called it—worked, he knew it would make his reputation forever, and not just in the military. He actually smiled at Somura. "The British called theirs the Mutton-boat because her aft gun running up onto the tower resembled a leg of lamb." Heiji laughed. "You know what I call ours?" Heiji quickly answered himself. "Boot on ski."

Somura, looking back at the long black craft, realized it was an appropriate description, the high ankle of the boot being the conning tower, its long rounded toe the hangar, and the long body of the sub itself, the ski. From where he stood, on the port aft side of the boat, the conning tower, the high ankle of the boot, appeared to be as wide as the sub, but as Heiji led him farther down the pier toward the bow that was bumping gently against the end of the pier and as he looked back he could see that while the dome-shaped toe-piece, or hangar, sat in front of and was integrated with the conning tower, the tower itself was not dead center but offset to port. Running for'ard, for a distance of eighty feet, from the closed hangar that formed the toe-piece was a narrow-gauge rail line that carried the catapult dolly for the M6 Seiran seaplane scout, which had carried out the reconnaissance for the big subs at Pearl Harbor and Sydney Harbor.

Before the war no one outside of the Japanese Sixth Fleet headquarters had known about the development of what was blandly listed in the Treasury allocation as:

Submarine: double hull design *Otsu-gata* (Type B).

Derivation: *Kaidai*.

Purpose: patrol.

The I-boat that Heiji was showing Tomokazu was I-43. Now that the war had entered its third year the type B I-boats were famous in Japan, their effectiveness in the early part of the conflict celebrated after one of them, three days following Pearl Harbor, had torpedoed the U.S. carrier *Saratoga,* which was salvaged only to be torpedoed again by I-26 in September, 1942, just six months after MacArthur had arrived in Darwin. In the same month I-19 under Commander Narahara had sunk the U.S. carrier *Wasp* in the Solomons and later Captain Yokota, in I-26, sent cruiser U.S.S. *Juneau* to the bottom off Guadalcanal.

Heiji had adopted a know-it-all stance, reminding Somura now of a pompous schoolteacher he once had had in Yokohama. "Not all type Bs have the special equipment," said Heiji. "On some you see we have removed the hangar and seaplane catapult so as to mount an extra 5.5 mm gun in addition to the standard 5.5 gun mounted on the afterdeck or to make room for piggybacking up to four of the type A midget subs. We did this for the attacks on Pearl Harbor and Sydney."

"Is it fast enough?" Somura tried to control his impatience.

"Twenty-three knots," replied Heiji, as though he had personally designed the I-boat. "Burst speed twenty-five. The Allies cannot match it."

Somura pointed to the thumblike projection sticking up from the long, domed hangar that formed the toe section of the boot. "Our radar is not good enough. Ten, fifteen miles at best. MacArthur's Seventh Fleet has much better." It was gross insolence to a superior, but Somura felt he'd earned the right. At Eta Jima they had been working him day and night to get him ready for CARP in time. He was exhausted, irritable, and it would be his life on the line. "They can hear us well before we hear them," he added.

"Yes," conceded Heiji. "But you forget our torpedoes make theirs look like toys. The Americans still have not corrected theirs. When they do manage to hit our ships most of them fail to explode."

Somura was not interested in torpedoes. All he could think of was that Brisbane was more than 1,400 miles south of

Rabaul—Japan's southernmost naval base—1,400 miles inside the enemy's sea.

Heiji took a small rice cake from his pocket, crumbled it and tossed it into the incoming tide. Gulls screeched down and began to fight it out. "Speed is not everything," Heiji said. "We must think constructively."

By now Somura knew that "constructively" in Heiji's vocabulary meant "deviously"—something the colonel, as part of Yamamoto's intelligence team for Pearl Harbor, was very good at.

"We will have surprise even more than speed. Speed, if we can. But surprise first! And the key is MacArthur's strict timetable. He rises at the same time, he leaves Lennon's at the same time. This is what he takes pride in, so this is his fatal weakness." Heiji hesitated, looking out across the gray, metallic bay. "Of course, Somura, we cannot pretend they will not be after you following the successful completion of your mission. Once you are revealed they will be everywhere." It was as if Heiji was testing Somura a second time. They had already been through this; Tomokazu had always understood it.

"It is the emperor's wish," he said. "It is in the hands of the *kami*."

"Quite so."

They strolled on beyond the huge submarine in silence. At the gates bearing the great naval insignia Heiji tossed out more crumbs onto the oily water. "There is something else . . ."

Tomokazu was only half listening, thinking of Cape Byron, of the curve of purple mountains beyond, the bright beaches, so bright they hurt your eyes—on a warm summer day walking hand in hand with her out to the black cape against the deep blue cleansing sea, her passionate kisses, their bodies in tight embrace. How perverse fate could be—that his intimate knowledge of this coast of the bay, the place of his happiest memories, should end up qualifying him to risk his life for his nation. He wondered if he would ever see her again.

". . . so if you are caught, being out of uniform you will be tried as a spy." Heiji offered his hand to Tomokazu, an affection seldom extended by any senior rank to a subaltern. "You are a good officer, Somura. Be sure your family will be proud. I will personally ensure the emperor hears of your action."

Tomokazu was moved at the thought that his name should actually be spoken in the Imperial Palace. It was, indeed, the highest honor. His family would forever be revered, but though he had been taught as a matter of course from the soldiers' manual that one must always save the last bullet for oneself, he had every intention of living beyond his mission, of seeing once again the fishergirls of Hekura, and if the *kami* were beneficent, to grow old in the shadow of Fuji with the woman he loved after the war was over. True, there could be no life without honor but nor was there honor in *useless* death. He would succeed. He would complete his mission and make his way back to the bay for pick up by the sub—the Byron Bay lighthouse as his beacon. Then after the war they would marry . . .

Somura then requested a leave. "You are bright, Somura," Heiji said. "But there is still much to learn. You may have a day but then you must return to Eta Jima to perfect your training."

Somura bowed with thanks. One day was sufficient. He could not share the great secret with his family, but they knew he was about to go on a mission of great importance for the outcome of the war and that it must be hazardous. There would be no formal farewells as such, only small talk to cover their concern.

Knowing he was about to leave, his mother had stood each

day in the village with the *mawashi,* the prayer belt, asking every stranger, as was the custom, to add their stitch. It was almost complete and when it had one thousand stitches she would present it to her son for luck.

CHAPTER TWELVE
Toowoomba

Just as he had said nothing when Elizabeth had dumped him for the Jap over a year before, Bruce Keely said nothing now. He was careful, too, not to talk about the war if he could avoid it, and had simply called around to pay his respects when he had heard the news of her brother's death. He had known Frank Lawson well, both of them having played in the high school's rugby union team—Frank always pulling the job of ruck, the front center man, in the scrums because of his smaller build, propped on either side by two taller forwards; Bruce himself, at nearly six feet, usually being one of them. When he had heard how Frank had held out as much as he could for as long as he could from the Japs Bruce wasn't surprised. He had been the same on the rugby field. Crashed into and piled on by a pyramid of opposing forwards twice their size, most rucks told you all about it after the game, touting their own toughness, but not Frank. His old man had taught him not to be a bloody whiner or a windbag but to go in, put your head down and your ass up and take your lumps and never mind broadcasting it.

Elizabeth noted Bruce's kindness. At eighteen, tall and blond, he somehow seemed more mature than the crude types who gathered downtown to leer at the girls and were struck mute unless supported by a gaggle of yahoos. Which was probably why, she reasoned, she'd said yes, though half-heartedly, when he had asked her to go to the movies on Saturday night. His civility and consideration reminded her of someone else.

Laurel and Hardy were at the Empire and Bruce had reserved seats upstairs in the lounge behind the balustrade out

81

of the way of the women with the bunch-of-fruit hats that now and then turned up to obscure the screen. The seats had cost him nearly five shillings, but now he had a part-time job as a bricklayer's assistant.

The first half of the show was the usual color-slide advertisements for fifteen minutes followed by the Tarzan trailer for next week, then the Movietone News. The broad black arrows grew fat as they moved across the screen showing how, in North Africa, Rommel had launched a surprising counter-offensive with panzers and Stukas, first beating the Americans but then being pushed back through the Kasserine Pass. Next there was footage of an endless column of German POWs stretching across endless snow following the collapse of Von Paulus's Sixth Army at Stalingrad:

> Our Russian allies move inexorably against the Nazi divisions pushing them back across the Ukraine. Meanwhile along the Burma coast Japanese forces continue to launch a strong counterattack against . . .

Between the rapid illumination of the flickering war footage Bruce watched Elizabeth, her head turned away from the screen toward the far, dimly lit pink balcony above the red EXIT sign. He reached for her hand. No response.

Now there were stills smuggled out of Singapore of thousands of emaciated POWs—British and Australian mostly, with a smattering of Canadians, East Indians and Americans paraded by the conquerors. It was said that they were down to eating rats, dogs, anything that moved, to stay alive. As Bruce watched the near skeletons shuffling through the dust he squeezed her hand again. She should know that he understood how she must feel. Little yellow bastards!. Now there was a clip of them "banzaing" or some such crap over a captured gun at Corregidor. When he saw the Yanks holding the pathetic white handkerchief on a twig and the defeat in their

eyes, looking up at the camera in shame, the Japs grinning in
their jungle caps and neck flaps, waving their rifles with the
long bayonets, he got so angry he almost cried. He wanted to
fight, to kill them. Everyone who'd seen what they'd done
wanted to fight. Being the only male in his family he hadn't
been called up, and he felt guilty.

They got off the bus at the top of Margaret Street and walked
down by the broken column memorial to the poet Lawson.
"Any relation?" he asked Elizabeth, already knowing the answer.

"No," she said quietly.

It was mid-April, autumn, and the harvest moon was high,
a huge bright disc over the undulating black folds of the
Lockyer Valley below and the gap in the Toll Bar Road that
pierced the lip of the range. A sweet breeze brought the ringing of the cicadas closer. Now and then the breeze drew out
Elizabeth's long blond hair. Above them the Southern Cross
lay serene, twinkling like crystal in the cloudless sky. The
moonglow was so bright that the crests of the far-off hills were
like a silver sea.

What did she feel for him? Nothing, really. But at least he'd
been decent. And her life seemed as empty, as silent, as those
distant hills, waiting for . . . For no one, really . . .

He turned her toward him. She moved stiffly. He pulled
her head toward him and kissed her. She leaned her head
against his chest and mistaking resignation for real interest,
he kissed her again, harder this time, until she pulled away.
He told himself to wait it out. Other guys had avoided her
because she'd had the hots for a Nip, didn't want to play
second fiddle to a Jap. He'd kept his mouth shut about the
Japs when he was anywhere within hearing distance of the
Lawson women.

"How about a picnic Sunday? We could go to Tabletop, if you like."

She hesitated. God, he was so earnest. Well, she reminded herself, at least he'd been kind, and for her these days that was a lot. A few people had come around after they'd heard about Frank and had asked about news of her father, but others had never forgiven her, and probably never would. "All right," she said.

"Great. Pick you up 'round ten."

"All right."

He'd get five twenty-six-ounce bottles of beer and maybe a bit of that Russian stuff. His friends said you could mix it with orange juice or lemonade and the women couldn't taste it— hey, he told himself, this was Elizabeth. She wasn't a tart. Still, he was pretty worked up about her, just being near her was enough to make him hard.

He went to the drugstore and waited till he was the only one left in the shop before he bought the condom. He could see the old man who sold it didn't approve, although he took the money quickly enough. He wouldn't hurt her for the world, and he respected her, but some nights just thinking about her drove him nuts. What was it they were telling all the troops before they went on leave?—a stiff prick has no conscience. Too right.

CHAPTER THIRTEEN

Waiting in Rabaul Harbor, the Japanese strong point in New Britain, 250 miles northeast of the New Guinea coast, no one aboard I-43 except Commander Osu, its captain, his first officer, the five-man hangar crew under Lieutenant Matsu, and the recently commissioned Tomokazu Somura knew the sub's mission and what had been loaded under wraps at the dockside. What the remaining hundred crewmen of I-43 did know was that Commander Osu would have their guts for prayer bands if whatever was under wraps in the hangar crew couldn't be launched by the crew faster than any I-boat in the Imperial Navy. The *Sho-sa,* the first officer who was a lieutenant commander, had politely pointed out to Commander Osu that standard TOL, time of launch, was twenty-five minutes after surfacing. Commander Osu replied sharply that there were only two kinds of TOL: that used by old women and the TOL for I-43. He reminded the *Sho-sa* that if he intended to attain the three full bars of a commander on his sleeve and if Lieutenant Matsu and the launch crew wanted leave on return home at Kure then they had better learn to surface and get Heiji's "surprise"—a folding-wing fighter—airborne and the sub submerged in record time in enemy waters or they might not return home at all.

"A sitting duck," Somura said in English, then translated.

The commander agreed, making the *Sho-sa,* at the risk of losing face, responsible for reducing the sub's TOL by a third in one week. During the next week the Sho-sa and Matsu became the most hated officers in the whole Sixth Fleet, but on the morning of April 15, a bleary-eyed *Sho-sa* informed Commander Osu that I-43 had not cut the TOL by a third but by a *half.* They could now launch in only twelve minutes.

"Seas permitting," Osu responded wryly, reminding the *Sho-sa* that he wasn't quite a superman yet, no matter what Tojo was telling them.

Somura smiled. Now that the intense training was over he found it easier to relax. He saw his reflection in the periscope column. He decided he liked the navy blue uniform, never mind the high scratchy collar. Studying himself he had to admire the cap, its anchor clustered by cherry blossoms, giving him an unexpected surge of pride in his graduation from Eta Jima, which in turn signified a new and momentous beginning in his life. And, with the enormous importance of his mission, a growing sense of power.

I-43 slid quietly out of Rabaul on the evening of Friday, April 16, at 1900 hours. Looking back at the thin green curve of Simpson Harbor, Somura watched the five volcanic cones slip over the sea's edge and then went below.

Cape Byron lay 1,400 nautical miles due south. Osu, silently monitoring the banks of pressure gauges, knew he could only be sure of eight hours complete darkness in every twenty-four during which he could run at maximum surface speed of 23.5 knots; for the remaining sixteen hours he would have to run submerged, making for a twenty-four-hour total of 316 knots. Accordingly the *Sho-sa* calculated it would take them just over four days to reach launch point, ten miles due east of the cape, far enough south to be out of the way of Brisbane's heavily defended coast.

But Commander Osu, a more experienced submariner, was not so sure of the *Sho-sa*'s estimate; he had been aboard as a junior officer during the first test run of I-26 off Honshu in October of '41, had launched a Yokosuka E14Y reconnaissance plane off Oregon, and before that commanded one of the I-boats off Pearl Harbor. He was bold but overcompensated in his planning . . . he had learned the hard way that all manner of things could go wrong once at sea and usually did. And now, entering the Solomon Sea, they would be within enemy bomber range. Once past the jade-colored slivers of the D'Entrecasteaux Islands to the left and Louisiade Archipelago to the right, they would be approaching the dangerous waters of the Coral Sea, where MacArthur's navy now ruled. He might have to slow to a crawl to avoid running into heavy traffic on the "Brisbane–Moresby Expressway" or wait it out on the bottom for a while, if it was shallow enough, running a long detour if it wasn't.

And then there were the riptides, cutting your speed in half, dragging and bullying you toward the treacherously beautiful coral reefs. Or, what if the German-designed snorkel, which allowed the diesels to breathe while the sub was submerged, fouled up, necessitating the draining of vital battery power? Any one of these could add dramatically to the ETA off Cape Byron. If there were delays, Osu told Somura, they might not arrive for nine days, until April 25. Somura said he didn't need to worry; April 25, he went on, was Anzac Day in Australia—a peculiar Anglo-Saxon celebration of Australia's and New Zealand's greatest *defeat* by the Turks at Gallipoli. The commander took it as a good omen. To add to his optimism in the predawn light he watched, entranced, as a school of porpoises crisscrossed the bow in fleeting blue green shadows, faces smiling.

A half-hour before the dawn on April 17, I-43, still rigged for red so as to see better at night should they suddenly have to surface, dived for safe running and trimmed off at snorkel depth of 100 feet. If for any reason the sub dropped a few more feet, a Ping-Pong–like float valve would immediately shut out the seawater from its breathing tube. The snorkel was actually leaking slightly, but it was small enough not to worry Osu unduly and he issued orders for the third officer on the 4:00 P.M. to 8:00 P.M. watch not to pump out the accumulated bilge until nightfall; the pumps could give away his position in a stream of iridescent bubbles.

The crew, their faces the color of lobsters, sweat glistening in the red glow of the sub, thought they had it all figured out. They were obviously headed south to one of the sparsely populated islands between Australia and New Zealand. The consensus was that it was Norfolk, but some of the "Hope" cigarette rations were bet on Lord Howe Island even farther south. The plane would be used as reconnaissance to locate any radar or radio station before the Imperial marines would land from the I-boats that were no doubt coming up in the rear of I-43. The big, fleet-sized I-boats, like I-43, had often been used for such spearhead amphibious thrusts. An island so far south would be an excellent sub base behind enemy lines from which to harrass MacArthur's U.S.–Australian supply line. Osu said nothing to deny the speculation, thereby tending to confirm it. Better they thought this, he told Somura and the *Sho-sa*, better they thought they had company in these waters than that they were alone in the vastness of the Pacific.

Chapter Fourteen

Bruce and Elizabeth rode their bikes to Picnic Point, left them unlocked in the rack by the kiosk, then headed east, walking over the lip of the range down through the wind-riven gum trees that sounded like running water. They followed the old dirt road until it became a rough track leading to Razorback, the sharply peaked hill covered by lantana bushes, rock, and tough vines that squatted before Tabletop Mountain. The steep ascent of Razorback over the wildly strewn gray-and-black volcanic rocks had to be made at angles often greater than forty-five degrees, and what passed for a path took sudden leaps over the granite boulders through the clinging bush. Although Bruce took care to stop often for a breather, Elizabeth was already tired by the time they reached the top, her face florid and covered with beads of perspiration.

Bruce steadied her down onto the rocky summit, handing her the khaki felt-covered water bottle. As she lifted it to her lips her breasts stuck to the faded khaki shirt she had worn along with matching cotton slacks. For a moment he thought she had no bra on and felt slightly shocked. But he was mistaken, the bra's outline being accentuated because of the perspiration dampening her breasts, pushing them into sharp relief whenever she moved.

They didn't talk as they sat back against the shaded stone and admired the view. To the north was the Lockyer Valley, its western reaches blocked from sight by Tabletop's northern face, but to the wilder south the distant hills were plainly visible, tumbling in purple toward the New South Wales border a hundred or so miles away. Elizabeth knew that beyond those hills lay Mount Warning, the densely timbered monolith, given its name by Captain Cook, who far out to sea had

used it as the fishermen still did as a marker for the treacher-
ous rocks of the cape. "You ever been to Cape Byron?" she
asked Bruce.

"No."

"It's beautiful, it's the most beautiful place in Australia . . ."

"Like you."

"We used to go there for holidays."

"Uh-huh."

"You must have seen pictures of the lighthouse."

"No. We go up north, to Caloundra."

She pushed her arms back slowly, lethargically, letting them
take her full weight, and breathing in the cool mountain air.
It was a delicious movement, and a rarity for her. "We always
liked the Northern rivers. It's so lush across the border
and—"

"It's lush further up north."

"It's different down at Byron Bay," she said, annoyed.
"Around Lismore and Bangalow. They're small pretty towns.
It's like Ireland, they say. Green hills and blue sea stretching
forever. So lonely but not lonely, you know?"

"Yeah," he said, but she could tell he didn't.

"You ready?" he asked.

"In a minute."

She closed her eyes and could see the long, lovely beach,
the sand grass fluttering on the dunes, and the dark, forbid-
ding Julien Rocks, black and surf-tinged in the middle of the
enormous bay, and behind, to the west, the dusky, lush mauve
hills covered in velvet twilight surrounding Mount Warning,
and the setting sun, its saffron rays bursting over the sea,
touching everything with gold, and through it all the salty
smell of ocean that was at this very moment crashing and
surging, frothy and clean, its spray a kind of benediction making everything new and good; and all of it swimming in the
dying light. She made herself think of the whole family; it

seemed safer, more acceptable, than thinking longingly, even wantonly, of someone in particular with whom the family, the country, was at war.

Bruce watched her face, her leaning back, and thought maybe she was teasing him. After all, it was the first time he'd seen her so relaxed, so sort of free, and yet intuitively he knew he wasn't really part of it. "Let's go," he said, standing quickly, shouldering her haversack along with his own.

They descended Razorback, down its eastern side, then hiked across the grassy ridge linking the smaller Razorback to its parent and began the long, backbreaking climb up the ancient spill of volcanic rubble that for thousands of years had defied the incursion of thick-veined bush that had long since covered the rest of the mountain. The stones kept sliding and Elizabeth felt as if she were slipping down an endless conveyor belt of sand. As Bruce came back to help her a sunbaking carpet snake slithered away into the lantana bush and a battalion of huge red soldier ants kept up the march, unperturbed, surging over a rotting cactus at the edge of the rock spill and rigidly bearing the half-eaten remains of cicadas, their stomachs gnawed away before being transported into the strange world of the dark green vines.

After they'd crossed the black rocks it became easier, a level, shaded path curving momentarily to the right, but not for long; the final ascent was out in the blazing hot sun again along a narrow gravelly ledge.

Near the summit they were both perspiring heavily, then suddenly she could feel the cooling east wind blowing across the mountain's undulating top, bending the long brown passpalem grass like folds of wheat. From the northern edge they could look down on the whole valley and, more importantly for Elizabeth, they could see farther south. Bruce moved ahead of her, looking down for snakes, and when he got to the northeastern edge stopped beneath a great pear-tree cactus that stood like a sentinel against invasion from the east.

Too hot to eat, Bruce said as he opened a beer and offered her some juice. "Would you like something to pep it up?" If he was blushing he knew she couldn't tell, his face already beet red from the climb.

"All right," she said, surprised at herself. Her mother would have had a fit—she'd told Elizabeth she couldn't drink until she was nineteen. "Just a little," she added quietly.

Like his buddies, Bruce was strictly a beer man, and spirits of any kind were a mystery usually consigned to the ladies' lounge. He poured a good two inches into the tin cup. It didn't look like much. He added some juice, and when she said it was too bitter, put in a little more. Tired and thirsty, she drank it down and lay back in the shade of the tallest cactus. Soon she began to feel . . . so relaxed, so good . . . she closed her eyes. The perspiration had now soaked right through and the khaki shirt clung to her like a second skin, the two top buttons undone from the strain of the ascent over the boulders. Bruce remembered only one button had been loose at the top of Razorback. All right, he knew she hadn't done it on purpose, she wasn't the type, but it did mean that now part of her bra was visible, not that he could see much unless he arched his neck at a painful and ridiculous angle. It was all right while her eyes were closed but he was almost a nervous wreck from trying to see more while trying to pretend otherwise. Heart thumping, he turned away momentarily and took another swig of beer. She heard the clink of the bottle and turned toward him, opening her eyes, saying nothing.

"After work, after play, after all—Bulimba Beer is best!" he sang out the commercial.

"That's Four–X," she corrected lightly.

"Yeah, yeah, so it is." She started to giggle. He wasn't sure why—maybe it was the vodka. Well, he told himself, he hadn't forced it on her, she'd agreed to it. She put her hand over her mouth to stop giggling but the more she tried the worse it became. Pretty soon she just couldn't stop and he happily joined, not really detecting the manic quality of her release. A finch suddenly appeared amidst the cactus flowers, seemed to inspect them, which hugely amused them . . . a fresh rush of wind ruffled her hair and he found himself kissing her and she put her arms around him, and pulled him onto her.

They were in a kind of frenzy, he calling out her name and she moaning softly, "I love you, I love you," but not really saying it to him. His fingers reached for his pocket but he knew there wouldn't be time, the moment would be lost. Her lips were wet, frantic, sucking his breath away. He was rigid against her and knew he couldn't hold out. She wanted to cry out for Tomokazu but managed to stop herself, even to push away the guilt. He fumbled beneath her slacks. She arched her back, bucking against him.

"Oh, God . . ." He wasn't inside her but he couldn't stop himself and shuddered violently, his body collapsing against her . . .

He rolled off her. All he could hear was the loud buzzing of cicadas. High above, a wedge-tailed eagle soared, a black dot against the blue. He turned back toward her. "Oh, God, I'm sorry I—"

"Shhh."

"I should have waited, I—"

She put her finger across his lips. "It's all right." He had nothing to apologize for. It was she who had encouraged it, had wanted it. She had cheated him, even if he didn't know it, and she could never tell him.

He, of course, was devastated by her apparent understanding—humiliated. "Elizabeth," he said, "I love you, I'd do anything, I—" And then he was kissing her again, frantically, as though somehow to prove himself to her.

Her eyes were open, staring beyond him at the cloudless

sky. And despite the yearning ache inside her she could no longer pretend that he was someone else. Reality was back.

By the time they reached home it was almost dinnertime—six o'clock on the evening of April 18.

CHAPTER FIFTEEN

At 3:00 A.M. on the morning of April 20, I-43 was running with the sea on the surface, making good speed under cover of darkness. Despite the early hour, inside the sub the temperature climbed to over 105 degrees as they entered the Coral Sea off Australia's northeast coast. The men stripped to the waist and soon the boat smelled like piles of dirty laundry soaking in diesel oil. As usual only the cooks and oilers, no more than a dozen men in all, were permitted to shower, the nozzles preset to run for exactly one minute to conserve the precious drinking water.

As the last oiler turned off the faucet he was aware of an eerie quiet that had suddenly invaded the boat. A veteran, he stood absolutely still, taking care not to make the slightest sound. He waited for the depth charges. There were none. At first he thought that the noise of the shower had drowned out the order to man battle stations, except this had never happened before. Then he saw men shuffling by in the artificial light like so many bloodied ghosts. They were not tense, as they would be during a destroyer attack, but something was very wrong. Their faces were like perspiring stones: shocked, stunned. He asked an armorer what was going on. The man stumbled on as if in a trance. It was the *Sho-sa* who told him the bad news that he had missed in the shower; the news that the most popular and revered officer in the whole Imperial Navy, the legendary Isoruku Yamamoto, had been shot down and killed by P–38s, American Lightnings, in an aerial ambush over the Solomon Sea as he was approaching a forward headquarters at Bougainville the day before. He had been found in the jungle still strapped into the seat of the Mitsubishi medium bomber, clutching his samurai sword.

The oiler sat down, as dazed as everyone else. Yamamoto was irreplaceable. He was not only the genius behind Pearl Harbor, he was the greatest tactician Japan had. Which, of course, was why the Americans had sought him out.

Commander Osu seemed particularly devastated by the news. Yamamoto had personally decorated him with the Golden Kite Medal for bravery, and Osu felt a profound anger at what the Americans had done. But his training quickly took hold and he managed to react to the implications of the ambush. Clearly it had not been by chance. They must have intercepted the radio traffic to know precisely where Yamamoto would be at precisely the right time. Osu gave two orders effective immediately: first, all communications with base were to be cut henceforth; from now on I-43 was on silent running. His second order overrode his earlier instructions to Somura and the *Sho-sa* and the hangar crew that they were bound to secrecy. As captain of I-43 it was his prerogative. He proceeded to tell the crew what their mission was—to kill MacArthur. He told them that it was surely the will of the omniscient *kami* that even before the Americans had attacked their beloved admiral, I-43, in a kind of inspired symmetry, had been ordained to cut out the heart of his opposite number in reprisal.

"Let our admiral's death stir our hearts," he told them. "Let it fill us with deepest resolve to avenge Nippon's loss and stop the Allied advance . . ."

The whole crew rose in the blood red light, hands thrust high, voices roaring the traditional *"banzai!"* Somura, never one to show his emotions, was so moved he allowed tears to mingle with the sweat from the now almost unbearable heat of the submarine.

With their true purpose known, all conditions aboard the sub became more bearable, and when Tomokazu Somura moved through I-43, the sailors regarded him in a new light, with new-found respect for his mission. As the commander, with his knack for the dramatic, said in another briefing, like the divine wind, the *kamikaze,* that had risen from the sea to wreck the fleet of Kublai Khan before his warships could touch the shores of Nippon, Somura would rise and destroy the enemy and turn the tide against the white invader. It impressed the crew, not to mention the once self-effacing Somura.

The crew offered him their rationed sweets, some even holding out as a sign of respect the rice cakes they had been given before their departure. And a delegation of *sho-i ko-hosei,* midshipmen, presented him with a white headband emblazoned in the middle with the red ball of the rising sun surrounded on either side by Shinto prayers.

Finally, through the others he had made peace with himself. Now he had accepted his mission not just as an order but as a holy command.

Yamamoto's death had also released in him a rush of memories of the whites' attacks on *him*: all those snide verbal asides he'd felt but tried not to show the hurt. In their way as devastating as bullets to the body. "Slant-eyes!" Petty schoolyard cruelties he had believed he'd buried with disdain were resurfacing, and he understood that Tojo had gotten to the heart of the matter, that the white man's time had indeed come and properly so—the ancient rulers of Nippon had been right after all—the whites *were* inferiors. Tomokazu, the former student, educated by foreigners, had become the convert. And like most converts, his belief was total, justifying any action— against the enemy, or friend, or even lover . . .

It was "Slant-Eyes" that would return, he thought wryly, not MacArthur. At times thoughts of Elizabeth pushed their way back into his consciousness, but they were too distracting, making him vaguely guilty when, he told himself, the guilt was, after all, on her side of the war. He was a soldier now, and vengeance was part of a soldier's code of honor. Vengeance for the death of Yamamoto. Without such honor a man, even the lowest outcast, the *burakumin,* couldn't live with himself or with anyone else.

So now he concentrated on the worst of the indignities of his time in Australia, how even on their last night together he had been forced to pull back into the protective darkness of a classroom, had retreated as though he had something to be ashamed of to escape the others' scorn, their cruelty about his color, the shape of his eyes. Such feelings had been stuffed down when he was with her, but now he saw that his apparent calm had been, like Nippon's volcanic cones, an inverse measure of the anger churning deep in him, ready to explode. And now so far from her, it flowed with no restraint. He had been ordered to kill MacArthur. Now he *wanted* to kill MacArthur in a most personal way.

In his cabin Osu heard the brassy clank of the voice pipe being opened about him on the conning tower.

"Bridge lookout."

"Control."

"Ship. Green bearing two three two."

"Range?"

"Six thousand yards."

Just over three miles. Osu knew that as long as the moon stayed hidden, I-43 was against the darkness, unlike this unknown ship on his port side, which he could see dimly through the search periscope and which was outlined to the east against the faint light of approaching dawn. But had the ship *heard* him? Its course remained steady.

"Perhaps it is not an enemy ship," said the *Sho-sa,* his face seeming flushed by the reddened control room. "A neutral. South American."

"Perhaps," Osu replied quietly, glued intently to the eyepiece. He turned as one with the scope, watching the ship. It was still too far off to tell.

CHAPTER SIXTEEN

Toowoomba

On the early-morning shift Constable Ellis was just finishing his report for the Criminal Investigation Division in Brisbane, which in turn would send a copy to the Australian Security Intelligence Organization, the ASIO, in Canberra. He told them that, as requested, the Toowoomba police detachment was keeping an eye on the Lawson girl. Elizabeth Lawson. Only new thing to note was that there was a Romeo, name of Bruce Keely, eighteen years of age, looks older, five feet eleven, twelve stone, blue eyes, blond hair, in the sub-senior year at Tech, part-time job as brickie's laborer. PMG, Postmaster-General's office, reported the Lawsons had no phone so naturally no phone tap. Only one letter received from the Jap —back in October, before war broke out, postmarked Moresby. Letter full of romantic stuff, sort of, but nothing since. Will keep up surveillance.

Surveillance, in Ellis's vocabulary, meant that he dropped around once a week to ask a nosy neighbor if she'd seen anything "funny" at 16 Ipswich Street.

"How d'ya mean, funny? Funny peculiar or funny ha-ha?"

He could hardly hear the woman above the din of her half-dozen dogs barking and snarling.

"Peculiar!" he shouted.

"Not so far."

"Okay."

Sealing his report and dumping it in the "Out" tray, Ellis sat back in the swivel chair, having a shot at the odd fly with the late edition of the tabloid *Truth*, and daydreaming. There'd been some tourists in town—God only knew where they got the gas ration coupons from—but other than that things were pretty slow. He'd been told by the super to pick up a couple of the town drunks down by the weeping willows of Gowrie Creek and now he could hear one of them crooning from the lockup, "And no more will I roam, far away from home, on the road to Gundagaiiii . . ."

"Hoy—give it a rest, Archie."

"Stone the bloody crows," protested the drunk's cellmate. "I can't sleep. He's been on the bloody plonk again."

"Rough Red, eh?" noted Ellis, slapping another fly dead. "Hitting the old Penfolds, eh?"

"Yeah, around the world for a dollar," said the cellmate.

"Wasn't Penfolds," began Archie indignantly. "It was metho."

Ellis banged at a blow fly. It fell dead. "I don't care if you drink methylated spirits or bloody turpentine, long as we get a bit of quiet in here. *Right?*"

Archie, dressed as always in an old faded navy blue football jersey and baggy brown pants, drew back from the bars and shuffled about the cell, an aged white scar above one eye testimony to a bad fall and cracked skull suffered while under the influence. They called him "Underbridge" because that's where he lived and no one knew his real name.

Ellis glanced at his watch. 3:10 A.M. Another two hours and he'd be off-shift and down to the Station Hotel for a breakfast of steak and eggs and a pick-me-up. He had nothing against booze but why some people got to hit the hard stuff, he didn't know. Well, that was Archie's problem.

"And no more will I roam . . ."

"Christ!" said Ellis, dropping the paper and scooping up his big keyring. He opened the cells. "Out!" he said. "Go on, piss off!"

"Thanks, sarge!"

Ellis knew that Archie was sober—the singing was simply a pressure tactic. And it worked. Ellis let both of them go, Archie's cellmate scuttling off toward the Empire Theatre, its huge, black, barnlike shape crouching over the sickly yellow glow of the streetlights.

When he hit the chilly air Archie immediately stopped singing and looked about him. He was dying for a drink but then he saw his hands in the lamplight. They were shaking violently from the DTs; he'd never seen them so bad and it scared him. It was time for a dry-out, and he knew for him there was really only one way to do it: to go bush. He'd take his matilda, a blanket, an inflatable pillow, a sack mattress, a bit of sugar, tea and flour for damper, and one bottle for emergencies, and then head down the range into the Lockyer Valley to his old boyhood haunt at the Seven Mile Caves. The farmers round about were decent sorts, and providing you didn't go starting a bloody bush fire they left you alone. He'd sit at the mouth of the big, wide cave and watch the cool, clear creek meander over the sandstone, catch a yellow-belly now and then for breakfast from the deep pools. It would be just the ticket, nice and quiet, with nobody bothering him, and if he wanted to sing "The Road to Gundagai," then he'd just go ahead and sing it. And the fish wouldn't mind. At night he'd lie on his back by the campfire, watch the iron bark turn scarlet, and look up at the stars.

He hid his hands in his pockets and told himself it would be good for him, a real nice holiday. He pulled the collar of his football jersey up and headed for the bridge, where he'd stay until dawn.

And then . . . a vacation to end all vacations.

CHAPTER SEVENTEEN

Through the earphone Osu could now hear the muffled rattling of the ship's propellers. They sounded louder. Or was it his imagination?

"Bridge to control. Ship. Bearing green two two nine. *Closing!*"

Osu didn't hesitate. "Stop engines."

"Stop engines."

Osu heard the gears splitting down. I-43 groaned hard astarboard, then was stilled.

"All engines stopped, sir."

He turned back to the voice pipe. "Identification?"

"Not clear, sir," came the bridge lookout. "Green bearing two three two."

Osu grabbed a headset. All he could hear was the surging of the ocean. Damn it—if only he could use the active pulse, except then they would know where he was. He'd just have to wait and listen on passive.

"Speed?"

"Twenty-five knots. Could be a U.S. destroyer, sir. Fletcher Class."

Everyone in control sat still, bracing themselves. Osu glanced at the chart—they were well into the Coral Sea. He felt like a soldier caught in an open field. Normally he'd have immediately lined up the sub, ready to fire torpedoes, but his overriding purpose this night was not to be seen, to keep his presence in enemy waters absolutely secret. But if he was spotted he would have to attack in self-defense. He couldn't dive, though; the sudden white effervescence in the dark tropical sea would signal his position as surely as a flare, and before he could get deep enough they'd have him in their sights and be racing at him, dropping depth-charge drums.

He left the *Sho-sa* in control and went topside. He felt the trade wind rustle his hair, the fresh smell of the sea intoxicating his diesel-soured lungs, and saw the moon hidden beneath a section of massively scattered cumulus. He was thankful for the clouds, but they were moving sou'sou'east, threatening to unveil pearl white light any minute that would light him up in stark silhouette for the destroyer.

It was then, through binoculars, that he saw them. More destroyers! A whole convoy moving north, the escorts at high speed weaving a constant defensive screen about the slower moving cargo ships. And dawn fast approaching. Quietly Osu spoke into the pipe tube: "Steer zero nine zero." He knew the sub, having been running with the sea, would still have enough momentum, a few knots or so, to turn bow on to the convoy, thereby presenting itself with only the dark pillar of the conning tower in silhouette rather than the full-length silhouette of the submarine. And in the last resort his for'ard tubes would be in a position to fire.

The Australian captain could not see him and was relying on radar. "Where is it now, Number One?"

"Steering approximately zero nine zero, sir."

The officers on H.M.A.S. *Grafton* knew there were no Allied subs in the area so it had to be a Jap. They were itching to go in.

"Our orders are explicit," the captain said. "Go to Moresby. Go *directly* to Moresby. Do not pass Go. Go being a punchup with a lone Jap—sub or anything else. We're not to break formation unless attacked. Our supplies must get to New Guinea. That's our priority. So we just watch him. Johnson!"

"Yes, sir?" It was the signals officer.

"Convoy can't break radio silence while under way, so use

the signal lamp. Signal convoy. Sub alert. Enemy position zero nine zero."

"Aye, aye, sir."

The one-eyed semaphore winked rapidly in the pale wash of the encroaching dawn, alerting the convoy to the enemy's presence several miles off the port beam. Back aboard the *Grafton,* only one of the seven escort ships of the twenty-ship convoy under the overall command of destroyer H.M.A.S. *Orion,* the sonar operators stayed glued to their sets, listening to the active pinging and the passive echo from the Jap sub, while the lookouts on the escorts from the crow's-nest down were straining for the telltale white streaks that would signal a torpedo attack, readying themselves should the steel shark tear through their screen into the convoy under their protection. They all knew that the convoy was part of the vital buildup for MacArthur's next push northward toward the Philippines, but for many of them, any chance to hit the Japanese navy was difficult to pass up—they prayed he would attack.

On H.M.A.S. *Orion* the junior officers were lamenting the lost opportunity even though they understood the reasoning behind their orders. "It's his lucky night," said one of them. "We'd plaster the bastard."

At that moment *Orion*'s captain emerged from behind the chartroom blackout curtain. "Ever seen a Jap's torpedo run?" he asked, lifting his binoculars toward the Jap's reported position.

"No, sir."

"Well, I have. They've got the best fish in the world, including Jerry. And the fastest. They come at you at over sixty miles an hour with 1,200 pounds of TNT, and they come straight. For 22,000 yards. That's flat-out for over twelve miles. Ours are smaller and slower and run for three miles max. It's *our* lucky night, mister."

Aboard *Grafton,* five miles to the *Orion*'s port quarter, the skipper saw that the clouds, dispersing at first, were gathering even closer now about the moon, hiding the Japanese sub. Good, the Aussies and Yanks slugging it out in the stinking jungles up north needed the convoy's munitions far more urgently than he needed a possible victory over a sub. What bothered him was what was a Jap doing penetrating Allied defenses so far south, 300 miles east of Cape York, Australias's northernmost point? Still, he recalled how they had penetrated 2,000 miles farther south when they'd hit Sydney Harbor. All right, but why hadn't the Jap attacked? And if he was out of torpedoes what the hell was he doing here anyway . . . unless . . . unless, like the Sydney operation, he was carrying Midgets for another attack on MacArthur's navy? In that case, where would the attack be? Brisbane, or even as far as Sydney again? Or was this as far south as he was patrolling out of Rabaul? *Grafton* skipper decided to play it safe. "Sparks, what's our next emergency transmission zone?"

"Mackay, sir. Two hundred and fifty miles north, sir."

"Very good. Once we're inside the zone . . . let's see, that should be around 1500 . . . I want you to send the following."

The radio officer flipped open his pad and wrote:

0330 hours, April 20 western Pacific time. Enemy sub. Latitude 22° 06' South, Longitude 153° 01' East. Did not engage. Sub could be proceeding farther south. Estimated speed on initial sighting 20 plus knots.

"Send it to SOWPAC. Copies from Brisbane to Coastal Command Sydney and Melbourne. Further distribution at discretion of SOWPAC HQ."

"Yes, sir."

The skipper recalculated his speed and position. By 1500, he figured, the sub would still be a long way off from doing damage to the Seventh Fleet—MacArthur's navy.

"Sonar contact fading, sir. Sub, red bearing one nine seven." Which put the Jap receding on the port quarter, making no attempt to turn and tail the convoy.

"Speed?"

"Dead in the water, sir."

"Zero speed," corrected the skipper. "Correct procedure if you don't mind."

"Aye, aye, sir. Zero speed."

"Besides, he's not dead—he's very much alive."

"Yes, sir."

The clouds broke momentarily over the convoy now six miles away, and watching the warships pass him by in the moonlight, slivers on the race of sea, Osu felt at once a strange sense of kinship with the enemy sailors and an enormous sense of relief that they hadn't seen him. He straightened up from the crouched position over the gimbals-mounted bridge compass, stretching the stiffness from his muscles, then gazed at the thick cumulus that once again was swallowing the moon. To the south the five twinkling points of the Southern Cross told him that he was far from home but on course. In the muggy tropical darkness that was skeined by the land-scented trade winds, he continued to ponder the brooding cloud banks that he believed had hidden him from the enemy's sight. For a moment he had worried about the enemy's sonar that was supposed to be better than his. Yet they had not detected the I-boats off Pearl Harbor either. Perhaps it was the old problem, the thermal layers below the surface of the tropical sea deflecting the sound waves upward before they could hit the sub and rebound. Whatever the reason, they had not attacked his sub. It was a good omen, for him and the men of I-43.

Soon he would be off Cape Byron, and the revenge of Yamamoto would begin.

CHAPTER EIGHTEEN
April 20

Bruce Keely couldn't sleep. The moment he closed his eyes he could feel her again, the warm, silky firmness of her thighs encasing him, pulling him, sucking him into a kind of whirlpool of lost control. After being with her that day he had felt so wonderfully satisfied and at peace that if necessary he could sustain himself just by the memory alone, in case he wasn't able to see her again. But that was only a few hours after it had happened, as they lay on top of the mountain watching the vast shadows shifting back and forward over the hills in a symphony of changing light. Now he wanted her again. He wanted to be with her every minute, wanted to make it good for her too. He *wanted*.

He heard a sudden raucous exchange outside his Newtown house. It was near midnight; some soldiers home on leave from the Sixth Division were making the most of it before they had to go back again to face the Japs. And that's what he had to do—make the most of it. For a moment he was resentful of the soldiers, a constant threat to a man out of uniform. Too many women were impressed by the uniform, justified their quick, easy surrender as a kind of patriotic duty to those who might not return. Elizabeth had told him about the senior girls at school saying how a lot of the men mightn't come back so what was the harm?

He thought now of the Jap—Somura. Would Elizabeth have given in to the Jap as she had with him or was he something special to her? No, to be honest he knew he wasn't, not yet, but even the idea of her making love to someone else was more than he could handle. He tried to evict it from his thoughts but the sound of the soldiers on leave, yahooing

outside, made that impossible. If one of those fed her a tomor-
row-we-may-die story . . .

Well, he would have to protect her, to be with her as much
as possible. But her place on Ipswich Street was three miles
away, clear across town, and like most homes it didn't have a
phone. At school he could only see her at eleven o'clock break
and then at lunch and he had to be careful to avoid being
unmercifully teased if they were seen together. Keely realized
his only real hope lay in restraint, in patience . . . he mustn't
be around so much he'd put her off. But just thinking about
her made him hard as a rock again—and the thought of her
being near the other males, sitting in class with other boys,
drove him up the wall. To make it worse, now that she knew
her brother had been killed she was talking about helping her
mother out by leaving school and going to work for the Commonwealth Bank. He'd see even less of her then.

Turning into the pillow, he gripped it until his knuckles
were white. Her breasts were high and firm, the nipples rising, pressing into him. Burying his face, he called out her
name, again and again.

CHAPTER NINETEEN

Osu looked at his watch. 4:00 A.M. As an added precaution he was now running submerged off the built-up coastline. "Periscope depth!" He reversed his cap and waited.

"Periscope depth, sir."

"Up scope," he ordered.

"Up scope," came the confirmation; the sleek column of steel slid up, its greasy, mirrored surface taking on the red hue of the control room. In the easy movement of long practice Osu's cap seemed to lock onto the eyepiece, his arms draped casually yet purposefully over the flip-down handles, his whole body turning as one with the scope. The sea was rising. In the distance between the trough of the waves he could see blurred shore lights twinkling.

"Two seven zero, sir," said the *Sho-sa*, plotting nearby on the chart table in the center of the instrument-crowded control room.

"Lighthouse flashing," said Osu. "Interval twelve seconds. Bearing two six five. Mark."

"Two six five. Mark."

Bending over the chart, the *Sho-sa* slid the parallel rules to the new line and drew it to bisect the first. They were dead on course but running late. The lighthouse was definitely Point Danger, just on the northern side of the Queensland–New South Wales border.

The string of lights a little farther north were those studded between Coolangatta and Surfer's Paradise, running northward to Brisbane. The intersection of the lines now put I-43 nineteen miles offshore, approximately halfway between Brisbane and Byron Bay. Osu looked at his watch. It was imperative that he keep I-43 well away from the heavy cluster of

shore batteries and searchlights around Brisbane along both
its northern and southern approaches. Byron Bay, eighty
miles due south of Brisbane, was perfect—far enough away
from the batteries around Point Danger but not too far to
affect Heiji's surprise.

"Down scope!"

"Down scope," confirmed the officer of the deck and the
column slithered out of sight. The *Sho-sa*, allowing for the
time lost during the encounter with the convoy, gave the new
estimated time of arrival off the cape. "ETA oh five hundred
hours."

Osu grunted his disappointment. It wasn't good enough.
"Too close to dawn," he said, turning to Somura. "We must
launch at least thirty minutes before sunrise. That way you
can have the best of both worlds. Flying along the coast, protected by darkness and running in with the sun behind you."

Somura knew all this. It was Osu merely thinking aloud.

The commander tapped the chart anxiously with the divid-
ers that looked like red daggers. "It's either go this morning
or wait the whole day submerged." He looked at the chart, the
perspiration heavy about his eye where it had rested hard
against the periscope. "Damn that convoy!" He pushed the
intercom.

"Engine room," came the acknowledgment.

"Chief, I want an extra two knots for a hundred miles to
Cape Byron. Can you do it?"

"No."

Those in control cringed. The planesmen grew more interested in their dials. The engineer was part Ainu, from Hokkaido, so that his insolence toward superiors was to be expected, but he was pushing his luck. Osu ignored it, too
preoccupied with the loss of an hour due to the encounter
with the convoy, and the danger if he had to wait out the
daylight hours in enemy waters.

"One point five knots?" he asked.

It sounded like an auction between the captain and the engineer.

"I'm not a magician," from the engineer. "We're already overheating. I can give you burst speed for thirty minutes. No longer."

"An extra knot for a hundred miles?"

"Only if you ditch the plane."

The *Sho-sa* could not believe the man's gall. He would have had the engineer court-martialed. Instead, Commander Osu was closely studying the map. He had no choice. He would have to run on the surface of the built-up area if he was to reach his destination in time. "Give us whatever you can."

"Yes," replied the engineer curtly.

Osu ordered, "Surface," and turned to the *Sho-sa.* "When we reach the launch point I want Matsu and his catapult crew so alert that they go out of that hangar like flying fish. Understand?"

"Hai!" The *Sho-sa* resented the captain's tone. Why didn't he tell Matsu himself, and why didn't he treat his second in command with as much respect as the engineer? The *Sho-sa* had no illusion that if he had spoken to Osu the way the engineer had he would already be on the charge sheet. He noted too, with some puzzlement, that Somura was not surprised by the captain's tolerance. Unlike him, Somura, Osu and the engineer, all from the Eta Jima Academy, were a breed apart, so confident and without fear. He wished he could be like them.

The *Sho-sa* could not, of course, understand that Osu's quiescence was more bravado than real, that he had been trained to assess danger quickly without letting it show and have those around him sense it and panic. Osu knew the submarine was 5,000 miles from home deep in the enemy's ocean. In the words of the old wise man of Honshu, "There must be no disharmony before the dawn." Everyone and everything must be undisturbed, in place. Especially the engineer; Osu knew that if any of the tail-end ships of the Allied convoy with their greater range radar had managed to detect him, if there had been no thermal layer as I-43 had passed the last ships, then the convoy must certainly have relayed his position to the south. Yet he could not alter course to any degree; to do that would be to lose even more time and the wait of another whole day in hostile waters was an even greater risk. He decided to compromise as best he could. Soon they would be leaving the lit-up stretch of the coast and he would alter course slightly, a degree or so, and come in closer to landfall.

Having given the orders, he contacted the fore and after sections, informing the chief petty officers that he wanted the six twenty-four-inch-diameter torpedo tubes ready for instant firing and reloading. His third instruction was that the 5.5-inch gun crew and the bridge's two 25 mm machine-gun crews were to be on standby till further notice.

CHAPTER TWENTY

On the bridge of destroyer escort H.M.A.S. *Bendigo,* which had received the convoy's sub warning, all was peaceful in the darkness, the only noises being the deep throb of the engines and the high pinging of the active sonar sending out its pulse northward beneath the waves. The passive radar was at rest, its lesser range to be used only if *Bendigo* wanted to listen without being heard. *Bendigo* had received the relayed message from CINSWPA headquarters, Brisbane, and was now steaming north from Coff's Harbor at twenty-five knots to join the search for the Japanese sub.

Fifty feet above the destroyer's main deck and directly over the radar cabin, Leading Seaman Ross fiddled with the thumbscrews on the range finder, making a mental note that one of the threads was worn and needed more pressure than the other in bringing the two images of a target together. He was practicing on a low-lying cloud, its lower edge broken silver in the moonlight. The swells moved the swivel bucket seat slowly from starboard to port. Getting drowsy, Ross sat up suddenly and started to hum to keep awake; the life of every man aboard *Bendigo* might well depend on how alert he was. Below him the sleek outline of the ship gave him a surge of pride. From the sharp determination of the bow his eyes moved over the twin 4.7s of the A and B turrets to the blunt toughness of the bridge. Directly below him, high on the rear of the bridge housing, he could see the gunnery control tower, and farther back, the dark circle marking the powerful thrust of the lone funnel. Then the searchlight mount, the fluted barrels of the two-pound Pom-Poms sticking up into the night and, flanking their circular mounts, a cluster of .303 machine guns, and further aft two wing platforms each housing a .20 mm Oerlikon. Finally there was the turret with its twin 4.7s and the V-shaped slipways for the depth charges and the deadly thicket of five-foot-long Hedgehogs ready to throw an explosion-on-impact pattern against subs.

Still, Ross knew that all this armament might be useless unless *Bendigo* spotted the enemy first. Perhaps the broken, mottled sea blue and haze gray camouflage scheme would help if *Bendigo* was caught in the moonlight. Now, as if reading his thoughts, the silver cloud was gone, the sea tar black, the moon temporarily hidden by storm cumulus. Ross saw it was time for his check-in, rang the bridge and reported, "Nothing in sight."

CHAPTER TWENTY-ONE

Although Captain Osu's eight-by-six-foot cabin was cramped, it was the largest on the sub and it was here that Somura set up the eight-millimeter projector on one end of the bed, watching the tiny four-by-four-inch image, its center line a row of bolts on the bulkhead. It was a poor-quality, coarse-grained black-and-white reel of Brisbane taken from the air by one of the Japanese consulate officers in early 1940 on his way home from Canberra on the Pan-Am clipper service through Sydney, Brisbane and Singapore. The sprockets on the film were worn and it jumped every second or so. A month before, this had not worried Somura, but now he found the fault irritating. This first part of the film was useless anyhow, but some "bright spark," he thought, had spliced it together with the footage on MacArthur, thinking the aerial shots of the capital would help. For a moment Somura was oblivious of the film's jerky advance because his memory was triggered by the phrase "bright spark." It was as Australian as "fair dinkum," which meant the honest-to-God truth, another colloquialism he'd unconsciously absorbed into his English vocabulary. It took him back to the golden days before December, 1941. The film skipped suddenly at the splice and Brisbane went into a long blur. He stopped, rewound and started again.

Now it was MacArthur, striding upright and tall, coming out of Lennon's Hotel into the limousine, the four stars on the front fender and on the pennant—beside him a U.S. soldier with a Tommy gun, another machine gun visible on the right-hand side of the screen, and one more directly behind MacArthur. He looked invulnerable. This portion of the film, a pirated copy of a U.S. Movietone newsreel, had been shot the previous winter in mid-August before MacArthur had stopped wearing all his decorations. He was wearing the darker chocolate brown jacket and tie with the thirteen rows of ribbons, including the Medal of Honor and a line of Silver Stars won for gallantry since his early days in the First World War, light khaki trousers and the famous gold-braided Bataan cap.

Somura recalled that Heiji had told him that MacArthur's determination to regain the Philippines, and not simply bypass it as he had so many islands, on his way to Japan had become such an obsession that when people rang B–3211, MacArthur's headquarters number in Brisbane, the switchboard operator had been ordered to respond, "Hello, this is Bataan." MacArthur's worn cap was a symbol in itself, part of the actor in him and part of his legend, as unchanging as his schedule. A varied schedule, Heiji had pointed out, would of course have made much better sense for his security, but MacArthur refused to alter it, believing, like the ever-punctual Yamamoto, that when your time came, it came. Accordingly his schedule was always the same, and Somura had memorized it from both the file and what he could see in the film.

Now MacArthur was entering the sleek black Packard at 10:00 A.M., having risen between 7:15 and 7:30, played the daily game of marching about the room with his son Arthur to their own military music, given a small gift to Arthur, then breakfast, then the reading of battlefront dispatches and news reports till ten. Then to the headquarters on the eighth floor of the AMP Insurance Building and at two o'clock precisely, returning in the limousine for lunch with his wife Jean in the three suites, guarded day and night, on Lennon's fourth floor. After lunch a nap, then back to his headquarters until eight in the evening, then back to Lennon's—either in the Packard or Cadillac—remaining on the top floor of the hotel till ten the next morning, when the routine would begin again. It was a Spartan, highly disciplined schedule, no drink, no parties, no socializing that might take precious time and energy away from his war with Japan. At sixty-two he looked much younger—close shaved, a face alive with the keen, sharp intelligence that had made him West Point's top graduate and at twenty-eight the youngest divisional commander in the American army.

Now Somura was watching the arrival of MacArthur back at the hotel and again, having been in August, the Australian winter, it was already dark but still MacArthur wore his sunglasses—like Patton's riding crop, Somura mused, they had become a dramatic prop. The lights reflected briefly off the general's ribbons, aides flanking him, machine guns bristling, the gold-braided battle cap and cane and finally on the Packard's rear bumper the license plate USA-1 all combining to create a figure of aloof theatricality, the arrival of a distinguished star at a Hollywood premiere. No wonder, thought Somura, that some of those who had served under him, like this General Patton who was becoming well known in North Africa, carried on in a like manner. The Americans loved it, the Australians loved it, the Allies loved it. Somura did not mind it either, because just as in Japanese opera, the prima donna's theatricality depended on timing, on precise arrivals and departures, all necessitating a rigid attention to schedule. It made them reliable—it made them the best possible target.

Somura watched the film end and disappear noisily into a white square of nothingness. He rewound the film, packed the projector carefully away and went back to the after torpedo room, where he had two of the catapult launch crew take down his prop from its bracket near the torpedo reloading pulley. A six-foot-diameter plywood wheel for its base, it was in fact a circular papier maché mockup of Queensland's southeastern coast, constructed with the help of early aerial photographs and sea-to-shore observations made by Japanese luggers plying the coast in the mid-thirties when they had ostensibly been looking for pearls on the Great Barrier Reef and coming into Brisbane for repairs. On the eastern rim of the wheel were the long spits of Stradbroke and Moreton islands and between them and the mainland the fifteen-mile-long stretch of Moreton Bay, with Mud Island in the middle, then the mouth of the Brisbane River. Inland another ten miles lay Brisbane itself and in its heart, Lennon's Hotel. What had Heiji said? "The surest way to kill a soldier is in his home, not on the battlefield but where he least expects it." It was a lesson well learned from the Tokyo assassinations of the thirties.

Sitting by the edge of the wheel but not touching it, Somura leaned over the tripod-supported bombsite, closed one eye and had the men spin the wheel. Then suddenly, at their own discretion, they would stop it, simulating Somura's run in from any number of angles, which might occur if he was harassed by fighters. A sudden evasive dive or bank could place him, in seconds, at 180 degrees to his original southerly approach and he would have to recognize the salient landmarks quickly so as to reorientate himself as fast as possible before the fighters had a chance to stop him. Of course he hoped there would be no fighters. But no matter how exhaustively they had trained him, no matter the endless practices, there was always the unexpected, and so, alone in his cabin, Somura laid out his headband, the short samurai sword that by tradition he would strap by his side, and his prayer belt, placing them before the sub's *omikoshi*, the small, portable Shinto shrine. He would not have time when all efforts and attention had to be focused on the impending launch of Heiji's surprise. He clapped his hands sharply, to gain the attention of the gods, and prayed that the sea would be calm, the sky clear for his run; that the rising sun would bring a victory for Nippon and new honor to his family, and himself.

*   *   *

On top of the bridge in gunnery control Lt. Cmdr. Gordon Smythe, Royal Australian Navy, *Bendigo*'s gunnery control officer, had been working hard to get his crew into top form. He was not liked because *Bendigo*'s seamen considered him the worst kind of RAN officer–the kind who had been trained in Britain, at Whale Island, and now was more British than the British, his Australian drawl all but buried in a plethora of "chaps," "jolly good shows" and "you theres!" all wrapped in an air of superiority that wafted like a bad smell through the lower deck. Behind his back they called Smythe "Bligh," but grudgingly, as Bligh's sailors had, they admired his skill. He could work the intricate bank of machines that clattered away like heavy typewriters—more accurately, primitive computers —which ingested all the variables of wind, condition of sea, humidity and temperature, and could direct the heavy guns with great accuracy.

This didn't mean that Smythe's twin 4.7s in the two forward turrets, A and B, and the after turret, X, were dead on target *all* the time, since in the split-second changes of wave and trough this was impossible. But while some gunnery officers could only manage to have their crews hit a target "once in a wet week," the moment Smythe found its range, a target was going to get its share of shot and if it stayed around long enough it was going to look "bloody sick," as Leading Seaman Johnson in A turret well knew. The problem was, would the captain get them on target? In any event, the gunlayers were ready. Under Johnson's attentive supervision and lathered in sweat, they had hauled away on the chain and cradle, bringing up the armor-piercing high explosive shells from the magazines through the shell room three decks below, stopping only when the safety balance had been struck between the number of reserve shells held in the turrets at any one time and those stowed for safety in the magazines between decks.

Captain Willoughby was a different kind of officer from Smythe, made to fit the happy cliché "fair but firm." Above all he was cool, an old-timer who'd seen action in the 'fourteen– 'eighteen war as a midshipman aboard H.M.A.S. *Sydney* when the Australian cruiser had sunk the German raider *Emden* off Cocos Islands in the Indian Ocean. Japan had been his ally in that First World War.

"Number One."

"Sir?"

"If the Jap is holding to his heading as reported, how far off is he?"

The first officer's calculations had been ongoing ever since they'd left Coff's Harbor. Besides, by now the first officer could almost anticipate the old man. "Forty plus miles, sir. Beam on to Point Danger. If he's running on the surface."

Willoughby did the rest of the calculations in his head, remembering that the maximum reliable range of the active sonar, much better than radar for detecting a sub if it was submerged or suddenly dived, was give or take twenty miles. But Willoughby wanted to play safe. Without turning to the assembled officers, his eyes fixed on the moonlit horizon, he told them: "Plan is as follows, gentlemen. We will cross the Jap's heading two three two to a point five miles beyond—that is, closer in to the coast. Then we cut all engines and drift. That'll put us on the landward side of his heading so that as the coastal current and tide push us back out, away from the coast, we'll be drifting back onto his bearing. If we cut engines here, we'll only be pushed further out to sea and have to start engines up to maintain position. Understand?"

Apparently they did.

"Good. Now when we move in, cross his line, and cut engines we'll shift from active sonar to passive. Got that, Number Two?"

"Active to passive. Yes, sir."

The first officer nodded in appreciation. The trap was beautiful in its simplicity. Once they were across the line of the Jap sub's heading and drifting seaward in silence, having switched from active to passive sonar, the inferior Jap sonar, with a much shorter maximum range of only twelve miles, wouldn't pick up any engine sound or an active pulse, because there wouldn't be any from the *Bendigo*. And even if the Jap wasn't staying on his original heading, at around fifteen miles, the *Bendigo*'s passive ears would keep Willoughby alerted to the Jap's approach before the Jap's shorter range sonar and radar would be able to pick up the blip of the destroyer's bulk.

It was a brilliant example of the destroyer using its longer electronic arm to best advantage. By the time the Jap had *Bendigo* on his scopes, Willoughby would have had time to start the *Bendigo*'s engines and would be charging in for the kill. Then it would be a race—whether the sub could dive fast enough before Willoughby, with overwhelming firepower, could get the winning shots away from the surface. But Willoughby was far from overconfident; the trap might be sprung by *Bendigo*, closing it would be another matter. His element of surprise would only be momentary at best, and despite all of *Bendigo*'s guns, depth charges and torpedoes, the Jap had a much lower and sleeker profile and had the deadly accurate torpedoes, called "white lightning" by those of *Bendigo*'s crew who had seen them ravage the Allied destroyer squadrons of Guadalcanal.

On I-43, slicing through the waters off northern New South Wales, the catapult launch crew was in a state of high tension, and the torpedo details fore and aft were ready to fire instantly. The 5.5 inch and two .25 mm machine-gun crews were likewise ready, clustered in the lee of the conning tower's bridge, away from the billowing spumes of spray thrown back by the bow cutting into the heavy Pacific swells. It was cramped but no one complained. They knew their commander was obliged to run on the surface to save time, to get it done. The air was cooler now and the decreasing cloud gave way to sheets of moonlight. In the tight conning-tower space Osu looked at the two machine-gun crews and the crew of the sole deck gun mounted astern out of the way of the hangar. If there was any trouble they would be on the deck in seconds.

On *Bendigo* the sound of the buzzer made the third officer jump. Captain Willoughby pressed the intercom bar. "Bridge."

"Radar contact, sir. Bearing two four zero. Range twenty miles."

"Switch off radar at fifteen miles, move to passive sonar mode."

"Aye, aye, sir."

Willoughby then rang the crow's-nest and gave Leading Seaman Ross the bearing.

Chapter Twenty-Two

Several miles south of Toowoomba, stretched out like a go-anna lizard, his shadow cast in enormous relief on the cave's wall by the deep red iron bark fire, Archie Underbridge lay listening to the sounds of the bush and leisurely taking in its smells. He was separating the pungent odor of the lantana bushes from the gentler, more refreshing eucalyptus that wafted across the wide mouth of the cave, varying in intensity as he fed the fire, altering the flow of air against the cold sandstone face. Six feet away, below the mouth of the cave, the U-bend of the coffee black creek was sprinkled with stars and beyond it the blackness became absolute, taken over by the sounds of cicadas, owls, the odd splash of a platypus, and in the distance, a long howl of a dingo, and once, the short, haunting cry of fox. Archie wondered if the animal was fed up with the world or caught in a trap, which he concluded was about the same thing—both were lingering deaths.

It was because Archie wasn't afraid of death that he was enjoying life better than most. He knew that if the metho didn't kill him something else would, but that once you fell hostage to the fear of death you became a slave to some kind of routine, embracing a risk-free routine as the guarantor of longevity. Archie had given up the fear and its offspring long ago when he had turned his back on the establishment and dropped out from a high-stress middle-management position at the General Post Office and decided to go walkabout. To bloody hell with them one and all . . .

And he had left a wife in Armidale, south of the Queensland–New South Wales border, because she had driven him near insane with constant harping about her legion of ailments. Archie had decided there was nothing really wrong with her, and one cold night in August five years ago had up and left. Occasionally he felt bad about it but consoled himself in the belief that she was better off without him, convinced that his passivity only encouraged her, that what she'd needed was someone to say "shut up" to save her from herself, to pull her out of her morbid self-indulgence. But he hadn't the strength or the disposition to shout, to lecture or cajole. And his supporting her, he thought, only gave her more time to feel sorry for herself with her imaginary ailments. If she had to work perhaps she'd be so busy making ends meet that she'd pull herself out of it. Or was he only excusing himself . . . ?

His thoughts were distracted by the gurgle from the Nestlé condensed milk can, blackened in a side pocket of bright orange coals. He'd punctured the tin so it wouldn't blow up, but a piece of ash must have fallen on the hole from the burning bark above. He prodded the tin farther out to the perimeter of the fire, the flames singeing one sleeve of his old beloved football jersey. Another hour, he told himself, and the condensed milk would turn to caramel. That and a cup of tea for breakfast was about as posh as a man could get, camping out in the bush. After that it would be tea and damper, flour and water baked in the coals.

The longer he listened the more sounds he could distinguish from each other, the far gurgling of a small waterfall and the lapping of the creek against the shore of clean-polished pebbles invisible in the dark. Above the cave the heavily bush-crested ridge along which he'd had to walk before working his way down through the lantana groaned softly in the breeze. They were called the Seven Mile Caves in Toowoomba, but the cave he was in was really the only one of any size, about twenty yards wide and twenty deep, the others being little more than pockmarks in the fifty-foot-high limestone cliffs that had been carved out by the timeless journey of the creek. Archie believed that a man could tramp the world and find no serener place than here. Now and then, during the day, you might hear the distant whack of a shooter after roos or maybe wood duck and quail or a far-off growl from a tractor echoing through the hills from some lonely farm, but in the main this was the best you could get and it was only seven miles down from the range.

As he dozed in the fire's ruby glow and a gust of wind moved through the heavy timber above like an onrushing sea, his mind built fantastic cities in the coals and watched them fall like Troy. It vindicated his feeling about all civilization, that sooner or later—in this war or the next—it would all collapse and disappear so why worry? Only the land like Australia's ancient bush country would remain. They said it was the oldest country on earth, few mountains over 6,000 feet, the rest already worn down by wind and erosion into the vast red deserts of the center and the hill country of the coastal belt.

He heard a loud rustle by the creek, and opened his eyes, staring. It sounded again and this time it was closer.

CHAPTER TWENTY-THREE

On I-43's deck the third officer lifted his sextant toward the Southern Cross, using celestial navigation to confirm the sub's heading. Jutting out beneath him he could see the wide, bulbous toe of the hangar, and running from it the inclined rail tracks glinting in the moonlight as they stretched toward the bow on the slight incline, seeming to converge above the fluorescent bow wave eighty feet away.

An oiler had told him that he'd overheard one of the five catapult launch crew and that every bit of unnecessary standard equipment, including extra forty-eight-gallon drop tanks and all armor plating, had been stripped from the plane. And someone had counted the number of aviation gas drums taken aboard. The gas, he figured, would allow for only 200 miles, to and from target, and fifty gallons more for "unknown contingencies." Half the normal gas load had been sacrificed so that Heiji's surprise could now carry more ordnance, including more than 2,000 pounds of high explosive fragmentation bombs, smoke canisters and wing rockets.

Soon there were experts and strategists everywhere aboard the sub, submariners who had never been near a plane until now arguing the merits of this plane versus that. The only common agreement among them was that Japan had the best fighter in the Pacific—the new navy type "O" fighter, an updated version of the Mitsubishi folding-wingtip Zero Sen, model 32: maximum speed 341 miles per hour, at least fifty-seven miles faster than its main opponent in the Pacific, the U.S. Navy's folding-wing Wildcat. It also had a much higher climb rate.

The *Sho-sa* let them babble on; it was good for morale, their talking an escape valve for the mounting tension aboard I-43, so thick you could cut it with a knife.

Chapter Twenty-Four

Byron Bay

The trick, old Bill Reardon knew, was to beat the other fishermen back to the pass with the first catch of mackerel of the
day. This way you could sometimes sell most of the catch to
the campers who came down onto the beach from the Palm
Valley camping ground above the bay. If you were lucky and
sold all of your catch you not only saved a trip to the fish
shops but you could set your own price. But you had to get up
early.

From his fibro-cement cottage nestled behind a rampart of
grass-veined dunes, Bill could see the two long white arms of
light, the body of the lighthouse between them, sweeping ma-
jestically high above in the darkness out over the township,
over St. Helena Hill and beyond, toward Mount Warning,
northward over the seemingly endless curve of beaches, eastward over the foam-ringed peaks of the Julien Rocks jutting
up from the middle of the bay, then further east out to sea,
the beam visible for fifty miles off the Australian coast, then
back to start the endless sweep again. It was two hours before
dawn and if he didn't get cracking he knew he'd miss the tide
at the pass and couldn't launch his boat unless he wanted to
risk bogging the Ford pickup in the wet low-tide sand. He
woke up his boozy son, Len. "C'mon, boy. Mackerel to catch."

Reardon Junior shivered in the early morning chill. "Jeez—
already? It's colder'n a fish's tit."

"Ah, rats, it's just a bit nippy that's all. Put on your jersey.
I'll make a cuppa."

In the darkness Reardon Senior made his way to the small,
functional kitchen, filled the kettle and pumped up the
Primus stove.

Len, shivering, rolled out of bed muttering a long list of obscenities, prefaced by "bloody" and finishing with "brass monkeys" as his feet hit the cold linoleum floor.

"Stop your moanin'. You'd think you were crossin' the pole."

"Feel a bit bloody frail this morning."

"Serves you right. How many times I have to tell you? Don't mix your grog. But no, you're the know-it-all. Tossing it down your gullet like a flamin' dump truck, then you winge all flamin' day."

"Ease up, dad—me head's breakin'!"

It was because Bill Reardon knew his son would be slow with a hangover that he had risen a half-hour earlier, estimating that by the time their pickup reached the pass, hauling their fifteen-foot inboard, they'd be ahead of the game, getting out a good hour before dawn, at the tide's high point.

He was right, no one else had yet put out to sea. Bill switched on his running lights, giving Len the tiller—Len'd be no use till the sun was up—and began cutting bait for the long lines they'd trail for the mackerel. Suddenly he saw a series of white flashes in the darkness—long, elegant taylor fish shooting the rollers—and he studied the sky, able to tell it would be a fine day and not just because he'd heard it on the radio. The wind had died and he could see there were few clouds about the moon. He put the state of sea at about a three—deep swells but long and easy with nothing much to worry about. "Pretty calm," he predicted.

"I'm goin' on the wagon," said Len, one arm stuffed in his windbreaker pocket, the other grasping the tiller reluctantly as the fifteen-foot boat crashed through the first line of breakers. The bow hit the next one off point and Bill Reardon grabbed the gunwale for support. As the bow swiveled to port the moon seemed to jump across the sky like a meteor. "C'mon, Len. Pull your finger out. You'll bloody capsize us if you're not careful."

"She'll be right. Don't get your balls in an uproar."

"And where's your bloody lifejacket?"

"Stowed."

"Well put it on."

"Half a mo. I'm just waking—hey, what's that?"

"What?"

"Out there. Looks like a . . . a bloody destroyer. By the cape."

Bill Reardon looked out along the moonlit sea. "Can't see anything."

"Well, course you bloody can't. We're in a trough now, aren't we?"

As the boat rose high on the incoming swell Bill looked out toward the high black cliffs of the cape beneath the lighthouse. "No destroyer out there."

"Must have just gone past the cape. About six miles out, I picked 'er up in the moonbeam."

"In the booze beam, more like it. Sure you're not seeing pink elephants?"

"All right, all right, how much you want to bet?"

"A dollar."

"Oh, big spender. Come on, make it two."

"All right. You're on."

Suddenly Len had more life in him, his hand gripping the tiller more resolutely, his body upright, waiting for first light. "You've done your coin," Len said, "I'm in the money."

It wasn't the size of the bet, but he was sure he had seen something. Problem was, if the destroyer was running with lights out it would be practically invisible with the black cape behind it, even in moonlight. They'd have to watch for it as they were passing to the side of the cape. He figured that would be in about thirty minutes.

Bill Reardon was grinning in the darkness and slicing more bait. He might lose a couple of dollars but now at least Len was paying attention. He'd bet on a sunrise if you let him.

*   *   *

At fifteen miles, Leading Seaman Mulvane, *Bendigo*'s sonar
operator, could see that the sub's heading was the same. As
instructed he turned the radar off, switched on the passive
sonar and informed the captain, piping it through the loud-
speakers so the bridge could also monitor the sub's advance.
They could clearly hear the hollow pinging of the sub's twin
shafts but there was a problem; although the passive sonar's
listening range of twenty miles was eighteen miles greater
than the active sonar's, the passive did not send out a ping
and could therefore not time the return of an echo to the ears
of *Bendigo*'s hydrophones. Which was where Leading Seaman
Mulvane's experience would tell, since a skilled sonar man
could tell from the slight variations in the doppler, the tone of
sound, approximately how far a target on a steady course was
closing or departing. It was still only an approximation but it
was better than nothing.

"What do you think, Mulvane?" asked Willoughby.

"Getting closer, sir. I'm clicking him, sir," by which
Mulvane meant that he had started a stopwatch, taking a beat
count of the sub's props to give him the rpm of the target's
propellers and thereby help him confirm the sub's speed.
"Plus or minus twenty knots, sir."

Twenty knots told Willoughby that the sub must be running
on the surface and he knew that, contrary to public belief,
over ninety percent of all successful torpedo attacks by submarines were made on the surface where the craft had three
times the submerged speed to maneuver, not to mention infinitely better vision. Willoughby had seen two destroyers go
down in as many minutes in the face of one such I-boat attack.
Now he conned a new course, and his destroyer swung two
points to starboard—the bow heading to intercept.

CHAPTER TWENTY-FIVE

Archie stared into the bush, the wind above the cave grown wilder now, signaling an approaching storm that was moving quickly eastward from the vast plains of the outback. The rustle sounded again by the creek. It was too brief to be a roo, a hare possibly, but Archie stayed rigidly propped up on one arm, fearing a snake. One thing he couldn't stand, he told the cave, was bloody snakes. Red-backed spiders, stone fish, both deadly . . . all right, but *not* snakes. Most were poisonous and around here they were mainly tigers or red-bellied blacks. First it would be paralysis, then convulsions.

Logic told him he was being ridiculous and he should go back to sleep. Even if it was a snake it wouldn't come near the fire. Would it? But logic had a way of fleeing the bush in the early hours. What happened when the fire died and they felt the warmth from the ashes beckoning them like the warmth of the sun they loved to sunbake in on the hard clay of the drying creek beds? Slowly Archie lay down but couldn't sleep, determined as he was to keep the fire well stoked. They gave him the wimwops.

No wonder Archie Underbridge was bone weary in that hour before dawn on April 20, when, 140 miles to the southeast, fifteen miles off the Australian coast and approaching Cape Byron twelve miles off its starboard quarter, I-43's catapult-launching crew in the control room made their way forward under the command of Lieutenant Matsu.

They passed through the watertight hatch of the pressure hull from the control room at the base of the conning tower to the aircraft hangar. Once the five men were inside, the watertight hatch was closed and Matsu ordered the lights on. Three of the four catapult-launch crew carefully took the protective tarpaulin sheet from the plane and rechecked the trolley mounting and its cradle for salt encrustation. Going up on deck the fourth member of the CLC, secured by a safety line to a U-bolt by the hangar's door, proceeded cautiously along the rails toward the black knife of the bow slicing open the moonlit swells, Using two wire brushes, one in each hand, they scoured the eighty feet of steel tracks, carefully removing any salt deposits, flying fish carcasses or sea cucumbers, the thick, slimy, sluglike creatures that, having attached themselves when the sub had been submerged, could momentarily deflect the trolley into disaster.

With the wind changing slightly from the northeast, Commander Osu on the conning tower bridge rang down to alter course two degrees starboard. He felt good; the sea wasn't too rough, despite the swells, and in the warm Australian waters the bridge was the best place to be. Besides, now he was well south of the heavy traffic zone of the Brisbane–South Queensland coast and approaching the cape. It had been selected as the best possible ditch marker by Somura for his offshore pickup by the sub. Osu acknowledged that it was the perfect choice because the lighthouse was an ideal landmark and if Somura for some unforeseen reason was running behind time on his return following the mission, he could easily pick up its beam at night after ditching with parachute and using a signal light from the rubber dinghy.

Noting the beam flashing high above the cape, Osu rang control and gave a new heading to compensate once again for the wind. The *Sho-sa* confirmed and plotted it, informing the captain that as they had passed south, off Point Danger, the tides had been stronger than anticipated and that they were still five miles from the cape launch point. Now Osu was worried; dawn was barely fifty minutes away. The launch would take a maximum of ten to fifteen minutes but to give young

Somura as good a start as possible he needed a half-hour of darkness. At this rate he'd be taking off in the daylight. Osu rang control and gave the order: "Launch in ten minutes."

In the dim yellow hangar light Somura, in his immaculate U.S. Navy lieutenant's uniform, tightened the prayer belt about his waist and the band the crew had given him securely beneath his leather helmet and climbed the ladder into Heiji's surprise—an American Wildcat captured intact in the Philippines, complete with U.S. naval white star insignia. Holding the short sword close to his side, Somura lowered himself into the cockpit and heard them roll the ladder away.

He felt calm. After all the hours of training at Eta Jima he was ready. He had been through it a hundred times. As the sub changed direction slightly the roll increased, but he knew that when the time came the captain would steady her for him. He must not think about the risk, only the procedure. When the time came the catapult-launch officer would order the trolley lock removed. A crew member would confirm this, showing him the lock held high in his hand. The launch crew would start the engine and under the dim hangar light Somura would begin his own checklist, starting with the life raft stowed aft of the aerial support down to his instrumentation, finally setting the flaps at thirty-five degrees for takeoff and the right rudder at one-third arc. The launch officer would then order the hangar light "off," push the button for the hydraulics to lift the hangar door and take the Aseki pistol grip pin-bulb flashlight whose black barrel prevented anyone from seeing the tiny red light unless they were looking directly into its cone. Meanwhile Osu would be bringing I-43 into the wind and the red pin light would begin winking at takeoff minus five minutes. Somura would run through his checklist: oil pressure, rpm, flaps, and finally he would pull the specially rigged release so that if he wished, each of the two landing wheels could be operated independently. When the red pin light ceased its blinking he would open the throttle and the engine would begin its scream into full rpm. He would tighten the shoulder harness, pushing himself back as hard as possible to counteract the enormous G-force of the eighty-foot, three-second run.

Now in a dry run he pulled the joystick hard to the right, then used his gloved left hand to anchor it, pushing the right elbow into his waist harness to counteract the shock-thrust of the fourteen cordite rockets on the trolley mounting below him, which, once fired, would propel the trolley and thereby launch the plane in three seconds flat. He touched his sword for luck.

H.M.A.S. *Bendigo* was across the line.

"Stop engines," ordered Willoughby.

"Stop engines. Aye. All engines stopped."

"Secure the ship."

All auxiliary machinery, including the air conditioning for the magazines between decks, was immediately shut off. "Ship secure, sir."

Silently, the *Bendigo* waited, hidden just south of the cape but forward enough so that its lookouts could see the northern approaches to the bay. Willoughby, unperturbed by the tension he could feel behind him in the plotting room, calmly ordered, "Action stations," and forbade any smoking. One flare of a match across the open sea was all it would take to alert the Jap.

Mulvane's voice came over the pipe. "Target speed increasing—twenty-five knots, sir. Changed heading two degrees."

"Very good." The Jap was falling for it.

In the two forward turrets, A and B, and the X turret petty officers and men sat perspiring heavily in their asbestos clothing and helmets. Leading Seaman Johnson in A turret announced that right now he would kill for a cigarette. Nobody told him the obvious.

Ten miles to the north of the cape, Osu lifted his binoculars and swept them through a long arc from the port bow to port aft and then from starboard aft to—

He froze. Five miles off the starboard bow coming out from the great dark mouth of Byron Bay he saw three dots of light: red-white-green. A ship's running lights. A civil craft? It didn't matter. If it saw him it would report his position and the launch would be lost.

He rang for general quarters at the same time as his sonar operator picked up the faint hum of the boat's prop. "Prepare to attack. Full speed ahead. Forward tubes."

"Prepare to attack," came the *Sho-sa*'s voice. "Full speed ahead. Forward tubes ready."

"Bearing, mark!"

"One eight nine. Range six thousand."

"Short fuses."

"Short fuses, sir."

"Bearing. Mark!"

"Bearing one eight seven. Range five thousand."

"Hold position."

"Hold position, sir."

"Range?"

"Four five zero. Small target, sir. Trawler perhaps."

Osu now realized he was in more trouble than he thought. He couldn't use a torpedo, which would be difficult with such a small target anyway. Of greater concern, however, was that the torpedo would cause such an explosion that it would alert the lighthouse keepers—it would alert the whole bay, and the .25 mm machine guns would take forever to put enough holes in the boat to put it under. He couldn't ram it either. Such a small boat could maneuver much faster than he could. The best way, the only way, was the deck gun—much less noisy than a torpedo and unlikely to be heard the six miles away over the surf. In any case he *must* launch in five minutes. He ordered the heavy 5.5 gun crew into action.

CHAPTER TWENTY-SIX

Three things happened almost simultaneously. I-43's deck gun fired at the Reardons' boat, which was now midway between the sub and the destroyer, hidden by the cape, to the south.

On the destroyer *Bendigo*, Leading Seaman Ross in the crow's-nest saw the red flash from the sub's 5.5-inch gun, gave the sub's position to the bridge, and *Bendigo*, starting engines, leapt forward, quickly reaching twenty-five knots, pressing for thirty-five, her A and B turrets firing the first salvo of 4.7-inch shells.

Osu, seeing that he was discovered, ordered his machine guns into action as well.

Bendigo's second salvo was guided by radar when the flashes of the sub's guns were momentarily lost to *Bendigo* as she smashed through the swells, heeling hard aport for the turn, firing two parachute flares three miles ahead on the port quarter, hoping to pick up the sub while still invisible herself. But the flares fell short and all that Willoughby could see in the phosphorous glare of undulating swells was a small fishing boat, its wake a crazy **S** surrounded by an exploding sea as the high white columns of the sub's 5.5 spewed up about her midst a rain of machine-gun fire whose white tracer was coming from some hidden point in the vast blanket of darkness eastward of the cape.

Bendigo's lookouts tried to pinpoint the position from which the graceful tracer was arcing in long, broken white curves, but the destroyer's bow was forging ahead at such speed the waves, exploding over the forecastle, clouded binoculars and eyes with spray. Ross turned on the wipers in the crow's-nest but it didn't help and the destroyer's shuddering charge made his job of holding a steady image on the range finder an impossible task.

His machine gun still firing at Reardon's boat, Osu now swung I-43 around to face the orange flames erupting from the Australian's A and B turrets as they bore down toward him. It was the worst possible angle. The destroyer—he presumed that's what it was from the speed readings coming from his sonar—was knifing toward him, offering him only the narrowest of targets. Now, that I-43 had turned to meet the destroyer head-on, the problem would, of course, be the same for the destroyer, but at this range of four miles the Australians' four forward guns had a decided advantage in maneuverability over the I-43's torpedoes.

Penetrating the armor plate of the control tower twenty feet below the crow's-nest, the deep thunder of his four forward guns gave Gunnery Officer Smythe his familiar surge of exhilaration. All 'round him he could hear the clicking of his machines making the instantaneous corrections when Leading Seaman Ross came through on the intercom with a visual fix on the flash from the sub's 5.5. Quickly Smythe punched in the corrections and gave the order: "Fire!"

Ross reported seconds later that from the spumes it looked like two "overs" and two "shorts."

Smythe punched in the correction for "straddle" and ordered "Fire" again, the 4.7s sending a shudder through the entire ship, rattling the galley's pots and pans in a headsplitting din that echoed unheeded by anyone; now that the ship was in action all hands were employed in the combat, including ship's cooks and helpers assigned to auxiliary tasks on the chains and pulleys in the shell rooms.

"Why doesn't he dive?" It was *Bendigo*'s first officer. Willoughby couldn't make it out either, unless the Jap had decided to bet all his money on a torpedo attack, but a destroyer bearing down at thirty-five knots against a sub's twenty-three had a decided edge and then once they got close enough the Pom-Pom and Oerlikon guns could open up and—

Osu could now see the white V of *Bendigo*'s bow wave.

"Fire one!"

"One away."

"Torpedo!" yelled *Bendigo*'s lookout. "Red, bearing three five zero! Four thousand!"

Willoughby saw it at once—the ugly white scar racing toward him in the darkness. Six seconds later he could see it was on a collision course with his starboard bow but he still couldn't see the Jap. Now wasn't the time for another flare; at three thousand yards away, the Jap would get as full a view of *Bendigo* as *Bendigo* would of him. The radar, though, showed him nose on, on the port side. "Hard aport," Willoughby ordered.

"Hard aport, aye."

"Stand by for hard astarboard."

"Stand by for hard astarboard, sir."

From his conning tower Osu was pleased to see that the Australian with the torpedo coming at him from the starboard quarter could only turn hard to port with any safety, and if he did that he would expose the destroyer's entire starboard side, all 350 feet of her, for Osu to shoot at. From her speed and two twin turrets forward Osu had guessed that she was of the Marksman class, maximum speed thirty-five knots and, all-important for a sub captain, a draught of thirteen and a half feet. With the destroyer closing in for the kill, Osu couldn't get I-43's bow into the wind for Somura's launch, but if Somura was to stand a chance the destroyer and all her machine guns that were now opening up had to be silenced, if not permanently then at least diverted long enough to allow Somura to get airborne. That was I-43's first responsibility— her own survival was secondary.

Somura waited, heart pounding. Matsu, fighting to steady his hand, holding the pistol grip lamp, waited anxiously for the *Sho-sa*'s command from control to launch as soon as Osu told him the sub was in position. He had shut the hangar door, keeping it closed until the very last minute out of fear of flying shrapnel.

The torpedo's wake shot past *Bendigo*'s starboard side not fifty yards away, clearly visible to the sailors manning the Pom-Pom. "Come on, come on," said one, eager to have *Bendigo* beam on for his guns to be operable. "Let's have a go at the bastard."

The men in the after turret also waited their turn for Willoughby to bring them broadside on for a line of sight. Instead, Willoughby ordered, "Hard aport," swinging *Bendigo*'s bow back again, aiming straight for the sub, no longer a shaky radar blip but a sharp orange image on the screen, its conning tower throwing back a full echo. Outside, its bridge was now visible in a sudden wash of moonlight that also sharply silhouetted *Bendigo*.

Seeing the destroyer brought back quickly to collision course so as not to expose her starboard flank, Osu, at 2,000 yards, fired Number Two torpedo. The fish leapt out from the bow tube, hitting the water at sixty miles per hour, its high explosive warhead aimed two degrees to the left of the oncoming destroyer, running for her port side. Then he fired Number Three, two degrees to *Bendigo*'s right, aimed at her starboard side, the two torpedoes streaking in a narrow V only feet apart, and only yards apart by the time they would reach *Bendigo*'s position, making it impossible for the Australian to turn either starboard or port without exposing his ship's sides to at least one of them. Now Osu ordered, "Hard astarboard one eighty. Hurry!"

I-43 turned tightly, ploughing into a heavy swell, trying to head into the wind for the launch, her deck gun now firing at a range of 1,000 yards at the destroyer, whose four forward guns were already sending out their next salvo.

"Two shorts. Two overs," reported Ross as towers of foam

climbed skyward a hundred yards beyond the periscope sheath of the turning sub.

Smythe corrected to straddle the sub, aiming his guns for the median position between the shorts and longs.

"Fire!"

The 4.7 tore through the sub's bridge, exploding in a deafening roar on the port side, churning the sea, knocking the sub off course. Osu died instantly and the machine-gun crew followed.

The hangar shook violently from the hit, as did the entire boat, and through a manhole-size gash in the hangar's roof Matsu was privy to a most incongruous sight—a peaceful disc of moon sailing calmly through fleecy cumulus. He rang the bridge, got no reply, and knew he now had full responsibility for the launch. He ordered the hangar door reopened, and it rose with growing reverberations, revealing to Somura a square of moonlit sea erupting in shellfire. The *Sho-sa,* dazed, made his way through the wreckage to the bridge.

Somura lifted his gloved hand, and Matsu's lamp began the count.

The torpedoes were now past *Bendigo,* whose starboard .20 mm Oerlikon, now in line of sight, began its staccato dance, its mid-barrel spring recoiling from the chump chump chump of the gun's assault on I-43's port side. With the sub beam on, the starboard four-inch gun opened up, then the Pom-Poms, pumping the stream of two-pound shells at the long black shape 300 yards away. The moon slid behind a cloud—into pitch blackness—and Willoughby, unable to see the sub clearly enough for a ram, with a risk he would angle too sharply, run into her prematurely and smash his own props, ordered half speed and "on, forward searchlight."

The beam reached out, holding the sub's stern, then there was the tinkle of glass and a sound like hail hitting *Bendigo*'s bridge as the searchlight was quickly extinguished at 200 yards by the sub's remaining .25 mm. Now that he had seen her, Willoughby knew the sub would turn again if she could, and so ordered "hard aport" to bring to bear all his starboard guns, including the aft 4.7.

The *Sho-sa* heard the sonorous boom of *Bendigo*'s rear turret, its shells screaming above the chatter of the destroyer's machine guns. Echoing Osu's last command he called out above the cacophony of gunfire, "Starboard one eight zero! Burst speed!" and I-43 gave all she had in an exhausting spring of thirty knots to bring herself into the wind.

The red pinhead of light now vanished from Matsu's lamp, replaced by the green. They were all clear—into the wind.

Somura pulled the stick over, pressed his body back, and dropped the white-gloved hand. Matsu waited a moment for the bow to rise on the swell, pulled the circuit breaker, and the fourteen rockets ignited. The trolley shot forward in a volcanic roar, Somura reaching a hundred miles an hour in three seconds, the G-force threatening to black him out. The whole world shook, the plane dipped, spray splattering on Perspex; he punched the supercharger, saw the trolley smashing white into the sea. There followed another gut-wrenching dip, a black mountain of water rushing at him, the nose lifting —he was airborne, the Wildcat climbing steadily toward the cumulus.

He saw I-43's lone deck gun still firing and in the moonlight a small boat drifting toward the doomed sub.

Watching his radarscope Seaman Mulvane suddenly saw two orange blips instead of one. A double echo? He knew everything went haywire in an attack, you couldn't be sure exactly where—no, the second blip was still there, its distance from the sub rapidly increasing, heading south.

Unable to dive, the *Sho-sa* brought I-43's bow around to face the destroyer and fired all six tubes. There was, after all, nothing to lose. The moon came out again, and now I-43 was clearly silhouetted, the moon a god-sent flare for Gunnery Officer Smythe. "Fire!" he ordered, sending the full salvo crashing into the sub's after quarter, ripping apart the engine room, lifting the sub's bow high into the air, the sea flooding her, her deck gun and remaining machine gun still firing from an angle of fifteen degrees even as the bow kept rising. The burst speed had taken her farther away from the destroyer, but no more than 300 yards, and now Willoughby unleashed a pattern of fifteen Hedgehog depth charges, then immediately brought the destroyer around to ram. As long as she was afloat with her six bow tubes intact Willoughby knew it wasn't over, never mind the crazy angle. Japs weren't finished till they were dead. He proceeded to give conning orders to the helmsman and engine room. "Half ahead both engines. Prepare for ramming. Port ten, midships, port ten, midships, starboard five, midships, starboard twenty—"

"Torpedoes!" someone shouted. "Four degrees starboard— four degrees port!"

The Reardons' boat, barely afloat, its running lights long swamped, its Johnson inboard flooded, was wallowing in the heavy swells, both men hanging onto the gunwales, only Bill with his life jacket on and praying that the concussion of the battle would scare off sharks—one of the Hedgehog pattern hit their boat astern, blowing them to pieces, the explosion a mere dot of light on Seaman Mulvane's radar screen, which quickly was gone.

Bendigo's starboard quarter buckled, then jumped hard aport with the force of the detonation, the torpedo striking just forward of the magazine. Willoughby knew they were sinking but the props were still moving, screaming in an agony of bent steel but moving. "Starboard twenty . . . starboard thirty, midships . . ."

The *Sho-sa* had ordered "Abandon ship," but there was no point. No one heard him—all communications were dead. Acid pouring out of the shattered batteries in the engine room mixed quickly with the seawater, forming dense clouds of chlorine gas that killed half of the remaining crewmen, the rest dying by drowning, concussion and in a hail of shrapnel. The deck gun fired one more round.

There was another tremendous explosion, and the Australian destroyer suddenly bucked and dropped, leaning precariously to port, another gaping ten-foot hole at her waterline, reducing her thirty-five knots to ten, her forward boiler room flooding with foaming torrents as if monstrous fire hoses had been thrust deep into her wounded side, her crew wading desperately for the ladders as damage control tried vainly to counter the destroyer's list. The second torpedo had struck her below the forward port storeroom near the forepeak, starting fires raging in the canteen and threatening A turret's magazine. Willoughby ordered the magazine flooded and listened as the damage reports came in, even as he continued the ramming run, reduced now to ten knots. Ahead he could see the *Sho-sa,* the twisted conning tower looming up. "Port twenty, midships . . . Stand by!"

She hit I-43's forward casing with the sound of a steamroller on gravel.

"Full astern!" Willoughby ordered, buying time, protecting his props even as H.M.A.S. *Bendigo*'s mangled bow rose high, crushing I-43's spine, the destroyer's Oerlikons, machine guns and Pom-Poms continuing the assault while the 4.7s, unable to engage at this close angle, became silent.

Remarkably the machine gunner on the sub's bridge—it was Matsu who had taken it over—kept raking *Bendigo,* knocking out the Oerlikon crew, then trying for the bridge but failing as the bursts were absorbed by the shrapnel pads skirting the superstructure.

As *Bendigo* withdrew from the agony of twisted steel her shafts and props, thrown out of kilter by the sub's attack, jerked the destroyer astern in gut-wrenching spasms. Willoughby heard the Pom-Poms still at it in an obsessive duel with the sub's lone machine gun. It was only seconds before I-43 finally rolled over, her back broken, that Willoughby spotted the trolley tracks. "Make a note," he said matter-of-factly. "B–1 class with hangar . . ."

Finally the Japanese machine gunner fell silent and with no more danger to his men, Willoughby gave the "Cease fire." Then with the same calm as he had begun the battle he turned to the first officer. "Stand by for possible survivors."

"Aye, aye, sir."

There were none. Willoughby was unmoved—he had seen the Japanese use heavy guns on Allied seamen floundering for life in the oil slicks off Guadalcanal. Within five minutes it was totally clear from the damage reports that *Bendigo* too was finished. Willoughby ordered, "Abandon ship," and had the radio room send out the last two messages of *Bendigo*'s life. One was a Mayday giving her position off Cape Byron, and the second signal, after conferring with Leading Seaman Mulvane, was a message to CINSWPA, Brisbane, that a Japanese plane had taken off from I-43 and was moving inland on a southerly vector in the general direction of Sydney. Willoughby knew that the southern heading was far from conclusive; as the wind had been coming from the south, the southern heading was probably only the direction of takeoff. It was impossible to determine anything further since the plane was flying so low that its blip was soon lost amid sea-wave scatter. For a moment he'd thought it might even be the fish boat that had started the engagement, but the blip was moving too fast to be any kind of boat. And there were those trolley tracks for a launch . . .

As Somura switched off the supercharger and looked back into the void from which he had come he saw the light from Cape Byron sweeping hypnotically round and round as if nothing had happened, and he spotted the boiling white blanket where I-43, his only means of escape from Australia, was dying. He was alone, except for the *kami*. He would need their help . . . for his mission, to avenge his comrades lost in I-43 . . .

Now, turning north in the darkness above the southwest Pacific where the Coral Sea meets the Tasman, Somura made his first crucial decision of that early morning. He had come too far, over 2,000 miles south from New Britain, to be foolhardy. He knew that Heiji's planned northward course to effect a westerly attack on Brisbane would be the shortest route, ninety miles in all, flying northwest with the coast, then nor'nor'west over thirty-five miles of flatland from the southern tip of South Stradbroke Island into Brisbane a few miles from the coast.

The planning of this route, however, had assumed coastal batteries that wouldn't have been put on red alert by the din of a naval battle between I-43 and the enemy destroyer. Now the equation of risk had been radically changed; the coastal batteries, whereas they would not have been unduly concerned earlier by a lone plane flying overhead from the south, from the opposite direction of any anticipated northern Japanese attack, would now be roused by the furious fight off the cape and would be suspicious of anything, everything. Besides, a modern samurai who was afraid of changing his superior's plan, who did not use his initiative to adapt to changing circumstances, was no more than a Chinaman, a stupid coolie.

No, he told himself, he would keep low and well clear of the coast. This way if the Australian ship's radar *had* seen him launch—they couldn't have heard him over the noise of the fighting—he should still surprise Brisbane, since he had launched on a southerly vector. They didn't, after all, know about his mission; all they *knew* was that a Japanese sub had been sunk off Cape Byron. If anything, they would think the sub was intercepted on the way to Sydney and that its plane, its shape indiscernible, had been forced to take off rather than be sunk. In any event he would fly as low as possible, as planned, to avoid the coastal radar.

He swung away from the originally planned northwest heading of 285 degrees, out further from the coast on a bearing of 360 due north. As he altered course he could see the long white fingers of searchlights far to the north of the cape probing the predawn sea for any other Japanese ships. Possibly, recalling how I-boats had been used elsewhere, the Australians might well think the I-43 was the spearhead of the long-feared invasion.

Somura felt better, breathing in deeply, flexing and unflexing his muscles in a rigidly predetermined pattern. If he headed due north on 360 degrees he could maintain a safety moat of thirty to forty miles from the coast until the moment when he would bank hard left and head in, running at Brisbane from the east through the gap between Moreton Island to the north and Stradbroke Island to the south, using the wide mouth of the Brisbane River as his initial aiming point. By flying this L-shaped course, due north then west, he would add another fifty miles, another ten minutes, to the original diagonal nor'nor'west flight, but the change should preserve the element of surprise.

He banked the Wildcat hard right, its tail in line with the dark hump that was Mount Warning, keeping well below the heights of the coastal mountain range to better avoid radar detection as he continued on his northern course from Cape Byron to Brisbane, the faintly visible curve of beaches to his left forming his western horizon in the predawn gray. Even with a full bomb load reducing his speed to 250 miles per hour he estimated he should reach the mouth of the Brisbane River in twenty-four minutes, at 0619, then swinging hard left he would make his run in from the mouth of the river just as the sun was rising.

CHAPTER TWENTY-SEVEN

It was almost 5:30 A.M. Elizabeth was running to her mother's room, where Sarah Lawson was screaming for Bluey, dreaming again of the Japanese invasion, complete with yellow hordes rushing for the white lonely beaches, overwhelming Bluey, and then one of *them*, bucktoothed and grinning, wearing one of the bowl-shaped camouflaged helmets, materialized right out of one of the posters that were all over showing the "Yellow Peril," sword drawn high above the khaki uniform, wearing long wrapped puttees, striding southward on the island chain through a sea of blood . . . Just the day before she'd overheard the latest reports of the Japanese cruelty to allied POWs. By now it was known that the Japs had publicly beheaded U.S. airmen who, under General Doolittle, had flown on the militarily ineffectual but, for the Japanese, infuriating raid over Tokyo.

Elizabeth tried to comfort her mother but she could not tell her it wasn't true, only that not all Japanese were like that and that her father was strong, fit as a lion from cutting the cane, and if anyone would outlast the war he surely would. Sarah didn't hear and began crying again as she had every morning since the telegram about Frank had arrived from the post office. Again she asked Elizabeth to "fetch Frank," to "find out when Frank will be coming home." The ID tags, Sarah said, were not his. "They must be someone else's."

"Mum, they're his, they're Frank's . . ."

"*No*, there's been some mistake. I know there has. It's been a mixup. I *know*. I prayed last night and I know . . ."

Elizabeth walked slowly through the cold darkness of the hallway to the kitchen and put on the tea kettle. For company she switched on the radio to 4GR and stood there watching the steam rising in the early morning chill. Everybody hated the Japs. Some people still wouldn't talk to her. But she knew they weren't all the same. She knew . . .

There were cruel Australians too, and Americans. She'd heard stories about them taking gold rings from the Italian POWs in the Middle East by chopping off their fingers. War did awful things to people.

The kettle began to whistle. In the background she could still hear her mother talking to herself and the announcer giving a prenews weather forecast of cloudy with showers, "a good thing for the downs. Much more of this drought and the farmers . . ."

She reached up over the stove's alcove to the tin of Bushell's Tea and carefully measured two teaspoons into the teapot. While it was brewing she went to the front-door steps, brushed off a mass of tiny brown sugar ants that were smothering the cardboard tops of the milk bottles, and picked up the Toowoomba *Chronicle,* quickly scanning it for any bad news from New Guinea or the islands. Whenever there was such news Elizabeth pretended that the paperboy had missed the house again. Her mother never pressed the matter, the only conscious chink in her self-deception.

In a little while the morning's six o'clock news would start and Elizabeth knew that the announcer would lead off with the war bulletins. She turned it off. The *Chronicle* this morning was mainly concerned with the preparations for April 25, Anzac Day, when Australians from Melbourne to Sydney, from Alice Springs to the back of beyond, would quietly gather in the dawn by the broken column memorials in the main streets, and in the most unceremonial of all countries the most serious ceremony of all would begin with the "Last Post" sounding as the sun rose and the eulogy "Lest We Forget," as old "diggers" marched to the sounds of bagpipes, brass and drum, the Gallipoli medals chinking in solemn memory of

fallen comrades in the wars of empire and in the present battle to save Australia itself.

Elizabeth folded the paper and put it on the mantelpiece,
next to the old sepia photograph of her grandfather in the
dashing ostrich-plumed hat of the Light Horse. She noticed
that the photograph had been shifted from the edge of the
mantelpiece to the middle on an alabaster square; it had become a shrine. Elizabeth looked with affection at her granddad and told herself she too had to be brave, or try to. What
was it her father had told her before he'd known about Tom?
Not to run with the crowd; "Make up your own mind, Liz,"
he'd said. "And stand your ground."

Now her mother was walking somnolently past her to
Frank's room. She would look in and then turn toward the
kitchen and stand there nursing her tea in silence. It was the
same ritual every morning of every day of every week. Even as
the sun rose higher, its warmth dispelling the morning cold,
Sarah Lawson's pallor remained, as gray and lifeless as
crushed stone. If *they* came, she warned Elizabeth, she must be
sure to hide.

In the darkness, with the margin between himself and the
coast varying from thirty to fifty miles, Somura passed the two
big crescents of beach, the first having curved the twenty-five
miles from Cape Byron to the rocky, surf-pounded snout of
Cudgen Headland off Kingscliff, its phosphorescence dimly
visible in the dark, then the next great curve twenty-five miles
into Kingscliff and Point Fingal, past the jagged blackness of
Point Danger on the Queensland side of the Queensland–
New South Wales border, past the sprinkling of lights violat-
ing the blackout at Miami and Surfer's Paradise, flying parallel now to the choppy shoals off Nerang Head, thirty-three
miles due west.

As the early blossom of sunlight turned the blackness into a battleship gray eighty-five miles due north of the sub's launch point, Somura swung the plane westward toward the gap between Stradbroke and Moreton islands thirty miles dead ahead. Beyond the gap there was another stretch of eighteen miles to the wide mouth of the Brisbane River and then . . . he would make a final twelve-mile run over the winding river right into Brisbane's heart.

CHAPTER TWENTY-EIGHT
MacArthur's Headquarters

Stretching eight miles back from the sea, the cold morning mist hung like gray cotton wool over the wide, meandering course of the river. High in the city's center on the U-shaped river peninsula bordered by Town Reach on the seaward side and South Brisbane Reach on the other, CINSWPA duty officer Melvin Pelowski plugged in an extra heater. One of the things Pelowski missed most about the States was the lack of internal heating in most Australian buildings, especially here in the ten-story AMP Insurance Building, the city's tallest, where, in the lonely hours of the dogwatch, he paced the top floor, trying his best to keep warm. The Aussies, many of whose houses were on stilts in Brisbane, argued, with some justification, that it was never cold enough for long enough in the vast, sprawling subtropical city to warrant furnaces, but now and then, before the sun came up, April's fall weather drove a chilly damp up from the river like an unwanted ghost that seeped into the very marrow of your bones.

Looking below, north to south, up and down Queen Street, Brisbane's main thoroughfare, Pelowski could see tram conductors in their white Foreign Legionnaire–shaped kepis leaning out from the long, open-sided silver tram cars, as well as a horse and cart clomping along, the jingle of its wire milk crates only faintly audible on the AMP's tenth story. He watched the mist starting to rise and the olive-colored river growing lighter, more friendly, then suddenly its surface was dappled by moving cloud and it quivered in response to phantom sea breezes. He heard the faint sound of a car honking, then another. Soon the rush hour would start and the sound of traffic would become a steady roar.

He heard the bell, and holding one hand over the glowing bar of the heater, he used the other to tear off the incoming message. It was in "plain" language, as the *Bendigo* had had no time to code it. It said that a Jap sub-launched plane was heading south, possibly toward Sydney. Personally Pelowski believed the Australian destroyer had been mistaken and had probably spotted one of the Allied coastal air patrols, but as a matter of course he sent copies on to Sydney and Melbourne stations.

As he plugged in the kettle for coffee, he wondered whether he should bother the duty officer at Archerfield Air Base seven miles away on Brisbane's southern outskirts. It certainly wasn't a thing worth bothering General Sutherland about. As chief aide to MacArthur, Sutherland had enough to worry about, helping solve the massive logistical problems necessary for the supreme commander's northward thrust. If MacArthur's island-hopping strategy kept working he'd soon have air bases that would be within striking distance of the Japanese home islands. Pelowski was sure that it was no longer a matter of whether or not the legendary commander could do it, only a question of when. Everybody said all MacArthur needed was time . . .

But as Pelowski looked out from the AMP Building over the white sprawl of the still sleeping city, slits of lights winking here and there behind the blackout curtains as men and women readied for early shifts, he thought of the attack on Pearl Harbor and the three attacks by the same carrier force on Darwin. What if there *was* a Jap seaplane on a southward-bound reconnaissance for a massive aerial assault on, say, Sydney Harbor? They had all heard about the luckless officer on Oahu in Hawaii who'd been given the report from Kahuku Point that a formation of planes was approaching from the northwest, but having mistaken it for the imminent arrival of B–17s from the States, had told the radar operator to forget it. Pelowski stirred his coffee slowly. And what if . . .

He looked again at the message. What if the plane wasn't heading south but north, what if it was a Jap and he *was* the reconnaissance point for a massive attack on the Brisbane docks to be launched from a carrier force that had somehow slipped through the Coral Sea to destroy Brisbane's vital naval installations *and* air bases so as to cripple MacArthur's advance? Jesus—that was precisely why the Japanese had attacked Darwin, to eliminate it as a supply base for New Guinea. Why else would a submarine launch a reconnaissance patrol this far south of the Coral Sea? Damn it—that was just what the Japs had done at Pearl, sent in advance I-boats with their small reconnaissance planes to scout around, and some with midget submarines to penetrate the harbor defenses as in Sydney.

Still, it was only one plane reported. Well, hell, he wasn't going to do a Kahuku Point. He wasn't in the army for the duration but for a career, and he badly wanted to stay on MacArthur's staff. The leaden sky over Brisbane was now becoming a lighter gray as the sun started to rise and Pelowski lifted the phone and got through to the Aussie duty officer at Archerfield.

"Hi, Chuck. Have a possible Bandit approaching Brisbane area. Destroyer picked him up off Cape Byron. Think we'd better send some of your 'cats up to have a look-see."

The reply was a sleepy, "Got a bearing?"

"No. Report was pretty vague. Could be on a southern or northern vector."

"Bit of a needle in a haystack, mate."

"Yeah, well, he could be on photo reconnaissance. All I know is if one turns up over Brisbane and the general sees I got a notification and did nothing it's my ass in a sling."

"Righto, mate. No sweat. I'll send four 'cats up. We'll do a sweep down the coast if you like. If it is a bloody Nip he should be hugging the coast trying to beat the radar. That's what I'd do. Anyway, that'll put you in the clear. All right?"

"Thanks, Chuck. I owe you a beer."

"Bloody right. What we looking for—Zero or Nakajima?"

"They didn't say. Only saw it on the radar, apparently."

"Sure they weren't pissed?"

Pelowski could hear a background guffaw on the other end.

"No. They were guys from the *Bendigo*. No one's had time to debrief them yet—far as I know, they've still got the fishing fleet at Byron Bay picking them up."

"Okay. Hey, the missus is dying for a pair of stockings. Any chance?"

"I'll see what I can do."

"Thanks, sport. Ta ta! See you at the rubbity."

Pelowski replaced the phone. He'd been in Australia damn near three years and understood about half of what they said.

At 0605 four Grumman F4F Wildcats, piloted by two Australians and two Americans, took off from Archerfield, their white U.S. Navy stars catching the sun as they climbed in diamond formation above the thinning fog into the cloud-bossed sky over southeastern Queensland. The flight plan was to cover a rectangle straight out to Stradbroke Island off the mouth of the river, a ninety-degree turn south down the coast to Cape Byron, then sharp right, inland over the Northern Rivers to Lismore, another right turn and back up north again to Brisbane. It *was* a needle-in-a-haystack job but if it was a Jap and he'd gone low to escape the radar, Pilot Officer Oakes thought they might pick him up. Two minutes later Oakes thought they had him, but it was a Beaufighter that had taken off from Amberley Field, its red, white and blue rondel only dimly visible in the gray dawn.

Pelowski, taking no chances that the report was correct and there was a Jap plane on a reconnaissance flight for some carrier force, now alerted the Brisbane AA battalions and the Seventh Fleet's duty officer, who as a matter of course notified all ships in harbor to keep a sharp lookout. In a way Pelowski began to hope that the dot on *Bendigo*'s radar screen was heading his way. Things were pretty dull in Brisbane. Sure, his was important work in MacArthur's headquarters, but here there were no actual hostilities and he hadn't yet been given the opportunity to go along with MacArthur on one of the general's on-the-spot battle observations. He craved some action.

Just over a quarter mile to the southwest in the penthouse of Lennon's four-storied red brick hotel near the corner of George and Queen Streets, in suites 41 to 44, the MacArthur household was stirring. It was 6:07. The general, half-awake, could hear his son Arthur talking to Ah Cheu, telling her that he and Mr. Watt's son, the hotel manager's boy, were planning to go over later and play in the Supreme Court gardens across from the hotel.

The general wasn't sure—it was difficult to tell in the darkness—but from his bedroom he thought he could see a scud of menacing clouds, black on black, sliding in over the northern part of the city. By way of compensating his son for the possible disappointment, he decided that today his gift for Arthur, a daily ritual with them, would be a 1901 Australian penny—the year of Federation. Ah Cheu would give Arthur some fruit juice, tuck him back in, and after he'd slept another hour he would come in and they would march about the top floor to the impromptu bellowing of military music. Then breakfast at 7:30. And afterward, until 10:00 A.M., MacArthur would study maps and read the most urgent battle reports. His study desk was already piled high with intelligence reports, and he had developed a new idea for the forthcoming CARTWHEEL operation—an amphibious left hook bypassing a ten-thousand-man Japanese garrison in the Solomons. It would save the Allies thousands of lives, isolate the enemy garrison and hasten the capture of Imamura's troops at Rabaul in New Britain, a major Japanese roadblock standing

in the way of the recapture of the Philippines and the capture
of air bases from which he planned to pulverize Japan.

Jean was still asleep, and so the general, always careful not
to wake her, moved silently toward the bathroom, frowning as
he passed the dresser mirror at a slight paunch that threatened to interfere with his uniform. There and then, as was his
custom, he scribbled a note to Ah Cheu: "No potatoes for a
month." He glanced out again at the weather. He wanted it to
be fine, Arthur needed to get out—any five-year-old boy who
had been through the hell of Bataan and Corregidor needed
all the play and good weather he could get, but you couldn't
control the weather even with four stars on your collar. Like
war itself, there was always the unexpected storm.

Back in bed he shut his eyes and listened to the low whine
of the elevator. Was it ascending or descending? Who would
have thought that the great general would have had such an
idle thought?

Pilot Officer Oakes watched the other three Wildcats, one on
each side of him, tail-end Charlie behind, all banking in unison over the long, timbered spit of Stradbroke Island that
from 4,000 feet resembled nothing more than a green excla-
mation mark sliding downhill on a dark blue sheet of sea.

Oakes admitted he might be prejudiced, but for him the
Wildcat was simply the best aircraft ever. So it wasn't as sleek
as the British Spitfire Supermarine and it wasn't as fast as
some claimed the Curtiss P–40 was, but it looked and was
every inch a fighter. The line from the cockpit to tail was a
continuous graceful slope, a natural extension of the cockpit's
contour, curving up slightly into the tail at precisely the right
point aerodynamically and aesthetically, the pilot sitting in the
cockpit looking as if he had come with the plane, so balanced
was the symmetry between man and machine. Even the Spitfire, its carburetor intake bump like a fish mouth gaping out

beneath the engine, didn't look as good as the Wildcat in a dive. Well, yes, he'd have to admit you could wish for better in some turns but it had killed more Japs than any other in the early days and had held the line for the navy when other faster fighters existed only in blueprints.

Oakes in his Wildcat looked down now and saw that the northeastern tip of Stradbroke was already touched by the sun's early rays but the southern part of the island was still in deep shadow because of the battalions of big cumulus moving in from the Pacific, piling up by the minute, stretching all the way from the coast westward over the Lockyer Valley and beyond to the Darling Downs.

A voice came over the radio on the combat channel: "Archerfield to cat leader. Aircraft bearing zero four two."

Oakes flipped the mike button and acknowledged. "Aircraft bearing zero four two. Understood." Oakes saw it immediately, a dot on the seaward horizon, so low it looked like a fast-moving bug on the flat surface of the ocean. "Let's have a look, wing."

The Wildcats again moved in concert, increasing speed, streaking eastward toward the dot.

Somura saw them as soon as they turned toward him, one of their wings catching a glint of morning sun. Unless he used the supercharger again, which he didn't want to do until absolutely necessary, he estimated that at 250 miles per hour he was about sixty miles slower than the approaching aircraft. But if the sight of an American plane could hold them for six minutes, no more, that would be enough. At 250 miles an hour and thirty miles from Stradbroke to Lennon's Hotel, the supercharger would jolt him to 300 miles per hour and get him there in six minutes. But their confusion about the true identity of the plane must last till then. Would it? Now that they'd seen him, flying low to evade radar would no longer help, so he pulled the joystick back and climbed into the high cumulus.

As he disappeared up into the white monolith he saw the other four dots coming from the west in the opposite direction, also climbing, no doubt convinced that he was trying to gain height for the best possible defense—or the best possible attack. He leaned back, pulling the leather helmet forward and the goggles down. He touched the sword.

Oakes saw a wisp of black smoke, and the dot seemed to hiccup two or three times and the smoke became a thick stream trailing back from the fly-sized aircraft and spreading into a wide, dirty cone. The other three confirmed his sighting. Maybe the pilot had no choice but to go into the cloud, trying to gain altitude to nurse the aircraft down to land. Besides, MacArthur's duty officer had said the destroyer had given a *southern* heading for the plane, directly opposite to this pilot's course. In any case, until he was sure it was a Jap he couldn't alert Brisbane base. You didn't want a reputation in the squadron as a "panic merchant."

CHAPTER TWENTY-NINE

Above Somura, with a base of 3,000 feet, the ten-mile-wide cumulus kept piling its ice cream into the blue to over 10,000 feet and growing by the second. Now in the lower regions of its southern extent, he caught a glimpse of the four dots some seven miles away and still heading toward him, gaining, then disappearing as he entered the misty entrails of the cloud, a last glance at its top summit showing him that it was flattening out from the brilliant white anvil, bruising quickly into a thunderhead. Somura shut off the smoke canister Heiji had had installed beneath the engine's cowling. In its swirling opaqueness the cloud momentarily transported Somura back to the great fir forests of Honshu, lost as a boy in the fog, fearing to move in the zero visibility lest he vanish into the dragon's abyss . . .

On the northern side of the cloud, Pilot Officer Oakes's diamond formation was climbing as a unit. At 2,100 feet per minute they would reach the top of the cloud in 5.6 minutes, providing they could all maintain their respective compass bearings and distance between each other. Not yet close enough to the dot, they wanted to get as much height as possible for a diving attack if this were their man.

On the starboard wing, one of the two American pilots didn't know what to make of the lone plane's maneuver into the cloud. If it was the Jap, the Aussie tail-end Charlie said, it was a bloody cunning move for him to go into the cloud, because while one pilot only had to worry about himself in the domain of zero visibility and sudden dangerous updrafts, the diamond formation of four planes was committed to maintaining a strict course lest even a slight variation by any one of them threaten the whole formation with a collision . . .

After three minutes of rough climbing, the swirling eddies bucking the airframe violently at 5,000 feet, Somura knew that the enemy diamond somewhere in the cloud's northern sector would still be climbing in the ghostly regions to reach maximum height and break into the clear. And so at 5,400 feet he leveled out, swinging three points to port to bring him on a direct westward heading with the river mouth, and began rotating the radio channels. It was unlikely he'd get the broadcasting frequency of the interceptors, which was frequently changed and often one Allied wing never knew another's. It was a lesson learned from the Japanese having confused Allied pilots early in the war by using English messages on a common frequency—exactly the tactic Somura was now trying. But he could find nothing; there were too many possible frequencies. The only thing he was receiving, on 1300 kHz, was broken chatter from a Brisbane radio station, some commercial for a soap opera, "When a Girl Marries—for all those who are in love and can remember."

He flattened himself against the backboard and headrest as he had when catapulted off I-43 and let the supercharger have its head. The plane shot through the blinding gray white haze at 320 miles per hour, streaking for the island gap, the river mouth and the Brisbane target.

He knew his pursuers would not see him until they flattened out at around 15,000, another seven minutes at least. When they did, though, all hell would come down and from that height their dive would give them more speed than his supercharger was giving him now. All he could do was hope that by then he would be over the river mouth, over Lytton Reach, skimming the stubby, hilly suburban sprawl, over the chunky forest of office buildings, then the dive with his cluster of HE bombs that would reduce Lennon's Hotel to dust-shrouded rubble. It would be over in minutes. This time MacArthur would not escape.

*   *   *

Oakes had been chosen as diamond leader because he was able to think ahead, and two possibilities were now playing tug-of-war with him. He couldn't reach the lone plane on their radio frequency and the plane had been trailing smoke. Was it an Allied plane too shot up, its radio out, or could the pilot hear Oakes asking him to identify himself and for some reason wasn't answering? If it wasn't a Jap, the plane would probably have found its way into the cloud because it was so disabled it couldn't do much else, or if it was the Jap, was it a deliberate tactic to keep Oakes's diamond together, to lure it into the cloud—but why, if on emerging, the single plane would be confronted by the four? Unless—

"Cat Leader to wings. Peel off. Repeat, peel off. Get out of the cloud. Possible Bandit may have broken cover. Make sure he *is* a Jap before you fire. Repeat, get a visual ID before you shoot."

"Roger, Cat Leader," came in the starboard, then the port: "Roger. Peeling now."

As Oakes and the tail-end Charlie continued to climb above 10,000, straining for the fibrous light of the cloud's summit, the starboard and port Wildcats banked sharply in a wide Y to avoid collision and dove, their altimeters falling rapidly, engines screaming to 400 miles an hour, the wind tearing at the cockpits as they plummeted, bursting through the cotton-wool margins at 3,000 into the clear opal blue, the starboard fighter now on the port and the port fighter now on the starboard a mile behind. The starboard pilot, an Australian, was the first to see the unidentified plane ahead and below, a mere scratch above the sea, heading fast toward the gap between Moreton and North Stradbroke Islands and the glinting bar of the river's mouth twenty miles farther west.

In the glare that was now flooding the southern tip of Moreton Island with early morning light but obscuring northern Stradbroke, the Australian took a few seconds to realize that the plane was still smoking. "Closing for ID," he reported to the port pilot, and cocked the six .5 Brownings. "You stay back. Cover the rear just in case."

"Roger."

As he dropped at 400 miles an hour, the smoking plane previously just a dot and now the size of a dragonfly was taking on a discernible shape, the wings rocking amid the increasing black smoke, with only one landing wheel down.

Seeing the Australian closing, Somura jettisoned the 500-pound bomb cradled beneath the cockpit. He was still left with 1,500 pounds of high explosive, more than enough to do the job, and the lighter load immediately increased his speed by another twenty miles per hour, bringing him to 340 miles per hour without the supercharger. It also allowed him to rock the wings more freely in the universal pilot's signal for "radio out—unable to receive or transmit." Five miles to his starboard Somura saw the Australian was still gaining but Somura figured that by the time the Australian reached him, he would be over the target area.

When the Australian saw the bomb drop and the wings rolling he decided the pilot of the plane was in trouble, dropping bomb weight to gain altitude and speed to reach land. And when he saw the bomb hit the metal glint of sea followed by the small white spume, brilliant in the sunlight, he was barely two miles from the unidentified aircraft. Now for the first time he could see its shape and markings clearly. It was as if he was looking in a mirror: nonspecular blue gray upper surface, pale gray undersurface, the thirteen red-and-white horizontal stripes on the rudder, the "F" fighter marking and a number; and the star on the port wing's upper side and the starboard's underside. The white U.S. Navy star.

The Australian flicked his R/T switch on the mouth mike. "Not to worry, it's one of our mob."

"Cat Leader to starboard. Repeat?"

"Starboard to Cat Leader. He's one of us. It's a Wildcat. F4F—folding wing. We've been up shit creek. It's a flamin' Wildcat. Must be off a Yank carrier. He's in real trouble—only got one wheel and smoking. Looks like he was shot up. Probably ran head-on into that bloody Jap."

Oakes's voice came in on a rush of static. "Okay, starboard. Close and escort. You too, port. Repeat—close and escort."

"Archerfield or Amberley?"

"Wherever he can make it. Poor bastard's on fire and one-legged. He hasn't much choice."

"Keep your shirt on, Cat Leader."

The American on the port a mile back shook his head at the banter. The Aussies were like Americans. No matter what you did you couldn't get them to stick to the book on radio procedure. They said what they felt, which could get a fella in trouble.

The Australian was now off Somura's starboard wing. He could not miss seeing Heiji's carefully spaced bullet holes in Somura's side. He was waving.

Somura, in his U.S. flyer's uniform, complete with the orange Mae West, his face still well back in his helmet, goggles down and sheepskin collar up, waved back. He had to be thankful to Nippon's army that had captured intact so much American equipment, including his Wildcat.

The river mouth was rushing up at him. Could the deception last? He knew the other two from the diamond would now be joining the Wildcat off his starboard wing and the port Wildcat a mile behind. He didn't know if the approaching pilot on the port would be smarter and ask himself why hadn't the Wildcat jettisoned its 500-pound bomb earlier if it was in trouble? Why hadn't it jettisoned all five bombs? The other four, two 375-pound bombs under each wing, were plainly visible. Of course it was possible, he hoped, that after a bad strafing, the results of which he was imitating so well, not only would a plane's radio be out and one wheel jammed but the bomb release mechanism would be damaged, too.

But if his deception had worked so far, he knew that it would be over the moment he began his bomb run. And one burst from the Wildcat on his starboard wing would finish him. No more time to think . . . He reduced speed, letting the Australian Wildcat overtake him, then kicking the rudder into a starboard slip he swept across the Australian's rear, the enemy's tail a blur through his props. He squeezed the scarlet button and his Wildcat shook violently with the Browning's hammering recoil.

The Australian's plane shuddered, the cockpit was a red balloon streaked with gray—the pilot's brain—then it disintegrated, a hard confetti of bloodied Perspex whipping back in the slipstream and splattering Somura's Wildcat like hail. Knowing the remaining pilot would be after him, he banked sharply and using Amity Point, the northern tip of Stradbroke Island, on his left and the southern tip of Moreton Island on his right as markers, he pointed his Wildcat's nose toward the island gap, with the supercharger, despite the bomb load, thrusting the Pratt and Whitney 1,200 horsepower into a howling 344 miles per hour down toward the river mouth. He glimpsed the starboard pilot streaking after him and then, below and behind, the prop and engine of the downed Wildcat hitting the sea, bouncing high, then shattering in a shower of sparkling debris, the three-bladed prop cartwheeling across the swells, finally and slowly disappearing, two of the three props intact, sticking up like outstretched arms.

From high above, Somura saw the other two Wildcats that had burst out of the cloud to join the pursuit. With the airspeed needle quivering around 344 miles per hour he was now twenty miles, barely four minutes, from the river mouth, another twelve miles to target, six minutes if his luck held. Racing across Moreton Bay, then over the mangroves, over

the spiky yellow pandanus trees toward the silver stretch of
Lytton Reach, toward the glaring white- and red-bricked city
of bungalows, toward the high tarred stilts of the wooden
houses, toward the tin roofs reflecting the sun, along the
broad snaking river, his eye caught a glint from the south,
and three minutes from target he saw the swarms rising from
Archerfield. He glimpsed a twin-finned tail. They were sending up Lightnings, grounding all Wildcats except the three
already in action to avoid further confusion among the pilots.

"The Jap's got this far pretending to be one of us," said
Oakes, trying to control his anger over his downed buddy.
"But no further. He's *not* to get near any of our ships—or the
big dry dock at Kangaroo Point."

"I'll get the bastard," the tail-end Charlie was saying.

"Not before I do," added the other American from the port
side. "I'm the nearest to the son of a bitch."

At 6:15 the duty officer at Archerfield had informed MacArthur's headquarters at the AMP that apparently some kind
of Japanese bombing-reconnaissance raid was in progress
against the Seventh Fleet elements in Brisbane's naval docks.
Lightnings and Thunderbolts were being scrambled to intercept.

Pelowski thanked his Australian counterpart at Archerfield
and hung up. There was no need to ring Lennon's Hotel and
wake the general—it was the air force's problem now. He
went over by the window and looked a half mile eastward
toward the battleships moored at the Eagle Street wharves.

The Wildcat was no more than a speck over the beaches
when the air-raid siren began wailing. Pelowski's heart beat
faster—it was the first time an air raid had been made this far

south. The phone rang. It was Collins, one of MacArthur's aides, calling from Lennon's. What the *hell* was going on?

Somura was now down to 1,000 feet, the sea below him a blur, the giant cumulus extending far inland, blocking the sun. He saw the black puffs of smoke coming at him, then felt the jarring as the AA shells began exploding all around him. Suddenly there was a thick field of black smudges against the white of the cloud that was crowding him. He worried it would obscure his bombing run. He was sweating and could feel the prayer belt clammy about his waist. He dropped to 500 feet, the wind screaming through the bomb racks.

Then the AA firing stopped. He must be too low, he guessed, for the antiaircraft guns to deflect any further without endangering the city buildings and their own shore installations.

Now he was two minutes from target; he could see the silver trolley buses, open-sided tram cars in the middle of the streets, the traffic on the left-hand side of the roads, palms swaying by the Roman columns of the city hall . . . all tilting crazily as he banked. Then the target—the four-storied red brick hotel a mile away, skirted with sandbags, guards posted around it looking incredibly, as he abruptly leveled for the final run, like the toy soldiers Heiji had used in the mockup site he'd practiced on so many times in Eta Jima. All moving as it should, speeding, rushing into his bomb site.

It was a sound like rain, a torn sheet flapping. The fuselage on his starboard wing was torn, the two Australians firing, coming in fast, trying to lock him on either side—which was why the antiaircraft guns had stopped firing. The attack planes were too close. He'd have to overshoot and come in again. He lifted the nose and hit the supercharger, rolling to starboard over the Roma Street rail yards, dropping, then suddenly climbing again, leveling out over the sprawl of Bal-

moral and Bulimba Reach, below right, coming about to get
Lennon's back in his sights.

It was only when he saw the Wildcat turning, its American star
visible in the plummeting dive toward him, that MacArthur
realized this was no Pearl Harbor attack on his ships. They
weren't after his navy, they were after him—again. He spoke
quickly, told Ah Cheu, young Arthur and Jean to go to the
bomb shelter immediately. They had been with him all the
way from the attack on Manila, the retreat to Bataan, the escape from Corregidor. They didn't hesitate, and in moments
were out the door, Arthur in Ah Cheu's arms, still clutching
"Old Friend," his favorite toy rabbit.

The general, in his blue and gray West Point robe, stayed
with Collins, handing the aide the secret battle plans from his
desk.

Collins was watching the fighter approaching. The moment
he saw the two black blobs dropping from the Wildcat his
natural impulse was to run, but you didn't run in front of
MacArthur, whom you'd seen continue a briefing in New
Guinea when everyone else had been diving under the table
for cover. It was impressive. It was annoying, at times agoniz-
ing to be with so much courage in the face of death. You tried
to think of reasons to call it inhuman, false bravado, to justify
your own fear. What gave him the right to think the enemy
wouldn't get to him? Everyone had to die. They called him
Supreme Commander, with reason. The four stars had been
earned from Vera Cruz to this moment.

Collins asked the general to move away from the windows.
"Sir, please, if you don't—"

He saw the sparkle, like six white headlights, coming at him
—the Wildcat's cannons firing at Lennon's top floor, the exploding bullets raking the hotel's side, red brick and plaster
filling the air with a dusty fog. Then the bombs exploded—

cutlery dancing off the white tablecloth, windows imploding in showers of glass.

To hell with it. The aide dove to the floor under the mahogany chart table. "General! Sir, please . . ."

The general, still standing by the living room doorway, answered with an order to "bring him down."

Collins shaded his eyes with his left hand, shaking his head. The two craziest men in the South Pacific at that moment, he decided, were Gen. Douglas MacArthur and the Jap flying the Wildcat. Crazy or brave or both.

Then the Wildcat, its guns still roaring, swooped over Lennon's, the wings' black shadow momentarily hiding the general's face. The aide couldn't see or hear the Jap or the other three Wildcats swooping in chase, the rumbling staccato of their machine gun fire—and then, by the door, a heavy thud hitting the floor. It was the writing desk, papers flying everywhere. Despite his head being rammed hard against the floor Collins was still alert enough to notice the time was exactly 6:20. MacArthur, near-incredibly, had struck a match and was sucking on his corncob pipe, its rich-smelling tobacco giving off a pungent odor, its smoke billowing to the roof. At least they still had a roof, thought Collins, still under the chart table and intent on staying there.

Once he'd seen the two bombs fall short, Somura climbed, banked to his right, the Australians still with him. He had used two HE bombs, now had only two left. But just one, square on the top of Lennon's, would do the job. Now that MacArthur would be alerted he *must* finish it quickly. He dropped to evade the other three Wildcats, looked into the mirror. Blue sky behind him. He made a 180-degree turn, coming at Lennon's from the other side. He glanced into the mirror, heard a sound like the patter of hail on his right side —probably back near the stabilizer—and saw that Lennon's had shifted abruptly to his right. Having no time to alter course, he released the left-side bomb and banked hard right, hitting the black smoke button.

The bomb hit the right corner of the hotel on the third floor and blew it away, a bed and other furniture toppling into space, a terrified woman, naked, suddenly sucked away from the door to fall, her mouth agape in a silent scream as she sped to her death on the hard, black bitumen below.

The cone of black smoke blinding the pursuer back on his right, Somura suddenly climbed and cut the smoke trail. Before the Australian pilot could realize what had happened he was passing through a billowing black cloud and Somura was diving, firing. The Australian Wildcat's right wing was chopped to pieces, sending him into a spin and plunging down over Queen Street. Now the Wildcat out to Somura's left was rushing in on a half-thatch weave attack, its guns firing at Somura, the remaining Wildcat 300 yards to his right. But by then Somura, slamming the joystick and rudder pedals hard as he could, was in a tight right turn going back at Lennon's.

The remaining enemy pilots were still hard on his tail. Somura hit the supercharger as one of his pursuers fired. Suddenly his plane felt slack, the joystick jamming, and he knew he couldn't finish the run. He would crash the Wildcat into Lennon's top floor, if he could only control it—but he couldn't. He'd only have time to strafe the top floor and release his remaining bomb . . . His Wildcat's six .50 caliber guns winked in the gray morning light and their fire moved from the third floor to the fourth, trailed by a shower of powdered masonry. The windows shattered right across MacArthur's suite, the bullets thudding into the far wall, two or three exploding in the door of the small elevator used by MacArthur and his staff. MacArthur hadn't flinched in the first attack and he didn't flinch now, but noted with anger that a shard of flying glass from one of the penthouse's French windows had embedded itself in his son Arthur's favorite stuffed koala bear, nearly decapitating it. Fragments of glass had also hit the general, but had done no more than lacerate the right leg of his trousers, drawing almost no blood.

Collins watched as the man some considered a god, above human feeling, picked up his son's koala, muttering in very ungodlike language his anger at the Japanese's attack on his son's toy. The Japanese had pursued him and his family, down through the islands—all the way from Corregidor to Darwin, chasing him by sea and by air. That only bothered him. Attacking his family infuriated him.

With the last bomb gone, Somura's plane immediately gained height as he watched the bomb bursting against the hotel almost at ground level, a tram jumping its tracks, careening wildly into the gutter, passengers spilling from it, its overhead wires sparkling in soft, bluish white flashes. Somura knew his best course was to get to 3,000 and head into the long line of cumulonimbus stretching westward from the city. Now he gave way, fists smacking the side of the cockpit in his frustration. So close to MacArthur . . . why had Yamamoto not been so lucky? Or maybe he, Somura *had* been lucky with his final strafing run and when the dust had cleared . . .

Now the two remaining Wildcats had disappeared in cloud, but he had to forget them for the moment and, as he entered the long scud of cloud extending from the city's west end out beyond Indooroopilly over the Lockyer Valley, concentrate on his own situation. He knew he had used too much fuel in the evasive actions so that even if he headed southwest, before he got anywhere near Byron Bay the American Lightnings would get to him. As for I-43, it must have been sunk. The cloud bank would only delay his end in the sights of the closing Lightnings from Amberley Field. But with his fuel already low he couldn't hide in the graying line of anvils forever. Even if he played fox in the cloud bank and kept circling with them unable to see him and not entering out of fear of collision among so many fighters—he figured there were over thirty in all—all they would have to do was fly outside the cloud bank and pounce when his fuel was exhausted or his failing controls sent him into a spin. It's what he would do if he were in their place. Besides, he had no idea how *wide* the cumulus bank was. In a few minutes he could be through to the other side, and an easy target . . .

He slid the cockpit back, the cold slipstream whipping his breath away, forcing him to gasp for oxygen like a drowning man as he unclipped the harness. His left shoulder beneath the strap felt wet. It was blood that he hadn't noticed in the heat of the action, and only now was he conscious that he had no feeling in his left arm. He could see the altimeter dropping dangerously to 2,000, hear the engine coughing, then spluttering to little more than 200 miles an hour. Like most of his instrument panel, his compass was out, but so far as he could tell he was heading due west and by now should be halfway over the valley. He couldn't, though, be certain. He had looked over the eighty-mile valley between Brisbane and the edge of the Darling Downs plateau a hundred times not more than two years before, but now, forty miles over it from the Brisbane side, he could have been over another planet, the Great Dividing Range rising in mailed fists on the western rim and beyond it, west of the downs, he could see the mottled brown blue bush of the Condamine Basin, and far to the south the rain-blurred smudge of the McPherson Range marking the Queensland–New South Wales border.

And then he could see nothing. Searing his face, the icy wind stole his breath as he gulped for air, feeling nauseated from swallowing the mixture of engine oil and vaporized gas that was streaming back in a fine aerosol from beneath the cowling flange. He wiped his goggles but it was useless—he was flying blind. Then the engine stalled. He had no choice.

CHAPTER THIRTY

Brisbane

The sirens of fire trucks and ambulances dueled in their rush down Queen Street, past the office of the Queensland and Northern Territory Aerial Service known as Qantas, then right past the opulence of the Odeon and Winter Garden on George Street and right again to the corner of Ann, the lead fire engine hitting a man-sized pothole, jumping, skidding across the center line into the right-hand lane, stopping just short of ploughing into the yellow ambulance now stationary and swallowed together with the hotel in a hundred-foot-high shroud of red brick dust made bloody by the sun.

"They got the general . . . where's the general . . . ?"

The reporters pressed about the hotel entrance, shoving, swearing, straining to peer through the steam of burst water pipes, over the piles of gutted sandbags still spilling their innards onto the sidewalk. The blue white striped awning was in shreds, fluttering exhausted and dirty like the torn pennants of a defeated army. As the dust settled, the hotel rose from the ashes, two of its broken penthouse windows staring eyeless from the debris.

Two stringers for the *Courier-Mail* came to blows with a young amateur photographer, knocking his box Brownie into the air as he tried to capture the chaos for the noon edition of the *Telegraph*. The camera smacked into the crossed rifles of the U.S. guards, whose dirt-powdered faces were streaked with rivulets of sweat. More trams and trolley buses came to a halt, quickly emptying their passengers, swelling the crowd already gathering across the street beneath the purplish blue jacaranda trees in the Supreme Court gardens. The crowd, in

contrast to the reporters, stood staring silently across at the
hotel. MacArthur, after all, had been their big hope . . .

An Australian infantry officer, the rising sun badge on the
upturned side of his slouch hat shining brightly, bent down
and picked up the Brownie. The boy took it, scrambling to his
feet, blowing the grit off the lens, "Thanks, mate."

And then he saw the general—or rather he saw the cap, the
worn gold braid on the peak holding the early daylight cap-
tive, and below the gold, the startlingly calm eyes of his Ro-
manesque face, corncob pipe in the right hand, and on the
stiff yet somehow casual collar, the four silver stars. There was
silence—then a relieved cheer erupted from across the street,
and clapping.

The general moved forward out of the dust and waved
briefly at the crowd, now several thousand. The sound of
horns, more cars stopping, cameras clicking. A flash. "Con-
gratulations, general."

"Congratulate the Almighty," MacArthur said.

A reporter from a Sydney paper laughed. The general
stared at him, then turned to the boy. "Get your shot, son?"

"Yes, sir. I think so."

"A close go, general," someone called out.

As the aide saluted and the four guards with the Tommy
guns closed in, MacArthur gave one last wave, turned and
reentered the hotel. There were still the battle reports Collins
had collected that had to be read before his departure for his
headquarters at the AMP, where there was more work to do
in preparation for Operation CARTWHEEL. He had just finished three days of talks with Adm. "Bull" Halsey, who, it was
agreed, would advance on the right flank into the Solomons
while the general would strike on the left against Salamaua on
the way to wiping out the large enemy garrison at Rabaul—a
body blow to the Japs and one more step closer to Japan.
That, at least, was the grand plan.

CHAPTER THIRTY-ONE

In the cave seven miles below the lip of the Toowoomba range, Archie Underbridge heard the crackle of the fire collapsing, the gray ashes now white in the morning light. The weather couldn't make up its mind whether to stay overcast or be fine. The early morning noises were much louder now and Archie looked into the long grass for the snakes.

The next instant he was sitting upright, startled by a tearing sound filling the air, as if some enormous tin roof was being ripped off; then the trees above him were snapping, sending lantana bushes over the front of the cave's mouth in a thick green and brown rain. A giant "whoosh" overhead. He felt a wind. Seconds later he heard a distant bump, followed a while later by a soft "whoof," and he could see a long finger of black smoke rising high above the gum trees. At first he guessed it must be only a few hundred yards away, but in fact it was over a mile from the cave. As he started out toward it, he was diverted by a strange sight, at least for Archie. He had never seen a real parachute before—only the ones in newsreels. And he was dead sober.

For a split second the tail of his Wildcat had rushed at Somura, a black knife in white. He yelled and could not hear himself, falling, tumbling uncontrollably in a vortex of ice-cold mist, updrafts and downdrafts battering him as he tore at his vest for the rip cord, the flying suit flapping crazily. He remembered the line of kites flapping, the multicolored carp-shaped kites, the carp who bravely swam upstream. He must not panic . . .

The wind was screaming through every opening, his eyes

watering profusely despite the goggles. He found the ring
and pulled. Nothing. The sound of kites—the silk—then the
jerk, the reversal, rising not falling in the mist, then falling
again but now more slowly. He regained control, then
speeded up again as he looked below. He could see nothing
except a cauldron of dry ice, its enormously long white
tongues eddying round him as he descended, and he guessed
the truth: the cloud was reaching all the way into the Lockyer
Valley, blanketing it in fog. He would not see the ground coming up to meet him; he would be broken against the hard
volcanic rocks of Tabletop or Razorback, ensnared by the giant pear-tree cacti that crowned the eastern rim; or worst of
all, impaled on drought-dry spears of naked gum trees.

He was wrong on both counts. The cloud was thinning as
he dropped through the mist. About 700 feet below he could
see the green and yellow jumble of lantana bushes standing
out clearly. He had been going in the direction of Tabletop,
sixty-seven miles west of Brisbane, but the southerly wind now
carried him north over the Warrego Highway that wound its
way eastward up to Toowoomba and he was coming down in
the bushy apron of foothills squatting seven miles beneath the
heavily timbered bluffs that formed Toowoomba's rim. Tug-
ging hard on the chute's left toggle to level his descent, he
almost blacked out with pain.

At first he told himself to be thankful, never mind the pain.
He was alive. But then the odds crowded in about him—the
sub was gone and the Allies, now alerted to his presence and
mission, would be after him once they found the crash site
and the empty plane.

He had to survive. He had to try again.

Though he'd lost part of the chute, ripped out by a scraggly
ghost gun, he came down in a relatively clear patch, its rocky
red earth contrasting with the bottle green of the passpalem
grass. Twenty yards away his vision was blocked by a tall stand
of gums. First, attend to his arm, bandage it. Above all, get

some rest, gather his wits and get something to kill the pain. He wished that Heiji had completed the deception by including an American flyer's combat first-aid kit, which was superior to anything that Nippon's pilots had. He must fight the pain, subdue it long enough to get help; it could be as much as twenty miles westward to Toowoomba on the trails that meandered through the foothills.

He reeled in the chute with his right arm, the left hanging uselessly by his side. As he began digging a hole in the dry ocher-colored earth so as to bury the silk, part of him said plainly that it was far too risky going to her, the other half replied, just as plainly, that there was no one else to turn to. He was hurt and he was 5,000 miles from home. Besides, wasn't it the great poet of Hokkaido who had said that

Even in war the love of her for him is an island, unassailable by the angry sea, forever lasting.

And if he told her how much she meant to him, how much . . . But would he be able to get to her?

He had heard the dull thump a few miles to the east as the Wildcat exploded, ending its short journey on Australian soil. He lay back exhausted, dispirited. The plane must have dropped like a stone and was now burning. What better signal to the Allies? They would get to it in a few hours. He cursed the Australian or American pilot who had paralyzed his controls. If only the plane had crashed farther away, he'd have more time for his escape to the purple vastness that was Toowoomba's eastern wall, where the high cliffs lay wrapped in dense bushland that clung as tenaciously as vines to the outer walls of the ancient Bushido castles. Clenching his teeth in his agony he continued digging—

"Hey!"

Somura swung around.

"Hey! Where are you?"

It was Archie coming up from the caves from which he had first seen the parachute descending. Somura swore. Someone had seen his chute coming down, someone who was now approaching through the bush no more than fifty yards away.

CHAPTER THIRTY-TWO

The Wildcat's explosion, a momentary orange glow through the low cloud, wasn't seen by the plane nearest to it, the tail-end Charlie of Oakes's original diamond, but by Oakes himself, who the moment he spotted it radioed the position to Archerfield. He and a squadron leader of the Lightnings considered making a strafing run but decided against it; a descent below 1,000 feet could take them smack into Vinegar Hill or any other in the amphitheater of hills below Toowoomba's range. Besides, if the Jap had stayed with the plane he would almost certainly be dead and if he wasn't he'd bailed out, and then it would be for the army and civil police to organize a search. If the Jap wasn't dead, Oakes, who had just lost two of his squadron, hoped he was crippled enough to be immobilized. Hikers frequently got lost in the wild bushland and trying to find them even when they wanted to be found was a monumental business involving hundreds of volunteers coming down from Toowoomba and the tiny towns sprinkled throughout the wide Lockyer Valley. The vastness of the thick bush could hide a whole division; one man could disappear forever if he didn't know the trails. If the bastard was alive and could walk, they might never get him.

The authorities at Archerfield aerodrome knew this too—if they didn't find him by nightfall, ten hours away, it could take weeks before hunger and thirst would weaken him enough to get careless. They didn't even consider that he might give himself up—that was just something the Japs never did. Besides, it was now April, and this Australian fall might well bring rain, unlike the summer heat that could be depended on to finish him off.

While the two remaining planes of the diamond formation

joined the Lightnings for the seventy-mile flight back to Archerfield, six three-ton trucks were already moving out from Toowoomba loaded with search troops. Moving eastward down the red dirt range highway out of the cool, fragrant breeze of the rim's flower gardens, they descended into the sticky mugginess of the bush valley as another 120-man infantry company heading west sped out of Enoggera Camp in Brisbane, its mud-colored trucks packed with armed recruits. In the lead jeep of the Brisbane contingent Captain Sloan of the Intelligence Corps and a veteran of the Kakoda Trail sat rolling a cigarette with a studied deftness.

"Whadd'ya reckon, captain?" asked the driver. "We'll find him?"

"Well, we've sure got him outnumbered, but we're the ones looking, he's the one hiding. One man dug in in heavy bush'll take ten to root him out. If he's alive he'll try to take a few of us out, you can believe me. Coming in that Yank plane makes him a spy. He knows he's got nothing to lose. He'll fight."

"If he's alive," added the driver.

Captain Sloan, unlike the gung-ho recruits, hoped the man was dead. A Jap on the run wasn't his idea of being sent back from the front for R and R, what the Yanks called rest and recuperation. Besides, Sloan knew that if a Jap *was* loose he wouldn't be able to leave it alone until he'd run him down. Somebody once called him obsessive, some head doctor in Brisbane. Well, about the Japs he guessed he was. Not just because they were the enemy but because, from first-hand knowledge, he knew the individual Japanese soldier when cornered was the most fanatical fighter in the world, bar none. The desk-jockeys who called them yellow-bellies had never met one face-to-face. They'd swallowed a lot of propaganda about *hara-kiri*. Man-to-man, the Jap was shrewd and tough as they came. Face it, he told himself, the idea of the chase and confrontation damn near possessed him. He hated it, he couldn't resist it.

Forty miles on, climbing the 300-foot Minden Range half-way between Brisbane and Toowoomba, Sloan noticed the scarlet bougainvillaea still in flower by the roadside. Beautiful and thick, as thick, he told himself, as some of the under-growth would be near the reported crash site. He'd been or-dered by headquarters to capture the Jap alive, if at all possi-ble, so that headquarters could answer some of the questions that, following the Jap's raid, had Brisbane alive with rumor about impending massive air attacks. Although MacArthur was pushing north, the deep fear of a Japanese invasion had not been put down. Sloan could understand headquarters' position. He also understood the Jap's point of view and moved the canvas holster forward on his side, pressing the heavy cloth until he could feel the hard steel of the Colt .45.

With the convoy moving westward down from the Minden Range and the Toowoomba convoy of a hundred men moving eastward along the Warrego Highway, the two groups would rendezvous in the search area at Helidon.

In two hours the few telephones that serviced the isolated farms that dotted the bushland below Toowoomba's eastern rim were ringing, warning the half-dozen or so farmers to be on guard. If anyone saw any sign of the Jap they should re-port it to the nearest telephone exchange. Actually Brisbane's army headquarters was hoping that the farmers wouldn't see anything. The "cockeys," as the farmers were known, didn't exactly observe military discipline, and after the big at-tempted breakout of Jap POWs in central New South Wales a year before and the invasion scare still fresh in their minds, the farmers, the only civilians allowed to carry firearms, had their own rules for dealing with errant Japanese.

CHAPTER THIRTY-THREE

Archie put his left foot on the top of a fallen iron-bark tree, pushing himself off the trunk rather than simply stepping over it where a sleeping snake could strike at his heel. Past the log through the sepia-colored bush he could see the white bloom of silk draped over a stubby lantana bush. He worked his way around a patch of stinging nettles past a half-dozen man-sized ant nests, his boots finding a worn kangaroo trail marked here and there by the small black pellets of old excrement. There were some cow patties as well, and in parts the grass had been flattened where the cattle had lain. He looked at the silk again—he'd thought there were supposed to be ropes or some such things hanging from a parachute but he couldn't see anything trailing from the silk and realized that the white cloth had torn right out of the parachute, hanging now like a huge handkerchief stretched over lantana branches to dry. Higher up in a gum tree at the edge of the bush clearing he could see another patch of silk.

He picked up a fallen branch, using it to push aside a lantana that was reaching out for his throat. "Hoy?" he called and stood still.

No answer. Only a slither—a blue-tongued lizard scuttling through the dry passpalem grass.

"Hoy?"

He heard a muted groan. He bashed away more nettles, walking quickly through them, raising the stick waist-high to keep them from touching the bare flesh of his hands. Then he saw the body, in a khaki flying suit, blood splattered and face down in the clump of straps that had been gathered about the head like a monstrous growth of green cord.

182

He dropped the stick and moved forward. "You okay, mate?"

He bent down by the body and carefully began removing the chute's cords from around the pilot's head. The body rolled, Archie saw the face, pulled back, but it was too late. Somura's right hand flashed out and across, the Nambu pistol butt knocking Archie off his feet so that he fell back into a sitting position, stunned, like a clown in a circus, shaking his head as if he had water in his ears.

Somura, on his feet now, his left arm bandaged and supported with a makeshift sling from the parachute, motioned to him. "Get up. Up!"

Archie Underbridge staggered, then fell.

"Up!" Somura commanded, waving the gun at his face.

Archie steadied himself against a small wiry pine.

"Bury the parachute," Somura told him.

When Archie, still wobbly on his feet, had finished, Somura ordered him to "walk ahead."

"Ahead where?" Archie's swollen lips made it painful to talk. He leaned against the ghost gum to catch his breath.

Somura motioned northeast toward the high, thin column of black smoke. "That way. Quickly."

Archie saw the Jap's immobilized arm. The Nip looked a bit bloody wonky, he thought, and if he walked fast enough maybe the little bastard would black out and that would be his chance, the Nip'd never hit anything with that revolver once you were a few yards into the bush.

Archie began trudging toward the smoke column. Of course, he told himself, if he walked slowly it would give the old farmer by the caves, or whoever else would be investigating the crash, more time to get to the plane before he and the Jap arrived.

"How come you speak English so good?" Archie asked.

No reply.

When he looked back he saw the Jap was pale, down to a

sort of pasty yellow. He quickened his pace. A tawny goanna, at least four feet long, startled by the footsteps, rushed through the tall brown grass, shot up a coolabah tree in a shower of loose bark, and stopped, invisible.

Archie wished he could join him.

CHAPTER THIRTY-FOUR

Toowoomba

Spreading her fingers out, she ran her hand through the nylons once more. Surely there had to be two without ladders to make a pair. It was eight o'clock and she had to be at the Commonwealth Bank on the corner of Ruthven and Little Russell Streets in half an hour. Finally she found two stockings to make a rough match; the shades were slightly off but nothing anyone should notice at any distance. Drawing them up over her long tan legs beneath the white cotton skirt and attaching the garter clips to them, she let her fingers trail unhurriedly, smoothing the nylons between her thighs, lying back on the bed, closing her eyes, dreaming about—

"Why don't they leave her alone?"

Elizabeth sat up. It was her mother talking to herself in the kitchen, quite different now from earlier that morning; no longer morose, but angry.

Walking into the kitchen for her lunch bag Elizabeth saw it was an old Woman's Day that was the problem—an article reopening the argument about the Toowoomba nurse, Sister Kenny, whose exercise treatment for poliomyelitis continued to raise the wrath of MDs from Melbourne to Alice Springs, doctors who believed that polio victims should be immobilized in iron or plaster casts.

Elizabeth had at first encouraged her mother to follow the controversy as *something* to divert her from her losses and to get her back in reality. But now Sarah was praying "Frank won't get polio in that awful New Guinea. Germs everywhere . . ." Elizabeth was close to the end of her wits. She was tempted to take the car, a '36 Plymouth she'd learned to drive after she and her mother had found themselves alone, but she knew it was a waste of the gas ration and so instead dutifully caught the bus.

Looking out from the window along the Tourist Road by the range's rim, she felt as if she'd already put in a day's work. The bus passed the broken column monument to the town's poet and she glanced through the gap, down the old Toll Bar Road that was now the Warrego Highway, and saw the leaden cumulus dispersing slowly over the valley. It would be a hot day after all, but she could hope thunderclouds would build later on and there'd be a heavy shower or two to cool things down.

Her thoughts began to blur with the view over the Lockyer into the middle distance. Maybe it was selfish at a time like this, but she had to wonder what would become of her. She had gotten to like Bruce more now but doubted she could ever love him. Still, with so many men in the service either fighting or about to be shipped overseas, how choosy could a girl be . . . ? And he *was* kind and wanted children and she'd heard of marriages that had begun without love but had turned out all right. She brought herself up short as she thought of the job she was going to. One thing she *did* know . . . she didn't like working in that bank. If only she could have been a teller, but in Australia that was a man's exclusive preserve. They said it was different in America but that was thousands of miles away. She had to deal with the here and now.

Gradually she became aware of someone watching, or rather staring at, her. It was a boy of about sixteen, trying to act like what he considered a man, his eyes undressing her as the drowsy hum of the bus moved into a steady throb down Margaret Street, past the Grammar School oval on the left, where Tomokazu had held her hand what seemed a century ago when they'd walked home in moonlight. The damn kid was still leering. She wasn't so much offended as overcome by a feeling of deep loneliness. She thought how ironic it was that she and Tomokazu had never been physically intimate though she had been with Bruce. Some needs just overcame any logic. Still not quite nineteen, she felt much older.

Two soldiers about her brother Frank's age, wearing the blue and khaki diamond of the Twenty-fifth Battalion, the Darling Downs Regiment that had been blooded at Milne Bay, hopped onto the bus at the stop by the public baths across from the high-school parade ground where Tomokazu had told her he loved her and where they'd watched the young Australians drill for war. She could remember the cool, sweet smells of that summer night. And, shuddering slightly, she closed her eyes and prayed for him, wherever he might be. She had secretly done it every day. Of course she wanted her own country to win this war. She knew the Japs had started it, but Tomokazu wasn't the *Japs*—he was *Tomokazu,* a man whose skin was different, whose eyes were different and whose embrace was different from any she'd known.

She closed her eyes, and the young boy smiled, mistaking the act as an attempt not to notice him. How could he know it was Elizabeth's only escape?

Chapter Thirty-Five

Below the range the two search companies met at 0811 by Helidon Spa, the huge, dark square of artesian water still and peculiarly lifeless beneath strings of Christmas tree lights that were only used on weekend nights for the bathers from Toowoomba. In one long, snaking column the khaki green trucks, their tires churning the volcanic loam into a fine powder, at times red, then black, threaded their way along the bush track toward Captain Sloan's map reference fifteen miles northeast in the hills below Toowoomba. Augmented by police from the small town of Gatton and an aboriginal tracker, the convoy had now swollen to over 300 armed men.

Sloan realized that if the Jap was alive he'd see the convoy's dust trails for miles, and from the size of the cloud he would know it was a large force. Nevertheless Sloan was confident they'd get him if he was trying to hike out in search of food or water at one of the nearby farms. And if he was hiking anywhere, Billy, the black tracker from Helidon, would run him down. You could say what you liked about the Abos, but they could see a trail when you saw only virgin bush. And it wasn't only the visible signs, a broken twig or a blade of kikuyu, that would alert them; it was the smell, the faint odor of a burst nettle, undetectable to the white man's nose but as pungent to an aboriginal as a bruised passpalem stalk with its trickle of sap or a rasp of gum bark slowly bleeding.

If Archie Underbridge owed some dues for his self-indulgence of the last five years he was paying them now, he thought. They had already traveled two miles without stopping and he couldn't remember when he'd needed a drink so bad. Hell, he'd even swallow water if he had the chance, and his determination to hold on could be measured by the fact that while he knew where the creek lay off to the right of the dry timber, he didn't tell that to the Jap. Maybe thirst would wear out the wounded Nip faster.

Archie stopped abruptly, Somura all but running into him, and Archie saw that the Jap's face was now even more sallow with fatigue and loss of blood from the gashed arm.

"Time for a break," offered Archie, who the moment he'd seen the convoy's dusty wake realized that it was important now to drag things out despite the fact that the Jap looked as if he was about knackered anyway.

"Keep going," said Somura hoarsely, and waved the Nambu. *"Go."*

Somura tried to displace the pain with the image of the carp, the brave carp . . . he'd seen them struggling upstream against all kinds of odds. He jabbed the Australian with his pistol. "Faster." A smudge of red against the opal blue sky was telling him that an enemy convoy was about ten miles to the south. The most they could do, he guessed, was twenty, thirty miles an hour on the rough back tracks.

Nearing the crash site, the black smoke wider now over a clump of scraggy hardwood, Somura couldn't see any road nearby, which he figured meant that the Australians would have to hike in from a back road, and in the time the search party fanned out for the sweep line he would gain maybe half an hour.

Soon he was only 500 yards from the crash site, the glinting, twisted metal in sharp contrast to the pale greenish brown bush. Then he heard a faint droning noise and saw the Australian looking up through the widening gaps in the low cloud, smiling in anticipation.

"Into the trees," Somura gasped.

Underbridge dutifully moved into the nearest stand of iron bark. As the slow spotter plane, sent in now that the low cumulus was clearing, flew over, Archie watched the Jap closely. He was leaning against a tree, his face mottled by the scant shade, his left arm immobile, kept in close to his body as was his short sword in the belt, the free hand that was holding the pistol drooping with fatigue. But then as Archie stepped to his left to rest on a termite-hollowed stump, the Jap's right arm came up.

"Hold on," Archie said, "just taking a breather. Don't panic . . ."

Somura lowered the gun. The Australian was right . . . he must never panic. To do so was not only unworthy, it was dangerous. He must think of more than the moment, plan ahead. He saw the carp in his mind's eye, the cool water, the sparkling sunlight, the clear air—and a calmness came on him and he knew what to do.

Somura was the first Japanese Archie Underbridge had ever seen and he was thinking that what he'd always heard was true. You couldn't tell what they were up to. It wasn't their almond-shaped eyes, the near squint, that gave them an inscrutable look. It was the way they refused to look directly at you, always off to one side as if communing with your shadow. The little bastard had guts, no question, Archie'd give him that. By all accounts he should have been down and out a half-hour ago. "Stubborn bugger, aren't you!" Archie said, growing braver. Clearly the Jap was afraid to fire—to give away his position. Archie saw a stony dip ahead. If the Jap, with one good arm, stumbled, he would have him before he could blink . . .

The spotter plane was gone, but now Somura could hear the distant sound of the army convoy growing louder. He told Archie to continue walking, and as they emerged from the trees at the edge of the dip he noticed, a mile to the right, an emerald green slash in the fawn scrub that marked a creek

that began westward, high on Toowoomba's rim, and wound
eastward down past the caves, which were by now several
miles behind them to the south. With the sun climbing, the
clouds were burning off quickly and it was still over 300 yards
before they'd cross an area of small volcanic boulders to the
downed Wildcat. Somura moved on over the rocks, forcing
the Australian ahead of him. He stopped. He could no longer
hear the trucks. By now the soldiers would be pouring out,
lining up, slamming home the first round into the breech.

The Wildcat was a charred shell, its tail recklessly intact but
the nose shoved up so hard by the impact that the engine's
cowling was practically in the cockpit, the Perspex having
shattered, shining like broken glass on the rocky shale. Here
and there a dozen or so small fires trapped in the rocks were
burning themselves out, their faint smoke trails rising lazily
overhead.

"Stop," ordered Somura as they neared the port wing, its
folding strut sticking out from the gashed fuselage, snapped
and naked as protruding bone.

Archie had to admit it was a good plan for the Jap to hold
him hostage, but what did he want from the plane? Was it
emergency rations he'd forgotten in the rush to bail out? Clas-
sified maps, orders? More ammunition?

Somura told Archie to take off his boots and clothes. Smart
bastard, thought Archie. A man without protection from the
fierce Australian sun and bootless in the unforgiving bush
would make the perfect prisoner, not able to go anywhere.
The perfect hostage. Well, maybe not . . .

He swung about, and the Jap's sword flicked toward him,
just missing his throat. Archie tried to say something, his arms
flailing, but he fell backward, then was back on his feet with
surprising speed for his age and condition. There was nowhere to run, he was surrounded by a U-shaped lantana bush
six or seven feet high and more than ten feet thick. The Jap's
pistol was back in his holster but his sword flashed through

the sun, missing Archie but decapitating the outgrowth of lantana bush he'd ducked behind. Now the sword came back, nicking Archie's right arm, drawing blood and making him back farther into the sharp-barked lantana. "Hey, *hey* . . ." was all Archie could manage in his stumbling shock. The sword came sweeping back again. With nowhere to go, all Archie could do was lift a broken stick of gum tree, which Somura promptly kicked from his grip, then on the back swing sliced into Archie's right arm, cutting to the bone. Archie, like a tormented bull, ran at Somura, crashing into his legs and knocking him down. Archie heard the ridge of the sword strike the naked metal of the Wildcat's wing, and kicked at Somura's head, catching him hard on the left side, but not before Somura had retrieved the samurai blade from the plane's ashes.

Archie, cradling his left arm with his right and realizing that the Jap didn't want to use the pistol and risk alerting the search parties, half-stumbled, half-ran out of the U of the lantana bush and made for a dark green slash that told him where the stream was and where he could escape—Somura, the pain of his own injury in his face, came after Archie. Suddenly a herd of wallabies were bounding heavily through the bush, and as Somura, startled, kept up his chase, other creatures stirred—from magpies diving to peck at the two men to brown snakes slithering through the waist-high passpalem grass. Archie made for the creek, lantana bushes flashing past him, his face now feeling the cool breeze from the shallow artesian stream that only a few feet across meandered underneath a wattle tree, a spill of light green maidenhair fern hanging down from the creek's far bank. Archie felt his left foot slip on one of the rocks, somehow managed to regain his balance and make a big step for the far bank, slipped again, this time in the black mud, his right hand reaching for a fist-sized rock. He turned, threw it at Somura, and in the dappled shade of the bush saw a last glint of sunlight before Somura's

sword sliced his jugular, his life's blood spurting forward into
the creek where he fell.

Somura waited until the bleeding subsided, the blood
quickly carried away by the stream, then proceeded to drag
the Australian back to the crash site, only fifty or sixty yards
away although it had seemed much longer in the chase.

He dragged him over to the burned-out cockpit, put his
near-severed head on the cockpit rim the way his father used
to lay the gills of big fish on the boat's gunwale, then behind
the cover of the surrounding lantana bushes, his left arm in
great pain, changed his clothes for the Australian's, slitting the
left sleeve of the dead man's football sweater to accommodate
his swollen arm. He took off his Imperial Japanese Forces ID
chain, dropped it over the Australian's neck and tried to push
him over into the cockpit, but the body slipped nose first,
falling into the soft ash of the smoldering cockpit fire so that
Somura had to go around to the other side of the plane, lean
over and drag him one-handed back into the cockpit. He noticed that the Australian's face, blackened by the ash, looked
like one of those American vaudeville actors, the whites of the
eyes strangely comical. If there was no gasoline left in the
plane he would have to use the dry lantana, but luck was with
him, the starboard wing, because the motor had died, had not
caught fire like the cockpit. Well aware that the search party
was advancing on him, he quickly stabbed the wing's tank
with his sword and used his leather flying helmet as a bucket
to pour the gasoline over every part of the Australian's body.

Next he strapped the corpse, still warm and now dressed in
the Allied flying suit, into the pilot's harness, careful to clip
the radial buckle before slashing the face with his sword so
that it was unrecognizable. Then he threw some of the blood
on the grass and lantana, as if on impact the cockpit had
smashed the pilot's face beyond recognition. He rammed the
broken control stick into the late Archie Underbridge's stomach, then stood back and threw a lighted match. The match

went out in mid-flight. In the distance he could hear a slight clanking noise, like a cowbell—the sound of battle packs advancing in line? He tossed the second match lower down. The cockpit erupted in an orange flame and soon the Australian, his skin already melting, was being incinerated. A river of flame raced back from the cockpit to the wing. There was a "whoof" as the residual gas caught fire, and Somura, though standing twenty feet away by now, felt the searing heat from the pyre as tongues of flame spread out and about the plane down toward the creek.

Somura regretted that he had to leave his American flying boots on the Australian; whoever saw a pilot without flying boots, even if they would soon be just black blobs with steel heel and toe tips. His thoroughness, however, meant that he had to wear the Australian's ankle-length boots, two sizes too big. Already limping after only thirty yards, he headed for the dark green outline of the creek, which he intended to follow up to Toowoomba's rim.

CHAPTER THIRTY-SIX

The long khaki line of some 300 soldiers, spaced between ten and twenty yards apart, stretched for almost three miles through the rolling bush, parts of the line disappearing now and then as troops vanished into clumps of thick trees and undergrowth before emerging moments later to rejoin the line.

Somura, in the tramp's clothes and grabbing a moment's rest, could see some of them, scarcely dots on the horizon, coming from two miles away, the crash site midway between him and the line. He hid in the bushy lip of a creek where he had splashed his face and drunk, careful not to take too much water. His left arm was numb below the elbow and he was worried that perhaps he'd bandaged it too tightly, doubting that gangrene could have set in so early. Whatever the cause, the numbness at least meant it was no longer painful. The Australian's clothes reeked of stale tobacco smoke, and the baggy pants and jacket were constantly catching on the lantana and wild rose. His disguise was too good, he thought.

Sloan saw the spotter plane returning eastward from its reconnaissance. He waited with his radio operator as the rest of the line moved on, trigger fingers itchy. The spotter plane's pilot told him that apart from what looked like a bush fire starting around the crash area, there had been no sighting. Sloan wasn't surprised. Over this wild foothill country that spilled down from Toowoomba's range into the valley, aerial reconnaissance wasn't likely to be effective. Its purpose was mostly harassment, to excite the quarry, panic him, if he'd somehow survived the crash, into making a "blue," a blunder.

The most important thing that the reconnaissance pilot told Sloan was that another search line from Esk, in position ten miles to the north, was even now moving south to meet Sloan, the two search lines forming a shrinking corridor, closing in like two railway lines from opposite sides of the crash site, the western end of the corridor blocked by the thick, bush-covered bluffs of Toowoomba's rim. Headquarters in Brisbane had decided that if the pilot had bailed out or walked away from the crash he would most likely try to reach the Warrego Highway to his south, which he could then follow east or west, or he might try to go farther into the mountain wilderness of the north, away from the highway. The odds were against his trying the much more difficult route against the Toowoomba rim. Still, "to be on the safe side," as he'd told his sergeant, Sloan requested that another company of militia from Too-woomba man the cliff tops overlooking the valley.

But when he got to the Wildcat he saw it was all for nothing, that the pilot was burned beyond recognition, the heat of the blaze so intense that the black skin, or what was left of it, was stretched tight over the bones, thin and fragile as burnt news-paper, the features impossible to make out because of the multiple injuries that the Jap had obviously suffered on impact, especially in the area of the eyes and nose, which were no more than charred lumps.

"Better him than me," said the lieutenant, trying to sound tougher than he felt and turning quickly away.

Sloan halted the line, the men farthest away on either side of him mere specks that kept moving for several minutes after his order was given, and some only now joining the line after making their way up the uneven depressions and having to use their bayonets to make a firebreak before the flames from the crash site could spread further and become a full-fledged bush fire.

As Billy, the aboriginal tracker, moved about the gutted plane—something he'd never seen before—Sloan used the barrel of his forty-five to ease off the Jap's ID tag, ordered the sergeant to have the corpse buried and told his radio operator to contact the spotter plane. But there was nothing but static, the radio being blocked by the amphitheatre of hills and the Toowoomba range to the west, encasing them now in what was in effect a huge box canyon of wild bushland.

"Unless the spotter plane flies directly over us again we've lost him, captain."

Sloan shrugged. It just meant that the line from Esk would needlessly keep trudging south toward the smoking remnants of the Wildcat, and that the Toowoomba rim would be needlessly patrolled for a few more hours until Sloan could notify the troops that he'd found the Jap dead in the wreckage.

"Do them good," said the sergeant. "Better than sitting on their asses playing poker."

When Sloan saw that the shallow grave was filled in, he waved his arm over his head in the about-turn circle. The line turned back and moved off in the direction of the trucks to the south, the men noisier, less cautious now, the unblooded recruits among them complaining that all they'd been used for was to fight a bloody bush fire.

When Somura saw them move off he headed into a sunlit patch by the creek and lay down, resting for the first time since he'd left the sub at five-thirty that morning, only four hours before. It seemed like four days. Four years.

Sloan was trying to make out the Japanese writing on the ID tag. "Well, no need for track, Billy. He's finished."

"Yeah. But two fellas there, boss."

"What?" Sloan stopped and offered Billy the khaki-covered water bottle.

"No thanks, boss. Yeah," he continued, pointing back at the plane, "two fellas by plane. All way round. Pretty damn soon."

"What the hell you on about?" It was the lieutenant.

"Two fellas by plane."

"Farmers," the lieutenant said disgustedly. "Couldn't bloody wait for us. They were told to stay put if they came across anything. Typical."

Sloan had drunk from the khaki-covered blue enamel tins for six months in New Guinea and he was convinced that no matter what you put in them it would end up tasting of enamel. He corked the bottle. "Well, what about it, Billy?"

"Only one fella, he go away, boss."

"The invisible man," said the lieutenant, winking at the sergeant. The lieutenant didn't think much of Abos. For starters they couldn't handle their booze. Then, of course, they had the wrong skin color.

Sloan ignored the lieutenant. "You *sure*, Billy?"

"Plurry oath, boss. Two come. One go."

Sloan rolled a cigarette. "Well it's got me beat. What do you think, Billy?"

"Don't know, boss. Debil man, maybe."

The lieutenant lifted his eyes heavenward at the sergeant and shook his head. Abo superstition . . . they believed any-thing . . . like pointing the bone at you would kill you.

Sloan halted the line and turned to the tracker. "Maybe two farmers, Billy, or a couple of hikers. One got hurt, busted a leg or something and the other piggybacked him out . . ."

"No, boss." Billy hadn't missed the lieutenant's contempt, and while he spoke to Sloan he was looking at the lieutenant. He knew his only real weapon against the white man's so-called superiority was his knowledge of the bush. "No, boss. No piggyback. Track not so heavy. Not for two fella. Only one fella going."

"Maybe the other joker's up a tree?" said the lieutenant, wittier by the moment.

The search line was broken now by soldiers squatting here and there, others seeking shade, and all waiting for Sloan to give the go-ahead back to the trucks.

For Sloan it was an impossible equation if Billy was right. Two men come to the plane, see the dead pilot, and one walks away.

"You really sure, Billy?"

"I bet baccy allowance, boss."

Sloan knew he couldn't get more serious than that. Squinting into the sun, he said nothing as he drew heavily on the cigarette and squatted, poking idly at a trapdoor spider with a wattle branch. After a minute or two he looked back toward the crash site and went over it in his mind. The plane had been burning, the smoke column visible for miles, then the smoke had died, then sprung to life again, the fire obviously having reached something else that was highly flammable. Unless . . . he recalled the lieutenant's queasiness, the sight of the pilot's mangled face. The welt on Sloan's forearm flared angrily as he scratched it. "Lieutenant!"

"Sir?"

"I want you to go back and dig up the Nip. We'll take him back to HQ."

The lieutenant went pale. "What good'll that do?" Silence. "Sir?" he added.

"I don't know," Sloan replied honestly. "We'll see."

The lieutenant's fingers were doing a nervous dance on his holster. "Ah . . . we've got nothing to carry him in."

"Use your head," Sloan told him. "Got a ground sheet, haven't you? If you haven't, Billy'll lend you his. Right, Billy?"

"Not to worry, boss."

"There you are. Take three men. We'll leave a truck for you. Think you can handle it, *lieutenant*?"

Sloan didn't wait for an answer as he signaled the line to move on to the trucks. "You think he can handle it, Billy?"

Billy smiled, said nothing. Sloan had to consider that Billy

had misread the signs. The Abos were good at bushcraft but
they could make a mistake too. What Billy was probably reading were signs confused by the scattered debris of the crashed
aircraft, something beyond Billy's experience. In any case it
would even things up for the tracker. Pompous lieutenants
could do with the exercise.

The lieutenant watched sourly as the shovel scraped away the
stony red soil. "Be careful," he shouted, "don't go at it bull at
a gate. You'll go right through the—"

"Oh, *hell* . . ." One of the diggers stumbled back from the
grave. Back from the corpse that was copper red, already
seething with thousands of red ants.

Moving cautiously, following the course of the creek, Somura
found it necessary to rest every ten minutes. The pain was
returning in the arm and his thirst was increasing, the creek
having dried up, what water there was being confined to stagnant pools, billabongs, in the gulleys with long stretches of
cracked baked clay in between. He didn't dare drink any of
the evil-smelling billabong water, figuring it could poison him
or at least cause severe stomach cramps. He cursed himself for
not having drunk more of the spring water that had been
running in the lower part of the creek; now, ahead of him, lay
the high, winding climb up the range. He had hoped to be at
the rim by nightfall, coming up by the town's stone quarry, a
massive gray slab amid the green bush. From there it would
be about three miles by road to her place. To keep going, to
take his mind off the exhausting ascent, he thought out loud,
trying to place the house as he'd remembered it, and thinking
how he would approach it; above all, what he would say.
Would she even still be there?

He stopped, listened. Beyond the sound of his own breathing the dense bush surrounding the billabong was silent; the birds, small rednecked finches and wild green and blue budgerigars that had been flitting here and there in the deep shade, had suddenly vanished. At first he thought it was because the creek bed had widened, with less shade over the stagnant pool that was all but overgrown with reeds. He saw a water rat clambering hurriedly up through the scraggy bank and in place of the bird sounds he now heard a shuffling, multiplied many times to his left and right. And then a crash not ten yards away, followed by another, brown leaves falling, a hole in the undergrowth on top of the creek's bed. Another crash and the dull glint of a bayonet.

Somura slid down the moist bank into the green slime of the reeds. The water was only a foot deep but the reeds towered above him. Steadying himself, left arm wrenched out of position, right hand holding the gun, he saw that behind him the muddy creek bank showed the mark of his slide, and behind the slide a bootmark clear as a plaster imprint. Voices. The Nambu had nine shots, no time to reload. Stay calm, as still as the crimson carp asleep in the lily pond.

They passed him—three of them. All he could see was their backs. More were coming from the north, but the sounds were fainter.

A crash. He swung around, a brown blur in front of him: a wallaby escaping the passing soldiers. After he had hauled himself out of the scummy reeds he saw that his left arm was thick and lumpy with leeches, already fat with his blood.

At 4:00 P.M., when their C.O. received the message from Brisbane headquarters that the Japanese pilot had been found dead, the soldiers on the rim were picked up in twos and threes by the army trucks and taken back to the Toowoomba camp. Burned up in his plane, they said. Relieved smiles all around.

CHAPTER THIRTY-SEVEN

The bank manager told Elizabeth that the new tally hadn't balanced and they'd all have to stay late, until seven if necessary.

Too tired to object, she tried to phone Mrs. Murphy, who lived a few houses up from hers on Ipswich Street to take a message but there was no answer. She remembered it was the day for meat-ration cards and everyone was staying out shopping to get the best cuts.

The manager ordered in fish and chips for the staff and during tea break they listened to the radio, Station 4AK in Brisbane, which was full of the news about a naval battle off Cape Byron early that morning and a Jap bombing raid on Brisbane.

"Another Darwin," a junior teller said.

"He crashed," someone else said in the excited din.

"Good bloody riddance."

Elizabeth took her tea and went back to her desk. Cradling the tea close to her, she shut her eyes. In Japan it would be early afternoon on the same day—

"Elizabeth!"

She started, as if from a dream.

"Someone to see you. Side door."

It was Bruce, who said he'd wait and drive her home no matter how late it was.

"No," she said, "I'm tired. Really. But thanks."

"Okay," he muttered, and turned to go.

She touched his arm. "Bruce?"

"Yeah?"

"How about tomorrow night. We could go to the Strand if you like. There's a movie about—"

He didn't care what it was about. "Seven?"

"All right." She shocked herself a little then . . . thinking how she wouldn't let Bruce go all the way, she'd just lie on top of him, her tight panties sliding back and forth while she pretended it was Tomokazu, hard against her the way he'd been on that night before he left . . .

CHAPTER THIRTY-EIGHT

The closer Somura got to the range's rim the more the billa-bongs petered out and the pancake-baked creek bed was marked by the graying skeletons of cattle and the stench of a disemboweled kangaroo caught in a barbed-wire fence trying to reach a now dry water hole. Five miles in front of him, the dusty track made his throat feel rougher with acute thirst. And though the sun was still up, the bluffs facing east were in deep shadow with only their extremities bathed in the golden light, their shade creating the illusion that there must be wa-ter nearby to support such dense growth. There was, but it was artesian water feeding the subtropical forest from far be-neath the earth, the surface streams long gone in the drought. The soil, black and spongy, added to the illusion of surface streams, the fine maidenhair ferns, cool and delicate to the touch, reminding him of the forests of Honshu. Everything else was alien in spite of his Australian experience a couple of years before. The only known was Elizabeth, his vision of her unchanged, unchanging.

The cicadas began their ringing chorus in anticipation of the coming night, and the dark smells of the eucalyptus range filled him not with memories of his Australian time but with a longing for Japan, where a man's soul could be in harmony with the land. Australia was different. Australia was too big; one was swallowed by its vastness. In this single northern state of Queensland, Japan could fit many times, but beyond the sheer size of the country it was the lack of water that had made it always so strange to Somura.

Inland from the sea the first thing you noticed was the ab-sence of water, putting you on the edge of disaster. How many times had he heard the stories while studying at the

Toowoomba Tech of the newcomers from Europe who having
run out of petrol on the outback roads had foolishly wan-
dered from the car for help only to be found dead a few miles
away in the waterless bush . . . It wasn't just the ever-present danger of thirst but the speed of the dehydration in the
Australian bush. You could survive a week or more without
food but not without water. If it weren't for his wounded arm
he figured he could survive a day or so without liquids, but
with the loss of blood and the exertion of the last few hours
and the climb in front of him, his body desperately needed
fluids. He thought of his survival training at Eta Jima. If he
could kill an animal he would gladly drink its blood, but to
fire his pistol was to risk detection and he had no time or
strength left to set a trap.

He looked up at the brooding bluffs; they seemed determined to defeat him, the ear-ringing noise of the cicadas the
first onslaught in the battle to unnerve him. In Honshu the
softer-toned woods had been home to him, their silences com-
forting, his loneliness absorbed by their solitude; but here the
thick, wiry woods of the bluffs were hostile, the wind in the
high white gums malevolent, teasing him with the sound of
rushing water, the dry, crusty bark of the gums harsh and
hard like the faces of angry old men staring at him, and everywhere, under everything, insects that bit and stung and
poisoned.

Finally, his tongue swelling, his vision already blurring, he
took off the left boot and shook it, ridding it of any dirt and
dried leaves that had worked their way down past the socks,
urinated into it and drank. He forced himself to swallow it all,
smacked himself hard with the pistol, telling himself that if he
dared to be sick and vomit he would have to punish himself
like a samurai. He kept it down.

He strapped his boot back on, feeling defiant. His people
were the most urbanized on earth but they had become the
best jungle fighters the world had ever known because they

could adapt. They were natural survivors, and he would survive. He had to, for his still unfinished mission. *"Honto-ni bakarashii,* no nonsense," he clutched his left arm, and set off again. He didn't walk on the cattle trails that twisted up around the cliffs but kept parallel to them, moving through the cover of the bush.

Now and then he stopped to listen, it being several minutes before he could hear anything above the thumping of his own heart and the ringing of cicadas. He thought he heard a rustling—a rat, a possum, some other small animal? He waited, no longer heard it, and moved on.

Ahead he could see a black spider at eye level, its web, suspended from a coolabah branch, invisible in the dusk. He slipped and a rock tumbled noisily behind him. Again he heard an unfamiliar sound. He gripped the Nambu. He didn't want to use it, but if they rushed him he would have no choice.

CHAPTER THIRTY-NINE

By the time they discovered the error at the bank it was almost sunset.

"It was a folded five in a deposit," the manager explained to the accountant. "Elizabeth Lawson spotted it. Some depositor folded it and put it in a pile of fives and the new lad counted the two edges as two fives instead of one."

"Didn't he turn it around, count both ends?"

"No, he was in a hurry. He's not a bad kid. Anyway, I put him right."

The accountant shook his head. There was no way they could prove the depositor had willfully put one over on them. They'd have to carry the loss and it had taken them over an hour to discover it. It was now dusk and from across Little Russell Street he could hear the buzz of peak hour in the pub. He watched Elizabeth, her breasts sharp in the sweater as she pushed her shoulders back to put on her coat. She'd certainly developed in the past year or so. After the long hot day the evening was turning chilly and in the far west the cloudless sky was deep crimson, the sun a red orb through the filter of dust blowing in from the outback.

"Need a lift home, Elizabeth?"

She hesitated a moment, knowing the accountant's reputation for wandering hands. But she was worn out, and the thought of the long bus ride home was depressing. Besides, she was an adult, grown up in a hurry, she thought wryly. She was no little innocent anymore. She was a woman at eighteen, thanks to . . . what? Somura? Bruce? Maybe more than anything else, the war itself. War made the boys into men before their time. Why couldn't it happen to girls too?

She accepted, and on the way it occurred to her that, knowing Bruce, he'd probably gone into the Commercial Hotel across from the bank for a few beers after work, and maybe had seen her . . . Bruce. How did she really feel about him? Well, he was decent and kind even if he was too possessive. And seeing her drive home with another man after she'd refused him . . . It interested her, the way she was thinking about Bruce despite the tiresome chatter of the accountant. At first it had been a physical thing, that moment on Tabletop. Back then she really wouldn't have cared or worried about him seeing her with someone else. But now . . . well, obviously he was more important to her. Maybe it was possible, the way they claimed but she never quite believed, to learn to love somebody. At first there might be mostly pretense, but you could pass beyond that to genuine deep feeling, even love. Maybe.

Anyway, these were her thoughts as the car stopped and she realized they'd arrived at her house. She thanked him for the lift, feeling she really hadn't been very polite to a man who'd driven out of his way to take her home, never mind what his reasons might be. She shook her head and half-smiled as she walked up the stone path to her house.

What you need right now, girl, is a good stiff drink, and stop thinking for a while.

It was a long drive back to Brisbane, and Sloan could taste the beer he would have at the officers' mess. Behind his lead jeep he could hear the green canvas of the trucks flapping and the chorus of raunchy songs from the troops who were all young and full of spit and vinegar, bursting with enthusiasm to close with the Japanese now that MacArthur was readying for the big push up past Rabaul to the Philippines. MacArthur would need them. It was still a long way to Tokyo and still a balancing act as the general prepared the next CARTWHEEL strike, which was to shatter the Jap perimeter.

Captain Sloan didn't much feel like singing this late afternoon. It was Billy's story. It hadn't worried him until they'd
dropped him off at Gatton Police Station along with several of
the police constables and he had casually asked one of them,
"Billy a good tracker?"

"The best, mate."

"Ever made a blue?"

"Yeah." The cop laughed, his beet red face growing redder
in the late sun. "He came to this place. Should've stayed on
the bloody reserve. Too many temptations. Half a bottle of
rough red and they're off."

Sloan looked back to the west along the narrow two-lane
dirt highway. "But how about when he's on the job? He told
us two people were walking around up near the plane but
that only one walked off."

The cop took off his wide-brimmed slouch hat, its white
pleated band stained with sweat and streaked with dirt. "Well,
mate, all I can say is that if Billy says there were two then
that's how many there were. Don't give a fish's tit how many
walked away. He's got an eye like a bloody wedgetail eagle,
has Billy. Course, don't they all? How about a quick ale?"

"No, thanks," Sloan said, and looking beyond the hotel he
saw Billy, unable to drink at the white man's bar, already
walking alone down the dusty street.

CHAPTER FORTY

Strewn grandly like a frost across the cold night sky the Milky Way glistened above the Darling Downs as Somura reached the top of the moon-washed range. He heard a wallaby thumping off to one side, and he felt safer now, once he saw there was no traffic on the road leading back from the stone quarry toward the lone northeasterly side of the town's rim, and he recalled how the few houses, in this one of Toowoomba's most scenic and expensive areas overlooking the valley, were set well back from the road.

Most of the land was still wild and uncleared, and trudging along the side of the road beneath the tall bunya pines he paused between the Fairholm School for Girls and Webb Park. He could see Tabletop rising from the valley floor a few miles away to the southeast, its grassy summit silvery in the moonlight. Once in the small triangular park, its peak a grassy knoll from which the scrub fell off gradually to the valley below, Somura, eyes searching the dark, hunched over a fountain and drank. The wind, a westerly growing stronger by the minute, was piercing but invigorating.

Resting on the bench above the swings and teeter-totters, he looked down at the twinkling points of light that marked the valley farmhouses 2,000 feet below him, the lights growing indistinct around the Marburg Ranges. He relished the night air, fragrant and cool after the muggy heat of the climb, and the fragrance of Toowoomba's mountain air heavy with gum and camphor laurel brought with it a rush of memory. They had never come to Webb Park. It was near the Church of England Boys' School, the Prep, as they called it, and there was always the risk of someone calling him slant eyes, or some other slur, the kind he and Elizabeth had in a way gotten used to but which, however it was handled, ruined the mood between them. At least at Tech, where the students had been older, the racism had been more circumspect. Tojo was right —in the end it was a fight between the yellow man and the white man, who'd had his own way for too long—

Above the sound of wind in a nearby willow there was another sound—voices—directly in front of him. But he could see nothing, only the edge of the grassy knoll, then the slope disappearing into the darkness. There was laughter, a girl's, and somewhere above it another sound, a soft whirring—then suddenly below, a flashlight penetrated the night, its beam coming from the knoll, sweeping left to right, then disappeared.

Frozen in place, Somura gazed intently into the blackness, and then he saw where the noise was coming from—a mushroom-shaped air ventilator sticking out of the ground about a foot above the knoll, purring in the strong westerly. An air-raid shelter! They'd built one into the knoll, probably for the boys' school.

Slowly he got up from the park bench, his body stiff from tension and fatigue. Backing carefully up the park's bank to the circular roundabout of road, he crossed over to the school side and began making his way down Campbell Street, hobbled now by a blister that had burst on his right heel. He turned left at the end of the block and began walking, or rather limping, along the remaining two miles to Ipswich Street. He felt better when he saw that the lamp lights were just as he remembered them, few and far between and weak, casting a yellowish glow arcing over the kikuyu grass. A bulb on a loose pole was scattering its light like a fish lantern swinging high in the wind, and he couldn't avoid walking beneath it without moving into the middle of the road. In the pale fringe of light he saw his arm was bleeding again, the new blood a strange chocolatey brown in the faint yellowish glow. Every fifty yards or so he found it necessary to rest again, leaning against a fence or tree well away from the lampposts.

A dog barked some fifty yards into the trees where a house light shone brightly. A door opened. "Half-pint, be quiet. *Quiet.*"

The door slammed, the dog still barking.

Somura eased himself away from the fence, falling, his boot stumbling over a branch brought down by the wind. The tree-tops were swaying and roaring with the sound of the increasing westerly. This was nothing new to him, unlike the air-raid shelter in the park, which had served notice that there were some things that had changed, that it could be a fatal mistake to assume everything had stayed the same as before the war. Ipswich Street might not be the same—nor the people in it. He must be careful to risk nothing without thinking it through, and realized the Lawsons might even have moved.

Thick and gluey, the sap from the cypress penetrated the tattered football jersey he had taken from the tramp. He could feel it squashing over his back, and his arm was bleeding more after he had slipped on the gravel road, but he didn't dare move, just sat there in the dark, the wind shaking the heavy dark needles above him, his arm throbbing, the gash bleeding as he waited for Mrs. Lawson's bedroom light to go out. If she spotted him, well, he knew what Australians thought of Japanese *before* the war. He was banking on Elizabeth understanding, no matter how bitter she might feel toward his country. But Mrs. Lawson would be far more than hostile. She would turn him in, without question.

For a while one of the windows was open in the bungalow on the north side facing the street and he could hear the tinkle of a radio, then caught the aroma of beef, a faint fried-onion smell laced through it, wafting out but quickly torn away by the westerly. Ground beef, he thought, which the

Australians called mince. The smell of the food was so enticing that in a moment of irrationality he was actually tempted to hobble to the door and take his chance that Elizabeth and not her mother would answer and protect him.

CHAPTER FORTY-ONE

Brisbane

The lieutenant had hung onto the railing, fighting the impulse to be sick as they'd carried the corpse up the stairs of the Green Slopes Military Hospital mortuary and a leg, the flying boot still on, had snapped off from the bloated carcass, sliding out from the ground sheets and bumping down the stairs. He badly wanted to drive out of the military hospital right then and only Sloan's order kept him waiting around for the results of the autopsy. He was convinced it was a waste of time—Sloan's petty revenge on him for his fun with the Abo. And then there'd been a mixup: the Green Slopes people, thinking he was bringing in a live victim, directed the squad to carry the body into 4B, the burn room, ready with ice tubs and tubes. It took another twenty minutes to straighten out that mess. He tried to get hold of himself by walking about the manicured hospital grounds, swallowing frequently to keep his lunch down, but finally had to give it up. He was finished in the men's room when an orderly appeared outside.

"Sir?"

"Yes," he mumbled, trying to maintain his dignity from inside the lavatory.

"Chief MO is ready to see you."

His face the color of pea soup, the lieutenant walked stiffly over to the chief medical officer's annex. The colonel, still in his white garb and skull cap, didn't waste time. He had three amputations scheduled, all grenade cases flown in from Moresby, the result of a Jap counterattack at Lae. "Here's your report, lieutenant. A male, though that's only an educated guess, given the condition of the corpse."

214

The lieutenant waited.

"Well?" said the colonel.

"That's *all*, sir?"

"Listen, sonny, we were lucky to determine that much. What you brought me was burned meat. You've been reading too much Buck Rogers. It may come as a surprise to you but in this day and age that's all we can tell, male or female. Can't tell much more when there's no skin left. When that's gone it's near impossible to tell race, especially when they're puffed up like this. Anyway, even if we had skin it probably wouldn't confirm anything. A white man with a good tan would look the same as an Oriental. Color really is only skin deep, you know."

The colonel flipped over the file. "All we've got left of any use for further examination is a skull. Might be possible to tell something from that, but you'd need an osteopath. You could send it over to St. Lucia, the university, if you like."

The lieutenant realized it was up to him. He could check with Sloan but that would take time and besides Sloan must have a reason, surely he wouldn't carry a grudge *this* far . . .

"Lieutenant, the flight from Moresby has just come in. We've got over twenty men waiting in the OR. Yes or no?"

"Yes, sir. Much appreciated."

The surgeon lifted the phone. "Sister—the burn corpse— have the skull tagged for records, send it over to St. Lucia for examination. Attention Dr. Anthony. Results to . . ." The surgeon turned impatiently.

"Carmany, sir. Lieutenant Carmany. Victoria Barracks."

"Right. Results by phone. Carmany, Victoria Barracks. Confirmation sheet to follow. Yes, thanks, sister."

As the surgeon opened the door for Carmany, they were pressed up against the dark brown plasterboard while the train of stretchers rolled by.

*   *   *

Mrs. Lawson's bedroom light, finally, went out. Now only Elizabeth's bedroom lamp on the west end remained, casting a soft, peach-colored beam out onto the rockery, whose dwarf cacti and volcanic stones created the effect of a small island in a dark sea. On top of the rockery there was some kind of shrub, a dune plant he remembered they'd brought back from Byron Bay.

The rockery had always fascinated him, its stubby solidity nurturing an air of immobility and security, the kind of place a small boy thought of going away to and defending against the world. Frank Lawson had liked it too; in a way it had been more like the Lawsons than their house. But the more Somura studied it the more he realized that something had gone wrong, that the west end, farthest away from the house, was inundated by weeds, runners of morning glory choking it, spearing through the topsoil, threatening to strangle the dune plant and take over the whole rockery. It had been abandoned. Now it vanished as Elizabeth's light went out.

The bungalow, unlike so many Australian homes, wasn't high off the ground, only four feet, but the house itself was on a rise, and from her southerly facing window Elizabeth could gaze over the dip south of Ipswich Street all the way to Middle Range, a black bulge of verdant trees six miles away in the moonlight. Several houses up, Somura heard dogs barking. Fortunately they were upwind and so shouldn't be able to catch his scent.

CHAPTER FORTY-TWO

Sloan complimented Carmany—the lieutenant had used his loaf, he said—and then rang St. Lucia to have the reports phoned through directly to him. The lab technician at St. Lucia, a middle-aged woman by her tone, told him that Dr. Anthony had left for Brisbane General Hospital to assist in a mandible resection. "No," she said emphatically, "the skull can *not* be interpreted for two to three days. Dr. Anthony is extremely busy with . . ."

Sloan pressed. She became pompous. Sloan hung up and dialed B–3211.

The voice this time was polite, crisp. "Hello. This is Bataan."

"Captain Sloan. Intelligence. Victoria Barracks. Duty officer, please."

"One moment."

Dr. Anthony was met by Captain Sloan at Brisbane General at 9:30 that evening with a written request from headquarters, Commander Southwest Pacific, asking him to look at the skull immediately. It was extraordinarily white—the bones stripped clean to a porcelain sheen by the enzyme bath of collagenase. "Whose is it?" Dr. Anthony enquired wearily, his accent distinctly British.

"That's what we want you to tell us, doctor." And he explained the urgency without going into any detail that would prejudice the doctor's examination: If you were looking for someone and they'd successfully faked their death, then you'd stop looking.

The doctor leaned forward for a closer inspection, the white of his lab coat not so white by contrast. "The Jap pilot, is it?"

Sloan didn't answer.

"I do listen to the news occasionally, captain."

The doctor quickly noted the frontal bone; there was an old fracture, small but distinctive, about a half-inch long directly above the right eye.

Elizabeth could hear the westerlies howling about the eaves, bashing the bamboo against the window like flailing grain, and below the window the plaintive moaning of the wind, and as her eyes became accustomed to the night she could dimly see the billows of linoleum where there was no liner underneath.

In the next room she could hear her mother crying, but tonight she was just too tired to go in. She felt guilty about it, but sometimes her sympathy gave way to anger . . . she too knew the pain and loneliness and above all the awful late night fear of what it would be like to be alone for the rest of her life. But if her father had taught her anything it was that you couldn't keep on harping, you couldn't, as he'd put it, be a dingo, a coward, you couldn't drop your bundle. You had to go on.

Still, she understood what her mother was going through—an Australian woman without a man quickly became a charity case if the old man hadn't left much, and if Bluey didn't return he'd leave only his memory and a small army pension. Elizabeth saw the years stretching out before her, of looking after her mother, trapped by "doing the right thing" until she could no longer do it and would have to put her mother into Eventide or one of the other places where people went to die. What man, after all, wanted to live with you and your mother?

When Elizabeth first heard the bamboo branch swishing against the window by her bed she thought it was a strong gust of wind, but when it sounded again she looked up and saw a cypress branch scratching where no cypress grew. Had it been blown off from one of the trees by the sidewalk down over the roof?

It moved again. It wasn't hanging from the top of the window, it was sticking out from the sill, moving across the windowpane. Slowly, she lifted her head from the pillow and looked down into the pale moonlight.

It wasn't possible, but there he was . . . what did she feel? No time to sort that out now . . . she had to face the immediate . . . She couldn't bring him into the house, not with her mother dozing fitfully in the next room. He had to eat. She could handle that. On the pretext that she couldn't sleep, she fumbled noisily in the kitchen, her nerves raw with excitement and fear. She rattled the cup and saucer, putting on the black kettle, before she realized she'd put out the stove's fire an hour before, at midnight.

When the tea was ready and a sandwich made and remade then stripped and made twice as big, lunch sausage piled on top of the Vegemite, she moved cautiously toward her mother's bedroom. Sarah was still dozing, turning, teeth grinding, subdued by her pills. In the morning she would complain of a terrible headache. Normally Elizabeth woke her up in an attempt to break the cycle, but now she turned, quietly shut her mother's door, spilling some of the tea, and moved back down the hall, praying her mother would sleep until morning.

Morning! It was only six hours away. Where could she hide him then? Dear God, should she hide him at all? She put the tray down, hands shaking, gathering her long red nightrobe about her, then as quietly as she could she went to the bathroom, shutting the door before turning on the flashlight and opening the medicine compartment, not risking the overhead bulb out of fear its light might spill from the worn doorsill and cast a glow under her mother's door. Reaching for the roll of cotton, she almost started an avalanche of pill bottles and cosmetics, a shampoo bottle teetering dangerously. She quickly pushed it back and took out a gauze bandage and some iodine for his arm—she'd use a pillowcase for a sling—stuffed them along with the cotton deep in her nightrobe pocket and made her way out the back door down the five wooden steps into the laundry annex.

She stood still—all she could see now was the big copper cauldron squatting in the black stand and across from it, below the only window, the two cement tubs used for bluing and rinsing the wash. Then she saw him. He had moved in further, leaning against the detachable rubberized wringers for the tubs. His breathing was labored, his body reeked of sweat and wood smoke.

"I've been . . ." he began but didn't finish, his right hand reaching, grasping for the sandwich like a starving animal. The tea was so hot he spat it out.

She added some cold water, turning the tap as quietly as she could. Looking at him, it was hard to believe it was really him, the Tomokazu she'd known . . . he had said almost nothing so far. Neither had she. Now they stood there looking at each other and she couldn't stand the silence any longer. "Tomokazu, where have you—I mean, are you—?"

"You haven't heard yet?" He looked up, astonished, wild-eyed. "They haven't broadcast it yet?"

Before she could answer he swallowed a hunk of sandwich and washed it down with the tea. He was feeling better, collecting himself . . . "Elizabeth, you're the only one I can trust, I'm sorry to put you in this position but . . ." Get her confidence, reassure her, he told himself. Tell her a story . . . "I was on a submarine . . . we were attacked off the coast. Byron Bay." He looked up at her, an exhausted man. He looked down at the sandwich as if someone else was holding it, then slowly back up at her. He put down what was left of it, wiping his right hand on the rough woolen jacket, her father's, that she had brought out to him. "Elizabeth . . ." His voice was subdued, respectful now, the way she remembered it. The wind hadn't let up its howling but in contrast his voice was now calm, reassuring, as if it came from the quiet heart of the storm. "I'm sorry, Elizabeth, I've frightened you, I've been running like an animal . . ."

Her hand, without her willing it, went out to his face. At the last moment she turned it, the back of it resting coolly, on his cheek. "I never thought—"

"Nor I," he said quickly. Strange, but of all about him that was familiar to her, the most familiar was his impeccable English, perhaps because everything else . . . his swagman's clothes, his smell, his savage hunger . . . were so foreign to the Tomokazu she knew. Only now did the voice tell her it was really him.

His fingers spread into the tight small of her back, gently pulling her down to him. ". . . I volunteered as soon as they asked for a crew who knew anything about Australia." He kissed her softly on the cheek, moving his face across hers, kissing her more strongly each time. "I thought about you Elizabeth. I did not stop—"

"It was the same for me," she said, her voice so taut he could barely hear her above the wind. "I have your letter, the last one you wrote . . ."

"From Moresby. On my way home?"

She nodded, allowing tears for the first time. He pulled her in closer, put his face against hers as she knelt down beside him, his lips pressing into her hair.

"What happened? I had all these awful dreams, fantasies . . ."

He pushed her slowly off, as if what he had to say could only be said face to face, not hidden in any way. "The submarine . . . it was attacked . . . Elizabeth, are you sure you haven't heard anything about it? They must have reported it. The radio?"

"Reported what? All I heard at the bank was something about a naval battle and a plane attacking Brisbane."

"Nothing about a submarine?"

"Were there men killed?"

"Yes."

"Then the censors won't say what kind of ships were involved or anything until the next of kin have been told first. That's the rule." Anyway, she told him, even if there had been anything on the radio about a sub she purposely avoided as much war news as she could, for her mother's sake. The less she knew, the less she might be forced to tell her mother. She wanted to tell him about her mother, what the war had done to her. About herself, what it had been like without him. About Frank, who had liked him. About her father, who had never met him. She could ask him more, how did he get here, why had he . . . No, don't ask, it didn't matter.

She felt him, hard against her, and she didn't care where he'd been or why. He was *here*. Fantasy had turned into reality. This was no time to question it, to risk losing it . . . She could feel her heart pounding, her cheeks burning. Her hands were cradling his head, her lips searching for his, his for hers, his right hand moving beneath her robe, feeling her thighs, the damp warmth of her. Her breath got shorter, responding to him, and he drew her more tightly toward him. She felt him, physically aching for her. He heard her moan slightly, and took her hand, pushing it between his legs. Trembling with excitement, her own and his, she undid the buttons on his fly and held him, then thrust forward as he entered her moistness . . .

They lay exhausted in each other's arms, and only now did the pain in his left arm reestablish its grip on him.

"Darling?"

"Yes."

"Tell me what happened."

What he had felt moments before was displaced by annoyance. "I was on a reconnaissance submarine. We were attacked by an Australian destroyer off the coast. Many of my friends were killed, Elizabeth. Some of us escaped. I don't know how many, it was very dark, about five o'clock yesterday morning. I and a few others managed to get ashore, somewhere near Kingscliff, I think. The breakers threw us near the rocks. That's how I hurt my arm. We split up for safety." His sudden grimace was not affected—the pain stabbed at him. "I had to steal these clothes, from some washing line. I have been . . . Elizabeth, try to understand . . . I have been running ever since. To you . . ."

She was trying to take it all in, and in spite of herself felt vaguely troubled.

"Why? I mean, the clothes, why did you need to steal them?"

He relaxed. The question was reassuring, its very irrelevance confirming that this was the Elizabeth he remembered, the schoolgirl . . . She was the same, she still loved him. And *everything* depended on that. He did not, of course, answer the question.

"Oh, God, Tom, I'm glad you're here, but . . . what are we going to do?"

His silence seemed immense, and when he finally spoke he did so calmly. "I want to give myself up. I have been thinking it through, Elizabeth. I want to be with you, *after* this war, after all this is ended." He looked carefully at her. "If you will have me—"

"Tom—" She reached out for him but he held her away. So honorable.

"Understand, a Japanese soldier is disgraced if he surrenders. You must help me. I will not go to them alone, Elizabeth, not to some army post where I will be another accident before I get to a prisoner-of-war camp, like so many of my comrades in New Guinea. And I am in civilian clothes. They could say I was a spy. I cannot trust anyone but you. Darling Elizabeth, you must take me in. I must have someone with me, then I can surrender as a *soldier*. And I must go only to a major command post. I cannot drive with this"—his head indicated the injured arm—"but not to some minor outpost where they will not know what to do, where they might shoot . . ." He gasped with real pain.

She placed her hand on his forehead. "Tom, what do you want me to do?"

"Brisbane," he said. "You must take me to MacArthur's headquarters. I will be safe there. He is a man of honor. He respects a soldier loyal to his country."

She had heard of the Japanese killing themselves by the hundreds rather than surrendering to the enemy. So this seemed an act of love, of trust in her. "I'll help, Tomokazu, but we should get a doctor for your arm. You must—"

"No." He tried to be calm as he said it. "A doctor would have to report it. He would have to inform the Toowoomba garrison." He thought of the Darling Downs Regiment and the fierce battle of Milne Bay. "They would make sure I never got to a camp. Believe me, Elizabeth, the arm will have to wait till Brisbane. We will put on a fresh bandage here. Give me the iodine."

He took off Bluey Lawson's coat that she had given him and the old football jersey, its slit arm blood-soaked and badly scratched by the lantana. She took the jersey from him and threw it into the clothes basket. As he poured on the iodine she could see his body jerk rigidly with the shock of the antiseptic.

"Have you enough petrol in your car?"

She had to think how many ration cards she had left. It was nearly a hundred mile four-hour trip on the dirt and gravel roads. "Yes, there are enough coupons for six gallons. That will get us to Brisbane."

His face was still twisted with the pain of the iodine burning into the open wound. He drank a mug of water. "Can you bring me some . . ." He had drawn a blank, not able to remember the Australian brand name of pain medicine. "Bex," he finally said. "Anything that will kill the pain."

"Yes," she said, upset to see him in such agony. "*Yes* . . ." And her head snuggled into his chest.

CHAPTER FORTY-THREE

"Can't honestly say."

Dr. Anthony, disheveled after taking off his white coat, was leaning back on his desk, his red tie clashing with a green tartan sports shirt. He flipped off the overhead light to heighten the contrast of the bone structure beneath the examination lamp. "There are minor differences between an Oriental and Caucasian skull, but that's just it, they're minor. And in each race there are bound to be individuals who don't fit the mold. You only have to take a walk down the street to see that. Small whites, big Orientals. Right?"

The smoke from Sloan's third cigarette in half an hour wafted across the skull. "All right, doc, but if you were forced to bet?"

"Sorry. I'd be giving you a line if I said I had more than a guess. Might as well flip a coin." The doctor pulled down his tweed coat from behind the door. "Puts you on the spot, does it?"

Sloan thought for a moment, watching the glow of his cigarette. "Don't really know," he said.

"You don't think it was the pilot, I take it?"

Sloan shrugged. "Well, either I'm right and an Abo's wrong or it's the reverse. Back where we started."

Walking down the hall, their footsteps echoing loudly off the old stone floors, neither spoke until they were approaching the main portico. "I am sorry," Anthony repeated. "Wish I could have helped."

"That's okay, sir, at least headquarters won't think I'm a fool if you can't be sure."

It was nearly midnight as Sloan disappeared into the headquarters staff car. Dr. Anthony, feeling vaguely uneasy with his nondiagnosis, lingered a minute on the portico to steal a glance at the Southern Cross, the brilliance of the stars in the Southern Hemisphere never ceasing to amaze the Englishman, whose native land rarely saw a cloudless day or night. But now the clarity and peace were marred by the diffuse edges of searchlights and an air-raid siren wailing somewhere in the Gabba district. He couldn't hear any planes, but they were increasing the drills following the Japanese attack that morning. He wished he could have been more definitive with the captain. It would have allowed Sloan to mobilize more help from the already critically strained security forces and police. He turned and was on his way for a last-minute check of his patient in Recovery when he decided to take one more look at the skull. He owed himself, and Sloan, that much. He opened the door, moving cautiously into the semidarkness, switched on the light and turned the skull around, this way and that, and walked around it. Sometimes a different angle could help you interpret a problem, like rearranging the same cards in a poker hand.

In West Toowoomba Bruce Keely lay in bed brooding, waiting for the dawn, though it was only 1:00 A.M. Damn it, he wanted to punish, to hurt her. He'd felt humiliated when he watched her driving off from the bank with another man, and, he learned, a married man at that. It had been no accident that he'd spotted her . . . he'd purposely positioned himself at the pub, waiting for her to leave the bank, planning to surprise her. Well, the surprise was all his. He felt like a first-class idiot. After what they'd had on the mountain . . . it had been special, he'd *thought,* to both of them. Apparently not.

He couldn't wait to see her, to tell her how he felt. He lifted the pillow, driving his fist hard into the accountant's face. Jesus, an *accountant.* How romantic . . . Yes, he wanted to tear into her but he knew, when it came to it, he wouldn't. He couldn't. Damn it, he was crazy about her . . . which was why he was so bloody mad at her. But why had she lied? Maybe there was an explanation, maybe her mother had been sick and she'd had to get home in a hurry. But they had no phone for her mother to call the bank. Damn it, he was no drongo, if she didn't want him, better now to cut it clean. But why that bloody *accountant*?

A hundred miles east in Brisbane General Hospital Dr. Anthony sat staring at the skull and wondered for a moment whether it might even be a woman's. After all—it was only the word of the Green Slopes MD that it was a male, and the corpse had been totally broiled in the fire. Contrary to popular belief, sometimes it was difficult even to determine the sex when the genital area had been consumed by fire. Maybe he should just guess. A lot of physicians made their reputation by guessing, by going out on a limb and only being proved right afterward. He rejected the temptation. It just was too irresponsible.

He studied the skull a while longer, shook his head and switched off the light.

At 6:00 A.M. Sloan woke up to the doleful sound of reveille echoing through the Brisbane hills. The magpies were already at it high in a rose gum, and a flock of galahs, flexing their red and gray wings over the parade grounds, were squawking their parrot talk while the usual smell of powdered eggs moved relentlessly through the camp.

In one of the outer huts, Sloan grabbed his razor and towel and made his way down the hut's narrow hallway toward the showers, where the moans of early morning resentment mingled with the laughter of kookaburras outside and sharp shouts inside as carefully adjusted faucets were thrown out of sync by a sudden surge of cold, brackish water, thanks to which the soap would not lather and formed a white scum driven gurgling down the open drains.

"Captain Sloan?" The voice came from somewhere beyond the steam.

"Here," said Sloan, lifting his head up.

"Call from Gatton police. Urgent."

"Tell me."

The corporal, uncomfortable around so much naked authority, read through the message, the steam enveloping him in a humid fog and causing the message pad to droop.

"Local copper, uh, I meant the local sergeant, sir, says one of his cockeys, a dairy farmer near a Six Pile Creek—"

"*Mile,*" corrected Sloan.

"Oh, yeah, well the line was a bit scratchy."

"Go on."

"Well, sir, the cockey reports seeing a bit of parachute in one of the trees."

"Parachute? Where's the farm?"

The corporal glanced down at the scribbled message. "Near some cave, Seven Mile Caves, I think the copper said."

The towel disappeared completely from Sloan's neck and was now pointing at the corporal. "Who's the duty officer for today?"

"Lieutenant Felbury, sir."

"Get him to contact Toowoomba headquarters. I want a platoon, full battle dress, two transport trucks, and I want them down that Toll Bar in twenty minutes and a thorough scan of those caves. And I want every detail of everything and anyone they find. Tell them C rations for lunch. They can grab a mug of tea and slops before they shove off. Got it?"

"Yes, sir. Toowoomba headquarters—platoon—battle dress —two trucks—grab quick breakfast. Departure twenty minutes. Search caves."

Sloan lifted the corporal's hand to look at his watch. "At 0630, right?"

"Yes, sir."

Sloan sat down on the bench. Now he had a parachute *and* a body. He got dressed, rang Archerfield and asked whether any Allied pilot had bailed out over the area.

"No," they said, no Allied pilot had gone down in the area.

It didn't make sense, except if . . . and he thought of Billy, what he'd said about two people's tracks around the plane, and only one moving away.

CHAPTER FORTY-FOUR
Toowoomba

Elizabeth's note was a short lie: "Mum, took car, might be working late. Have to leave early. Anzac Day rush. See you this evening. Love, Liz."

She took one of Frank's white shirts and a large tartan blanket, two cans of baked beans, a half packet of Arrowroot biscuits and a bottle of Seppelt's brandy from the medicine cupboard. She decided not to take anything else for the four-hour drive over the narrow valley highway and through the Marburg Ranges. It was almost seven and any more activity might wake up her mother. She could call the bank on the way.

With Tomokazu hiding well below the car windows in the big green Plymouth, she let the old '36 sedan roll gently down the Ipswich Street dip before starting the motor. But her mother did hear it. So did the dogs a few houses up, barking loudly, and by the time the car had traveled the three-quarters of a mile up Ipswich Street and swung left along Tourist Road to the monument heading down the Toll Bar, Sarah Lawson was reading Elizabeth's note. She seemed not to comprehend it. She went into the kitchen, turned on the tap and sat waiting, staring as the thin trickle of water from the drought-struck tank slowly filled the kettle. She made a pot of tea and toast, put it carefully on the old cane tray, and took it to Frank's room. Frank would appreciate it. Frank . . .

In the Plymouth's rear-view mirror Elizabeth could see Tomokazu stretched out in the back seat, his bandaged left arm resting by his side, some blood on the white shirt, his eyes staring at the roof. To the right, five miles south of the highway, she could see Tabletop's sunburned summit poking high above the blue, dew-spangled hills. She caught his eye.

He tried to touch her shoulder from the back seat but couldn't reach her. In the early morning his skin seemed as golden to her as the light that was now suffusing the valley floor, his gentle almond-shaped eyes quiet and unperturbed, just as she had remembered him. In the light of day it was as if the Tomokazu she'd known a year-and-a-half ago had never left.

Beyond his image in the mirror she saw three trucks about a mile behind rounding a curve at the base of the range by the black sheet of Helidon Spa. One of them was a semitrailer, a cattle transport from out west, the other two, pulling out to pass him now that they were on the flat, were three-tonners.

"I see them," he said. He had raised himself up and was watching the rear-view mirror too.

"What'll I do?"

"Pull over," he said. "Let them pass us."

"Why don't you give up to them? Now that I'm with you—"

"Elizabeth," he said, changing position so he could lower himself from view again, "I only trust MacArthur. He is our enemy, he *was* my enemy, but he is a man of honor. He will make sure I am given a fair trial."

She watched the trucks approaching. The khaki canvas contrasted against the early morning haze of mists and irrigation sprinklers reflecting silver through the sunlight.

Elizabeth pulled off to the left and stopped the car. "How can you be sure?" she asked. "I mean about MacArthur? Why don't you give yourself up here, with me? I can speak for you . . ."

He could see her looking at him in the mirror, the back of the front seat suddenly a wall as formidable as any rampart between them. He felt the sudden suspicion rising. It was only a few seconds that they sat there, wordlessly, but it seemed much longer. Especially with his new thought about her.

The trucks passed them. "Believe me, Elizabeth." He sat up and reached out for her again, his right hand managing to rest on her hair. He was sure she would pull away but she didn't. "I'm telling you the truth, Elizabeth. Please believe me." He paused. "I love you, I have never stopped . . ." He stroked her hair. "Trust me, Elizabeth. Take me to Brisbane, it's my only chance."

She wanted to believe him, she *had* to believe him . . . all this time she had told herself he was different, she *knew* him. Was that possibly a lie? She couldn't believe that, never mind her doubts. He'd never lied to her. He was in an enemy country. The least she could do was trust him, trust *herself* and her feelings for him . . . She nodded. "I'm not sure where it is."

"It's on the corner of Queen and Ann Streets," he said quietly. "Every Japanese soldier is taught that."

As she pulled out, he lay down. A car coming the other way from the direction of Brisbane, hauling a trailer, passed them, children waving as if there was no such thing as war.

Somura glanced at his watch. 8:21. Ahead lay the Minden Range, then the dirt road flats before the Marburg Range, then Brisbane. He knew they would lose time on the slow climb up the western side of the Minden and then by having to brake hard again going down the eastern slope. Even so, Elizabeth was making good time. Off to the left he saw a red trail of dust created by the two army trucks that had turned off left near Helidon.

An old haversack, the sacking one-third packed with dry pass-palem grass for a mattress, three old moth-eaten blue blankets, a black billy can encrusted from long use standing forlornly amid a soft pile of white ash, tea leaves scattered about the edge of the dead fire and the punctured can of condensed milk, its edges already rusting, were all that was left in the cave. The farmer who had led the soldiers from the two army trucks to the cave now stood back, batting a gnarled briar pipe on his cartridge belt, a shotgun broken open across his left arm. He pushed back the broad-brim felt hat and waited until the officer in charge of the platoon crossed the creek, watching his reflection in the deep mirror green stream, its sandstone sculptures curving below the mouth of the cave. "Looks like 'e done a flit," said the farmer.

The sublieutenant clambered up the six-foot slope between the water and the cave's entrance and poked about the fire, using his swagger stick as one might on a particularly nasty carcass. In the thirty-man line that was now shaped like a boomerang around the wide entrance of the cave a soldier made a loud hiss just as the sublieutenant gingerly lifted the blankets. The officer jumped back, followed by a snigger in the ranks.

The sublieutenant turned around. "Right! I want that man's name. Now, right now!"

No answer.

"Right. Detention parade 0400—the lot of you."

The farmer puffed the pipe, calmly watching the antics of the army. "It was me," he said finally.

The sublieutenant glared at him, but at least he was off the hook with his ridiculous threat. "Well, I reckon," he said, trying to regain some face and finally justify his jumpiness, "the joker who was camping here got bitten by . . . a tiger snake, panicked, made a run for it. Probably's delirious from the poison. Dead somewhere up there. In the bush."

The farmer looked up at the sky, his amusement hidden in the sun's glare. "Don't think so, son. No crows." He blew heavily into the pipe. "Whoever was camping here was scared off by your mob, I reckon. A bum by the looks of it, travelin' light. Just wanted to be alone, I'd say. He's probably gone walkabout until your lot come through. Probably a metho drinker."

"A metho? What makes you think that?"

"When 'e dropped by the house to get the okay to camp 'ere he smelled like a flamin' paint can."

Remembering the emphatic and detailed instructions from Victoria Barracks to search the cave thoroughly for every detail—full description of everything and everybody he came across—the sublieutenant lifted the flap from the haversack. "What'd he look like?"

"Oh, medium height."

The officer waited impatiently. The farmer was sitting on a worm-eaten gum now, making spitting noises in his pipe.

"Any distinguishing marks? Eye color? Hair?"

The farmer struck a match. "Didn't take much notice of 'im, to tell you the truth. I was milking when he came by the house." He blew out a long trail of smoke, the rich smell of the flake combining with the pungent lantana. He waved a green blowfly off his mouth. "Like I say, didn't take much notice of 'im."

"He give you his name?"

"Nah. Didn't ask."

The sublieutenant pulled out a brown bag of white flour, no label, and an old Rogers syrup can of coarse brown sugar, ants thick about the rim. There was also a bottle in the haversack—an imperial quart of methylated spirits: "Merv's Hardware—Ruthven Street. All your garden needs. From our shop to your home—free delivery."

The farmer grinned. "A hair of the dog, eh? Thought 'e was a metho. Told the wife I did. Said, 'May, that fella's a metho. Smell 'im a mile off."

Two hours later, at 10:37, the sublieutenant told Sloan what he had found. Sloan was quickly through to Toowoomba, asking the manager of Merv's hardware which of his customers was in the habit of buying methylated spirits to drink.

The manager said no one did.

Sloan told him he wanted to know who bought methylated spirits to drink or he'd report Merv's to the gas-rationing board and Merv's would have to deliver by donkey.

The manager said they suspected, but only "suspected, mind," three bums. Sloan took the names, then rang the Too-woomba police station.

Sergeant Ellis shook his head when he heard the captain's request for addresses. "You must be jokin', mate. Methos don't have addresses. One of them lives under the bridge, the other two knock about North Toowoomba, Mount Lofty area somewhere."

"Can you check them out? Right now?"

"Well, I don't know about the Lofty ones, but Archie's been gone . . . oh, for about a week now."

"What's he look like?"

The policeman gave a very good description—five feet ten inches, late forties, slight build, blue-eyed, brown hair, "Looks emaciated, which is no surprise. Scar on right side above the eye . . ."

Sloan tried to remember the skull in its detail. He couldn't. He told Ellis he'd call back. Next he tried to get Dr. Anthony on the phone. It was the huffy secretary again. Dr. Anthony was en route to Brisbane General for morning surgery.

"Corporal!" shouted Sloan.

"Sir?"

"Motor pool. A jeep on the double!"

When Sloan found him, Dr. Anthony was scrubbing up for the first operation of the day. The doctor quickly confirmed the size and exact position of the scar on the skull.

"Right!" Sloan said. "Then the Nip is loose!" He headed for the door.

"Anything else I can do?" asked Anthony.

Sloan turned. "Well, if you could ring headquarters personally it might help convince them to lend me a few extra men to look for him."

"Glad to," said Anthony. "Good hunting."

Before he left the hospital Sloan rang up the farm near the caves but the sublieutant had left on his way back to Toowoomba garrison. Sloan then called Sergeant Ellis, first to tell him that the body they had was definitely not the Jap's but a bum named Archie, that the Jap must be on the run and that Ellis should intercept the sublieutenant's two-truck convoy as it returned from Helidon up the Toll Bar and tell him to set up a roadblock on the highway west of Toowoomba, an escape route that would take the Jap away from the big airfields of the coast. It was just possible, Sloan said, that the man had some crazy idea of stealing a plane from the interior and flying north beyond Alice Springs on to Darwin and then a short hop to one of the Japanese-held islands off New Guinea. Crazy, "but a hunted man will try anything," he said.

"What about east of Toowoomba between here and Brisbane?" Sergeant Ellis said. "Down your way? Sounds more likely he'd head for the coast."

"I agree," said Sloan. "But don't worry about that one. I'm ready for him if he comes my way. Let me know if anything happens on your end."

Ellis, catching Sloan's excitement, said he would and slammed down the phone. He'd been waiting for something like this since the war began.

CHAPTER FORTY-FIVE

Bruce Keely was in no mood for the dogs up from the Lawsons' house. Usually the snarling pack, Alsatians and blue cattle dogs, straining at their chains, scared him even though they were tied up, but this morning he felt he could kill them all with his bare hands.

He saw Elizabeth's car was gone and after Mrs. Lawson . . . out of it as usual . . . showed him the note Elizabeth had left it took him less than five minutes, during which he rehearsed his speech to Elizabeth, to cover the three miles from the top of Ipswich Street on Toowoomba's rim to the Commonwealth Bank of Australia in Ruthven Street.

Her car wasn't outside the bank—she'd probably parked behind the building.

The bank doors were locked so he knocked on the glass panel. A teller, a short fat man, came out from behind the Foreign Exchange window, obviously annoyed, his mouth moving silently behind the glass like a goldfish, his hand pointing imperiously at the hours of business, 10:00–3:00, written in gold letters on the door.

Keely searched the pockets of his red plaid shirt for a pencil. He couldn't find one. He gestured for the teller to wait and ran back to his red pickup parked illegally in the taxi stand in Little Russell Street.

The teller was gone when Keely returned and he had to begin hammering all over again. The teller ignored him until he began thumping really hard on the glass, and it was the accountant who came sauntering out from behind the teller cages. The accountant looked at him, said something to the teller, who shrugged. The accountant hesitated, then came to the door.

Bruce slipped a note under the door, explaining that he wanted to see Elizabeth Lawson, that it was urgent.

The accountant surveyed him, said something again to the teller and opened the door slightly. "Why the panic? We'll be open at ten."

"Can't wait. I'm working out at Harlaxton. Got to be there by nine."

"You're late."

Keely turned supplicant. "Look, mate, give me a break. I'm not going to rob your bank."

The accountant eyed him carefully. "Seen you before, haven't I? You a customer?"

"No," Keely said, ready to strangle him. "I'm with the opposition—Bank of New South."

"Wait here."

It seemed forever until the accountant returned, the cold shadows of the Greyhound bus depot by the bank shortening as the sun climbed higher over the downs.

"She hasn't arrived yet."

"You *sure*? She left a note with her mum, said she had to get here early. Something about an Anzac Day rush. You sure she hasn't arrived yet?"

"I'm sure. Where'd you hear about this Anzac Day rush business?"

"I *told* you, she left a note." If she wasn't there, where the hell was she, and who the hell was she with?

"Well," the accountant was saying, "she hasn't arrived and that's all I can tell you."

Keely didn't hear him. Something was wrong. If she wasn't home and she wasn't at the bank, then where? And why the note about the Anzac rush if there wasn't any? He started the pickup, pulled out of Little Russell into Ruthven, heading toward Margaret Street and the range top. Up by the Grammar School he stopped at a telephone booth and called the Harlaxton site and said he was sick, he'd try to get in later.

He didn't know how he'd handle Mrs. Lawson, she didn't have all her marbles after losing her son Frank and not hearing any news about her husband Bluey. But something fishy was going on, and he'd have to talk to her again about the note.

Sarah Lawson was dusting the mantelpiece for the third time that morning when Keely arrived, running up the crazy path. She invited him in for a cup of tea. He declined, then was sorry he hadn't accepted. It would have made it easier to talk, to question her.

"Ah, Mrs. Lawson, did Elizabeth say when she'd be home?"

"You know about Miss Kenny?"

"What?"

"The nurse!" she said irritably. "Y'know, polio nurse."

Oh, Christ. "No, no, I don't. Sorry. Look, Mrs. Lawson, I . . ."

The note was still on the table and he asked to read it again: ". . . Have to leave early . . ."

Why? Who with?

"Those doctors hate Sister Kenny. Afraid they'll lose money."

"Ah, yeah . . . look, I have to run, Mrs. Lawson. See you later."

How he'd missed the blood, or rather spots of it, on the way into the house he didn't know . . . probably because he was so angry, so overcome with jealousy he'd been literally blinded to anything on the crazy path that wound in from the base of the cypress tree. And there was also a faint red trail on the grass leading across the lawn to the rockery. Now he followed it around the west side of the house to the crushed pebble walkway leading to the washhouse. Inside the washhouse he saw a darker smear by the washer and on the floor more blood spots. She'd had an accident! There was a strange smell too—iodine. She'd gone to the hospital and didn't want to panic her mum. That would explain the note and the car not being there. The nearest hospital was St. Vincent's a half-mile away by the Grammar School.

He ran to the pickup. The dogs started barking again and he could see a nosy neighbor peering at him from behind curtains. To hell with all of them.

The nuns at St. Vincent's told Keely that the only patient in emergency was a little boy with a severe gravel rash. Maybe she had gone to her family doctor, he thought. No, it would have been too early for office hours.

He went up to the information desk and phoned the police station.

When Ellis arrived at 9:30 accompanied by a doctor, in response to the call, and met Keely outside the house he was already curious because it was the girl's place, just up from the nosy neighbor with the dogs—the one the two Australian security and intelligence men had asked him to keep an eye on. The blood on the grass could have a number of explanations but when he followed the trail to the washhouse and found Archie's blood-stained football jersey in the laundry bin everything changed.

As promised, he called Sloan. "Something's come up," he reported. "Your man on the run."

After questioning Keely, Ellis gave Sloan a description of Elizabeth's car—1936 green Plymouth. He checked with the neighbors and asked if anyone had seen the car and could remember the time. The nosy one told him her dogs had awakened her early as the Lawsons' car had driven off. Going east.

"Are you sure?" pressed Ellis.

The neighbor was indignant. "Of course, I'm sure. I saw it

with my own eyes. First it passed the house then made a U-turn and went back up the hill again."

By the time Ellis had finished, Keely had gone, his pickup hitting forty-five, a dangerous speed for anyone heading down the range along the switchback Toll Bar Road. It was 9:47 A.M.

Driving by Helidon Spa at the foot of the range, his foot flat to the floorboard, Bruce Keely leaned hard on the horn, but the herd of Jersey cows, accustomed to crossing the highway at their leisure, took no notice, seven of them, water still dripping from their shanks, stopping on the center line, staring imperiously at the pickup as it ground and rattled to a halt, the rust-colored dust sweeping over it, its pistons thumping and banging.

"For Christ sake, *move!*" Keely yelled.

One of the cows lifted her head skyward, half closing her eyes, and bellowed indignation. Keely edged the pickup forward to bully them. Which only increased the Jerseys' intransigence.

In the distance, across the field by the spa, a boy with what looked like a stick in hand was ambling along, skirting a green island of tall, sticky passpalem grass. Keely got out of the pickup and tried to shoo the cattle on. A few moved a pace or so but the others, as if by some prearranged plan, took their turn at standing, staring and blocking his way. Perhaps it was the warmth of the road after the cold chemical trough.

"Fuck!" shouted Keely in utter exasperation, giving his front tire a violent kick for good measure. Behind him he could just make out the flat summit of Tabletop, where he'd been with Elizabeth what now seemed a million years ago.

CHAPTER FORTY-SIX

So much had happened in the last six hours that Elizabeth had had no time to think about things, but now on the road, tires humming, she finally had a chance to collect her thoughts and decided that what had seemed acceptable in the passionate rush of the previous night now, in the sharp morning light, seemed more like a dream . . . terribly convincing at the time, unreal in the light of day.

It didn't come on her all of a sudden but rather sidled up, like an old fear sneaking through one's defenses. It wasn't just the question that if he trusted her to witness his surrender to guarantee his safety, then why wouldn't he trust her here with the troops that had turned off by Helidon? Did he really expect to surrender to MacArthur personally? Earlier she just hadn't allowed herself to confront such an obvious question. Because if she did, if she couldn't believe him . . . And why his insistence on MacArthur's headquarters?

But in the end it was a mundane detail that got to her, that destroyed her rationalizations and denials. How had he traveled the 150 miles from Byron Bay to Toowoomba between the time of the submarine battle in the early morning . . . around five, he'd said . . . and midnight when he appeared by her window?

In the distance she could see rows of sprinklers casting rainbows over the emerald green fields of vegetables, and far to the northeast, but still northwest of Brisbane, the blue humps of the D'Aguilar Mountains.

"Tomokazu?"

"Yes?" His eyes were closed with exhaustion.

"Did you catch a truck, a semitrailer, from Byron Bay?"

"No."

243

Silence. His eyes opened, and he was staring into the mirror.

"No," she said, answering her own question. "Otherwise you wouldn't have needed my car." No sound but the whine of the tires. "How did you get to Toowoomba then? You couldn't have walked in one day. It's impossible."

No answer.

"You didn't walk," she said, and forced a tight laugh.

He sat up.

She jerked the wheel, barely missing a rabbit scampering across the highway. The Plymouth slowed.

"You . . ." She thought of the news broadcast she'd heard at the bank about a Jap plane. "My God—*you were the pilot.*"

"Yes, Elizabeth."

The car shuddered to a stop, the only sound now made by the wind across the Lockyer Valley.

His voice was calm. Deadly calm. "I didn't tell you earlier, Elizabeth, because I was afraid you wouldn't believe I really wanted to surrender. If I were you I probably wouldn't believe it. But I swear—"

"*No,* damn it." She turned around. "My God . . . you're going to kill him like the other one tried to do. We've heard rumors but . . . oh, God, you've been using me . . ." She buried her face in her hands, slumping back, then collapsing forward against the wheel, the horn blowing.

"Elizabeth," Somura said. "Elizabeth, I know it looks bad, but believe me, I want to be with you, my only chance is to be taken into custody by the general or his people. Public anger is so strong, I could be shot by anybody else." He put his hand gently on her shoulder.

She was dead still now. He watched her closely in the mirror, her head bent.

"I'm telling the *truth,* Elizabeth, I've always told you the truth, how I felt about you. Think back, remember how we were. I'm the same man. Just drive me to Brisbane, you'll see." He reached out and touched her hair.

She said nothing.

After a few minutes she started the car, her face a pale mask. He sat back. There was nothing more to say if she did not believe him. And if she did not believe him, then she became a different person. She became an enemy who could threaten his mission. He had known this was a possibility ever since the crash but hadn't wanted to think about it. Now it had happened and there was no turning away from it. Just as there was no turning away from what he must do.

CHAPTER FORTY-SEVEN

Somura braced himself as Elizabeth pumped the brakes down the narrow curving road on the eastern side of the Minden Range where the road headed into the Marburgs. Purple and crimson blobs of bougainvillaea swept by, and inside the car it was becoming hot and muggy as they descended. Winding down the window he could smell the sweet black soil of the valley and see the fields to the north and south stretching toward the ranges that enfolded them like two great rugged arms.

It was 10:07 and everything was going well. Now and then cars passed them, most of the drivers giving a wave, so common, he remembered, on the Australian roads beyond the capital cities. They passed tropical fruit and vegetable stalls, some unattended, a money box placed out in front on an honor system. For the first time since he'd bailed out Somura felt almost comfortable. The Bex powders he had swallowed had stalled the pain. If he moved the arm the throbbing would surge, but if he kept it relatively still it was a bearable throb rather than a sharp stab. A line of four cars had built up behind them, the road being too winding and narrow to risk passing. Far below he could see a farm nestled by a field of milo, the wind moving it like a chocolate sea against the mauve hills.

"Pull over," he said. "Let them pass." He was afraid they would see him if they kept so close on the Plymouth's tail.

As she pulled off on the unpaved shoulder a flock of rainbow lorikeets took flight and a cloud of sandy loam dust enveloped the braking Plymouth and floated out over the valley. The sun, reflecting off the grains of dust, for a moment reminded Somura of his youth, when he was ill and bored, watching the particles of dust from his sickroom, amazed that each single speck had its own life as did each person, and how insignificant one life was in the large scheme of things and yet how one speck of dust could in the end tip the balance. As he was now destined to do.

Now the Plymouth was the last car of the line, a square Ford sedan, originally behind them, in front. The line slowed in obedient convoy as the road dropped a hundred feet or more into two shaded S-curves. For a moment in the shade he saw a sweep of green become lighter, as if from reflected light and looked at the hillside for a shiny surface—there was none. The car in front, the Ford, pulled off on a siding, the driver waving. Somura rubbed the right side of his face, hiding it from the Ford as they went by. Elizabeth did not acknowledge the man's wave, intent on negotiating the turns, the Plymouth lurching again as she kept pumping the brakes, an annoying clicking sound accompanying each lurch every time the brake shoes gripped. Soon the Ford was behind them again, and now it swung out and passed them.

Whether it was the driver of the Ford not waving as he had done before or whether it was his unusual haste in overtaking the Plymouth Somura wasn't sure, but the sudden, erratic behavior of the Ford sharpened his senses. Had the driver seen his face? Did it matter? Might not the driver mistake him for Chinese? Would the side of his face be enough? In a country whose fear of Orientals was now paranoid, perhaps it was. Did the Ford have a radio? Were they broadcasting a description of him? But they couldn't possibly know—but then why the two troop trucks turning off at Helidon?

The road was dropping off gradually, leveling out along the valley floor. Elizabeth had stopped pumping the brakes. It was the cessation of the rhythmic braking, the clicking, that told him something was wrong, explaining the Ford's sudden, urgent spurt ahead, the determined, anxious look of the driver not bothering to wave any longer at the Plymouth. The very absence of the rhythmic braking and clicking, like the sudden absence of a familiar sound, made him realize what the noises meant—and why he'd seen the dark green in the shadow become lighter.

"Faster," he ordered.

"What's wrong?" She hoped something was, that it would somehow help her out of this nightmare.

"Faster. Pass that Ford. Quickly!"

As they passed the Ford the driver appeared grim and unnaturally careful not even to glance at the Plymouth. Which confirmed Somura's suspicion.

Soon the Ford was 100 yards behind, then 200 yards. Ahead Somura saw a long curve passing a small roadside cemetery and beyond it a blue green field of lucerne. As they rounded the bend, Somura told her to stop and turn the car at right angles from the left lane, which would block the road.

"Why—what are you doing?"

"Turn."

She pulled the car about. He looked to the east. No one was coming. Behind them the Ford would be rounding the bend in a few moments. He reached over, jerked the keys from the ignition, pulled the hood release and, grimacing with a stab of pain, got out the back door.

"What are you . . . ?" He ignored her, lifted the hood with his right hand, sticking the pistol in his belt, and ripped out the horn wire.

The Ford was traveling at over forty miles an hour as it came swaying round the bend, skidded and, rocking precariously on the gravel, finally screeched to a stop in a shower of stones and dust by a grove of black wattle trees.

Somura stepped forward, quickly covered the six feet between the Plymouth and the Ford, lifted the Nambu, and fired three times.

The Ford's windshield imploded, Elizabeth screamed, and the driver was flung back against the seat, staring up at the

Ford's roof, two bullets in his face, the third having torn through his windpipe.

His left arm still immobile with pain, Somura stuck the pistol back in his belt, used his right to open the Ford's door, and using all his strength, dragged the driver out and back to the Plymouth's trunk. He opened the trunk and grabbing the dead man's trouser belt, lifted him into a prayerlike position against the Plymouth's back bumper, then with his right arm tumbled the body forward. After closing the trunk, Somura had to take hold of the handle and stand still for several seconds to catch his breath, the effort having made him momentarily dizzy. Now he could feel the sharp, stabbing pain, running along the full length of his arm and deep into his shoulder blade.

He walked back to the front of the Ford and, holding the barrel of the pistol, smashed the windshield with the butt so as to remove any evidence of a bullet hole for anyone passing the car—making it look as if flying stones, common on Australian roads, had done the damage. He used the short sword to unscrew and finally pry off the Ford's rear and only license plate, exchanging it for the Plymouth's. Then he opened the Plymouth's hood again and ripped out the headlight connections. Now she could click the high-low beam switch, on-off, on-off, in sync with her braking and there would be no headlights. Half-stumbling to the trunk, he smashed the taillights for good measure before getting back into the car.

"Do not try to signal again," he told her. "In any way. I do not want to hurt you, Elizabeth, but if you force me . . ."

She forced herself to keep quiet. She was damned if she'd let him see her break down. But as she eased the car off, her leg shook so badly that the clutch jumped, causing the old Plymouth to shake in protest.

In the rear-view mirror she could see him, his head on the folded tartan blanket, swallowing another Bex powder dry. She also could see the gun, its barrel having made a black powder stain on Frank's white shirt, and the elaborate handle of the short sword, and a stranger, unrecognizable to her now. It was the same face but it was a mask. Everything was the same and everything had changed.

This stranger meant to kill MacArthur. This man with the mask of Somura was the enemy.

Somura looked at his watch: 11:17 A.M. They would not be in Brisbane now till 12:30. Still enough time. He had allowed for some delay by having her leave Toowoomba so early. Mac-Arthur would be at his headquarters at the AMP Insurance Building until 2:00 P.M., when he would return for lunch to Lennon's a few blocks south near the corner of George and Ann. That would leave ninety minutes to prepare his attack. It would be enough.

Back along the highway the last cow finally ambled off, protesting with a long low moan, and Keely was off in a shower of pebbles. He drew alongside the boy now approaching the road, stopped and reversed, the tires spinning furiously in the valley's black soil.

He had been mistaken. The boy herding, or rather strolling lazily behind the cows, wasn't carrying a stick but a .22 Hornet, the rifle that fired the long-jacketed .22 bullet with an accuracy prized by farmers and hunters who were reluctant to use the bigger and costlier .303s for the smaller game of fox and rabbit hunted in the valley. Keely only had a ten-shilling note but he threw his watch into his offer.

"How many jewels?" asked the kid, turning over the watch.

"Seventeen," Keely lied. The kid was no fool.

"What else?"

"I only want to borrow it for a few hours," Keely said. "B'sides, you've got my license number for security. I'll bring it back."

"What do you want it for?"

Keely's nerves were raw. "You heard about a Jap running loose?"

The boy's eyes brightened. "From the prison camp? Another breakout?"

"Yeah."

The boy gave him the rifle, refused the payment and returned the money and watch.

"How many left in the mag?"

"Six, I think. Wait, there's one in the chamber."

Keely waved his thanks. "I'll bring it back," and drove off. The Hornet, he thought, was a beautiful weapon. No kick to speak of, highly accurate at 200 yards, lots of punch for its size.

Ahead he could see the green and purple slash of the Marburg Range rushing forward to meet him.

Somura had been shaken earlier by the sight of the two army trucks turning off by Helidon on what must, he decided, be a second search, as well as by the SOS Elizabeth had sent out. But along with it was a sense of freedom from pretense, with the exhilaration of commitment to an irreversible course of action. There was no way back now that she'd seen him kill; there was only time to stick to his plan, to the alternate plan that had begun the moment he'd slashed the tramp's face into an unrecognizable pulp.

From time to time he saw her shoulders heave, no doubt out of fear, and guilt over the unknown driver who had fallen back to get the Plymouth's license number. She had signaled him, and was responsible for his death. Somura felt no sympathy. He had seen a ship of a hundred men die in as many seconds, cut to pieces by the relentless pounding of the Australian destroyer. A hundred widows, thousands of miles away, would be more courageous than she was over the death of a stranger. In the end, Tojo was right—they were different.

They had neither the inner strength nor understanding to see death as it was, a mirror in a maze of mirrors. Death made them inferior. For the Japanese it ennobled.

He looked ahead into the quivering haze of heat washing across the black road like a distorted mirror, another illusion of the earthly journey. To steady himself he invoked the tall, sacred *sugi,* the Japanese cedar; the *torii,* the gates to heaven; the *miki,* the sacred wine; the prayer scrolls fluttering from the juniper. And he heard again the haunting song of the Naval Academy: "If I go to sea . . ."

Through the shimmering heat over flats at the foot of the Minden and Marburg hills, the last range before Brisbane, he could see three bumps stretching across the road. Two miles farther on he could make out that two of the bumps were dark green jeeps—the other, gray—and then when the Plymouth was a mile from them he saw a red line in front of the two green jeeps, and above the line, rifles slung on the shoulders of the soldiers.

A roadblock. Four soldiers in all. The gray bump in front, its trunk facing Somura, was a taxi sedan being searched by two of the four soldiers from the two jeeps, the other two stationed on the other, the Brisbane side of the roadblock. He sat up further and nearly blacked out as the pain pierced his shoulder blade.

On the far side of the red barricade he could see two more cars approaching from the direction of Brisbane. Shaking his head to clear it, squinting in the harsh sunlight, he refocused. The jeeps and taxi appeared to be coming toward him.

Elizabeth was speeding up.

"Slow down!"

She did not.

"Do it, or I will kill them."

The Plymouth slowed.

Three hundred yards away, the jeeps took on distinct shapes; two Willys, their spare gas tanks prominent on the rear, each jeep effectively blocking one of the two lanes. For several moments it seemed the two vehicles were touching nose-to-nose, but at 200 yards, the Plymouth now slowed to twenty miles an hour, Somura saw it was an optical illusion . . . in order to let the traffic through after being inspected the two jeeps were in fact parked about ten feet apart, one across each lane, so that on being waved through, a car would have to slow to about ten miles an hour in order to negotiate a sharp S-bend between them. On the Brisbane side one of the soldiers was bending now, opening the trunk of a black sedan, the first of the two cars pulled up on the other side of the barricade. The other soldier coming up behind peered inside the car before waving it on. It maneuvered slowly through the gap between the jeep and passed the Plymouth, increasing speed.

The Plymouth was nearing the barricade. "Slower," said Somura. "Wait until the second car comes through from the other side, then be ready."

Elizabeth said nothing, her shoulders rigid. She could still see the blood-covered face of the dead man in the trunk. The Plymouth slowed to a crawl.

"Do you understand?"

"Yes."

He was closely watching the two soldiers on his side of the barricade, particularly the one searching the trunk of the taxi twenty yards in front of them. The soldier was doing a thorough job of it, leaning low to examine the contents of the trunk.

Elizabeth turned, her face still pale. "We can't run through, they'll shoot. You can't—"

"Do as they say." He surprised her. "If you give any signal, any alert, I will have to kill you."

She looked at him. She did not know him.

He was still watching the two teams intently. Army style,

both teams searched each vehicle as it halted before the barricade in exactly the same way, one soldier approaching the driver on the right side to inspect the trunk, the other a few yards behind approaching on the left to look inside.

Twenty miles behind, Keely cursed the big blue Greyhound bus as it lumbered down the long hill past the bunya pines toward the flats that ran to the foot of the Marburg Range. No room to pass, and a Greyhound driver as usual obeying every rule in the book. Keely hauled the pickup over the center line, pushing the accelerator to its limit. The pickup, its radiator low on water and unaccustomed to the punishing speed, was spewing a rusty torrent, splattering dirty steam onto the windshield. He flicked on the lone wiper. Now doing forty miles an hour on a stretch no longer than 200 yards, he drew alongside the Greyhound, an old lady's face horror-stricken at his attempt. Beyond the bus there was a spill of purple bougainvillaea on top of a sheer drop. Dead ahead, coming 'round the bend, he saw a giant Farmall—a tractor as high as the bus and twice as heavy.

He stabbed at the brakes; the rifle jumped forward, its A-sight narrowly missing his eye and crashing against the dashboard. The pickup bucked, wobbled and slipped in behind the Greyhound with only a second to spare.

The farmer didn't bat an eyelid, a blue cattle dog panting contentedly at his shoulder, the bus driver and two whey-faced passengers shaking their heads in a chorus of disapproval as Keely again pulled out, touching fifty around the bend, overtaking the bus and speeding toward the flats.

The only other witness to the near head-on collision was Robert Friedman, a motorcycle constable from Ipswich, which is thirty miles to the east. Usually the army preferred its own to deliver the telegrams to next of kin, but in country areas it often was left to the policeman. Friedman was drawing a map for the farmer in the dusty yard by a small, man-made dam of silty brown water when he saw Keely's pickup flash by.

The farmer, hands in his pockets, was staring at the map. His son had been killed in the New Hebrides and he wanted to know where it was.

"Will they bring him home?"

"No, Dave . . . the heat and all . . ."

"Yeah . . ."

"Your missus home?" Friedman asked, turning as he spoke, watching the pickup.

"She's in Brisbane," the farmer said. "At her sister's place."

"You want me to notify her?" Friedman saw the pickup disappear over a rise.

"I'll ring her, I'll tell her."

"Yeah, right you are . . . Dave, can I use your phone for a second?"

"Help yourself," said the farmer without taking his eyes off the map.

Friedman turned the handle briskly and lifted the short, cone-shaped earpiece. "Marburg. Constable Friedman here, number 132. There's some ape in a beat-up red Chevy carving it out along the flats, heading your way. Bloody idiot'll kill someone. Send a bike out will you? Should stop him before he hits the next range. He's probably pissed. What? No, I'm tied up here for a while."

When Friedman returned to the front yard chickens were wandering across the powdered loam and the farmer was still looking at the roughly drawn map of New Guinea and the surrounding islands. "New Hebrides." The old man shook his head. "Geez, thought they was in Scotland."

*   *   *

At twenty yards Somura could see the second car approaching the gap from the other side. The driver of the car coming through gave Elizabeth a wave.

Somura stuffed the blanket against the small rear window of the car to block the view of anyone from outside and sank low into the space between the front and back seats, jamming himself tightly up against the bottom rear of the high front seat directly behind Elizabeth, out of view of the first soldier, who would inspect the trunk and who was now casually walking toward them. Somura was glad he had exchanged number plates with the Ford.

"Wind down your window. Tell him the trunk's open," he whispered to Elizabeth. "If you make any sign, say anything more, he will be dead."

The pain in Somura's left arm was almost unbearable as his right arm inched the rear seat up and he pulled it out just far enough so that the back panel of the seat fell slightly, creating a slit no more than two inches wide running the breadth of the car and through which he could see a part of the corpse in the trunk. He could hear the approaching footsteps crunching on the gravel. They stopped.

"G'day, miss."

"Hello."

"Mind if I look in your trunk? Carrying out a search. Okay?"

"No . . . I mean no, it's all right," she said. "It's open."

"Thanks. Switch off, please."

Somura could hear more crunching as the boots passed along the right-hand side of the Plymouth. They stopped again and turned directly behind the trunk. Listening intently to the Australian's lazy accent, Somura, pistol drawn, lay still and low, hard against the right back door, straining to hear what the soldier was saying and who he was saying it to.

Then almost simultaneously he heard two sounds: the first soldier who had just spoken opening the trunk, and the second soldier a few yards away approaching on the left side. As the trunk opened, the long slit of darkness between it and the back-seat panel exploded into a ribbon of white daylight, revealing the vertical struts that supported the seat back and the dark shape of the corpse hunched and silhouetted against the soldier's uniform.

He planned to fire once through the slit, swing around and up and fire twice more at the other soldier approaching. But he quickly saw it was no good. The other two would be alerted, the distance between them and the Plymouth too far for him to beat them before they could use their rifles. In another instant the short sword was at Elizabeth's throat. Could he do it if they called him on it? He didn't know, but neither did they.

"Drop your rifles. Now," he ordered.

"Shit . . ." It was the first soldier, discovering the body. The second Australian was raising his arms, his rifle clattering against the running board and onto the bitumen. "Drop your arms!" he shouted to the others. "For Christ sake it's him! He'll kill the girl!"

The man at the trunk hesitated; he could glimpse Somura's back through the strip of light, but he realized that the slightest movement and the girl would be dead, her throat slit by the weight of the Jap falling back, if nothing else.

Elizabeth tried to speak but the blade was taut against her throat.

Slowly, the four soldiers dropped their weapons. First Somura heard the man behind him at the trunk drop his rifle, then the other three, armed with Owen submachine guns, let theirs slip to the ground next to their jeep.

"By the roadside," Somura ordered. "Together. Hurry." He knew that if he did what he was thinking, the authorities would not know for sure whether he was heading east or west.

Now he knew that the hoped-for deception of the tramp's body in the plane finally hadn't worked, but it had served its main function—it had bought him time. Now he needed to buy more if he was to stay ahead of them. Quickly returning the knife to his belt, he waved the Nambu at them.

The four soldiers moved to the roadside. One of them, his arms falling slowly, tired from the effort of holding them up high, said, "He talks like one of us. I'll be—"

"Shut up!" The Nambu now rested against Elizabeth's neck, its black snout level with her chin.

Before she could even turn to protest, he fired four shots, point blank range. The first two fell, the third and fourth, though hit, broke and ran. He shot the third again as he turned, but the fourth, stumbling into the gravel, was now crawling a few yards from his jeep, trying to reach one of the Owen submachine guns.

Somura fired again, pushed Elizabeth aside, ran forward and fell. He pulled the trigger again. A click, out of ammunition. He dropped the pistol. The soldier's hand moved forward, revealing a hole in his chest. He pulled the Owen gun to his side, but Somura was on him and one blow of the sword to the man's neck finished it.

As he got to his feet he saw Elizabeth with the rifle from one of the dead soldiers, blood-spattered, her hair matted by one of the soldiers' blood. The rifle was too heavy for her to hold properly and she held it like a lance under her left armpit, supporting it in front with her right arm. Of all things to note at that moment, Somura saw something he had long forgotten —she was left-handed. Breathing hard, he looked straight at her, moved toward her.

"I'll shoot . . . I will, damn you . . ."

He walked forward. Her eyes closed and she pulled the trigger. Nothing happened. For a moment Somura froze in disbelief, looked down, then smacked the rifle aside.

He reloaded the Nambu while he looked at the .303. As in

all armies, the safety catch had been put on while the rifle had been in the port position.

Stuffing the reloaded pistol into his waistband, he picked up one of the Owen guns and took an extra magazine from the other gun, then slipped the firing bolt from each of the .303s and the remaining Owen and tossed them into the sunflower field.

It was 11:47.

He listened. In the far distance he heard no traffic approaching, only the low rustle of gums in the light breeze. Someone, of course, would report the dead soldiers but the road was rough and by the time anyone got out here to investigate it it would be at least two o'clock and even if they made it out before that they would not know where he was. He could have taken any of four side roads to all points of the compass. As far as the enemy was concerned he was merely a Jap on the run, not a Jap with a mission to fulfill. He still, he reminded himself, possessed the advantage of surprise.

Elizabeth was crouched on the roadside, hugging herself, not making a sound. He was glad he had steeled himself to use her, if necessary, from the moment he had bailed out. There was no time or purpose in feeling for her now. If the warriors who had attacked Pearl Harbor had thought too much, courage surely would have deserted them.

Before he left he helped himself to a grenade and a pair of binoculars from the nearest jeep, then lugged one of the jerry cans of gas from the jeep into the Plymouth. He undressed one of the soldiers, left him naked in the ditch of brown grass that ran by the roadside, and put on the dead man's uniform. They buried his civilian clothes in the brush.

CHAPTER FORTY-EIGHT

Not a sound from Elizabeth, which was beginning to unnerve Somura, as she drove up the Marburg Range thirty miles from Brisbane. Her shoulders had a set to them. He was concerned about the near-blackout earlier when he had sat up at the roadblock and again when he had had to exert himself when the two soldiers broke and ran.

The loss of some blood could be overcome, but the long sleepless run from the caves to here, the loss of sleep before that in the tense air of I-43, the nervous energy spent waiting in the cockpit during the early part of the battle with the Australian destroyer . . . any of these things alone might not have exhausted him, but together they demanded a tremendous effort if they were to be overcome, and he had to overcome them if he was to succeed.

He opened the Seppelt's brandy to help him relax, but the fatigue made it difficult to think clearly and concentrate on recalling the aerial vista over Ann and Queen Streets with Lennon's halfway along the block facing south. He could visualize the sandbagged entrance, and opposite the hotel, south across George Street, the gardens of the Supreme Court buildings. But as confident as he was of the general layout, he knew that since the bombing there might well have been changes he couldn't anticipate. The final details of his attack could not be definite until he was actually there.

He looked at the Owen submachine gun, its magazine high on top of the barrel, its awkward, ungainly appearance belying the gun's reputation for simplicity and power. He felt hot, then cold, a hollow wake of fear that followed the surge of anticipation as Brisbane came closer. A special daring had shot Yamamoto out of the sky, he told himself. The same kind of daring would get MacArthur—

It lasted only a moment, a flash of light, a glint of metal in the sun and then it was gone, a car a mile ahead just visible on the range's summit, turning around now and heading away from them in the direction it had come from. Tired as he was, Somura's raw nerves were monitoring everything that approached, that was a possible danger point. Now the car was a mere dot disappearing over the summit.

"Faster," he said, his voice raspy.

He cursed himself. How could he have been so stupid not to have realized that the taxi that was searched before them might have heard the gunfire and come back to look down the black ribbon of road along the valley flat to see what had happened? Then he heard another deeper noise approaching —a low, throbbing growl. The white Harley-Davidson, a policeman on it, eyes hidden by dust goggles, could be heard for a full minute before Somura actually saw it coming towards them. He flipped up the safety on the Owen. The motorbike flashed by. Surely the taxi driver would have stopped the policeman . . . Somura put down the submachine gun and turned to follow the Harley-Davidson until it disappeared around the bend. He took up the Owen again. *Zurui*, cunning, he thought, suspecting that the policeman had gone by so as not to show his hand. But even now he would be turning back.

In fact, the policeman was looking for Bruce Keely's speeding red Chevy pickup.

It was noon.

"General," his aide Collins was saying, "with respect, I suggest this is one day you ought to stay inside. With this Jap running loose . . . sir, he could still be trying to—"

MacArthur held up his hand. "Joe, I appreciate your concern. It is your job and you do it well. I have to do mine, which precludes staying locked up inside these walls. I really can't be concerned about some crazed Japanese on the run." He thought but didn't say how he felt when he was ordered out of Corregidor and they called him Dugout Doug. He did not propose to give that charge any credence. He had said he would return and, God willing, he would. "Joe, the men need a commander they can see. The public needs it, perhaps more than the troops. Anything less demeans our troops, our resolve. You'll do your job, Joe, and I'll do mine and we'll both have to trust in the Almighty."

Collins knew when it was pointless to go on. "Yes, sir," he said, but at that moment decided he would have to act alone, at least get someone's help in disrupting MacArthur's daily routine without the general knowing about it.

"Major, I've got sharpshooters that can drop a roo at 300 yards on an open sight," Captain Sloan was saying. "I promise you the general won't even know they're there."

Collins's sentiments were with Sloan. "All right. But keep them out of sight or the general will have my head. And Sloan . . . You never told me."

Sloan guaranteed it. He was pleased that the general didn't like the public being inconvenienced, because the public, always eager to see him, unknowingly provided an added ring of protection.

Unknown to MacArthur, Collins arranged for Sloan's first group of four snipers to use the general's private elevator so as to gain access to Lennon's roof. There was a guard outside the suite, because even though the general was in his headquarters at the AMP, Mrs. MacArthur and their son Arthur were at home. The guard was armed almost as heavily as the snipers and scrutinized their page-sized SC sheets carefully, making sure it was the Department of Defense's signature on each security clearance. The youngest of the four snipers, a South Australian, tapped the scarlet armband with the DOD stamp on it. "It's all right, mate, we won't steal the silver."

The guard was not amused as he continued to check out the passes. "Up you go," he said finally.

Being midday, the weakening autumn sun was directly overhead as the snipers spilled out onto the roof, water still lying in sheets on the tarred surface following an early morning thunderstorm. The shadows of their Lee Enfields were sharp, short and pointed, the usual protective wood forward of each .303's breech having been stripped to make for easier adjustments on the high-precision rifles. Each rifle had been selected to mesh with each sniper's idiosyncrasy. The heavy winter-issue coats were soon removed; not so much because it was warming up but because their prominent ivory white insignia, crossed rifles on the embossed white crown signifying that each marksman had qualified with extraordinarily high scores, might be spotted from the street below.

To the east and behind them they could see Queen Street; to the west, Ann. North of them on their left was the great wide dome and high sandstone clock tower of City Hall. To the south, in front of the hotel across George Street, they could see the flame and jacaranda trees outside the Supreme Court.

As each of the four took position, one on each corner of the roof, he pulled back the bolt, pressed a copper-sheathed round into the breech and slipped on the safety. There was no need to check the telescopic sights—they had been preset at the Enoggera Range when Sloan had given them the assignment. Two of the marksmen had seen action in the islands against Yamashita's troops, the other two in the Western Desert against Rommel. Now they heard a dull thump below, the elevator stopping, then someone walking up the short flight of stairs to the roof.

It was Sloan, tall and squinting in the bright light after the shadows of the city streets, the collar of his trench coat still high from the early rain storm so that only his eyes were visible. He called them to the middle of the roof.

"The big problem, if the Jap's crazy enough to have another crack at the general, is that he'll be hard to recognize. I mean he won't advertise, he won't be wearing Japanese gear. Most likely he'll be in civvies. Try to outthink him, how *you* would do it." Sloan had worked with snipers before and so he added, "And use your binoculars first, don't go sticking your bloody telescopes over the top to have a look-see. I know you lose valuable time, having to resight the target switching from binocs to telescope, but you might as well run starko down Queen Street if you show those .303s poking over the edge. Besides which, MacArthur's staff doesn't want any panic on civvy street. And remember, if the general spots you we'll be in more trouble than the Jap. He considers it demeaning to hide behind elaborate security."

"Any idea what the opposition looks like, captain?"

"He's a *Jap*, Terry," said one of the diggers who'd fought in North Africa.

Sloan glared at him. "We're not sure but we think he's with a girl from Toowoomba. About nineteen. She used to go around with a Nip before the war, so it could be him. We asked a neighbor, she said if it's the same one, a guy called Somura. He's short and stocky, so she said."

"Right," said the South Aussie. "That pins it down. A short Jap. Christ, ever seen a tall one?"

"I know," conceded Sloan. "It's nothing much to go on. Just use your loaf. The drill is, anyone who gets too close to the general cops it. Rather make a mistake and have a civvy dead if it comes right down to it. I know he'll be tough to spot from here. Could be anywhere. In a crowd—"

"Then what the hell are we *up* here for?" It was the young South Australian.

"Because, private, he might get on another roof along the general's route and our men on the ground won't be able to see him."

Sloan looked over the buildings that crowded in around Lennon's. "One more thing" . . . He was looking at the corporal who would be in charge . . . "We've sealed off all roof access in the city center so if you see anyone crawling about on any building but these . . ." He gave them a street map with four Xs on each of the four highest points, including the AMP and Lennon's. ". . . you shoot them, whether they look like a Jap or not."

The South Australian glanced unhappily at the map, one arm protecting his eyes from the sun's glare on the sheets of water.

Sloan undid the trench coat, his face now visible and flushed. "We don't know about the girl. If it is Somura, her old boyfriend, she might even be part of it."

The snipers, squatting on their haunches, the rifles in midposition, looked uneasily at one another. You didn't shoot women. On the other hand, this war was getting more vicious by the day.

"Well, the Russians use women, don't they?" said the corporal.

"What's that got to do with the price of rice?" asked another.

"Look," Sloan said, "I don't like the idea any more than you do, but if he's using this girl then she must know the score. Our only job's to keep the general alive without him knowing what we're doing. That's *all* that matters." He checked out the four faces. "Anyone's squeamish, I'll understand. I'll have you relieved and no questions. If you stay . . . you pull the trigger."

Silence.

Sloan nodded. "Okay, next team'll spell you at 1600."

He left then, the door to the roof banging shut behind him.

" 'Course," said the oldest man, one of the North African veterans, "the Nip could give it a miss. Probably on his way to Tokyo."

They watched the traffic crawling down Queen Street. The cars looked like toys. A quarter mile to the northeast, on top of the AMP now in the shadow of gathering rain clouds, they could see four other figures positioning themselves.

It was 12:15.

When Keely saw the mirage shimmering ahead he knew there was something very wrong; the lonely black road with the green Marburgs rising beyond was awash in debris. Slowing down, he heard the cawing of crows occupying fenceposts and trees.

Then he saw the white Harley-Davidson leaning heavily on its kickstand, the policeman standing nearby, stunned, arms akimbo, staring at something in the tall grass. At first Keely, following his gaze, didn't recognize the bodies because the ants and crows had already taken the eyes so that now the four men—three in one clump, the other naked in a ditch— stared blankly at the sky. The two jeeps stood silently nearby. The crows flew off as Keely moved closer.

The policeman turned around and saw Keely, whose face drained of color as he took in the carnage. "Jesus, the bastard's run amuck!"

Keely willed himself to look at the bodies, fueling his anger. "He's got my . . . he's got Elizabeth." His voice was almost inaudible.

The policeman wasn't listening, aware only of the scattered details—the empty jeeps, a half-dozen .9 mm magazines, a grenade missing from the egg-mold box, the rifles, their bolts gone. It all had a dreamlike quality, and at first only the red pickup—Keely's—that he'd been heading to intercept for speeding made any sense. And only after Keely explained himself did the policeman understand that Keely knew *who* it must have been who had killed the soldiers.

Keely wanted to go ahead alone for Elizabeth but the policeman saw the gun and pointed out that the Harley-Davidson would be much faster than Keely's beatup Chevy, so perhaps Keely should come with him.

Since the .22 Hornet didn't have any rings attached for a sling, Keely couldn't use one from the .303s and instead stuck it in the bike's right rear saddlebag, the barrel sticking high up by his head. The constable kicked the starter and told Keely he'd passed a Plymouth less than a quarter hour before. He twisted the throttle and the bike thundered off after the car, to catch up before it got to Brisbane, and to reach a phone so as to get his message to Brisbane that one of the dead soldiers he'd found was naked. Which meant his uniform was on the Jap.

Sloan got the message fifteen minutes later and immediately contacted all the snipers on the three-quarter-mile, reverse L-shaped route. On the walkie-talkie his voice could be heard above the honking of traffic surging about the AMP at the Queen and Edward Street intersection, telling them about the massacre. "So this Somura, if he shows up, will most likely be wearing an Australian infantry uniform. I'll try to have the general leave the AMP a bit earlier than usual if I can swing it, but we can't let him know why or he'll refuse. Anything we can do to throw the Nip off will help. So remember, if he's in Aussie gear he'll have a slouch hat as well, which will make him even harder to spot."

The South Australian shook his head. "That's all we need . . . a bloody Jap pulling his bloody hat down 'round his ears. He'll look like every flamin' digger in Queensland."

"I don't like it," said his companion. "We could hit one of our own."

"Well, at least it won't be the girl," the South Australian said, and the moment he said it realized the possibility it could be. After all, she'd been his girl, they said, before the war, and he had gone to her . . .

On the City Hall clock the shadow of the minute hand moved. It was almost 1:00. To the east the sea's horizon was dark as another thunderstorm rolled in over the Stradbroke Islands, heading for the mainland.

The Plymouth stood chattering beside the abandoned taxi, the taxi's passenger door wide open, the driver having fled across a brown milo field, his entrance into it clearly visible by windblown husks around the drainage ditch. Somura now understood. The taxi driver, having doubled back after hearing the shouting, seeing what had happened down below on the flats and the Plymouth coming toward him, had decided to stop and run rather than take the risk of being overtaken and joining the dead soldiers. A mistake . . . the taxi driver had missed the chance to stop the police motorcyclist. No doubt the taxi driver would reappear from where he was hiding as soon as he moved on into the outskirts of Brisbane, but by then he knew it would be too late for anyone to stop him.

Even so, he let the air out of the four tires and ripped out enough wiring to paralyze the cab. He also exchanged license plates again, telling himself that it was time to switch cars and plates, that even if the driver did manage to make a call in time, which he doubted, they would be traveling in an unknown car in the heavy Brisbane traffic. He had considered taking the taxi itself but the keys were gone and the risk of having it stall in traffic and him having to get out and hot-wire it was too great.

As he clambered back in the Plymouth, tossing its keys to Elizabeth, he realized once more the truth of what he had learned so well in the Academy—just how difficult it was for "pursuing forces to stop one determined man."

CHAPTER FORTY-NINE

By the time Sloan had asked for more police patrols and roadblocks in the most likely suburbs, Somura was already past the Mogill Ferry and inside the general metropolitan area of Brisbane, approaching the Valley, the city's busy commercial sector, with horns blaring impatiently all about him and hundreds of pedestrians dashing every few minutes to beat the lights and the intermittent showers. It was perfect cover.

When the West Brisbane police patrol found the empty green Plymouth abandoned by Mogill Ferry, the license plate number wasn't the same as they'd been told, but there was blood on the edge of the back seat and fenders were caked underneath in red soil from the Darling Downs. "And the radiator's solid with bugs," they radioed Sloan.

"All right," he acknowledged. "Check for every car stolen in the last hour."

"Hell, that's like trying to find a needle—"

"Check! And sergeant."

"Yes, sir?"

"Shoot the bastard on sight."

"And the girl?"

"Use your judgment."

The sergeant had never fired a shot in anger. The Jap was no problem, but the girl . . .

"Oh, *Jesus.*" It was one of the constables.

The sergeant turned to him. "What's wrong?"

The constable showed him the body in the trunk with two bullet holes in the head and one through the neck, small pieces of shattered glass embedded in the skin.

* * *

Elizabeth had done what he had told her for the last half-hour without even a hint of resistance, but he knew it was less acquiescence than a tactic. She would wait for the last moment; therefore he had to take it from her.

He refused himself more Bex—it tended to make him drowsy. Besides, he needed pain to keep him awake. Through the cluster of buildings pressing in from all sides he could see the sky to the north over Fortitude Valley. The earlier snow-white clouds had lost the shine of their creamy underbellies and were swelling into purplish black battalions over Town Reach, which formed the eastern arm of the U-shaped sweep of river running like a quarter-mile-wide moat around the downtown core.

Even without the maps Heiji had drilled him with, Somura knew that following the attack the quickest way out of the U was over Victoria Bridge, which as an extension of Queen Street crossed the river by spanning the western area of the U a block south of Lennon's Hotel. It was also the most dangerous exit. As the nearest to the hotel, it would be the one most quickly sealed off, and with City Hall, the District Court, the Treasury Building and Parliament House all within half a mile of Lennon's there would be any number of police ready to mobilize along the full length of South Brisbane Reach. The first sign of trouble and they would converge like crows to rotten meat.

The problem was timing. In the cream Morris that he had stolen at Mogill Ferry and which was now stationary, its motor running, on the left-hand side of Queen Street outside the general post office, Somura looked due south toward the bridge. He was sitting behind Elizabeth, holding the gun inches from her back as the traffic light changed and the Morris moved off.

He could see the layout clearly, looking directly down

Queen Street past the AMP not a hundred yards from him on the same side as the post office. Thanks to the long, exhausting training sessions at Eta Jima, he knew that from where he was it was 665 meters to the entrance of Lennon's, which was two blocks south and right on George, halfway down the block. The place would, he was sure, be swarming with police, some in rain capes—another shower had begun—some no doubt in plain clothes. There would be just as many or more at Lennon's. In any case, his best protection was that his was only one of thousands of cars moving through the city.

He could already see a small crowd gathering a hundred yards back down about the granite colonnade that formed the entrance to the AMP. The entrance being on the eastern side of Queen Street, the chauffeur, driving on the left-hand side of the road, would continue heading south, carrying the general the two blocks down Queen toward the river before turning right onto George and heading for Lennon's two blocks to the west. Allowing a maximum of three minutes for MacArthur entering and leaving the Cadillac, a possible word or two to an aide and the U-turn in front of the hotel, the journey should take no more than five minutes, possibly ten if a traffic policeman, preoccupied with jams at any of the four main intersections along the reverse L-shaped route, failed to wave the general's motorcade through right away.

The most difficult problem was that getting into and out of his car, the general would quickly be surrounded by the usual cluster of well-wishers and autograph hunters. And there would be a security ring about him provided by the four guards with the Thompson submachine guns stationed between him and the crowd. No clear shot at any distance. Added to all that, the Cadillac was armor-plated, so at no point would the general present a clear, unprotected or stationary target.

From the moment the general's limousine stopped at 2:00 P.M. outside the AMP and took him aboard to the moment it discharged him at Lennon's he would be moving, either in the car or on foot. To use the Owen gun efficiently Somura knew he would have to get in close for a controlled burst to catch him in an inescapable cone of fire. But how would he get in close? True, it was turning chilly with the squalls of rain coming in from the coast so that he could wear the captured Australian's coat with upturned collar like so many of the Americans and Australians were in the habit of doing, and this would help to hide the gun and his face, but by the time he pushed through the crowd and got into position the general would either be in the car leaving the AMP or arriving at Lennon's, safely in the hotel's lobby within some thirty seconds. He could push to the front of the waiting crowd—his wounded left arm, which no one but Elizabeth knew about, would support the gun long enough for him to fire the burst —but to be in position he would have to be so close to the security guards that he was certain to be seen. And he would have to be on the eastern side so as not to have the open door obscure the general from view as he got out of his car, but this was the side the security guards would be watching closely. He remembered how the Filipino Pacis had proceeded in this fashion, only to be gunned down. In any case, as the general alighted there would be a guard on either side of him in the same way as they guarded the U.S. president, so that they would be the first to be hit if there was an attack. And now that it was raining even harder, obscuring umbrellas would be everywhere.

In the abstract, ever since he had crashed in the Wildcat, he had been confident the gun plan would succeed. Now, the physical world was imposing its mundane limits on the clearest abstractions, robbing them of all their promise.

He would have to get MacArthur another way.

Elizabeth? Ironically, as he had seen his original plan of attack with the Owen gun become unworkable, he now saw that Elizabeth would not be a problem . . . providing he had at least fifteen minutes in which to launch his attack. After that any warning from her would be useless—it would be done, the general would be dead.

When he heard the swishing of tires on the rain-slicked blacktop and saw the long line of bright fire red delivery vans, each with its gold emblem, the insignia of the post office, coming in to park for the lunch break and saw that most of the drivers, while taking their keys with them, left the sliding doors of the vans open to cool down the vehicles, he believed he had the solution for Elizabeth. It would take him only minutes to tie and gag her and drive over to one of the open van's doors, which he would close after putting her inside. He reached for the brandy bottle.

"Here," he told her, thrusting the bottle of brandy under her nose, "it will calm you down."

"I don't want to be calm—"

"Drink it, Elizabeth," he commanded and let her feel the edge of steel against her neck. She drank, some of the liquid spilling over her summer dress. Suddenly she tried for the door. He jerked her back by the hair and threatened her with the Nambu. From across the street he saw the long row of radiators, smiling benignly at him from the delivery vans.

Three blocks away on George Street the lunchtime crowd of sightseers was congregating around Lennon's. It was 1:30.

The Harley-Davidson left the highway along the Mogill Ferry Road and headed into the sprawl of Indooroopilly, racing beneath the overarching trees four miles southwest of the city center. Constable Hill, with Keely behind him, waved a gloved hand at the police manning the roadblock. There were six of them, two wearing the armbands of special constables. All had guns.

"Off the bike," the corporal shouted. "Both of you. C'mon, hurry it up."

Always unarmed except in emergencies and even then with guns having to be especially authorized by the chief superintendent, Hill's fellow Queensland police looked odd, holding their guns without the easy confidence of the army types he'd seen. Hill blamed himself; it was a different world out on his Marburg Highway, along the stretches in the Lockyer Valley where a gun was as natural to a farmer as a cow, but once in the city it was a provocation, especially in wartime, and a .22 Hornet sticking out of the saddlebag . . .

"Look, mate, I'm Hill, a constable, Marburg Highway Detachment. Picked this bloke up near the bloody massacre at—"

"Get over by the car. Johnson, get Captain Sloan on the blower."

Corporal Johnson eyed them suspiciously, taking in Hill's uniform and memorizing his badge number. The thought of Australians who might be fifth columnists helping the Japs made him boil. They didn't look like fifth columnists, except he didn't really know what a fifth columnist was supposed to look like. Besides, if you did know there wouldn't be a need for any roadblocks. In any case, he wasn't about to muck up his next promotion by letting someone inside city limits with a .22 rifle while the MacArthur alert was on. And the radio bulletin had said the Jap had been traveling with an Australian girl. If so, there could be others involved.

Hill gave the corporal the details of the massacre in an attempt to convince him. "For God's sake . . ." He was shouting at the corporal now. "I'm the one who told Brisbane about the uniform being taken from one of the soldiers. What you should be looking for is a bloody Jap dressed in—"

Keely broke in. "The bastard'll *be* there by now."

The corporal fingered the trigger guard nervously. If these two were telling the truth he could be in the soup. "So how come you two know all about this massacre? You must have been there, eh?"

"We *were* there, you drongo," snapped Keely. "*After* it happened. We're only twenty minutes or so behind him. Now you're making it a half hour."

"Well . . . we were told to stop anybody who looked—"

"Corp?" It was one of the younger constables strolling over from the police car. "This fella's badge number checks out with the report relayed to Captain Sloan from Marburg, and the bike's license is—"

Before he could finish, the corporal lowered his gun. "Righto. Sorry. Off you go."

"Where's this Sloan?" Hill asked.

"Lennon's. Why?"

Hill kicked the starter as Keely slid back onto the back seat. The corporal pulled out the Hornet.

"Hey, what the—" objected Keely.

"Not in town, mate. We're the only ones allowed guns."

"Except the damn Jap!" Keely shouted, but his voice was drowned by the roar of the Harley-Davidson as it shot past the roadblock and roared out along the alabaster stretch of Milton Reach less than three miles from city center, passing from sunlight into rain into sunlight again.

It was 1:32.

CHAPTER FIFTY

Inside the darkness of the parked van, Elizabeth fought against panic and claustrophobia. He had no need to put a blindfold on her, but he had gagged and bound her. All around her was the reek of the spilled brandy that was evaporating slowly in the darkness of the van and had chilled her, her dress clinging to her, her bare feet ice cold. She did her best to block out the morning's blood, the dead staring eyes of the soldiers, the corpse in the trunk. To think of them threatened to paralyze her.

What mattered now was that somehow she must stop him. Concentrate. She began counting, carefully, slowly to calm herself in the darkness, then to try to find a way to break out. He had trussed her hands and ankles together behind her so that it was impossible to roll without smacking her head into the hard, slatted wooden floorboards.

Outside she could hear the rumble of tram cars moving up and down Queen Street. She tried to call out but there was only a smothered grunt, the gag hot and tight in her mouth and smelling of alcohol.

Now she heard a tram close by, squeaking loudly to a halt. A tram stop? Right outside Lennon's . . . What could be more natural—someone just standing waiting for the—

No. He would need the car to escape. By moving her bound hands and legs to one side and turning her neck she could just see her watch. 1:39—and suddenly she remembered what she and every Australian knew from the newsreels about MacArthur—that at 2:00 P.M. precisely, twenty-one minutes from now, the general's Cadillac would arrive at the AMP down the block, less than a hundred yards away. Would he try there?

She could hear voices outside. Some of the post-office driv-

ers coming back? She rolled her body, pushing hard into the
wooden floor; a sliver, stilettolike, pierced her face. Pulling
her bound legs up behind her, gaining an inch or so of slack,
she kicked against the van's metal side, hearing it buckling,
echoing like an empty water tank. Silence, then voices coming
nearer. She kicked again and again. A tram car thundered
past, its tremble felt by her in the van. The voices, mingled
with laughter, were receding.

Somura pulled back the sleeve on the Owen gun and flicked
on the safety. He would not try any of the roofs as vantage
points. It would be too far for the Owen's range—and once on
a roof, how to get off? They would surround him immediately. He was thankful for the bad weather as another shower
began. Collar up, slouch hat pulled down in the rain, it took
him only a moment to get out and open the trunk six inches
or so, a little longer to pull down the back-seat panel so that
from the back seat of the stolen Morris with its new plates,
parked nose in, as was the custom, to the Edwards Street curb
and diagonally opposite the reddish gray ten-storied AMP
barely a hundred yards away, he could see the granite colonnade entrance through the binoculars that he now propped
on the seat. Crouching below the back-window level, he used
the partially opened trunk as one would the slit of a bunker.
Hidden from view, he felt relatively secure. After the frustration of his failed aerial attack, he had new hope.

He was also grateful for the pain to keep him awake. In a
moment that threatened weakness he had taken two of the
Bex powders from his pocket. Momentarily they had become
an enormous temptation. Now he threw them down and took
up the binoculars. Waiting. They would expect him to try
when the general was stationary or walking, not in the car—
which was why he decided he would not.

CHAPTER FIFTY-ONE

The South Australian wasn't sticking his rifle's muzzle over Lennon's parapet, but he was ignoring Sloan's order to use binoculars. In late 1942, during the heavy fighting around Buna, he had missed a Jap in the time he had taken to switch from binoculars to scope and the sniper, lashed high in the palm, had shot his buddy. Never again. From his position on the northwestern corner of the hotel he could see ahead to City Hall, its tall Roman columns and high sandstone tower a golden amber against the cloud-mottled sky. Beyond, he could make out parts of the YMCA, a quarter mile to the northeast and about 200 yards to the left of the AMP on Edward Street. He lifted the rifle, targeting the clock tower with the scope's circle, watching the huge, black minute hand jerk forward to 1:40 P.M.

"Here they come!" It was one of the other snipers calling out.

The South Australian swung around to face Lennon's northeast corner and saw the older veteran's rifle pointing over Adelaide Street and another block to the intersection of Queen and Edward—at the AMP.

For a moment Somura was almost caught off guard. It was still ten minutes to two as he touched the focus wheel on the binoculars and saw the lead jeep arriving with its guns, officers in trench coats, rain capes on the MPs, high collars and steel helmets glinting in the sheen of the rain-slicked street. Now the crosshairs of the binoculars' range finder bisected the polished black Cadillac slowing behind the jeep to stop precisely in front of the granite colonnade.

In the binoculars' circle Somura could see the four silver stars on the stiff metal flag and behind it the long sedan's interior: a driver and a bodyguard in the front seat, and behind, another jeep, two men in its front seat, and behind them a high-mounted Browning .50 caliber, the gunner closely watching the crowd.

Moving the binoculars side-to-side, Somura could see that in addition to the four guards outside the insurance building there were now four outriders and two more military policemen posted on the street, on the far side of the car, obscured now and then by a flash of passing traffic heading south toward Victoria Bridge, while the usual crowd of some fifty or sixty people, perhaps fewer than usual because of the rain, were pressing in expectantly by the colonnade for a glimpse of the man who promised to defeat Japan.

He swung the binoculars to the rear jeeps and further on to the intersection of Edward and Queen, then back to the AMP, settling on the grayish pink Helidon freestone of the ground floor. There was a sudden stirring in the crowd, held back into two groups of twenty or so on either side of the colonnade. Though he could not see faces clearly through the rain, the umbrellas compounding the problem, Somura could sense the crowd's impatience, some of the faces turning toward one another, apparently annoyed at being pushed back, at being kept so far from the entrance.

He glanced at the intersection again, police in groups on all four corners, traffic moving smoothly, three trams running so close together heading south to the bridge that they seemed joined together like a train, an illusion caused by the angle and the binoculars' magnification. He looked back at the AMP —hands clapping, faces turning toward the colonnade. It was only a glimpse but it was enough . . . the MPs forming a defensive diamond about the man, his face and sunglasses obscured by the moving heads of the guards, his high trench-coat collar, the famous Bataan cap plainly visible as he bent slightly to enter the limousine.

"Hey, mate, your trunk's open . . . hey, you all right?"

A man's face was peering in through the driver's rain-streaked window looking down at Somura on the back floor.

"Hey, you okay?" He saw the bullet holes in the khaki tunic and opened the back door—

Somura swung around and up, the short sword sinking into the man's belly. He bucked, legs thrashing for a minute, then rose upright, mouth open. Somura jerked the knife up into the heart and out. As the man staggered back toward the curb, legs crumbling, he sat in the gutter staring down at the oozing gash in his stomach. A woman screamed. Somura rolled over into the front seat, teeth clenched against the pain from falling on his injured arm. He knew it was impossible to drive for long in his condition, but all he needed was the strength for a half-mile west down Edward as the general's motorcade moved south down Queen, then turning left on Adelaide going south, both of them heading south, a block's width between them, and then a block to the west, he would turn east at the corner into George while the general's motorcade, completing the other half of the square, turned right from Queen and west into George, the two cars heading for each other as the general approached Lennon's. It was then that Somura decided he would hit him, across the center line, broadside, hard and fast like the *kamikaze*.

It was 1:45. As he saw the jeep ease off from the AMP Building, Somura started the Morris, telling himself to obey every traffic rule. If by some mischance he was delayed at one of the intersections, then no matter, he would allow the general's motorcade to pass him, then fall in behind and swing across the center line in front of Lennon's as the motorcade made its U-turn across to the hotel entrance.

Driving west, turning south into Adelaide and running parallel with the motorcade a block to the east, Somura switched off the windshield wipers, bent forward, using his body to lend pressure to the wheel, steering the Morris as he wound down the windows, the driver's side only halfway, and unscrewed the cap on the jerry can of gas he had hauled from the jeep at the roadblock. Next he pulled the Owen gun closer to him and took the grenade from the bloodied jacket, wedging it within easy reach between his thigh and the seat. Only now did he realize it had stopped raining. He leaned back and switched off the wipers. He was ready. He could hear the wail of an ambulance. Too late—by now the nosy pedestrian would be dead from loss of blood.

With the general's entourage leaving the AMP five minutes early without incident, on top of Lennon's the corporal in charge ordered the four marksmen to change their positions so that now two men, the South Australian and his older mate, moved down to take up stations midway along the southern side of the roof overlooking the guy-rigged awning on George Street. If there was any trouble when MacArthur alighted, they would be directly above it. Just beyond the lip of the awning they could see parts of the sandbagged wall and the two guards with their Thompsons, now down from the shoulder-slung position, cradled at the ready for the general's imminent arrival.

The sun was coming out, the streets steaming. Everything looked normal, the crowd, growing by the moment, being politely but firmly pushed back by the hotel commissionaires, aided now and then by two Aussie privates, their blancoed canvas belts a light creamy green in the sunlight, the brass buckles flashing as they turned.

A commotion by the curb—a drunk singing "Waltzing Matilda." A police constable, hooted at by a couple of people in the crowd, tried to move the drunk on. From the roof, the

South Aussie could see some in the crowd clapping, a few of them joining in:

Once a jolly swagman
Camped by a billabong—

He heard a screech, a white Harley-Davidson skidding to a stop, its rear wheel sliding hard into the curb and a man getting off, standing for a moment immobilized, as if his legs wouldn't work, the crowd turning to stare at him. He was followed by the driver of the motorbike, a policeman who disappeared beneath the canvas awning and who could be seen arguing with the MPs.

Through the gag Elizabeth wheezed for more air. She should never have listened, should have used her head not her heart, should have known, should have realized from the beginning the real reason he'd come to her. She'd duped herself . . . She lifted her feet up behind her again, her thighs taut, arching as she kicked and kicked, again and again . . .
    Suddenly light was flooding into the van.
    "What the—?"

The South Australian heard the argument growing louder above the murmur of the crowd, and down by the gutter, as though some unseen hand had pushed it, the Harley-Davidson crashed to the ground.
    "What the hell's going on down there?" he asked the corporal.
    The corporal stretched forward over the parapet for a better view. "Dunno." He brightened. "Not to worry . . . there's the general now." He pointed eastward over Adelaide to the line of heavy traffic moving slowly south up Queen

. . . the Cadillac, small from this distance but much longer than all the others and looking as if it had been stretched, standing stationary, idling, flanked by the outriders and the armed jeeps in front and behind, all stopped in the long line of vehicles at the Albert Street intersection waiting for the policeman on point duty to give the go signal so they could continue south on Queen before turning right on George for the last 200 yards to Lennon's.

The sun disappeared in a squall, and in moments it was pouring rain again.

The corporal lifted his binoculars and swept the Supreme Court gardens directly opposite where a smaller crowd was clustered, umbrellas sprouting by the big jacaranda tree. Everything looked okay, and below, the altercation beneath the awning had ended. But then, moments later, they could hear the elevator moaning upward, clunking to a stop, followed by hard, running footsteps on the stairwell. The roof door burst open, banging hard against the jamb. It was Sloan, and directly behind him Keely and Hill, who had given him more information on the massacre site where they had seen some 9 mm magazines but no Owen guns. Also a grenade stolen.

"The Jap's on his way," Sloan shouted. "That Aussie uniform I told you about . . . this fellow says it's probably chopped up a bit, gunshot wounds, and the Nip's probably hauling an Owen. We don't know where or how he'll—"

He was cut short by the corporal. "Hey?"

They turned. Horns were honking, pedestrians stopping to look at the sight eastward on Adelaide one block over. There were loonies in any city, but this barefoot one was a beautiful loony—running through the rain, torn clothes stuck to her, oblivious to the cacophony of horns, catcalls, laughter and derision. She kept on running, moving out now from the crowded footpath to the center line, moving between the lanes of traffic toward the intersection of Adelaide and George, a block to the left of Lennon's, the noise increasing until the whole of Adelaide Street seemed to be rioting. She didn't waver, as if drawn on by a point in space that had to be reached but which no one could see but herself.

Sloan saw the traffic cop a block to her left, two blocks left of Lennon's, signaling "go" to the general's motorcade. It was 1:53 and Sloan figured the motorcade, though moving slowly in the rain and traffic, would arrive at the hotel in three minutes—1:57 at the outside.

The woman was still running toward the intersection midway between the motorcade and the hotel.

It was hard to tell a block away but—"Oh, Jesus, it's her!" Keely yelled. "It's Elizabeth . . ."

"Stop her," Sloan ordered, leaning over the parapet and calling to the guards below.

Keely's eyes went from the corporal to Sloan and back. "But she isn't the one that—"

"Corporal!" Sloan said, "come with me! *On the double!*"

They were on a collision course fifty yards from the hotel entrance when Sloan tried to stop her. As she ran into him, he fell backward, pulling her down on top of him.

Keely quickly was helping her up. "Elizabeth—"

"Where is he?" demanded Sloan, pushing Keely aside and retrieving his .45 that had skittered in the rain along the center line. "Where *is* he?"

She tried to catch her breath. "I don't know!" She saw the front jeep approaching, tires spinning up a fine spray, behind it the Cadillac, the stiff, metallic flag, the four stars, the lone figure in back.

"Where is he?" Sloan demanded again. Keely was holding her.

"I told you, I—"

"Leave her alone," from Keely.

"You were with him, damn it, you must know—"

"I *don't*, but he's in a Morris, cream color . . ."

They saw the Cadillac a block and a half from them, now stopping, an old man appearing from a clump of pedestrians at the corner, bent over, face hidden by his rain hat and slowly wheeling a wicker pram between the front jeep and the limousine.

On the roof the South Aussie had the old man's head centered in the crosshairs, trigger finger curled, poised. The old man kept moving, one hand reaching into the pram, then straightening up, its front wheels lifting up over the curb where the South Aussie caught a glimpse of a pink baby blanket through the scope and a rattle suspended halfway across the canopy. He moved the rifle scope away from the Cadillac south to Victoria Bridge, sweeping across the rear jeep, its gunner also watching the old man, and then the scope darted forward in a blur beyond the front jeep to Lennon's entrance below, the crowd filling the target circle. He slid the scope south from the crowd across to the Supreme Court, then left to the T-junction of Adelaide and George fifty yards from the hotel.

"Hey, corporal, look at the captain, he's cornered a loony."

When the corporal looked down he saw something quite different. Sloan was sprinting, revolver in hand, toward Lennon's entrance, Keely and Elizabeth just behind.

"Get inside. Please, Elizabeth," Keely was saying.

She had no breath to speak, could only shake her head.

Ten yards ahead, Sloan, informed by Elizabeth about the Morris and the gasoline can, was yelling at the hotel guards to disperse the crowd.

The tram had stopped at George and Adelaide some hundred yards to the left of the Lennon's entrance, disgorging its pas-

sengers, obliging Somura to stop. He felt nauseated from the
stench of petrol fumes. Beyond the disembarking passengers
he could see the lead jeep approaching Lennon's from the left
on the far side of the intersection. They passed him. The tram
had cost him precious seconds. There was still time. He would
wait until the motorcade began the right-hand U-turn across
George to the Lennon's entrance, exposing the Cadillac to a
broadside attack. The intersection cleared. Sitting low, he
sped forward, overtook the car, then slowed, making sure that
he was the first car behind the rear jeep.

"You asshole . . ." It was the driver he had cut off in order
to take up position. Soon it would be over—

But the crowd was breaking up and to his right someone
was coming toward him from the edge of the crowd.

On the road in front of the entrance Sloan, the .45 still in
hand, signaled urgently for the motorcade to keep moving
past Lennon's. The forward jeep, a hundred yards from the
entrance, reacted immediately, speeding up, the siren acti-
vated, warning the Cadillac not to stop but to stay in column.
There was a screech of brakes, traffic blocked the way eastward. The lead jeep swung in a sharp U-turn hard left away
from Lennon's toward the Supreme Court buildings opposite.
Two events happened at once. Sloan, watching the jeep turn,
saw the Cadillac begin to follow and in the gap between the
limousine and the rear jeep he saw the cream Morris surging
forward and Elizabeth running straight in its path, Keely taking after her, Sloan calling for the waiting crowd at Lennon's
to disperse.

Sloan lifted the .45 in double grip, held his breath, fired.
The crowd broke and spilled across the pavement. The jeeps'
machine guns were impotent in the heavy traffic, but the snipers above and the jeeps' riflemen opened up with rapid fire
and Sloan saw flecks of the Morris flung high into the rain, its
tires shredding, its chassis shaking but still rushing forward at
the Cadillac that was now caught in mid-turn between the two

jeeps, which only as the Morris got closer could open fire with less risk of hitting civilians.

Somura fired the Owen gun—its stuttering burst raking the rear jeep. The soldier on the Browning jerked back, crashing to the pavement, his helmet clattering as he lay dead in the street.

The left side of his face stinging from the shower of shattered glass, Somura could hear two bullets ricocheting about somewhere in the back, possibly the trunk. Now another smashed the right side of the windshield. He could not miss. He was too close. It seemed time had stopped. The crowd was breaking up.

When she stepped in front of him—between him and the escaping crowd near the front of the Cadillac—he saw only her face, nothing else, only her face. He jerked the wheel away from her and the crowd behind her, sideswiping Keely without seeing him. Elizabeth's face went past him like a slow-motion dream. He pulled the pin—the grenade rolled free.

The Cadillac's driver pushed the accelerator to the floor, swung hard right. The limousine leapt forward but the cream blur of the gas-soaked Morris still struck it beam on, exploding in a massive, rolling ball of orange flame, hurling Somura through the windshield and engulfing the rear of the Cadillac, lifting and throwing it, its doors springing open with the force of the blast, leaving it to rest against a semitrailer that was also now on fire.

Without Elizabeth's warning, passed on by Sloan, the whole crowd and not just the Cadillac would have been caught in the fireball.

Fire engines and ambulances were already screaming, speeding southward from Brisbane General as reporters on extended lunch hours hurried out of every bar within a mile of the crash. One, the first on the scene, from the Brisbane *Globe,* saw Keely limping in agony amid the dense black smoke, bending over Somura, pulling back the hammer of the dead chauffeur's service pistol, aiming its barrel at Somura's temple. The reporter saw the Jap, eyes still moving, staring fixedly beyond the broken corncob pipe at the still figure beneath the gold-braid cap. When the Jap made out the face beneath the cap, close enough to touch, he moaned. It was not a moan of pain but a deep cry of defeat. Only then did he understand why the general's motorcade had left the AMP Building ten minutes early.

"No," he said, and closed his eyes.

Keely stared at him for a few more seconds, the gun in his hand, then let it fall by his side. The man was dead. And only then, satisfied that there was no longer any threat to Elizabeth, did he look closely down at the man in the gold-braid cap. He was dead too—but there was something very wrong . . .

On top of Lennon's the corporal saw a Packard three blocks to the northeast drawing up outside the AMP. The corporal, terrified, heard the tower clock sound 2:00 P.M.—the exact time the general always left for lunch.

It took Keely, still stunned by the force of the explosion, several minutes amid the chaos of fire engines, police both military and civil, sightseers, army and ambulance men, to realize that close up, his sunglasses still in place but shattered by the impact, the general . . . the man, the body with the four bloodied Silver Stars, the high-collared army trench coat, the shattered corncob pipe nearby, was the same build, the same height . . . But it was not Douglas MacArthur. The stand-in lay dead on the rain-splattered street.

Sloan had decided he couldn't risk just having MacArthur

depart late to confuse his would-be assasin. He had to find a substitute for the general, he decided, and fast. He put out through the army personnel records department an urgent request for an unmarried soldier or ex-soldier, highly motivated, who was willing to take on a most secret and dangerous mission. What he came up with was the man who now lay dead in the rain-splattered street. His name was Raymond E. Piers, a fifty-five-year-old cane cutter from Childers, north of Brisbane who had lost a younger brother to the Japanese at Milne Bay. Piers had quickly agreed to stand in for the American general, and if it cost him his life, he was willing to face that too. His hatred and hunger for revenge and desire to *do* something were overwhelming. Of course, he had never expected anything like this . . . he had been exempted from military duty due to an old eye injury . . . but he welcomed it. He also had no family, his whole life had been devoted to his brother. Sloan had found his ideal man.

Sloan rolled Somura over with his boot to see the man's face for the first time. He had used a stand-in for the general just as Somura had used Underbridge as a stand-in to deceive him. "You showed me how to bait the trap," he muttered at Somura.

Watching the blood-stained rain washing away in the gutters, Sloan surveyed the burned-out hulk of the Cadillac. He had protected the general, but he had also lost the bait. He moved through the line of police and the crowds pouring in and about the stalled traffic, then into Lennon's lobby, where he rang headquarters.

"Hello, this is Bataan."

As he waited to speak to Collins he wondered what Bataan, the Philippines, actually looked like. He saw Keely sitting against a wall receiving first aid. Elizabeth was kneeling alongside him, allowing herself a last look at Somura as the ambulance swallowed his remains and the doors slammed shut.

"Who's the woman?" asked a reporter from the *Courier Mail.*

"Someone," replied Sloan, "who has a ton of guts. Put herself between the Morris and the crowd."

In Room 806 of the AMP they heard the explosion to the south. All ten officers watching the big multicolored wall map of the southwest Pacific turned from the boardroom table— except MacArthur. After the guns of Corregidor no explosion fazed him. ". . . So, gentlemen, thirteen amphibious landings in all."

The faces turned back to him. His pipe stem, one of the latest aluminum-ribbed types from the States, swept, or rather leapfrogged from one island over others to the next target, north of Australia across the Solomon Sea from the jade-shaded Trobriands in the southwest, 500 miles northeast to New Georgia and another 800 miles northwest and on over the barrier of New Britain to the huge Japanese airbase at Rabaul on the eastern tip, then into the Bismarck Sea. "In June, Woodlark, Kiriwina and New Georgia. In August, Salamaua, Lae, Finschhafen and Madang. In December, New Britain." The supreme commander paused, his gaze resting on Halsey's admirals and Kenney's bomber commanders. "The crucial factor is coordination of the naval bombardment and air support for the landings. Remember, the enemy will yield nothing once he has set his course. He is intractable. For him to surrender, to abandon his plan once decided upon, is anathema. Once we hit those beaches we must advance. We must therefore use the enemy's fanatical commitment to our best advantage; feint in the direction of his commitment, then outflank and attack." He paused. "Or as it is referred to in the vernacular, 'hit 'em where they ain't'!" There was polite laughter.

He stood, the fellow-planners of CARTWHEEL following him, the chairs making a din even in the muffled surroundings of the boardroom. From far below they could still hear sirens. The general lifted his cap. One of Halsey's aides noticed for the first time that the general was balding slightly.

"We will discuss the Australian thrust with Blamey's staff this afternoon." And then he was gone to his limousine—a Packard—waiting below.

He had no knowledge of the late Raymond E. Piers, who had saved his life.

EPILOGUE

Leyte Gulf, the Philippines, October 19, 1944

It was the largest fleet in history, more than 800 ships steaming through the night, and as he saw MacArthur gazing into the velvety darkness that surrounded the *Nashville* and the rest of the armada advancing into the gulf, Sloan was conscious of how he was no longer simply a member of MacArthur's security staff but part of a momentous, much larger enterprise.

At dawn the awesome bombardment for A-Day, Assault Day, began, Kinkaid's fleet, including six battleships and eighty-six destroyers, opening up in fiery support of Krueger's Sixth Army.

On the way in to Red Beach, shortly before 2:00 P.M., weaving its way through hundreds of other landing craft, one burning fiercely not far from it, with Japanese snipers adding to the usual confusion and thunderous din of a beachhead assault, the general's landing barge ran aground on a sandbar some distance from the shore. The general ordered the ramp down, and after it crashed into the sea he waded ashore on Leyte, not, as his critics would later have it, in a staged rerun of a rehearsed drama for the cameras but for the first time with the new Philippine president, Osmena, at his side.

In Normandy, four months earlier, the German army had lost 200,000, almost half of them surrendering and being taken prisoner, the rest killed or wounded. In the Philippines, the Japanese lost 450,000; a surrender by a Japanese was so rare as to be virtually unknown. Sloan, against the backdrop of a torn landscape of splayed coconut palms, watched as, amid gray curtains of tropical rain, William Dunn, a CBS radio correspondent disembarking from a weapons carrier, set up the microphone that on various wavelengths transmitted via the *Nashville* the news that Gen. Douglas MacArthur and President Osmena would soon speak.

With the rain still pouring down, the supreme commander of the southwest Pacific forces stepped forward:

People of the Philippines. I have returned. By the grace of Almighty God, our forces stand again upon Philippine soil, soil consecrated by the blood of our two peoples . . .

Sloan saw several veterans of the long brutal campaign in near-tears as MacArthur continued, his voice rising with emotion:

. . . Rally to me! Let the indomitable spirit of Bataan and Corregidor lead on. As the lines of battle roll forward to bring you within the zone of operations, rise and strike! . . . For your homes and hearth, strike! In the name of your sacred dead, strike! . . . Let no heart be faint. Let every arm be steeled. The guidance of divine God points the way. Follow in His name to the holy grail of righteous victory!

Sloan wondered if there would be trouble over the last words, invoking God, but he also knew that the general believed every word, and believed that the Filipinos would welcome him, and he was right. His speech galvanized the islands into unprecedented guerilla warfare against the Japanese.

Now Yamashita, who had been so celebrated for overrunning Malaya and Singapore, was on the defensive and decided to make his final stand in the mountainous jungle of Bataan. He surrendered to MacArthur's forces at the summer capital of Baguio on September 3. Found responsible for atrocities committed by Japanese occupation forces in the Philippines, he was hanged in 1946.

Sloan saw more tears again at the retaking of Manila when at the old Bilibid Prison, MacArthur faced 5,000 starving

POWs, stumbling, rushing to greet him. On March 2, 1945, Sloan witnessed MacArthur return yet again, this time to Corregidor, in four PT boats—the same number he had used on his escape to Australia three years earlier. Of the 5,000 Japanese defenders only twenty-six surrendered. Outside the shell-wrecked ruins of the old barracks the Rising Sun fell, the Stars and Stripes hoisted in victory.

On August 30, 1945, MacArthur, barely two weeks after the atom bombs had been dropped on Hiroshima and Nagasaki, flew to a Japan still a fortress, bristling with arms and inhabited by fanatics who had already besieged the residence of Prime Minister Suzuki, killing the general of the Imperial Guard. At Atsugi Air Base west of Yokohama the officer in charge informed his pilots that it would be treason to surrender.

En route to Atsugi, MacArthur's C–54, *Bataan,* stopped at Okinawa. MacArthur ordered Sloan and other nervous aides to take off their sidearms. To impress them, he said. If they didn't know they were defeated, this would convince them. On the fifteen-minute ride into Yokohama, Sloan, as part of the MacArthur entourage, was witness to 30,000 Japanese, their bayonets an endless ribbon of steel, facing away from the general, both in the final act of capitulation and as protection against those who, like Somura, considered it more honorable to die than to surrender.

In awed silence the motorcade made its way. On September 2, at 9:04 A.M., MacArthur accepted the instrument of surrender aboard the U.S.S. *Missouri* in Yokohama Bay and became absolute ruler of Japan. Tojo, shortly before he knew he would be arrested, tried to commit *hara-kiri* by stabbing himself in the heart, but unsure of exactly where the heart was, he sought advice from a physician. Tojo failed once, then the physician made an X with charcoal on Tojo's chest. Again Tojo tried but failed. He was hanged as a war criminal on December 23, 1948.

Sloan listened to aides advising MacArthur that Emperor
Hirohito should be immediately arrested and tried as a war
criminal. Others insisted that at the very least the emperor be
made to appear before MacArthur, symbolizing Japan's total
submission. MacArthur said no—to force the emperor to appear would be an unnecessary humiliation and counter-
productive to the peaceful conversion of Japan into a demo-
cratic state. MacArthur waited. The emperor came.

Sloan returned to Australia in December of 1945, but never
saw Elizabeth Lawson or Bruce Keely again. They became
engaged for a short time in 1946, but Elizabeth called it off
when news of her father's death in Malaya finally reached her
through the International Red Cross.

Bruce Keely was wounded in Korea on February 27, in the
fierce winter of 1951 as the Third Royal Australian Regiment,
while under the overall command of the Ninth U.S. Corps,
captured Hill 614, one of the precipitous high points overlooking a valley that lay in the path of the U.N. advance
toward the thirty-eighth parallel separating North and South
Korea.

Five months earlier, as commander in chief of all U.S.
forces in the Far East, supreme commander for Allied Power
in Japan and first commander in chief of all U.N. forces, General MacArthur, at seventy-one years of age, astonished the
world with his amphibious assault on Inchon, a left hook behind enemy lines to relieve the U.S. garrison at Pusan. In the
council of war preceding the plan his admirals and generals
advised against it. Inchon, an indentation halfway down the
western side of Korea's crooked nose, was, they pointed out,
besieged by some of the world's highest tides, and at low tide
the harbor was a vast mudflat, both conditions disqualifying it
from the highly complex business of amphibious assault for
70,000 marines. MacArthur listened to the objections and re-

plied that "the very arguments you have made as to the impracticabilities involved will tend to ensure for me the element of surprise. . . . The enemy commander will reason that no one would be so brash as to make such an attempt. . . . Surprise is the most vital element for success in modern war."

In June, 1952, Elizabeth, now twenty-eight years old, did marry Bruce Keely at St. John's, a tiny and, by Australian standards, very old church in Toowoomba nestled in the deep shade of tall gums and spreading camphor laurel. Elizabeth was given away by an uncle, and the couple spent their honeymoon at Caloundra north of Brisbane on the coast. They would have two children, David and Larissa, whose grandmother Sarah died shortly after Larissa was born. Larissa would marry a farmer on the Darling Downs. David would graduate from Queensland University with a business degree to become a consultant for Mitsubishi Electronics. No one considered the irony of it.

Raymond Piers, his name still unknown except as connected to a far-fetched rumor few put credence in, was buried in his hometown of Childers three days after Somura killed him outside Lennon's. There were no posthumous medals, but an old soldier named Sloan would never forget him.